Small Acts of
Kindness

As a freelance journalist for national magazines and newspapers, Caroline Day wrote other people's stories: happy stories and sad stories, stories of the greatest tribulations and triumphs. To do this right, Caroline spent many hundreds of hours trying to truly listen to what each of these people had to say. And although fictional characters are a little trickier to interview, Caroline loves spending time with them. Caroline lives in north London, with her husband, Ben, two greedy rescue dogs, and with occasional visits from her grown-up (but still lovely) children. Her debut novel, *Hope Nicely's Lessons for Life*, was a *Sunday Times* bestseller.

Small Acts of Kindness

Caroline Day

ZAFFRE

First published in the UK in 2024 by
ZAFFRE
An imprint of Zaffre Publishing Group
A Bonnier Books UK company
4th Floor, Victoria House, Bloomsbury Square, London, WC1B 4DA
Owned by Bonnier Books
Sveavägen 56, Stockholm, Sweden

A CIP catalogue record for this book is
available from the British Library.

Paperback ISBN: 978-1-83877-843-9

Also available as an ebook

1 3 5 7 9 10 8 6 4 2

Typeset by IDSUK (Data Connection) Ltd
Printed and bound in Great Britain by Clays Ltd, Elcograf S.p.A.

Zaffre is an imprint of Zaffre Publishing Group
A Bonnier Books UK company
www.bonnierbooks.co.uk

To Alexandra Lines. Because of all the fun we had.

NED

THIS IS IT. THE chance. The perfect cross – whipped, powerful yet controlled. Brilliantly angled. And I'm there.

I'm past the centre back and the goalie, already beginning my leap. Throwing myself towards the ball. It's heading for the back post. And I'm there. All I have to do is nod it in. This is *mine*. I stretch my neck muscles. Then a crack and a burst of pain in my head. And the world goes grey.

MAY 2019
KIKI

OUCH. OUCH. OUCH.

Do they not have any signposts in this country? Just field after field, and mud and rain, and cows watching you like they could tell you exactly where you should be going, if they could be bothered.

Squeak. Squelch. Squeak. Squelch.

Stupid boots.

I haven't slept for two nights and here I am, out on a tiki tour through the wop wops. Let's hope that smell is just the cows.

'When the time is right, little Kiriaki, we will go back to England,' my Yaya used to say. 'You will love it there. I know it.'

But, Yaya, now I'm here, my feet hurt, I'm soaked, I've already spent all my money and this backpack's like an elephant on my back and I've been tramping forever.

Squeak. Squelch. Squeak. Squelch. Ouch.

Remind me never to buy a pair of gumboots without trying them on again. So much for £1.75 in the Stratford Dogs Trust charity shop. So much for only half a size too small, so much for I reckon they'll stretch.

And that mean woman with her Land Rover, driving off like that and leaving me at that petrol station in the middle of nowhere. Crystal, her name was. No way she didn't understand,

'I'm just popping in to the loo'. Just as well I took my back-pack out with me.

Squeak. Squelch. Squeak. Squelch.

I couldn't not buy them though, these boots. Sitting there in the window, like they knew one day I'd come. Like they'd been looking out with their big froggy eyeballs, waiting for me. The Cinderellas of animal wellies. Because how often does that happen? You go out looking for some festival gumboots, and they're right there. 'Novelty wellingtons', the shop assistant called them. Fate, or karma, or – I don't know – just luck, maybe. The shop assistant couldn't believe that gummies like these even existed in size five – well, size four and a half. She was sure they only made them for children.

It's the right boot that's squeaking. And scraping my poor blister. Then the left one squidges around my toes. Like a wet sponge.

Why did I not just buy some sensible boots? Nobody else there was even dressed up.

Stupid cows chewing at me, with their big faces. And, this poncho – water resistant? And if I wipe my glasses it'll just make them worse.

Stupid ratbag Crystal with her, 'I can take you as far as Bristol if you give me the petrol money upfront.'

Ow. Ow. Ow. Ow. Ow.

She overheard me arguing with my mother while she was filling up with petrol, I reckon. Hardly a reason to dump me in the rain though. Mean old ratbag.

What is it with people? That Pete and Paul and their, 'We'll text you as soon as we've pitched the tent.' What was their problem, gapping it on me like that? Where did they disappear to? They seemed so nice in that pub in Stratford – the Hairy Biker? Scary Biker? – selling me the ticket even though they didn't know me. Although I'm not so sure about it being like the actual Glastonbury. Everyone at this thing seemed so agitated. All those people throwing themselves off the stage into the crowd, and beer cans flying over your head, and all those men shouting 'ribbit' when I walked past. And the music. Just screaming mostly. I can't imagine Yaya would have enjoyed that.

Yes, cows. I'm lost and I'm broke and I don't have a clue where I'm going. Not back to Stratford, that's for sure.

'Enjoy your festival.' That's what Siobhan-the-ratbag-landlady said. 'Oh, and if you could clear the bedroom. There's someone else arriving on Monday.'

It was a dingy room anyway, and the wrong Stratford. You'd think maybe she would have said something when I booked it. She must have thought I was pretty daft with my emails about Shakespeare and cottages.

This is pretty, though. Or it would be if it wasn't so wet. And there'll be a hostel or something soon, I reckon. Bound to be. If my phone had any charge left, I'd find a B&B just round the corner. Definitely there'll be somewhere. Because—

You're kidding me. That's not a puddle. How am I meant to get through that?

And what's that noise? From the trees over there? You heard that, right?

Is that howling?

NED

WHEN I WAS STILL me, I once dived from a cliff into the sea far below. In the moment before I leapt, I looked down and my insides lurched and rolled like the waves beneath. In the moment before, I felt the pull of death and life. I felt the warmth of sun on my skin and I heard the water below. I raised my arms until my muscles pulled tight, and contemplated what I was about to do. Scared. Excited. Alive.

Readying myself. Staring down at the white breaking through the blue far beneath me. Knowing I could turn away. Knowing I would not. Petrified but exhilarated too.

I dived.

Dove?

Dived. Yes, dived.

I dived.

I have known what it is to dive from the rocks into the ocean below, the crash of water as it split open to let me in, the slap of cold as I arrowed into it. I have known what it is to rise again, shaking saltwater drops from my eyes and hair.

The thrill of opening the door to death. Of staring it in the face and beckoning it closer. Of waiting until it's so near that you can feel its breath on your cheek, and only then slamming the door shut.

When I was still me, I dived from a bridge, much higher still, above a river, an elastic rope clipped to my ankles, and a group of friends with their phones held up to capture my moment. The air roared past me and time itself surrendered to gravity. Face first. All that existed was the falling. And then the snap and the bounce, and the laughter that was my return to life.

I laughed at death. I dived. I returned to life. To my wonderful, intact life. When I was still me.

Now, though, life itself ebbs and flows around me. The darkness comes and goes – voices drift, and I forget, and then I remember and I hear them say, 'We don't know. He may know that you are here. There may be some consciousness.'

I try to scream, 'I am here.'

And nobody hears.

MRS M

YOU NEVER WERE TERRIBLY fond of these tumblers, Roger. You would rather your glasses did not look as if they came from Amazon or IKEA you said, though of course they weren't from either. I don't even know how one goes about buying a thing from Amazon, though I presume on one of those iPad tablets. And I've never set foot in IKEA, as you well know, although parking is terribly convenient, I hear. They have a cafeteria too. Rather good pastries, Harriet always said.

John Lewis, in actual fact. These glasses. Look, if I hold this one up, no bubbles in the glass, good thick base, delicate sides. Classic, Roger. Good-quality glass. How clearly you can see the jasmine around the window through it? Goodness me, but it grows. I shall have to cut it back again. I do love the scent though. Here – when I open the door – heavenly. Even in this dratted rain.

See those eyes. 'Go on, dog,' I say. He's giving me that look, but one has to be firm and tell him, 'Yes, Wordsworth, indeed, it is wet. However out you go to do your business.' And out he goes, as if that was his intention all along.

Listen, Roger, if I tap the rim – granted, not the same ring as lead crystal. But still, you hear that? Good quality.

It was never you who washed them up, was it, Roger? Standing right here and looking out at the garden with your Marigolds on? It was not you who laid a tea cloth on the base of the sink, before filling it with water and detergent, because cut glass breaks so easily. I suppose you didn't know that. Or that I rinsed the glassware in a vinegar mix every other month to prevent clouding. And, you see, these ones – these basic ones – are dishwasher-proof. Not that you were terribly fond of the dishwasher either. Why waste the electricity, you said, when it took longer than my doing it by hand. Even though it was you who insisted we have the dratted thing in the first place and you who was ever so determined to have the most hi-tech model one could find. Too many programmes, if truth be told. Still, I've rather taken to using it now.

Anyway, Roger, happy anniversary, if you'll excuse the beaker. I thought it would be appropriate to have a little toast with your favourite . . .

Goodness me. Is one supposed to actually drink this? The smell, Roger. Where was it you brought this back from? The Isle of something? Neither of us imagined that would be your last golf trip.

The bottle does attract dust rather, rare batch or not. Though I should be a popular hostess if anyone were to call round for pre-dinner drinks. I'd use the best glasses then.

I did mention to the neighbours, actually, that they must pop in for some fruit cake or a sherry, you know, the ones who bought number four. I thought after that misunderstanding over the wisteria that it might be nice. I suspect he'd know a good single malt. I've seen golf clubs in their car. But I think perhaps they've forgotten.

Talking of which, I telephoned Faith last week. I hadn't heard a peep from her since she and Clive came for dinner and that was when you were still . . .

I'd been a little surprised not to have had an invitation back, and I wondered if it might have something to do with that silly discussion about those grandchildren of hers. You know how sensitive Faith can be, although, to be perfectly frank, it was about time somebody said something. Anyway – very sad – poor Clive died in February. Awful, of course, but you'd have thought she might have made sure that I knew. I should have liked to attend the funeral. After all, I invited her to yours.

Clive would have liked a glass of this Scotch, I suspect.

Anyway, Roger. Happy anniversary.

Sixty-four years. How can that be? It wouldn't stop raining, if you remember, a bit like today – just look at it out there – and Mother cried the whole way through.

Not that we ever made a fuss over anniversaries. Clever you for choosing a wife who was too sensible to bother about such things, you always said. Though you did give me that gift four years ago, if you remember. So much more economical not having to replace the bags when they're full. I won't repeat Harriet's words when I told her what you'd bought me.

She said surely it was a double bluff, and you had secret plans to whisk me away to Venice for a second honeymoon. Funny Harriet.

I said, 'How can one have a second if one never had a first?'

Platinum? Is that sixty years? No, no, sixty is diamond. Platinum, that's seventy.

Harriet said not to worry and that she'd make it up to me. She said, once mean old Roger has popped his clogs – sorry Roger, it was only a joke, and there was no way she could have known – then she and I should go to Venice. Italy wouldn't know what had hit it, Harriet said. Pasta and opera and gondolas and toy boy gigolos. That part was a joke, evidently.

I rather think I should have liked Italy though. I did so enjoy the television series with that chef who drinks all the wine.

But what have I been thinking of? Look at me, standing here. The poor dog.

Goodness me but it's pouring.

Wordsworth. Where have you gone?

I know, Roger. But Harriet was my best friend and nobody else offered to take him in. Penny, you might have thought. But these young people are so busy with their back-to-back meetings and their work–life balances. And just because you were never much of a dog person, it doesn't mean that I should not be. He is sweet, even if he does insist on digging up the lawn. See what a mess he's made over by the pear tree?

Where on earth can he have gone? He was right there a moment ago, sniffing around under the lilac. But, gosh, it's pouring out here. There is no way he can't hear me shouting for all I'm worth.

Don't say he's managed to open the side gate again. I shall have to ask that gardener boy to sort it out.

Oh, for heaven's sake, I thought as much. I always did say this catch needed tightening. Still, he's a dog. How does he do it? Naughty Wordsworth, don't you dare be digging around number ten's privet again.

Here I am, yelling through the rain, 'Wordsworth.' And the ground is so slippery down the side here. Silly old legs. I shall end up on my backside. Bothersome hound, making me come out in my slippers.

Not here in the front either, and I'm sure half the neighbourhood can hear me.

Well, not in number four. And not digging up number ten again. But where on earth . . . ?

Oh.

I see. There you are.

Coming out of the trees with a very unapologetic spring in your step. Have you been off hunting foxes again, you wicked creature? Look at how wet you have made me, you naught—

But who is this – person – and what is she doing emerging from the woods with my dog? The state of her. Has she painted her face green? Camouflage? A vagrant? Who else would wear such a ridiculous waterproof? And those plaits look like something a toddler might have. As for that handbag, it's like a green football on a rope. And those wellingtons.

I trust she's not dangerous. Foreign, perhaps. I had better address her slowly.

'Hello? Young lady, Yes, you. Do you speak English, girl? What are you doing with my Wordsworth, and why are you dressed as a frog ... ?'

THREE DAYS LATER
KIKI

I BET THAT FIRE LOOKS amazing in winter, with heaps of logs and real flames. Yaya would have loved seeing me here behind the bar, with these pictures of foxes, and the ones of dogs wearing jackets and playing cards. Because of the name, I guess – The Fox and Hounds. Yaya would have been so stoked.

And, look, I'm getting the hang of pouring a pint – see this one? It's harder than you'd think. Because of all that froth. I had a bar job back home once. I loved chatting to the customers. But they only did bottled beers. And then it turned out they didn't need me anymore, which was funny, because they always seemed so busy.

The boss was a grouchy old ratbag anyway, always saying things like, 'give me strength'. This one's grumpy too. Mervyn. His daughter's even worse, although she's not here tonight. She's at a party.

I don't think Mervyn smiles. He just sits at the end of the bar, shaking his head and asking if I don't have a job to do, which is funny, because, look, I've poured this excellent pint for the old man. It's not like I can't have a little chat at the same time. That's called multi-tasking. It's good customer service. You'd think Mervyn would be pleased. You'd think he might say something nice about this great pint I've poured.

If Sue was here – that's my old flatmate Sue from Auckland – she'd tell Mervyn a few things. Sue says motivational management is important for a happy workforce. Sue studied psychology so she should know. She didn't finish the course but still, she knows heaps about it. Like a conversation is not just words – there's a whole technique to it. If nobody is speaking, you ask the other person about something they're interested in. And see, I've been the only one talking for a while – telling the story about that dog, Wordsworth, howling outside the pub again this afternoon, and me taking him back to his owner, the old woman who looks a bit like the Queen. Mervyn's not said anything, just sat at the end of the bar, leaning on his elbows. The old man hasn't said a thing either, except for 'thank you' when I passed him the pint. So now I'm telling Mervyn how much I like the pictures of the dogs playing cards. I say, 'They're like your pub theme, eh?'

He shakes his head and asks if I don't have anything to be getting on with – *eh?* – so I say I'll collect up the empties.

Someone's left a newspaper on the table in the far corner. Table six, the one by the gents. An empty pack of salt and vinegar potato chips too. And I'm rolling the paper up to chuck it, but the word 'festival' captures my eye, so I open it up again for a quick squiz. But it's only about some cheese festival this weekend. There's a picture of the organiser – a bald man with a very round head – holding up a cheese the size of a bicycle wheel. It says for more news about this and many other events and festivals this summer including Glastonbury Festival news, turn to page seven. It's not the main article on the front page, though. That has the headline: BRAIN-BLEED MUSICIAN STILL UNRESPONSIVE ONE MONTH AFTER FOOTBALL ACCIDENT and a photograph of a man with a laughing smile and a soccer shirt with 'NED 30' written on it. The story below it is about a tree falling onto a car, though luckily nobody was in it at the time.

Mervyn can't see round this corner from where he is or he'd tell me to put down the bloody paper and get on with my job, I reckon. But maybe I won't throw it away. I'll have a look at the Glastonbury news later. You never know.

NED

E-n-t-i-c-e.
   Ten.
   Tin.
   Nit.
   Tic. That's five.
   Entices. Tens. Tins. Nits. Tics. And that's ten. Come on, brain.
Ten more.
   Cent.
   Cents.
   Sent.
   Exist. Of course. How many's that . . . ?

MRS M

WHAT DID I ALWAYS tell you? The roots come away so cleanly after heavy rain. Tidier already – see that. Just a few more – out come those naughty roots – and I'll have you shipshape and weed-free. There, that's better.

Look at these azaleas from the garden. And let me take away last week's daffodils. If these poor old knees will ever let me up again. Otherwise, Vicar will find me still down here when he arrives to prepare for evensong. I shall have to tell him, 'no, Vicar, not praying but weeding'. Mind you, at least then I should have the chance to bring up those ridiculous regulations against planting on the plots again. Why it's against the rules to dig in a nice bed of lavender or a rose bush, I can't comprehend.

Silly legs. Do excuse me leaning on . . . apologies, Harriet . . . only a stone when it comes down to it . . . I . . . shall . . . just one moment . . .

There. Goodness but it becomes harder each time.

Aren't they magnificent? The azaleas? A very you colour, I thought. Shocking pink, the fashion designers might say, like that scarf you wore to Muriel's funeral. Though the daughter didn't seem to mind.

I sent her a long letter, actually. I enclosed it with a Christmas card. I thought she might appreciate hearing a little about those afternoons her mother and I spent setting up the library for Vicar, although I was never certain how well suited Muriel was to the job. Her alphabetising left a lot to be desired and as for her idea of genre – well, I ask you. The daughter never wrote to thank me. But that generation seem to carry out all of their correspondence on Facebook, don't they?

Where was I? Oh, yes, Muriel's librarianship. Somebody brought in that *Joy of You-know-what* book and she filed it under romance.

Which reminds me, you will never believe what I found amongst my laundry.

The shock of it, Harriet. I'd never even seen one before, much less picked one out from my own wash pile. And how on earth it came to be mixed in with my linens, I simply can't comprehend. What if Roger had still been alive and glanced up from his newspaper, while I was pegging out the whites? He would have seen me pulling out this item and he would have assumed that it was mine.

Thankfully there was only myself and Wordsworth – who was every bit as bemused as I was. He had that expression. You know the one.

Where can it have come from, Harriet? That's what I don't understand. Such a thing can't have materialised during the wash cycle, now can it? And it gave me such a turn. Picture it, sunny afternoon, nice breeze, me in my housecoat with a handful of clothes pegs at the ready. Pillow case – peg, peg – hand towel – peg, peg – bath towel – peg, peg – flannel – peg, peg – giving them a jolly good shake because you know how important it is not to have any creases when it's going on the line. So there I was – you can picture me, tea cloth. Peg, peg. And, you know how one is with such chores, I wasn't concentrating because, well, one does switch off rather.

And then I spotted it. I didn't know what it was, of course. I thought maybe a piece of embroidery floss from my box, or an errant shoelace, not that I have any in that colour. It was tangled around my oven glove. How I missed it going into the machine, I don't know. I suppose I should count myself lucky it didn't run. But naturally, I was surprised to find this scrap of cotton caught up with my wash and, as I unravelled it, I saw that it was attached to a tiny triangle of – well, I don't know if you'd call that material. It wouldn't have covered my nose. 'What on earth have we here, Wordsworth?' I said. Because I could not for the life of me imagine. Then I held it up. Like this – up to the sky in case there was a pattern to make out. I thought at first maybe a rather strange sort of lacy eyepatch.

I dropped it the moment I realised. Why – I had to open Roger's whisky again to calm my nerves. And then I so very much needed to speak to you that I found myself walking to the telephone in the hall. I did feel foolish.

No doubt you would have found the whole thing most hilarious but, Harriet, I fail to see how any person would contemplate wearing such a thing.

I didn't like to throw it away though. Well, it could be some sort of evidence. Because it didn't summon itself into existence and throw itself into my washing machine. In the end, I sealed it in a freezer bag with a date label so I'd recall the time of finding, should it ever come to that. I have filed it away in my cabinet, with the household receipts and guarantees.

It was only afterwards, when I was applying my cold cream, that it occurred to me that in fact I really should have called 999, because for all I knew there might have been somebody in the house. And then of course I worried that there might still be. I crept down and took a rolling pin from the kitchen drawer and Wordsworth accompanied me around the house. We looked in every cupboard and wardrobe and behind the curtains and there was no pervert lurking. Still, it does make one feel so vulnerable.

Oh, look, there's Vicar. I must speak to him. But, Harriet, such a mystery. There hasn't been a soul in the house for weeks – unless you count the gardening boy, or that strange festival girl. Those preposterous wellingtons and with that handbag like an oversized tennis ball on a rope. She was probably on drugs, now I think about it. Although something about her reminded me of you when we were young. Pretty, but with a faraway expression.

I obviously didn't let her in any further than the hallway while I telephoned Mervyn Paterson to ask if the live-in bar position which he'd been advertising was still vacant. Apart from her there was – is it Ruby or Agnes? – one of Millicent's grandchildren, knocking on the door about some fun run or other. She seemed to think I should give her the money before she'd even done the running. I had to tell her, 'Young lady, this is not how a sponsored race works'. But she remained outside, and besides she can't be more than eight years old. So surely . . . oh, bother, there goes Vicar. Has he not noticed me waving? He can be so unobservant. One ends up having to shout.

'Vicar! If you have a moment . . .'

KIKI

FEEL THAT? The room shakes when the trucks go past. And hear that clanking and jangling, making The Fox and Hounds sign outside squeak on its chain?

It's mostly quiet. You don't see a car for hours, just maybe a bike or a tractor or someone on a horse. Then these enormous trucks come down the hill at some random hour. This one's a giant dumper truck with its headlights shining through the gap in the curtains onto the ceiling. The first couple of nights they woke me every time.

I'm awake now anyway, in the window nook, with my knees up and my laptop resting on them – well, my flatmate Sue's old laptop that she sold me. I'd sit at the desk if I could, because Sue says it's important to be ergonomic. But there's no room to pull the chair out. There's barely space to squeeze between the bed and the desk, nor between the bed and the window. Mervyn shouldn't say 'room and board' but 'cupboard and board'. And you wouldn't believe how much he charges for it. I'm going to have to work twenty hours every week before there's any actual pay, even though it smells like beer and chips and those pies they sell. It says on the slate 'home-made steak and kidney pudding' but I've seen the packets.

This room's smaller than my bedroom in the bus but this window is deep enough to sit in. It's pretty snug, too, because

20

of the thick walls and the pillow behind my back, so here I am in the middle of the night, watching the pub sign swinging and waiting for Sue to email me back.

My bus wasn't like a London double-decker or an – I don't know – Greyhound bus. It was a converted one with a shower and a loo and heaters and wall hangings and a kitchen. It wasn't a driving bus – or maybe it was when Gramps was alive, when I was too little to remember. But for me it was always just home. I had my bedroom and Yaya had hers. We had a little bit of garden too.

Sue won't email back straight away anyway. But at least the Wi-Fi is working after all of those 'account not recognised' and 'unidentified address' and then 'password incorrect' messages, and that thing with the portal and the not finding whatever it was it couldn't find. Sue would have laughed at me trying to work it out. She always said I was a digital dodo. But I'm sure it went through eventually because it didn't do that bouncing back like all the others. It's just the middle of the day over there so she's out, probably, doing something. And it wasn't an urgent email anyway. Just checking she's all right, because of all the texts I've sent since I've been here.

Hi Sue (I'm just giving my email a quick read back), Greetings from Little Piddleton (really!) the most typical English village ever. I haven't tracked down my Glastonbury ticket yet or learned anything about my mum or Stan Douglas. I've been too busy. I'm in Somerset now and I've got a job in a pub here . . .

She'll laugh about the festival though, I reckon, and me thinking it would be anything like the real Glastonbury. She teases me that I'm always getting the wrong end of the stick. She'll say I'm a muppet for mixing up my Stratfords too. But

Sue's going to love hearing about The Fox and Hounds and how I was lost in the rain and ended up here. I've told her what an old grump Mervyn is and how the daughter's even grumpier, with her eye make-up and rings and bangles. And all about the funny dog who keeps escaping from home and howling outside the pub until I go out. Maybe I'll send her some photos.

I didn't say anything about losing her good luck present.

It was in my pocket when I left that festival. Because I sneezed in the car and when I pulled a tissue out of my pocket, out came my good luck gift too. Awkward. Ratbag Crystal gave me a funny look. But I know for sure I put it back in my pocket, because it was there when I blew my nose later, too, after she'd dumped me at the petrol station in the rain.

So I don't know where I could have lost it. Dropped it, I reckon. But I can hardly ask Mervyn if he's found it in the pub.

Sue said it was a little something to bring me luck on my travels, but I still wonder if she maybe mixed up her gifts, because when we went to that hen's night before I flew, the hen, Sue's mate, seemed pretty surprised to be given a Saint Christopher pendant when everyone else was giving her wind-up willies and edible underwear. So when I unwrapped my gift later on the plane, I did wonder.

But I texted Sue to say thank you for the lucky gift. I won't tell her I've lost it. It'll turn up.

NED

IT'S TIME WHICH UPSETS me the most. Upsets me like an apple cart. Derails me and tips me over, so that my wheels are spinning in nothing. Turning in empty air. Because it's not as if I was ever unaware of time, or how indiscriminate it was. I knew its winged chariot was there at my back. I heard it behind me even as a little boy. I remember when Grandfather moved into an old people's home, those Sunday visits, when I wanted to be outside, kicking up mud and riding bikes. Even then, what bothered me the most on those overheated Sunday afternoons was not the loud TVs and the shuffling slippers of the old men and women, with their mouths chewing on nothing. What bothered me was the knowledge that the only thing dividing me from them was time. Even then I already understood time would make no exception of me.

Time lends us youth and strength. It will claim them back. There is the bargain. But I never suspected that time would not play fair. I knew that eventually it would drag me down, just not that it would come up behind me, while I was unprepared, and shove me from behind.

I never thought that time would be a cheat.

When I was still me, there was a woman. Smart, beautiful, sexy. She wanted to spend her life with me. And I said yes. But then I said no. Because I was not ready. Because my life stretched out with too much time to have regrets.

I had no way of knowing.

Now I know.

Time has taken everything. And it stretches on. A cartwheel spinning in empty air.

MRS M

THE WAG OF THE tail is decidedly hopeful so I have to tell him, 'Do not give me that look, Wordsworth. We both know that you are an extremely naughty dog who deserves no tea. There is no point gazing up as if you're the party to whom the disservice has been done. It will take more than that face for me to forgive you.'

Perhaps I should have let him be taken to the Dogs Trust after all. I still could do. I could take him there and tell them that I appear to have inherited a defective dog, and that since he seems so terribly keen on escaping from his home, perhaps he would prefer a cold, empty kennel. No, dog, I shall not forgive you. It was bad enough when you were first here: all that nonsense, carrying off my things and burying them. That lovely Jaeger scarf. I could not for the life of me think what I had done with it, until out it came from the vegetable patch when I was planting tomatoes last week. Pure silk, and the mud stains will never come out. And then there was my rolling pin. Do we remember *that* incident? Caught red-handed, you were. Or red-pawed I suppose one should say. With it beside you while you dug in my nasturtiums.

And my purse. Those things I said about that poor plumber. Not that I *accused* him per se, although perhaps I was a little hasty in making the call to his company. How could I have known though? I merely pointed out that I had left it on the hallway table and that he had had ample opportunity. How was I meant to have foreseen that a wicked hound might have relocated my purse to the fuchsias? What Wordsworth intended to do with it I cannot imagine. What conceivable use would he have had with my library card, travel pass, cheque book and loose change?

'Were you planning to take the number seven bus to Waitrose?' I ask him. The only response is a waft of something very unpleasant. 'Revolting creature,' I tell him. 'I'm sure that Australian frog girl thought it was me earlier. I should put you out in the garden, but you'd only do your Houdini act again. Honestly, it is becoming a little embarrassing. You're not a puppy anymore, Wordsworth. And you may still miss your old mummy – do you not think I do too? But why you feel so determined to go howling to that strange young woman is beyond me.'

There is a passing resemblance, I suppose, but to Harriet as she was many years before Wordsworth's four paws were on the scene.

He is still gazing up at me, with eyes that say he promises he'll never do anything bad again.

'Very well,' I tell him. 'As far as the field, but you shall remain on the lead.'

KIKI

T HE CHEESE FESTIVAL WILL include tastings and talks by local cheesemakers. It's one of a huge programme of exciting events in the area this summer. That's what the headline says: *Huge programme of exciting events.* And, to be fair, there are heaps. This weekend there's a cider festival with more than one hundred stalls. There's also a cross-stitch extravaganza, a yoga roadshow, a ceramics workshop and a country fair, featuring pony racing and a dog show. I'll be working, I reckon, but maybe the old woman with the basset hound might be interested.

I kept the paper from the pub because it said about turning to page seven for Glastonbury news, but it's not very helpful. It's only what acts have been announced and what new areas are being constructed this year. There's nothing about where to nab a ticket if you don't have one, just the website address to *find out more.* Even a digital dodo like me's already checked that with its *all tickets have now been sold* message popping up, however many times I refresh the page. And, yes, I knew there was a limited resale in April – so limited that they'd all gone by the time I'd even pressed a button on my computer. Like – whoosh – all gone.

It was daft of me, maybe, not to realise how hard it would be. I mean, I'd read about the tickets selling out in no time but I didn't quite realise just how fast. And maybe I sort of thought that it would be different for me, maybe because of

Yaya talking about all the times she'd been. It just sounded so free. And I remember local festivals from when I was little, back home, going with Yaya and Gramps, all the music and the food stalls and people everywhere. I remember shouting, 'Look at me. I'm at Glastonbury,' and Gramps and Yaya laughing and saying no, this was tiny compared to that. But to me even a little local festival felt huge.

'Maybe it'll be easier to sort out once you're over there,' Sue said. But in London, I asked everyone. Even strangers. Nobody had a clue where to find a Glastonbury ticket.

This bed creaks whenever I shift my weight trying to make myself comfortable. I'll have to talk to Mervyn about a new mattress because this one's heaps saggy and the springs poke you when you move. Trying to lie in a way where I'm not spiked in the night is giving me back ache and now I'm stretching and thinking maybe this yoga extravaganza day could help make my back muscles stronger.

And maybe it's because I'm thinking about yoga that I notice the words on the front page of the newspaper as I'm flipping it closed. It's next to the one of the man with the top that says NED 30. And it's him again, doing some sort of press-up but with one of his legs out straight too, and he's wearing a sleeveless T-shirt that says *Pilates, Passion & Practice*. So I'm thinking how Pilates is like yoga, but also that you can sort of hear a man's voice saying it in a really cheesy way: Pilates, passion and practice. And also thinking that maybe I shouldn't grumble about a dodgy mattress and not having my Glastonbury ticket when this poor man's unconscious in hospital.

He has a nice smile.

When I was younger I used to beg Yaya to let me have braces like all the girls at school had. Yaya said no, of course.

She said my teeth were what I was born with and that beauty was what nature gave to us. Pilates Ned had braces, I reckon, or else nature was kind enough for those lovely teeth to be born that way. Probably they were. I mean, look at him. Even his pot plant is perfect.

It says under the picture that Annabella Hopkins, fiancée of Norton Edbury – known to his friends as Ned – is raising money for therapies that might help him. To make donations go to a JustGiving page or check his YouTube channel, *Pilates, Passion & Practice.*

But I'm sorry, Norton Edbury. There are only three weeks until Glasto and I need every penny for when my ticket shows up.

NED

OFTEN THEY TALK AS if I am not here. Or here as nothing but a physical object of no other significance. They speak amongst themselves about my vital signs and my temperature, my scans, my catheter and feeding bag and my needing to be turned or washed or to have my sheets changed or my case discussed. They read out my consultant's notes and they talk of pathways and the demand for beds. They do not use my name. Not very often. 'This one', they say, or 'He'. Or 'Bed Five'.

'I've changed Bed Five's drip, but he still needs turning over.'

'If you could do Bed Five's vital signs. His temperature was a little on the high side earlier.'

'Keep the notes out for Bed Five. He's still waiting for Doctor to come round.'

'*I have a name*,' I want to tell them. '*I am here*.' Except I'm not, am I? Or here perhaps, but not I. I am not me.

The dreams are the worst, because when I dream, I'm running or dancing or fighting or doing whatever crazy shit we do in our dreams. Even in my most irrational dreams, it's me in my body and only the world that is warped. Then I wake up. And it is a few beats before I remember, and in those moments I'm thinking that I'm just about to sit up and then stand up, and I'm going to say, on my way to meet the day, 'What a mad dream I just had.'

But there is no sitting, no standing, no saying – and then I remember.

'We need to prepare Bed Five for transfer to the rehab unit.' That was the ward sister, KerryAnne, earlier on, talking to one of the other nurses, Paulina, I think it was. I wonder where I'm going next. Not that it makes much difference. Acute ward or rehab unit, it will smell the same. The lights will be bright and switch off at 7 p.m. The bed may have another number but I will still be the thing in the bed.

In the beginning, I tried so hard. I was certain that trying would make it happen – the saying, the sitting, the standing. Here I was – in my time of tribulation, my time to dig deep and find out just how exceptional the human spirit was. Everything had been taken from me. But watch me, world, I'd come through this to write my song of resilience. I tried and I tried and I tried. I tried to blink my eyes, to wiggle my fingers, to open my mouth, to make a noise.

And nothing came.

I sang songs in my head, ones that told me that we would overcome, that we could be heroes, that the only way was up, that whenever I felt afraid, I just whistled a happy tune and that I believed in me. And still I thought, beyond a doubt, that these things were true. Because good things come to those that try. I waited and I tried. Tried and waited. Tried and tried and tried.

I did anagrams in my head. Seeing how many small words I could make from a longer word. I wrote poems that only I could hear. And I waited. And I tried.

I can feel everything they do. The tugging and the turning and the sticking and the pricking. I ache and I hurt. My legs cramp and I want to yell and to rub my screaming muscles better. Pins and needles torment me. My bones are sore.

Physiotherapists manipulate parts of my body. I feel it being done. The physios always use my name – a little too much perhaps, and the wrong name. They tell me what they're going to do before they do it. The one I liked best was called Nathalie. Her accent was South African.

'So, Norton, I want to believe you can hear me and you can understand me, so I'm going to assume that's the case. Fair enough? But what I need is for you to show me. Can you move your eyes? Just look up or look down? Or can you blink? Norton, can you try and do that for me?'

How I tried. A thing as small as a blink.

'Come on Norton, just one tiny movement of your eyes, to tell me you understand. I know you can do it.' A warm voice and so encouraging. I wanted her to see how strong I was, what willpower I had. This was how it would start – if I could just move my gaze one centimetre – one millimetre – one tenth of a millimetre, she would see. In weeks or months or years to come, we would look back and talk about this moment. By then, I would have overcome all the obstacles as she helped me on my journey. I would have told her, nobody calls me Norton, at least nobody except my mother and my ex. I was going to try harder than any person had tried to do *anything*, ever. Nathalie would see how much I could make happen with my indomitable spirit.

My eyes *must* move. Move. Eyes. Move.

'OK, Norton. Let's leave that for now. Now, how about your fingers. I'm just going to lift up your left hand, OK? Like this. Good. OK, now I want you to use all your effort and try to press your fingers onto my palm.'

All my effort. All my effort. All my effort. By rights, my face should have been squeezed red and tight, with veins pulsing and eyes bulging. I once ran a half-marathon in less than an hour and a half. That was nothing compared to the effort I now put into moving a finger that will not move.

'Right, Norton, so great try. That's good now.' We both knew nothing had happened. 'Now, I'm going to take your right leg and just help it do some stretches. We call this mobilisation and what we're doing is hoping that we can help towards restoring some motion. OK, so Norton, you'll feel me lifting this leg up slowly and bringing it back towards your chest. That's good. There. And then let's straighten. Feel that? Right, and now the other leg.'

A thing being moved and pulled and pushed and that thing is me. Last week, Nathalie moved on to a paediatrics placement in Cardiff. She told me she'd written up my notes and the rest of the team would be just brilliant at working with me. 'But listen, Norton,' she said, 'I want you to keep trying, OK. You keep trying to move those eyes and those fingers, Norton, because I know you can do it.'

I don't know if she really believed it, Nathalie, but she sounded like she did. The other physios tend to sound less convinced. Or maybe they're just bored. Like that Becky who I can hear over in the corner of the ward right now – she's there with Bed Two, asking him if he can't squeeze just a little tighter, but with a tone that suggests she's thinking about whether she'll have pasta or pizza for dinner.

After this, she will move to Bed Four – Three is always wheeled out to a different room for his physiotherapy sessions. I'm not sure why, but I've given up trying to understand the logic of the hospital. Then Becky will come to me and she'll say, 'Right, let's start with your eyes. How about trying a blink for me please, Norton?' And she'll wait as if she's counting the seconds, and she'll scribble on her sheets.

I was so certain yesterday that I'd done it. Not a full blink, maybe, but something. A tightening, a shiver in my eye muscles. And I waited for the angels to sing hallelujah and for Becky to dance for joy and sob with relief, then run to tell the doctors the happy news. But if it truly happened, this movement of my eye – the culmination of weeks of strain and effort – she didn't see it, because she was already telling me to have a little go at moving my fingers, please, Norton.

Nobody calls me Norton. You don't even know me. You don't know the first thing about me. So don't call me fucking Norton.

'Right. Let's see if I put my hand into your hand here whether you can give my fingers a tiny squeeze. So, try that please, Norton. Big try.'

Don't call me fucking Norton. My name is Ned.

MRS M

HOLY FATHER, HEAR MY prayer. Look after Alfred Mortimer and keep him safe in your blessed kingdom. Why Vicar keeps calling him Alfie I cannot imagine. It's not as if Alfred didn't come to this very church every Sunday. Although he was a rather quiet person. One always had to tell him to speak up. Nice singing voice though, as I've told Vicar many times.

'A lovely baritone, that Alfred Mortimer. You really should invite him onto the choir.' You might have thought that Vicar would remember me saying that, even if he recalls nothing else about the poor man, because, for all my warning looks, on he ploughs with Alfie this, Alfie that, now let us all be seated for a moment of private prayer and reflection while we remember our friend, Alfie.

Poor Alfred. May he be at peace. Though if such music were to be played at my funeral, I fear that I should never rest. 'Abide With Me' and 'Jerusalem' were what we played for Roger. Respectful, appropriate hymns. None of this Robin Williams rubbish. Poor Alfred.

And that poem. Sweet of his granddaughter to try, but what is it about a death that makes everybody suddenly believe themselves to be Emily Dickinson?

'I have tears in my eye, because I did not want you to die.' I believe that was it. 'I never wanted to part, but Grandpa's forever in my heart.'

I trust nobody will throw together bad poetry to eulogise me. One blessing of having no children or grandchildren. And of course Harriet will not be there now, otherwise no doubt she'd have been straight up with some gushing words about friendship. No, Lord, give me Romans 8, 'Who shall separate us from the love of Christ'. Or John 14, 1–3 'Do not let your hearts be troubled'. Or else . . .

What are we to sing next? This order of service is rather blurred.

Ah, Frank Sinatra. I might have known.

I . . .

Silly old eyes. I don't seem to be able to . . .

Of course, it's time to . . .

. . . stand and sing.

Dear me. I feel a little . . .

. . . maybe if I . . .

I shall stay seated just a moment or two, yes that's . . .

. . . better. Just a passing . . .

Now where . . .

A migraine, perhaps. Harriet used to have them. I . . .

Yes, migraine. And isn't a lady allowed to remain seated for a moment or two?

I . . . where are we?

. . . be thy name.

. . . thy kingdom come . . . .

Yes, perfectly well. Yes, of course I can stand. Yes, I am most certain. No, perfectly all right. Just a passing migraine. Absolutely fine.

KIKI

'SILLY OLD WITCH. SPILLS her drink and then snaps at me about it. Not even a "Sorry". Just, "Get a dustpan, Meredith". And has the nerve to tell me my boots are inappropriate.'

Meet Meredith – Mervyn's daughter. And, yes, she always sounds that happy. She was in a foul mood already because Merv told her that researching an essay is no reason to not help out in the pub when they have a function on. There was a lot of shouting from the kitchen while I was putting out the plates for the buffet. Him about her taking his credit card to nightclubs, her that there was no point hiring me if I couldn't manage the bar on my own, and that he didn't have any idea what hard work a degree was.

She had a face like a dark cloud on her before any of the guests even arrived. Now she looks like somebody's snatched an ice cream out of her hand. She slammed that plate of cheese straws down. Look how it made Vicar jump. He was waiting for me to pour him his sherry, and saying what a good turnout it was for dear Alfie. Now he can't get away quickly enough.

'I'm not clearing up her mess. I was perfectly polite, offering her the sandwich platter and she makes this face at me, and drops her glass on the floor. Not even an apology. Stupid cow.' As she's telling me this, Meredith's making a face. 'So I ask her what the hell she's doing and she just stares at me like she

37

doesn't even know who I am. It's my pub for heaven's sake. Must be drunk, the silly witch, or overexcited about outliving another one of the old bastards. You only ever see her in here after a funeral. Taking notes, probably. Or maybe it's the free drinks. She was definitely slurring. And that look.'

The face again.

'You get the dustpan, Kiki. You're her friend. I'll mind the bar.'

'Whose friend?' Because I don't know anybody here and Meredith hasn't told me which old witch she's talking about.

'Her, of course. Poisonous old cow.' I'm not sure if Meredith is still mimicking or if this is her own expression to tell me how stupid I am. But I'm looking over in the direction she's nodding in and even though the pub is full of pensioners in black, I know who she's talking about. The pub is pretty crowded but there's a space around her. Maybe because of the broken glass.

She really does look a bit like the Queen of England, on a not-great day. She might wear one of those hats, although this one also looks a bit like those knitted things people put on teapots. And you never see pictures of the Queen with her hair sticking out like that. A bit like a wire brush. But still, she looks decent for somebody that age.

'Kiki. Get the bloody dustpan.'

I could point out to Meredith that she was only just complaining about people not saying 'please' but I'm not sure that would go down well, so I just nod and go to find it.

'No O.'

I don't know if this was the look that Meredith was talking about but it's pretty stern. Except I don't know what the old woman is talking about. No O? All I said was that I was going to clear up the broken glass, Mrs O'Malley, if she didn't mind.

'There is not an O in my name. Do I look Irish to you? My name is Malley, Mary Malley. No O. You may call me Mrs Malley.'

Let's not mention those times I've taken her dog back after he's turned up howling outside the pub and she's called me 'you' or 'girl' or 'whatever-your-name-is'. Instead I'm mumbling an apology and saying I've just come to clear up the glass she dropped.

'I did no such thing.'

I can't even look at her. 'But . . . Meredith said . . .'

'What Meredith Paterson says about anything is of no interest to me.'

I'm about to say something else, but maybe it's best not to. I'm trying not to stare at the broken pieces of glass on the floor. I'm trying not to stare at her either. Except, the more I'm trying not to, the more I can't help doing it. And the look she's giving me back is not friendly.

Like Meredith said, something does look a bit off. Like she's frowning, but with her eyes. And the words are out without stopping to think. 'Is something wrong, Mrs Malley?'

And of course now her face looks fine again. Except that it does look pretty angry.

'Of course there is nothing wrong. And I would most certainly remember if I had dropped a glass. I may be eighty-four but I am not senile quite yet.'

NED

I NEVER KNEW HOW FREE I was.

Don't get me wrong, I knew I was lucky, that I'd had a good draw in the old lottery of life. Without being big-headed, I had health and enough money, decent looks and brains. As people go, I knew that I was OK.

But I didn't know how free I was. I didn't know that luck was a smaller thing than having friends who enjoyed my company or YouTube comments from people who loved my videos. Luck was walking to the shops. Luck was lifting a toilet lid. Luck was answering a phone. Luck was googling.

Googling – silly word. Something that felt too easy to be of any value. Something that I thought as little of as breathing, not that I take that for granted anymore. The one glorious relief of this godawful time was my lungs frog-kicking back to the surface when they finally pulled out that tube.

When I'm feeling that nothing could be worse than my current existence, I remind myself of those days, when the air was being pushed into and sucked out of me. I could feel it and I could hear it, awake and aware, with my throat open like an inflatable doll. So things could be worse. I cannot do much, but I can breathe.

Luck is breathing. How did I never know that?

Luck is googling.

Back then I could have tapped in key words such as 'coma' or 'consciousness' or 'cerebral haemorrhage', 'paralysis' or 'prognosis'. Knowledge was at my fingertips. Now, I listen out for scraps of information and, when they come, I'm ready to pounce – metaphorically – so that I can store them away like a squirrel before winter. I hoard my snippets, stockpiling them in my head. If I can collect up enough of these jigsaw pieces, I will be able to put them together into the full picture. But I struggle to remember the words, I do not understand all the meanings and my only search engine is me.

All of those important early discussions happened when everything was so foggy. Was it the drugs? Or perhaps my damaged brain was still too bruised to focus. None of it felt like it could be real. My mother was there – crying, begging them to fix me, sobbing. That seems likely enough. But I was sure my father was there too, and he's been dead fifteen years. Let alone the children at the end of my bed singing nursery rhymes.

That had to be a dream. Sometimes I still think it all must be.

These things I know: there was a time which passed without me knowing – a period of true unconsciousness, I'm not sure how long – and now the doctors do not know that I have woken up inside. Because outside, nothing has changed. Nothing moves, nothing reacts. They cannot see the difference. They have not ruled it out, but they do not believe it. My mother – assuming she was real – insisted I must be able to hear her.

She had seen the film about the editor from French *Vogue*. Or was it *Elle*? About the butterfly. The one who wrote the book by blinking.

'His eyes are open. My baby can hear us,' she told them – with the delivery of the trained actress she is. 'My poor son, trapped inside his own body.' This must have been real. Such melodrama could only have come from my mother.

Unlikely, though not impossible, the doctors told her – yes, his eyes are open yet there is no sign of voluntary eye movement. Cases of actual locked-in syndrome are rare, and controlled blinking is the norm. Although the body will be entirely paralysed, the eyes retain vertical movement. Generally patients signal their awareness through eye control, which did not appear to be the case with me.

Magnetic brain imaging showed extensive trauma to the brain. They didn't wish to harbour false hopes. Recovery or a return to any form of consciousness was possible but not likely.

'She's right. My mother's right. I'm still here,' I was screaming in every part of me that made no mark on the outside world. 'I can hear you. I understand every word. Look – here I am.' I told those eyes that should have moved that they must move. If I could do that tiny thing then everybody would know. But the conversation continued around me in words which were becoming more familiar: brain stem infraction and unresponsive wakefulness syndrome.

If only I could have googled. Or if only I had studied biology instead of philosophy and music.

Bella was often here too, citing heroes the internet had offered up who'd spent months in a coma only to return to work or skydive or run a marathon. She took photos of me, insisting to anybody who'd listen that this would be her chronicle of her fiancé's road to recovery.

Fiancé? As if that discussion had never happened.

I could not ask her why she was there, after what I'd said. I couldn't thank her either, for not abandoning me.

Sometimes, both of them would be here at the same time, the mother I hadn't seen for years and the ex-fiancée who seemed to have forgotten that I'd ever said it was over.

'My mother's instincts tell me he will beat this. I know he will.'

'In sickness and in health. Darling, I'll prove I mean it.'

Often darkness returned. Time was elastic and unpredictable, with lashes of wakefulness and pain and relapses, waking up to a jolt like lightning with masked faces looking down, and a voice saying, 'We have a pulse.'

I do not remember the tube being put into my throat, just that it was there, nor can I recall why it was removed again – perhaps they were confident that I would breathe without it. Or perhaps they assumed I would not. I remember hearing sobbing.

But I did breathe. I do still breathe.

My mother does not come anymore. She will always love me, so she said, with the tears to prove it – her poor, broken boy. But there was a role, in Los Angeles, one she could hardly turn down. If it might have helped for her to put her life on hold, of course, she would not have hesitated, but . . .

Bella still comes most days. I learn a lot from what she tells her phone camera as she documents my new life – the doctors say that the longer I remain unresponsive, the smaller my chances of recovery, and that I may never regain any awareness of my surroundings. She refuses to believe it. She knows me better, she says.

When she is here I am at my most frantic with my attempts at eye movement. Because she must see, mustn't she? She who loves me enough to be here with me still, despite everything. She must be watching for the tiniest sign. And it would be recorded for the doctors to see.

I am the castaway signalling for all I'm worth at the plane flying overhead.

Move eyes. Move. But the plane continues on its merry way.

Bella sits on the side of my bed. I can only see her face when she bends into my field of sight. That is the scope of my vision – whatever position I have been placed into by nurses, I can only stare ahead. When Bella moves her left hand in front of me, which being left-handed she does to operate her mobile, the ring on her finger flashes and reflects light from its sharp cut edges.

She cried when I gave her that ring. She also cried when I told her how sorry I was, but that we should go our separate ways. I wondered then if I should ask her to give the ring back. But I couldn't bring myself to do it.

MRS M

D ON'T BE SCARED, LITTLE starling. I shan't hurt you and neither will Wordsworth. He's far more interested in that smelly old marrowbone than your seeds. Besides, his lead is attached to a stake in the ground. Tethered like a goat, and thus he shall remain, until he learns not to run off again. For that, I'm sorry to say, is how one must deal with a naughty dog. So you need not be scared of him. That's right. All that lovely birdseed just waiting to be pecked up. Oh, you handsome little bird. Yes, you eat all those seeds. You with your shimmering feathers.

'Hope is the thing with feathers.' Who wrote that? Elizabeth Barrett Browning? No. No. The American one. Harriet loved her. Eleanor? Emma? Somebody was talking about her earlier. Silly old brain. I never used to have these problems. A human encyclopaedia, Harriet called me.

Her great–niece recited it at her funeral, Harriet's, 'the thing with feathers, that perches in the soul . . .' She read it beautifully, in actual fact. A striking young woman, even if . . . well, Harriet always said the father was never mentioned. And she did bring that female friend to the funeral.

Great-great-niece I suppose, now I think about it. A lovely speaking voice, but a shame the poor girl was given that name. Summer, is it? Or Sunshine. Quite ridiculous. Had I ever had a daughter, I should have named her Deborah. A proper name.

And had I had a son, he would have been John. None of this Rainbow or River nonsense.

Harriet did love poetry. That's why Wordsworth is Wordsworth, of course. She was always keen that I should have a dog too. The companionship would be good for me, she used to tell me – which didn't say a great deal for her opinion of Roger, now did it?

I suppose she would have liked me to name mine Coleridge, then Wordsworth and Coleridge could have walked together in the woods.

Emily Dickinson! *Hope is the Thing With Feathers.* Just like you, little bird. Look at your expression. So fixed and beady. Reminds me of that frog girl. With the accent and the plaits. Such strange looks she was giving me earlier. I very nearly had a word with Mervyn. Not that there would be much point talking to Mervyn Paterson about politeness.

I told her of course that I was perfectly all right, as if it was any of her business. But she still kept giving me that look. Yes, little starling, very like that.

Maybe I did feel just that teeny bit peculiar at Alfred's funeral. I think perhaps I needed a drink of water. It is very hot today. I shall call for a check-up at the opticians, too, because things were a little out of focus. And—

Now, listen to you, Mr Starling.

How is it the poem goes – something about a tune without words. Harriet would have known. She wrote me that poem for my birthday one year when she was so annoyed with Roger because he'd forgotten. Not that I minded really. One reaches an age when one stops caring about such things. But Harriet did mind. She came round with the most exquisite bouquet of lilac and freesias, it smelt divine – and a card and the poem too. She said I deserved to have poetry written for me by somebody so she'd penned me a birthday bucket list.

'Harriet,' I told her, 'bucket lists are for the sort of people who read Sunday tabloids.' But she said it was perfectly fitting for marvellous old ladies such as ourselves to have them too. Although in fact she did not call it a bucket list, but something far ruder. It rhymed with bucket. Something that I should have said to Roger long ago, according to Harriet. She was awful.

I never showed it to Roger. I'm not convinced that he'd have seen the funny side. I hid it inside *Mrs Beeton's Book of Household Management* – no danger of him coming across it there. Such a naughty poem it was, but so terribly droll. Marvellous rhymes. Let me think, something about being old and past our prime and it being time for misbehaviour before we had to meet our saviour. What else? Driving in sports cars and being mutton dressed up as lamb. And going to the Ritz and ordering chips. And bathing nude on holiday. And about burying her in a tuxedo when she died. And stockings – that's right. Oh, dear Harriet – because, it rhymed with shocking. *Bury me in something shocking, a white tuxedo and some fishnet stockings.*

Of course, I never relayed that to Penny when it came to the actual funeral.

It was only a poem after all.

Oh, little starling, off you fly then. I suppose it's time for me to untether you too, Wordsworth. And I shall phone the optician before tea. They're doing it again, rather, my eyes. Which does explain why my head is aching so.

Righty-ho. Call optician, peel potatoes, grill chicken. But first I shall make sure that poem of Harriet's is still inside Mother's old *Mrs Beeton.*

KIKI

I SHOULD PROBABLY INTRODUCE YOU to my mother at this point. You can't see her, can you? I mean, not *see* see. But she's here. Just here by the bed. A little bit above the bed. She likes to mainly hover. And I know you can't actually see her – or I can't at any rate. Not with your eyes. But you can see her with your, you know, mind – and you can hear her, sort of, too.

Isn't it the sweetest little voice? Like magical bells in a Disney film and words which are singing but quiet. If you listen hard you can just make out what she's saying. There – you hear that? '*You know in your heart there's something wrong. Run and check she's safe – it won't take long.*'

She means Mrs Malley. But there's only so much you can upset an old lady in one day. I don't think she'd be pleased to have me turn up on her doorstep. She'd hit me with her umbrella or call the police or something.

'*If your instincts are kind then they can't be ignored.*' See the shimmering of glittery dust in the air as she speaks? It catches the light because her wings are beating the air, even if you can't see them. She smells like candy floss. It's faint, but sometimes you can smell it. '*A good deed is its own reward.*'

She's giving me her hardest stare. I can sense it on me, with those huge Disney eyes and those long eyelashes.

I'm not falling for it.

'Mother. I'm not going.'

You're surprised I talk out loud to her? I'd never do it when there are other people with me. I'm not stupid. Or not that stupid. But, yes, we have conversations sometimes when I'm alone.

You should see the way she's crossing her arms. She never likes it if I say no. But don't worry, she'll be all giggles again in a moment.

The funny thing is I've never even watched *Peter Pan*. I suppose I must have seen a poster when I was little. Or maybe another child at my playgroup had a doll or a book or a lunchbox. Because when she first started coming to me she was completely real. Not like a ghost or a whatsit. Not like now, when I'm not seeing her with my eyes just with my – I don't know, senses. Back then I really saw her: green leaf skirt, blonde hair scooped up. Apparition. That's what she wasn't. She was really there. No wand either. She's not a real fairy. Or a ghost.

Because, just so we're clear, I do know she's not real.

So, no, I'm not mad. And I don't have schizophrenia either, either, which I'm guessing is your next question. Everyone assumes it, if I'm ever foolish enough to tell them about her – which I don't. Not anymore.

Everybody's read stories in newspapers, and they reckon they know. They think people who hear voices or see things all have schizophrenia.

There was a woman back home. Tanisha. She had a unit, along the lake from Yaya and me. She had loads of photos of places in Asia and Africa and of people singing or playing instruments. And lovely incense. She was a photographer. And she also had schizophrenia except you couldn't see that. She was just normal. And nice.

It's what Sue thought too, first of all, when she heard me talking on the stairs. I'd just moved to Auckland after Yaya died. I had this tiny studio on the top floor of the same building. And I mean tiny, even smaller than this one, if you can believe that. And sometimes it just felt too small. I had to get out. Except there wasn't really anywhere to go. I didn't know anyone and I didn't want to sit in a cafe or bar on my own. Often I'd go for walks but this one time, it was raining outside, so I was sitting on the stairs because it felt better being there than in my own tiny room.

My mother popped up and was talking to me about something – probably about being stronger than I thought I was or not having to be scared about being alone. And I was talking back to her because I didn't think there was anyone else around. Except then Sue came out and asked if I could keep it quiet on my phone because she was studying. When she realised that I didn't have a phone and it was just me talking to myself, she was quite excited I think, because of having done that course in psychology and because she'd never met a person with schizophrenia, before.

She invited me into her flat for a coffee and wanted to know all about it. 'Don't worry,' she said. 'I'm not judging you.'

I think she was pretty disappointed when I told her I didn't have schizophrenia, but she must have decided I was still interesting because she googled it.

'Hearing voices is not so uncommon, actually.' That's what Sue told me when she invited me for another coffee the next day. 'And it's not just in schizophrenia, apparently. It's people with mental illnesses or people who've come through a trauma or just ordinary people for no obvious reason. This article I found said one in ten people hear voices at some point. Isn't it funny that nobody talks about it?'

Sue's theory was that people were scared of others thinking there was something wrong with them. I reckon that's right.

Anyway, that's how Sue and I got to know each other. She suggested I could move in to her spare room because her flat was expensive for her on her own, and she talked about writing me up as a case study and maybe even going back to finish her psychology course. She'd been training as a hairdresser but she'd decided that wasn't right for her either. She was going to be a life coach now. Or maybe a therapist.

So, no, I'm not mad, and other people hear voices too, even if they don't say they do. I like my mum being there, if you must know. Even when she does give me hard stares, like now – can you hear her? *'All it would take is one little call. What if she's hurt or had a fall?'*

Mother, there is no way I am calling Mrs M to see if she's had a fall. Anyway I don't have her number. So you can sulk, and rhyme, and shimmer all you like. I'm going to look out my notebook and start doing something useful.

Yes, this notebook here. And where is my pen? Because I'm not about to go round to Mrs Malley's house. Trust me, that would not go down very well.

NED

'. . . THAT NOBODY UNDERSTANDS what you are capable of like I do. I explained to them how sharing your journey could help to raise awareness of . . .'

The doctors are not being fair, so Bella feels. They've told her that it is not feasible to allow a film crew into the hospital even though she thinks it's important to capture this part of my 'journey'. What would she call it, I wonder, if the doctors allowed the filming of my documentary? Something enigmatic. *Norton's Struggle? The Day the Music Stopped?*

I'd forgotten just how formidable Bella can be when she's set her mind to something. And how loyal she is too. I first met her at a charity event I had no wish to be at. This was not long after my father died – though he and my mother had divorced years earlier. My mother had recently remarried – or should that be re-re-remarried – and she'd not yet become bored of the new game of being an English country lady.

Bella was a pretty teenager, a year and a bit younger than me. I was angry, grieving and rude and when she asked if I wanted to hang out with her and her friends, I was not very pleasant to her. But she found my telephone number somehow because she called the next day and the day after that. She invited me to go riding with her, and to the cinema. Every time I went away – to school, to university, travelling – she'd be there when I came back.

'You know you're happy to see me,' she used to say.

And I started to realise I was.

She's here now because I have been moved to a new bed in a room of my own on a new unit. The Sunshine Unit for Neurological and Stroke Rehabilitation has only been open a month. It's state of the art, and Bella's alternating between talking to me and turning to her iPhone to record her commentary.

When she reaches close in to me, she smells like my old life. I can picture her perfume bottle, round, with a gold cap. I bought it for her from a duty-free shop at Geneva airport after a skiing holiday with some old pals from university. Occasionally, she takes my hand and sits in silence, or sighs and leans in to me with a kiss on my cheek or forehead. But right now, she's in full Bella flow.

'. . . highlight the benefits of physical therapy and showcases this centre while also capturing the calamity of a consciousness disorder for such a young person . . .'

Along with the new location – not that one hospital ceiling is much unlike another – I am to continue physical rehabilitation sessions and physiotherapy, but I will also benefit from the sensory garden, weekly music therapy and, by next month, if all goes well, a spanking new aqua-therapy pool. Quite the five-star hotel.

Is that ungrateful? I know that this is landing on my feet. There is a team working to keep my body from shrivelling. They are trained and devoted and they want to help me. Not all hospitals are so fortunate as to have generous benefactors opening new units. This place is the product of a decade of fundraising by a very wealthy woman whose husband was treated here. I know this because the consultant was talking about it earlier, to the students who were following him as he swept in on his rounds. He stopped by my bed and he addressed me as Mr Edbury.

'Good afternoon, Mr Edbury,' he said. 'I trust you will not mind my explaining that you have recently come to this unit from the acute neurological ward. As you can see, Mr Edbury is now breathing unaided.' He proceeded to talk to them about a 'pontine haemorrhage following traumatic injury and subsequent period of induced coma and ventilation' and about complex evaluations and something called the Glasgow Coma Scale, before one of the students asked a question which I didn't understand and which led to a lengthy discussion on cortical function which was way beyond me.

One student said then that she had seen my eyes move when he'd said my name and the consultant gave a reply which was something about observational assessments over weeks and months and about how such involuntary reflexes didn't necessarily indicate any significant level of awareness.

'From my experience, Ms Zwicki, it is often the case that upon seeing such uncontrolled physical reactions, relatives will infer a higher level of consciousness than is in fact present. Understandable, but as doctors you will find that the majority of reported interactions can be ascribed to wishful thinking rather than to actual cogent activity.

'In genuine cases of pseudo-coma, or locked-in syndrome as it is widely known, one will generally find that vertical eye movement remains intact, despite otherwise total paralysis, due to sparing of the reticular formation. Thus the patient will be able to communicate his conscious state, although this must be confirmed by consistent correct responses to questions, rather than anecdotal or occasional and inconsistent reflex responses.'

I swear I was moving my eyes at that very moment. But the consultant – I believe his name is Mr Douglas – continued his lecture.

Come on Ms Zwicki, I willed her. Ask me something. Test me. Ask if I can hear you. Ask me if I know where I am, or what my name is, or what two plus two makes.

But the consultant thanked me for my time and off they all went.

And now, here is Bella, clutching my hand while telling her mobile telephone how she'll never stop fighting my corner. And I am moving my eyes again. I swear I am. Like a flag waving above my head. I can feel them. Why can she not see it?

'. . . my Norton is too loved and too talented and has too much to offer for the world to give up on him and . . .'

Bella, look. Annabella, look. Look, Bella. Bella!

When I was still me, I kept myself in shape. As well as the running and the football and the Pilates of course, I went to the gym three or four times a week. I cycled too. I never imagined that the thing I needed to be exercising would be my eyes. Before I ended our engagement, Bella and I would go riding on her parents' estate at weekends. I liked my body to ache at the end of a day. Then, my muscles were taut and firm. Afterwards, before I'd even showered, she'd tug up my top and kiss me. Her perfume smells of those kisses.

Pilates, Passion & Practice. All of that was her idea. I was dismissive at first, but it was fun to do, and I clocked up twenty-thousand-odd views, which felt pretty fantastic. She's a doer, Bella.

Chanel. Her perfume. Not No 5. Something else. Fresher. Younger.

'. . . and Norton's story shows how a life can be overturned in the blink of an . . .'

Eyes, Annabella. Look at me. Please.

Like flowers and apples and lemon zest and sunshine. The smell of her body against mine. Breathing it in as her eyes locked onto mine. *Chance*. That's what her perfume was called. I would nuzzle into the soft hollows of her neck and breathe it in. All those times, snuggled against her, listening or half-listening to some recounting of a work project, or some story about something a friend had done.

Bella. Look at me.

She has beautiful eyes. More grey than blue. And her skin is pale and even. No freckles, just one little mole on her right hipbone, peeking down at her appendix scar.

Oh please, Bella.

Such soft skin. I loved to rub my cheek across her, smelling her and—

My god. Now this is unexpected, and a little embarrassing, but I'm feeling the swell of a desire that's been absent since all of this. If I could, I would be reaching inside my hospital gown, to check if my body is doing what it believes it is doing. Surely Bella can sense this.

'. . . the message I suppose that Norton would want to give to the world is to never give up, however bleak the future seems.'

For pity's sake, look at me.

Finally. She is standing and leaning in so that her chest comes into my field of vision. She is wearing a white T-shirt and I can just make out the contrast through the cotton of her bra against her skin. From my bed, with its top end slightly raised, I am watching her bend into me, into my line of sight, and smelling her perfume. Is she going to touch her lips onto mine?

I feel a sudden surge. Will she press her body closer? Thread her fingers into my hair. Would she dare hike up her skirt and climb onto me here? Surely not, when a nurse could walk in at any moment?

'Poor Norton.' She gives my forehead a kiss. 'But you'll come through this, darling, wait and see.'

No, Annabella, no. *You* wait. Look. You must see the SOS that my eyes are flashing, that my body is throbbing? I'm a human distress signal for Christ's sake. Annabella . . .

'Sleep well, my love. I'll be back tomorrow.'

MRS M

HERE WE GO. *MRS Beeton's Book of Household Management.* Do stop looking at me that way, Wordsworth, you shall have your tea in two shakes. Patience, dog, is a virtue. Goodness me, but this book does bring back memories. Standing on a chair at Mother's side, while she beat and creamed and whipped and rolled and folded, and I would be pleading with her to let me help, and secretly hoping that she might permit me to lick the bowl.

The book had once belonged to her own mother, and she remembered standing on her own chair. 'One day it will be you teaching these recipes to your daughter,' she'd tell me. Though of course that was not to be.

Mother's sponge pudding was a thing of beauty. I can almost taste it now. And there is nobody here to appreciate this fact except Wordsworth, so I address my thoughts to him.

'Do you know, dog, I cannot for the life of me understand why nobody cares for a pudding anymore?'

Not cosmopolitan enough, I suppose. No Asiatic influences or Mediterranean twists. Everything now must be a fusion of something or other. Although, she made a rather nice-looking spotted dick the other day, the one on BBC2 that Harriet liked. The one who's always licking her fingers. And I thought to myself how many years it was since I'd eaten one. Roger never liked them. And the ones they gave us at school were simply awful. But Mother's was marvellous. And her custard never came out of a packet.

'So, Wordsworth,' I say. 'If I . . . if I—'

Oh, yes, here it is. Harriet's . . .

What was I saying?

Mrs Beeton. I—

'Oh, Wordsworth, this blasted headache. I should have taken a nap when I came back from – where was I again?'

Maybe if I – oh bother! That noise. That—

What on earth is Mrs Beeton doing down on—

On the . . . ? Down on—

Did? Did I think I . . . I . . .

KIKI

*I*OANNA MOON. FACTS.
   This is what I have written at the top of the page of my notebook. The one I found in the pub. It's one of those ones with the pages held together by a wire spiral.
   Then I've written:

Born – Glastonbury (roadside, near Pilton festival).
DEFINITE.
   23rd June 1971. DEFINITE.
   Died – Glastonbury, or nearby? (Van? very near. Yaya said near stone circle said NOT festival.)
   Stan Douglas – who is he? Poison? Why? Came through window?

I have this notebook in my left hand. On my right knee, I'm balancing another one. Its cover has a picture of three cartoon puppies. On the first page, in pencil writing: *Kiki Moon, I am 6. My secruts.* There is a box drawn around the word *secrets*. On the second page. *Big secrut — Gramps is my favurit.* But below it, in purple coloured pencil, is *Yaya is too* with lots of badly drawn hearts. I must have felt guilty.

   'Call back if I can help any more.' Pam at the Glastonbury register office told me, when I phoned before the wake earlier. And also, 'You're welcome, Kid.'

Gramps used to call me Kid. Or Babber sometimes. 'All right, Babber? What's that you're playing?' And it's like Pam calling me Kid with her accent from here has brought his voice back into my head. I'm here, in my window nook, looking out at The Fox and Hounds sign, with these two notebooks on my knee, and there's an ache in my gut. Gramps, with his cuddles and his calmness and his 'grab your sleeping bags, girls, the stars are too lush for roofs tonight'.

The three of us – him, Yaya and me – would lie in a row, each in our hammocks stretched out between the wooden poles he'd hammered in by the lake edge. I'd try to stay awake while they talked about other nights and other countries and other times. If they thought I was asleep, they'd start whispering.

I'd listen as long as I could, telling myself I must remember everything they said – names of bands and friends and stories of jumping in vans to drive the length of the country, and of tents blowing away in gales and acquaintances falling into ditches or leaping onto stages to perform with heroes.

If it was about my mum, Yaya might cry then too. I'd have to listen really hard to try to understand what she was saying.

Yaya never learned English at school, only after Gramps brought her to England. You never quite knew if her words were the ones she meant to say or just ones that had come into her head. Gramps said she talked her own language. Yaya-ish, a Greek-Kiwi-Somerset mix. 'Your Yaya is unique,' he used to say. 'Never forget that, Babber.'

As if I could.

When Pam asked why I was calling, I said I'd ordered a copy of my mother's death certificate by email a couple of months ago from New Zealand, but I'd had an email back saying there was no death registered with the details I'd given.

'Oh dear,' she said. 'Let's have a little look.'

I'm holding the spiral notebook – it's one someone left in the pub, unused except for a couple of pages of doodles and some letters, like for working out a crossword.

Ioanna Moon, I've written. *Facts.*

Sue always says it's important to focus on the facts. So that's what I'm doing.

Ioanna is Greek for Joanna. I know where and when she was born because it's like our family legend. Yaya always loved to talk about my mum's birth, but if I asked her about her death, it was like suddenly she couldn't understand anything that was said.

My mum died when I was three which was 1997. I don't know the exact date, but Pam said the search would have allowed a couple of years either side, so that shouldn't matter if I'm sure of the year. She asked how certain I was about the place of death. Widening the geographical area could help, she said.

'Yeah,' I told her. 'Nah. I'm certain where it was.'

It was written in my book of secrets – or *secruts. Glasonby.*

There's a website with births, marriages and deaths – all the old certificates being put online. It goes up to 1997. I told Pam I'd already looked on that. Sue'd found it for me when she was helping me back in Auckland. When we looked on it there was an Iris Moon who died in Frome – not too far from Glastonbury – in the summer of 1997 but she was 78, way too old, and a Ioanna Free who was born in 1971, and her death was registered in December of the right year. But it was in a place called Penrith and I checked where that was. It's up in the north of England, almost Scotland. Miles away from Glastonbury. Anyway, their names were both wrong.

There were other Ioannas though their dates and places was wrong too. And none had the last name Moon. None were my mum. A Joanna Moonfleet died in Bristol in August 1997. But she was only five, poor thing.

'Do you have your mother's birth certificate? Passport? Any other paperwork?' Pam asked.

Yaya and I were burgled after she became ill. They took all our passports and certificates. Old letters from Gramps, too, and pictures my mum had drawn when she was little. It was the most upset I saw Yaya ever. But she said the thieves were stupid because they hadn't found her grandmother's gold earrings that she'd sewn inside one of the cushions.

After Yaya died, I cut open all our cushions and found enough dollars to pay for my plane ticket to England. I never found her grandmother's earrings though.

I told Pam I wouldn't bother ordering a copy of my mum's birth certificate, because I knew all of that information. My own birth certificate is the replacement Yaya ordered after the burglary. My mum's signature has the Os of Moon crossing over each other. That's how I sign my name now too.

The father's details are all blank, but it has my mother's place of birth and occupation and address when I was born. It says *student* and the address is on the Holloway Road in London. My place of birth is a hospital called the Whittington.

The first thing I did when I arrived in London – after dropping off my backpack at ratbag-landlady-Siobhan's and having a sleep – was check out the address. But it was more like a hostel than a home, and the man on the desk wasn't very friendly. I went to the Whittington too. I rode up and down the escalators and went into the shop and told a few people about me being born there. I told the woman in the information booth on the ground floor. She said, 'Oh, wow.' Then she said, 'How can I help you?' I didn't really have anything to say back.

Ioanna Moon. Facts.

My pen's in my mouth. Yaya always told me I shouldn't chew my pens and I can feel the plastic cracking as I do it now. I write down my own date of birth. And *London.* And *the Whittington, Holloway.* And *student.*

Yaya never told me anything about my father, except that he was one of the 'crusties' that Ioanna lived with. It wasn't Yaya being rude, she said, everyone called them that – crusties and new age travellers. Gramps always joked that he and Yaya were old age travellers then, but they weren't really. They had their barn which Gramps had converted all by himself.

My mum and her friends were arrested heaps of times but not because they were doing anything wrong. Mostly they were trying to save woods or forests from being cut down. They'd chain themselves to trees or dig tunnels and hide in them. That was how my mum ended up doing law studies in London, because she wanted to learn how to fight in court instead. But she'd only just started when she found out she was pregnant with me. The university said she could finish her studies when she was ready. Except she died too soon.

University of North London, I write. And *Who was my dad? Yaya said one of mum's crusty group. Other friends?*

I found the address of the old barn Yaya and Gramps lived in. My mum went and stayed back there with them after I was born. But I don't think there's any point going there now. I looked on Google Maps. There's just a big supermarket and car park where it used to be.

It's cosy here, with the pub sign creaking outside. And I'm trying to think what else I know for definite. I open my little girl secret book and turn the page.

Mumy did wen I wos 3. The 3 is the wrong way round, so is the *s. Somtims she toks to me.*

I had my own cushion, a yellow one. It had a zip on the back. I hid my book of secrets inside it – copying Yaya. After Yaya died, I found it again when I was cutting open the cushions. I'd forgotten all about it. My writing's pretty good for a six-year-old. Gramps was a great teacher. I reckon my spelling would be better now if he'd stayed alive.

I'm thinking of Gramps's voice. 'Your mum would never have chosen to leave you. It just happened. It wasn't her fault. She was sitting down, drawing pictures, and she went to sleep and didn't wake up.'

It was only after he died that I started to think, but why didn't she wake up?

'Your grandfather told you this a hundred times,' Yaya would insist, when I asked her. 'Don't make me talk about it. It brings everything back like it's today again.'

Later, when I told Sue, she said maybe Yaya was telling the truth. Maybe Gramps had told me. Children only take in as much as their brains can understand, so maybe that was why I couldn't remember what I'd been told.

Yaya seemed more and more upset each time I asked. If I carried on pushing her she'd say different things. I never liked to see Yaya sad, so mostly I stopped asking. But one time I confronted her. I demanded to know who Stan Douglas was. 'I know he killed my mother,' I told her. 'I heard you saying it to Gramps. You thought I was asleep but I heard you saying to him that Ioanna was poisoned by a man called Stan Douglas. Who was he, Yaya? Why did he kill my mother?'

What was I? Thirteen maybe. Old enough to ball my fists and say she had to tell me.

But Yaya said she didn't know what I meant, I must have dreamt it.

'I didn't dream it,' I told her. 'I remember you saying it. You said Stan Douglas came in and killed her. You said you'd have saved her if you were there. You said thank God I wasn't there too.'

That's when Yaya started sobbing.

'Who's Stan Douglas?' I asked her. 'Tell me.'

'You were dreaming,' Yaya told me. 'Or it was your imagination making stories. I do not know a Stan Douglas. Nobody killed your mother. It was just an accident.' I think maybe that's when she said about it being a fire. Or maybe that time it was the van accident. Or maybe the gas leak. Maybe all three.

But after Yaya died, I found my secrets book inside my cushion and it was there, written down in my best handwriting in blue pencil. I'm looking at it now. *If she closd the wido stan doglas wodnt hav posund her.*

And here I am, looking at the pages of little-me's overheard secrets from our hammock nights.

If she dint go to glasonby she wud still be her.

Yaya wil mis yona antil she dis. Gramps wil to.

Fank god Kiki wosnt wiv her.

dint ned a dep hol.

Kiki wil go to festivls wen she is gronup.

glasnby is best festivl I wil go when im gronup.

I am sory I et yayas choclat.

This last one is a different secret, I reckon.

I underline 'Stan Douglas' in my other notebook. I've googled the name heaps, of course. There are TV executives and bank managers and rugby players. But nothing came up when I googled it along with my mum's name or *murder* or *poison*. Sue had a go too, because she's not such a digital dodo as I can be. But she couldn't find anything either.

'Are you sure you heard it?' she asked. 'And wrote it down right? You were only six, and – let's face it Kiki – you do get the wrong end of the stick about things.'

But I told her I was certain. I did remember. I heard Yaya saying it.

'If I'd been there, I would have saved her.' Yaya wasn't really a whispering person. She was crying so much that she could hardly say the words. I was in my hammock, and I wanted to cry too.

NED

T HERE IS THIS BODY. I don't know if I can call it mine anymore. And there is Becky, the physiotherapist, yanking and stretching and pummelling. And the body has no option but to let itself be yanked and stretched and pummelled, because over none of these things do I have the slightest control. I cannot say 'stop'. I cannot tell Becky, 'Leave me alone. Go and find some other poor bastard to manhandle.'

What am I now?

My body is no longer me. I observe from deep inside my broken brain. I am a cave dweller.

I loved to sit with friends and contemplate life's questions. Philosophy, I felt, was not valued enough. I loved to debate and to examine. Not with the football team, nor with Bella, but with old pals from university days, over cups of tea or pints of beer.

Cogito, ergo sum said Descartes. I think, therefore I am. I wrote a dissertation on that once. Then there's the big old chestnut – if you'll excuse the pun – of the tree falling when there's nobody there to hear it. Does it make a sound? I'd mull over these perennial questions for hours at a time: an intellectual exercise. Now, thinking is the only existence I have. There may be plenty of people here to hear, but no, I do not make a sound, and if nobody hears the tree fall even though they are there right in front of it, does it even exist?

My moods swing. Inside, in the hollow depths of my mind. They swing up and they swing down. I try to rock them upwards. I picture beautiful places and beautiful people that I have known. I set myself challenges and games. Anagrams. Multiplication tables. Remembering the scores of football matches I've played; the lyrics of early Bowie songs. And then I try to compose music or a poem. But with no pen, no book, no sheets of bars and staves, it is like trying to write on air. I feel the whistle of despair, because the harder I swing myself upwards, searching for *something* to fill the emptiness, the steeper and faster the plummet is as I come back down.

Oh, to dive from the cliff and never resurface. To have the means to make the choice.

'OK. Just going back to the left leg. We're going to lift, and stretch. It's nice, this new unit, isn't it? I haven't been in here before.'

If I could answer, I would cut her off with some monosyllabic response. Mostly she doesn't bother with chit-chat, and I prefer it that way. 'Been anywhere nice recently?' my barber, Pete, used to ask. Sometimes I had, though I wouldn't tell him, because all I wanted was a trim and not a lengthy discussion about my trip to Ibiza or the stag weekend in Prague or about how Pete would have liked to have travelled a bit more if he hadn't had his family to look after.

What am I? What is I? How do I learn to not be me? Or to not be?

I am not able to dive. I cannot throw myself into a river or under a bus. I cannot go on hunger strike because my food comes through a tube. After they took me off the ventilator, I tried to hold my breath. 'Stop breathing,' I told myself. But my lungs continued working.

'OK, Norton, I'm just raising your bed a bit to get you sitting up more.'

I cannot die, but is this living?

'Right, so I'll see you later in the week.'

Does a falling tree know it is falling? If I could starve myself of thought, could I bring an end to this? If I do not think, do I cease to be?

'If it stops raining, I think one of the occupational therapists might get you outside later today or tomorrow.'

Outside. Air. Sunshine. Wind. *Outside.* It has been so many weeks of beds and corridors and machines that beep and curtains that draw, that I had almost forgotten there was an outside.

And, like that, the swing turns and begins to lift me upwards again.

MRS M

I NEED, PLEASE . . . I

. . . Harriet, I . . .

KIKI

DO EXCUSE ME, MRS Malley. Sorry to disturb you but I thought I might have heard Wordsworth outside the pub so I just wanted to check he was safe with you.

She'll shout. She'll say, 'Girl, do you not think one is capable of looking after one's own dog?' But then I can go back to bed and sleep. She's not going to shoot me.

Nearly there. It's the third cottage. The one with the white fence and all the flowers.

I thought I heard your dog barking outside the pub. It's better than, 'I know this is crazy, but I just wanted to check you were OK.'

Kiki Moon, turn around and take yourself back to the pub now before you make a fool of yourself and insult the old woman even more than you've done already. Sue says nobody gets the wrong end of the stick more often than me. And this is the wrongest end of the stickiest stick, I reckon. The lights are on. She's still up, knitting or watching that *Strictly* programme or making jam or whatever old people do. Are you really going to knock on her door because your imaginary fairy mum got you all spooked, and then thinking about your Yaya made you even more jittery?

You know what Sue would say? This is just a – what is the word she always says, like the ads on the radio about having had an accident, and like middle-aged men with big cars and little penises – compensation. Over-compensation. That's what

Sue would say. Kiki, you're over-compensating. It's not going to bring Yaya back.

She probably didn't even drop the glass. Meredith got it wrong, like she said. I should just go back now. I'm imagining it all. I'm over-compensating.

Except I am here now.

Might as well have a little peek in, just quiet like a mouse. If I see Mrs M sitting there with her cup of tea, I can sneak away and I'll know everything is all right. And if she spots me, I can say the thing – I thought I heard Wordsworth outside the pub so I wanted to check he was safe.

The gate is open. One teeny squiz and she won't even notice, probably. I'm not sure why her curtains are still wide open. At least it'll be easier to see inside.

Oh hell. Hear that? No mystery about whether the dog's at home now.

She's bound to come out now to see what he's howling about. She'll catch me standing here.

OK. In case she opens the door, I'm smiling and ready to say about the pub and the barking, except I'll also laugh and say, 'I guess I didn't need to worry, eh?'

Yep, smile. Tell the story. What's the worst she can do?

Where is she though? You'd have thought she'd be out by now.

Unless she's calling the police. Bugger. Wordsworth, can you shut up in there!

Where is she? Bugger, bugger. I'll have just a little look in. If I creep between these bushes – I'm just going to – whoops, sorry flowerpot.

I just happened to be walking past and I heard Wordsworth howling, so I thought I'd trample over your flower beds to spy on you through your windows. That will go down well.

But if I lean up over this bush thing, like – please, don't be gazing out at me, Mrs Malley. Whoops, sorry snail. Right, so, the telly's not on and you're not on the couch. Maybe you're in the kitchen and you've just left the lights on. Plan A then? I'll knock on the door. Smile. Use my line about the dog.

Wait.

What's that on the floor? An old book? Bent open. You don't just leave that open in the middle of the carpet. And what's that slipper – and another slipper next to it – and a leg?

Oh, God. Mrs Malley. I didn't think you'd actually be—

'Mrs Malley!'

I'm banging on the window now, like I'm trying to break it, but you're not moving. Please get up. Come on. Stand up. Hear this hammering on the glass. Get up off the floor. Tell me you were just – I don't know – tidying under the coffee table. Yell at me for sticking my nose in. Shout about the squashed flowers. Call the police. Just please stand up.

Bugger. Bugger. Think, Kiki.

Get a neighbour? Smash the window with a flowerpot? Scream the village down?

Don't you even think about being dead, Mrs M. You told me you were fine. You gave me that look. I asked if you were all right, and you gave me that look. Don't you dare go and be dead now.

Think, Kiki Moon. The side gate? Wordsworth is always escaping through it. Or try the door. Bound to be locked, but might as well try – if I just turn this. No. Or what if I push instead – oh, wow. Not locked then. I reckon Yaya would tell you that's asking for—

No, another time. Thank God it wasn't locked anyway, because I'm in, shouting, 'Mrs Malley. Mrs Malley, it's Kiki from the pub.'

And Wordsworth is running with me. Here she is. He's sniffing her cheek, while I'm kneeling beside her. 'Just let me lift your hand a moment,' I'm telling her, 'so I can check for – oh thank goodness. Now, don't worry. Everything's going to be fine. I'm calling for an ambulance.'

NED

I THINK SOMEBODY IN ANOTHER part of the ward may be dying. Something is happening out there. Not that I have any hope of finding out what it is. My light is off and I assume that even if I could sit up and look around, my door would be shut. But I can hear the swinging open and shut of other doors, in the corridor outside, and a bustle and a hurrying of shoes on hard floors. The clacking of heels tends to mean senior doctors who don't spend entire days on their feet. The nurses have softer soles, so you never hear them coming.

There are voices, not distinct enough for me to work out what is being said – though I'm fairly certain that I heard 'oxygen' and 'family' – but the hum is agitated and urgent and there is a phone that keeps on ringing. Despite myself, I would love to know what is going on.

When I was little, my mother had a regular part on a soap opera that was set in a hospital. She played a nurse called Roxie. We were living in California then and she must have still been married to my father because some of my earliest memories are of sitting with him, on a white leather sofa, dipping fries into melted cheese, while watching my mother delivering babies, performing CPR, or clutching the hands of sobbing patients. I was two or three years old perhaps – and it seemed to me that I must have two different mothers and that the one with the kind eyes and the gentle voice was never the one at the breakfast table telling me not to eat with my mouth open and not to play with my Cheerios.

This part of the hospital is quieter than where I was before. Most nights, there is nothing to listen to apart from the occasional siren outside. There, that's one now. The nights feel longer now, but maybe I'm just more awake. When I try to piece together my time here, I know there are blank stretches – days or weeks at a time maybe – machines and beds and people changing around me without me seeing it happen. Not so much now. The funny thing is I've never had to be in hospital before. As a child, I imagined them to all be like the hospital of my mother's show. *The Hospital of Eternal Hope* it was called, and my toddler self used to think it must be an exciting place. Everybody seemed to be constantly making new friends. I don't remember making this comment but I remember being told, by my father, about a time when I said to my mother that I wanted to go and live with the nice mummy in the 'turnalope' place.

Well, here I am, all grown up and living in my very own hospital. Except there don't seem to be all those new friends that I imagined. The non-stop excitement is lacking, too. Be careful what you wish for, little Ned.

I once trekked through the Amazon, sleeping in hammocks. I caught and ate piranha. Now, here I am, lying on an incontinence pad, with my ears straining to hear the voices outside my room, as attentive as any viewer to their favourite soap opera. The phone is ringing again and I want to yell for somebody to answer it. There is the squeaking of wheels outside too. A trolley passing by? A life lost perhaps. Or being saved?

I'm not even sure if this stab of sadness I feel is for the stranger being pushed past my room, or for me.

On balance, I think it is for me.

MRS M

A THING ABOVE

me, thing,

Thing. Light.

where am?

KIKI

WHERE IS THIS?

This smell is wrong.

It's not the damp beery smell of the pub. Not the scented candle smell of Sue's in Auckland. Not Yaya's smells of lemon and garlic and, well, Yaya.

This is washing powder. And wood polish.

I'm not quite awake, because I'm rubbing my eyes, but not opening them yet, and feeling the heavy quilt thing with my other hand. And stopping.

Something is licking my hand.

I haven't got my glasses on so I'm not seeing clearly, but there are two eyes looking back at me. I reach for my glasses from a little table beside me and the dog blur becomes a dog. Wordsworth looks like he's been watching me all night.

Of course.

Mrs Malley on the floor. Me phoning the ambulance, and not being able to get my words out. Blue lights. Sirens. Wordsworth howling as I left him. Me in the hospital, with no money for coffee and nobody telling me anything, and then me bursting into tears and the lovely nurse – Derya – saying Little Piddleton was on her way home and driving me back at 3 a.m., telling me she was sure my grandmother would be all right. I remember thinking I needed to tell her that Mrs M is not my grandmother, but being too tired to really talk by then.

The thing is, I didn't tell anyone that's what she was, or I didn't mean to, but the words kept kind of falling out of my mouth. When I called the ambulance. All I wanted to do was tell them I'd come round and found Mrs Malley because I was thinking about my own grandmother. But what came out was more just 'my grandmother', and lots of crying. That's why they asked me to go in the ambulance, I reckon.

Derya said I'd probably saved Mrs Malley's life.

When Yaya fell over in the corner dairy that time, everyone thought she was drunk. That's why the police took Yaya back home. Maybe she'd have recovered better if she'd gone to hospital quicker.

The doctor last night reckoned Mrs Malley had maybe had a mini stroke earlier, when she dropped the glass. She thought I'd arrived soon after she'd had a bigger stroke. She said that getting to hospital quickly will have been important. But she also said that older brains could find it harder to recover and that the next few days would be crucial.

Poor Wordsworth. I hope you aren't confused by me being here. I hope Mrs Malley won't mind either. But I could hardly leave him here on his own all night.

Poor dog.

I'll go in and visit. Perhaps the number seven goes past. Or Mervyn might drive me. Or Meredith maybe. I'll call the hospital to ask when visiting times are. I'll tell them I'm not her granddaughter, in case that's what they still think. She'll have a real family probably, who'll need to know what's happened. Hopefully she'll be awake today, anyway, and she'll just come home.

NED

'IT'S GOOD TO SEE you looking so much better, Ned, mate. You didn't half give us all a shock, you know, going and nearly dying like that.'

Toby is standing at the end of the bed but from the angle at which I'm lying, I can't see his face, only from his thighs up to his chin. He must have taken his tie off on the way in, because I can see it, curled into a spiral in his jacket pocket.

He is nervous. I know because he keeps laughing at his own jokes. He's always sounded like a goose when he laughs. Toby went to boarding school, he plays rugby and golf and drives a Volvo. He studied accountancy at St Andrews, where we were in the same halls in the first year and, during those three student years, he shaved his head, pierced his ears and took enough drugs to tranquillise an elephant. He voted Lib Dem in the local elections too. Then came the milk round and graduation, and he traded in his dungarees for a job in the City, married a fellow accountant (a woman, called Hilary) who's currently on maternity leave having had their second child. They have a Labrador called Henry. Toby, Hilary and Henry. Their children are Phoebe and Freddie.

'Honestly, mate, there must have been easier ways to get out of marrying Bella.' More honking laughter. 'After I came by last time, I said to Hil, "Goodness, Hil, lots of people get cold feet about their wedding, but it's a bit extreme to go and put yourself in a bloody coma".' Yet more laughing, though only from Toby, evidently.

'You know I'm joking, don't you, mate. Because, seriously, it's good to see that tube out of your mouth and your eyes open again. We'll be out for a few pints any day now, Ned, mate. More than a few, I bet.'

And then, just as I'm waiting for more laughter, Toby bursts into tears.

He apologises, and tells me he doesn't know what came over him. 'Just a bit exhausted, I suppose, with the new baby, and things being so crazy at work. And it's all so bloody difficult with Hil because, between you and me, I think she imagines that I go to the office to escape from them all. So, honestly Ned, don't think it's because of you. You're going to be *fine*. You've always landed on your feet. You just need to give it a bit of time. You know, rest up. You'll be out of here before you know it.'

Toby leads himself off on a painful tangent of how plenty of sleep is bound to do the trick, and anecdotes of times when I did other unlikely things at uni – mostly related to beer or women – that somehow prove to him that I'm *bound* to bounce back. Oh and he almost forgot, but he made me a playlist of my favourite tunes from those days, even though I always had the most abysmal old hippy taste in music (honk honk), and do I remember those parties we had and all the times . . .

It's strange, but his words seem to be floating to a further corner of my brain. I can hear the words. I understand the words. I know that they are there. But I'm finding it harder to . . .

*

'The Jean Genie'. David Bowie. I'm smiling and nodding my head and it's like a little rush of wonder, because there are still things that are perfect. Bowie at his best. Genius. I'll give myself a few minutes and then maybe I could go to the pub for a nice cold beer with Toby. He might be a knobber sometimes but he knows me better than I like to think. I want to say thank you for coming and talking and crying and laughing and bringing me Bowie. But I'll just listen to the music for a moment, and just . . .

*

'. . . scans indicate pontine haemorrhage combined with other areas of damage in Mr Edbury's nearby cerebral region. More recent periods of consistent wakefulness. Breathing unaided and we see from the notes here that both the physiotherapist and attending nurses have recorded signs of eye movement, though this looks more like a reflex than a voluntary response, or perhaps what they are witnessing is ocular bobbing or nystagmus, and in any case is more consistent with ongoing vegetative or minimally conscious state. No swallowing reflex. Nutrition is nasogastric. Observation and clinical assessment is ongoing, but as you see the patient is currently . . .'

I'm not sure where Toby went. But I should concentrate. This might be important. Even though my mind is a bit – a bit— Because everything the doctors say is so . . . I should stay . . . because . . .

'Good evening, Norton. I hope you don't mind me coming past to say hello. I'm Antony, the hospital chaplain. We have met before, last month, when you were in the acute critical unit, though I'm not sure if you'd remember that. Your mother was with you then. She and I spoke a lot and prayed together. I was passing by just now and I thought perhaps you might like a little company?'

His face comes into my line of sight. Curly hair and eager face. He looks a few years younger than me. Late twenties perhaps.

Would I like a little company? The company of this stranger in a dog collar? Well, it's not as if I have anything else much on at this precise moment.

'I've spoken to your fiancée too. Charming woman. Very . . .'

I presume the pause is not intentional, just a search for the right word to describe Bella. I'm all ears. Very what?

'. . . upset that you have found yourself facing such tribulations. But I found her also very full of hope.'

The chaplain stands with his fingers entwined across his chest. 'I encountered your friend Toby earlier, too. In the garden.'

Goodness me. It seems Chaplain has spoken to everybody I've ever met.

'Lovely chap. He was telling me about this playlist he's compiled for you and what fond memories he has of your times together. I understand you're a David Bowie fan? "Ground Control to Major Tom". I'm more of an Ed Sheeran man myself, I hate to say, though of course I do appreciate how groundbreaking Bowie's music is. Always searching for a message of some sort, I've always felt. There's such a spiritual side to it, isn't there, and a sense of how all of us play many roles?'

No. Don't do this, brother Antony. Don't go crowbarring some uplifting parable about how God is watching over me into a reflection about 'Ziggy Stardust' or *Aladdin Sane*, not while I'm lying here, defenceless.

'Actually my father met him in Budapest. Dad was playing at a festival there. 1997, I think. I remember him talking about it afterwards, though I was only little. He said David was utterly down to earth with a genuinely good sense of humour. Not like a lot of the other musicians he met who had more ego than talent. He said the true stars generally had the most humility.'

Hang on, Chaplain. Your father played the same festival as Bowie? And spent time with him? I need to know more about this. I'm sorry I was so dismissive.

'Although of course, he did come across a lot of very troubled people – the industry, I suppose. Who was that very sad young man, the one who – Kurt Cobain, if I'm not muddling up my musicians – my father said that when they were staying in the same hotel he found him every bit the . . .'

Kurt Cobain?

I want to ask him who his father is, what he plays, what other bands he's played with. I want to tell him about my guitar and my songs and my dreams. I want to tell him I don't believe in God but I do believe in music – I do believe in David Bowie. I want to tell him that I'm meant to be playing at a few festivals this summer myself, the small stages and the minor festivals, of course, but still, I was proud to have the bookings. Maybe if I'm better, he can come and watch. Maybe he could bring his father.

Before he leaves, Antony the chaplain says he doesn't wish to be presumptuous, but he hopes I won't mind if he remembers me in his prayers, or if he comes back again to see me.

I don't mind. I hope he senses this. And after he's gone, I play guitar in my head.

MRS M

THIS IS NOT WHERE I should be. I don't know where I should be but I know that this is not it. There are people and there are lights and smells and there are questions and places and noises and faces and I do not know what is right, but I do know that all of this is wrong.

This is a . . . a . . .

a . . .

. . . no, I will not dance with you.

I try to open the thing that I open. I want to do the thing. The thing that I know, that I have always known. I do not know why I don't know it. I do know it. The – thing.

And I want a thing. I want a thing and I don't know what it is and I don't know why I don't know, but I know that it is not here. I do not know what is right, but I know that this is wrong.

KIKI

Yes, Mervyn, I *should* be more gentle with the dishwasher.

It's just not very nice. You'd think she'd be a bit more caring, studying sociology or whatever. Social something. You'd expect she might care about other people a bit if she's so interested them. Because if it was Meredith who'd asked me to swap shifts because there was a poorly person in a hospital, I'd have said, 'Yes, of course.'

It doesn't even matter when you write a dissertation. It's not like visiting hours in a hospital which are actual rules.

I don't get what her problem is. Yes, Mrs M does sometimes speak to you a bit like you're a – I don't know – not-very-clever dog. But she's old. She probably doesn't mean it. Bitch is a horrible word. And that thing about her allowing all the other Brownies to laugh at Meredith's cupcakes must be years ago.

I should have told Meredith that she was lucky to even be a Brownie. Yaya didn't agree with Brownies. Yaya didn't agree with following rules and wearing uniforms. Yaya didn't even agree with making children go to school. After we moved to New Zealand, I was home-schooled by Gramps. He was a great teacher. We used to sit out in the woods for my lessons. But after he died, I had to go to school like everyone else. I was the only girl in my class who wasn't in Brownies.

Sometimes I used to pretend, but they'd ask sneaky questions like which pack was I in, and then pucker their mouths when I said something like Squirrel Pack or Yellow Pack. So I didn't pretend it for very long, or only on my own, making up songs and promises, like promising to eat with my mouth shut, and doing my own badge tests, like touching my toes badge and counting trees badge.

One weekend I washed eleven cars. I told people it was for my car-washing badge. I washed them really well too. I'd definitely have got it.

That's what I should have told Meredith. So what if people laughed at her cupcakes, at least she knew what pack she was in.

But I just said, 'Oh,' and, 'So you can't switch shifts just this once?'

It's not like she's even gone to the library. She's just there with her pile of books on the table like, 'look how hard I'm studying'. Except she's tipping her chair back and playing with her phone and eating barbecue beef crisps. I can smell them.

She could have looked at her phone and eaten her crisps behind the bar.

Merv is just as bad. I don't see why we couldn't have Wordsworth here while I'm working, or let him sleep in my room for a couple of nights until Mrs Malley's back home. The room stinks anyway and loads of pubs have a pub dog. It adds character.

Anyway, Mervyn didn't need to be so rude. I was only asking.

I don't think I'll mention staying at Mrs M's last night because probably I should tell her first. She'll be grateful though, because if I don't stay there again tonight, who's going to let Wordsworth out? You can't just leave a dog on their own.

Mervyn wasn't very helpful about Mrs M's family, either. You'd think that owning the pub, he might take an interest in the people who live here instead of making stupid jokes about broomsticks. But he must have phoned the vicar, because that's him coming in. He looks warm in that black frock, with his shiny head. Maybe he'll know about Mrs Malley and how to get in touch with her family or friends so that I won't have to look through any more of her drawers and boxes.

And at least the vicar is polite with his, 'Ah yes, we met at Alfie's wake yesterday,' and, 'What a shock it must have been to find poor Mary like that. Is there any news from the hospital?'

I can only tell him what they said on the phone, which is that it's too early to tell how seriously she might be affected.

The vicar says, 'Indeed. Indeed.' He's not very sure who in the parish is friendly with Mary, but perhaps one of the other library helpers will know better than he does.

'She was always so very close to dear Harriet, of course,' he says.

Harriet had been Wordsworth's owner. She lived just round the corner from here. Meredith told me about her after the first time he showed up howling on the green and I had to take him back. Meredith said Harriet was a mad old bat.

There's a big cardboard box in the bedroom where I slept last night that had *Harriet – Mary Malley / Oxfam?* written on it in marker pen. The tape had been pulled off so I had a look – just to check if there were any clues to Mrs M's next of kin – but it was all books and photos and some hats and a few clothes and things. There was a red beret and a straw hat and some colourful scarves. Maybe it would be all right to try some of them on, if they're going to Oxfam anyway.

That poem on the floor beside Mrs M was signed *Harriet* too. 'The Old Ladies' Fuck It List'. It was really funny with these choice rhymes. It must have been important, because otherwise why would that be the one thing that Mrs Malley had beside her? She realised she was ill and couldn't make it to the phone, so she grabbed that poem, like a sign for whoever found her.

She won't have known it would be me. She's lucky it was. Somebody else might not have realised.

There was that old cookery book, too, and that was open on a page about cabbage. I don't think the cabbage is a sign but I can ask her when she's better. I'll take her the poem. Because, no question, that's a message. Those things in the poem are the things she wants to do. That's what a bucket list is.

Poor Mrs Malley. You're an old woman with so much left to do.

The vicar is still talking about Harriet and how terribly upsetting it was for poor Mary. 'She takes fresh flowers to her grave every week. She gives me rather a hard time actually, about not being allowed to plant some roses instead.'

He's polishing his glasses and talking about lavender bushes and parish regulations, and I ask him, 'Do you drive?'

He looks a little bit surprised but he says, 'Why yes, but what . . . ?'

'Will you visit her with me tomorrow? I mean, would you be able to give me a lift, please? To see Mrs Malley?'

He wipes his head with his handkerchief, but he says, well, what a very kind thought, and actually he knows the new chaplain at the hospital – young Antony – and he had been meaning to call in and say hello, so why not tomorrow morning. Mervyn is watching us from behind a *Sun* newspaper at the end of the bar. He can't really say no when I give him my sweetest smile and say, 'Mervyn. I hope you can manage without me for a bit tomorrow?'

NED

I T IS AS IF my leg is being torn in two. This pain feels like the pulling apart of Velcro. *Critch! Critch! Critch!* Sharp and hot.

Please stop.

In my mind, I am pulling my knee to my chin to rub my burning calf. I am kicking it out into the air. I am jumping out of bed and stamping and hopping on it. I am yelling and shouting and swearing. Top of my voice. 'Shit. Hell. Fuck. Bugger. Bollocks.' Loud enough to wake every person in the hospital.

What would happen then? Everyone would rush.

'It's only a cramp,' I would have to say. *Only?*

When I was still me, I'd wake up with them. Cramps. I used to dance around the bedroom in the night, shaking my leg like I was doing some crazy sort of jig. Cramp after late nights and too much beer. Cramp after too-long runs and too little hydration. I'd massage it until it subsided. Or if there was someone with me, Bella or one of my other girlfriends from before, they'd do it for me, my foot nestled against their chest as they rubbed my leg, asking, 'Is that better?'

Oh, stop. Surely it would not hurt like this if I could touch it. It would not hurt so much if I could open my mouth and scream.

In football matches too, when hungover Sunday games stretched into extra time. Already knackered and sore and then pulling up from a run on goal when the pains sliced through me. Pats on the shoulder from sympathetic teammates.

Childhood growing pains. Waking and sobbing. My father hugging me tight and singing lullabies with a note of whisky breath; my mother groggy and cross ('Oh, Norton, it's just growing pains. You woke me up.'); one of the stepfathers – Austen ('Back to bed, buddy') or Keith ('Stop this now, pathetic child') or Maxwell ('How about I fetch you a hot water bottle and we put on some music?').

Stop. Please stop. I am not growing now so what pains can I call these?

I cannot stroke. I cannot shake. I cannot cry.

Sometimes I wonder if I am being punished. Not that I believe in fate, or karma, or retribution, but it is so hard to ask yourself the question, 'why me?' and come up with no better answer than, 'why not?'

Perhaps you don't have to believe in God to believe in hell.

What are the seven deadly sins? Lust. Number one. That's me right there. Ha. But I've always been caring too, I think. Although Bella might not have said so if you'd asked her a few months ago. I was making a terrible mistake, she said. I was meant to be with her. She knew I was.

To be fair, she's stood by it. What I am now – this, me – most women would have been long gone. Most women would not come and sit beside this useless body. She doesn't even know I know that she's there. But she still comes.

Greed. And gluttony. Two different sins. I'm not gluttonous. Even now, when food is pumped into me through a tube in my nose and meals have the consistency of wallpaper paste, I'm not missing red meat or cakes. Although a bacon sandwich. God, yes, a bacon sandwich. And greed? I like good things.

Holidays and a good sound system. Spoilt maybe. But I don't think that makes me greedy.

Oh – stop, leg, stop.

Let's think. Sloth. Good God, no. Slothful. Never. If I could stand up now, I would never sit back down again. I would run and spin and write and sing and squeeze every second dry. God. If only.

Lust. Greed. Gluttony. Sloth. One, two, three, four. Three more. That movie, Brad Pitt, Morgan Freeman – wrath, of course. Anger? I never was a very angry person. Not until now. Now – fuck me – who wouldn't be angry?

Critch! Critch! I'm angry because I don't deserve this. Because I want life and love and pain – but pain I can express. Not this. I did not ask for this. I am angry because – no. Stop. Stop, Ned. Let's not go there.

Think about the pain in your leg. Feel *that* instead. Because oh, God it hurts.

Envy? That's six. Pride. That's one too. Is that seven?

Pride? Is that my sin? Pride goes before a fall, they say.

Bella used to sing me that song when she caught me looking at myself in the mirror – the Carly Simon one. 'You're So Vain'.

Too much pride, perhaps, but no envy. I would never have wanted to be anybody but me. Now nobody would swap places.

'Norton. Hello there. It's Tammy. I'm just coming in to check your blood pressure. I thought maybe you'd like me to pop the television on for you for a little bit too? I was talking to your friend, Toby is it, yesterday and he said he thought you'd be missing *Schitt's Creek*. We can't actually get Netflix on the hospital TVs but I've brought in my laptop and I have all the seasons downloaded. I'll just put it here on your table. I hope that's OK?'

Blink, eyes. Blink.

It appears my eyes do not wish to blink.

Where Toby came up with *Schitt's Creek*, I cannot imagine. I've never seen a single episode. *Fleabag* perhaps? But this is OK. It's a long time since I've watched TV.

I've heard about it, of course, the story of a family of multi-millionaire Americans who have lost everything and end up on their own in a crummy motel, miles away from everything they've ever known. The joke, I suppose, is that they're up *Schitt's Creek*.

Oh, I see. This is Toby's idea of funny. Ha, ha, ha.

'So, I'll just take your blood pressure while this is on, if you don't mind, Norton?'

No, Tammy. You go right ahead.

MRS M

Y ES, DOCTOR, OF COURSE I *understand what you are saying. I may be eighty-four but I am not gaga yet, if you please. And yes, certainly, I am aware that I am in hospital. How could I not be with those nurses insisting on sticking their – you know – into my – oh, you know, my thing – every minute of the day? It does distract one so. As do those spiders, on your – and – and yes – of course – I know my name. For goodness' sake, man. My name is Mary Violet Malley, born Mary Violet Penhaligon on 27th March 1935. So as you can see, stroke or no stroke, I am of perfectly sound – oh, you know – you know, thank you ever so.*

I'm just a little – still. But yes, I can un-der-stand.

Yes, of course I can *answer I just – yes, I understand. I shall tell you as much just as soon as the – things – come back to my – you know. To my. The things in my—*

KIKI

H IS FACE NEVER LOOKS too excited, but that tail is super-stoked and he gives me a look when I tell him, 'Sorry I've been so long. Long shift at work,' like – yeah – he understands that.

I explain about needing to use my laptop while I was there and had Wi-Fi, checking the message I'd posted on a festival community site saying did anyone know where I could find a Glastonbury Festival ticket to see if there were any replies. I had one which just said, 'Join the queue!' And another which called me deluded.

'People aren't always very friendly, eh, Wordsworth,' I say, and he wags at me like he agrees.

Not that I could afford the ticket if one did magically turn up. The wages Mervyn's paying can't be legal, let alone how much he's ripping me off for that room. I tried to talk about it nicely. He said to bring it up with my union.

At least Wordsworth appreciates me. I'll take him for a nice walk in a moment. But on his lead. I don't think Mrs M would be happy if I lost him.

What's that look now? Hmm. An empty dog bowl? Yeah, fair point.

I'd love Yaya to have seen this house. She was always talking about English cottages and how pretty they were, and how 'spick and span'. All the flowers and lace and stuff.

Yaya used to call it *chitz*. I was twenty-four before Sue in Auckland put me right. When I told her to picture me over here in England in a flowery cottage with chitz curtains, Sue told me what the real word was.

Still, that was Yaya-speak. You had to fill in the gaps.

Yaya would have loved all the chitz here. The curtains with their ties, and the fringes on the lampshades. Wordsworth even has a crochet mat under his dog bowl. He's gazing at it.

There was chicken in the fridge. But he's had that already. 'Let's have a look,' I tell him.

The fridge is definitely spick and span, all these little Tupperware boxes with their labels. Calves' liver. Haddock (smoked). Sausage meat (pork). Don't dogs normally eat biscuits or something?

Wait, Wordsworth. What about this cupboard here?

Blackberry conserve (Sept 2018), strawberry jam (frozen, Mch 2019), and these are – what? – custard powder, cornflour, bicarbonate of soda, candied mixed peel. OK. Here under the sink?

Look at that tail. Telling me I'm warm? I used to play that with Yaya. She'd hide a lolly or something and she'd tell me, 'No, no, no, Kiriaki. Cold as icicles.'

Very warm now, am I? Aha! What about – nope, birdseed. Washing-up liquid, Brasso polish. This tin here? Let's see. Fortnum & Mason fine ginger shortbread – well, that's a funny place for it. Under the sink. I'm guessing it's an old tin with something else in it? Heaps of wagging. Really warm then? Could this be dog biscuits?

Shall I have a look?

OK, so, hold on, it's just a bit stiff this lid, it's – here we go – deffo not biscuits.

It's – it's—

Wow.

I mean, wow.

I mean, look at that.

How much is there here? It's – well – if I shake them out onto the top here, there must be – just look, there are six rolls. And they're – let's take off the elastic band on this. It's a £50 note. And in this roll, there are one, two, three, four – hang on now, Wordsworth, down. Nineteen, twenty. That's twenty notes in one roll so that's – let me see – two notes are £100, so, hang on, one-two, three-four, five-six – £100, £200, £300 – seven-eight, nine-ten – so £400, £500. That's ten and there are – that's £1,000 in that one roll. And there are six of them.

That's more than Yaya's life savings. It's heaps of Glastonbury tickets. It's a round the world plane ticket. It's £6,000. And Mrs M's keeping it in a biscuit tin under the sink.

NED

'BUT YOU UNDERSTAND', NORTON, my darling, that if I could, I'd be back with you in a flash. In less than a flash. A blink, a whisper, a . . .'

I think my mother will come back to 'flash'. It really didn't need rewording.

'. . . a flash, honey. You know you're the most important thing in my life. You know that. It's just that Sadie says – you remember her, sweetie, my lovely agent – that this casting next week is really exciting. You know, not just exciting-exciting, but *exciting*-exciting. The casting director requested for me to do it personally. Sadie says the role is made for me. And the script – oh, Norton, it's divine. So I think it's best if I stay here at least until then. Say you agree, my precious boy? I know you do.'

The funny thing about my mother is the more genuinely sincere she is, the more she looks like she's acting. Which isn't to say she doesn't mean every word. Her hand is on her chest.

'Baby, I worry about you every minute, honey, and I can't pretend it's easy being away from you like this. I talked to some people about flying you to a hospital out here. A specialist centre for neuro-you-know. But honey, the insurance was *im*possible. They say flying could be dangerous. Because of the pressure, I guess. On your brain. So I don't think that can happen. Not for a few months anyway.'

My mother frowns. Or her mouth and her eyes do.

'But the doctors there tell me you're doing well. And your Annabella called me last night to tell me about this new unit and all the rehab they're starting. She's a sweet girl, Nortie. Such a relief to know she's with you. And so committed to raising awareness. I've told her I'll help in any way I can. Not to boast, but I do have a few contacts.'

Superb, Mother. Why stop at Norton Edbury, the Channel 5 documentary, when you can go full out for Norton Edbury, the feature film?

'And I— Oh, sweetie, give me a moment, there's somebody at the door.'

Her face recedes and for a couple of minutes my view is of a tan leather egg chair and a glass coffee table, on which lies a copy of *Vogue*. Then the white trouser suit and blonde highlights come back into view, panning in to a close-up of the face.

'Sorry, hon, just my personal trainer dropping off this new Pilates ball I ordered. You know, Norton, got to keep your body in—' She runs her hand through her hair. 'Anyway, what was I saying?'

Let's see, something about how well you know I'm doing in here?

'Yes, I know you're in the safest of hands. And like this, I can talk to you all the time, anyway.'

Indeed, Mother. This modern miracle that is Skype. How did we live without it?

'Honey, there was something that I needed to talk to you about. I've been speaking with Maxwell. Well, he contacted me. He was very upset actually and not terribly pleasant, if you must know. He said he couldn't believe I hadn't let him know what had happened, and, well, I suppose I should have done, but darling I've been so distracted, out of my mind with worry, and I suppose it must have slipped my mind.'

Slipped your mind? Maxwell bought me my first guitar and taught me how to play. He also taught me to kick a ball and how to ski. He paid for my education. And it was Maxwell, more than anyone else, who put me back together after Dad died. He lets me live in his annexe and has never once charged me a penny. He's probably the person who knows me best in the entire world and, on top of it all, he happens to be a qualified doctor. But it slipped your mind to tell him that I was on life support while he's away in his French hideaway, or that I've remained apparently unresponsive for – I don't even know how many weeks.

'I accept he's right to be angry. Not that he had to say the things he said. I've just been trying to hold myself together. I know you're the one in the hospital bed, but do you not think this has taken its toll on me too?'

There is a tremor in her voice and as she looks away from her screen it's hard to hear what she says, but it sounds like 'I'm sorry'.

It's a moment or two before she looks back. Maxwell always said that she and I have the same eyes, green, with flecks of blue and amber.

'Baby, I hope you're not angry too. If you can hear any of this, honey, don't be mad at me. I know you and Maxwell have always had a very special connection. And maybe sometimes I've felt resentful of that. I said to José – I told you about José, right? – I said to José, "What if subconsciously I chose not to tell Maxwell? What if subconsciously I was punishing him for Norton loving him more than he loves me?" But José helped me see that I've just been exhausted and that it doesn't help anybody for me to start blaming myself for what's happened to you.'

Two green-blue-amber eyes blink, full of feeling that does not translate to movement in the surrounding muscles. I beg my eyes to do a blink back. And it's not a blink, but a – something. Can't she see it? I'm asking her, 'Tell me more about Maxwell, Mother. What did he say?'

'You wouldn't understand, my darling, what it is to be a mother. You're thirty years old but you're still my baby. Even when you were a little boy, toddling out in the yard, every scrape, every graze, every cut, a mother feels it.'

Her hands have lowered out of shot. My memories of childhood tumbles are more the howls of, 'Norton, you've ripped your pants again!'

I'm tired suddenly. It's strange when there is nothing to do, when my body only moves if it is moved, that exhaustion still batters me like waves. But I need to concentrate. I want to know what she has to say about Maxwell.

'You try to do your best, because that tiny child is the world to you, but it's hard, baby.'

Mother. Please. Maxwell?

'Maxwell wasn't very happy. He called me selfish. He wanted to know everything that the doctors had said, you know what he's like, and I tried to tell him, but it gets so confusing. All this about the differences between minimally conscious and fluctuating and contusions and so many tiny details about what this scan shows or whether you might have had a voluntary or involuntary whatsit, and if you're not a neuro-you-know yourself, how can you be expected to understand it all? He asked me who was here with you, liaising with the medics. And I tried to tell him that you were in the best of hands and that I sleep with my phone on the pillow – but, well, you know Maxwell, hon. Always has to be in control.'

I don't know how much more I can listen to. I want to know about Maxwell. But it's so hard to keep concentrating on the words.

'Of course he was packing his bags even as we spoke. I hope that's OK, Norton. Because we've had our problems, but he does love you and you're what matters here. So I've told the doctors I'm happy for them to talk to him about everything and that . . .'

The words are losing me. But Maxwell will be here soon. Maxwell's coming. And I'm not able to – I'm not holding onto much anymore but it's fine – and for the first time in a very long time, it feels a little bit like I'm being held in a mother's hug.

MRS M

*I*T WAS JUNE 1951. *I don't remember the exact date but it was a Saturday and school had finished. The week before we had taken our General Certificate of Education. I was hopeful that I had performed adequately, and in fact I'd achieved the highest marks in the school, whereas Harriet did not give a hoot one way or the other. She already had an offer of a receptionist position at a doctor's surgery whilst I had a place at a secretarial school and was looking forward to learning typing. We felt modern and grown up and free. We were sixteen years old.*

My mother was visiting her sister in Herefordshire so I was on my own for the weekend with food for myself and the cat and instructions to do nothing stupid. Not that Mother expected anything stupid from me. I was a very sensible girl.

It was one of those days when the sky was blue and there was just the right amount of breeze. I can still feel it in my hair as we rode our bikes up Milk Hill and then freewheeled the whole way back down to the river in search of a perfect spot to unpack our baskets.

*

'Mrs Malley. Or can I call you Mary? Is that OK, Mary? If you could try to squeeze my hand, please.'

*

Cheese from the West Farm and apples from the orchard. Slices of thick ham in doughy bread with salty butter. Biscuits that Harriet had made – grainy because of her lazy beating, and cake which I had baked, and which was far better, if I do say so myself, and bottles of beer which she swore her father wouldn't notice had gone. We wore our bathing costumes beneath our dresses. We paddled on stones, until we felt brave enough to swim. We laughed at the minnows zipping around our legs. Then we lay on the grass until we were dry again and we talked and talked and talked.

*

'And if you can just try to lift up this arm, Mary. Can you lift it at all?'

*

She was trying to persuade me to go to a dance with her and Eric and Roger. Roger was Eric's friend and her mother would only allow her to go if I went too. Her mother trusted me more than she trusted Harriet, which was very wise of her. Harriet had introduced me to Roger and I wasn't keen. His main subjects of conversation were cricket and his prospects in the insurance company where he worked. His boss there was a Mr Scarigrew and Roger was particularly fond of repeating every blessed thing Mr Scarigrew ever said, and telling me how much it hinted at prospects for promotion. Harriet was very taken with Eric though. We both knew she'd talk me into going to the dance eventually but for now, I was refusing to discuss it, because the last thing I wanted to talk about was Roger Malley. I wanted to think about sunshine and the picnic and the fact that Harriet and I were grown up now and out of school and able to jump on our bikes with a lunch we'd made ourselves and to stay out for as long as we chose. I was sixteen years old and everything felt so terribly exciting.

I think perhaps that was the happiest day of my life.

*

'Now Mary, if you could try to stick your tongue out for me. Can you try to do that please, my dear?'

KIKI

'I'M TE'BLY SED TO hear thet. Poor Mrs Melley.'

'Mrs Malley,' I say.

'Indeed. Norman, d'you hear thet? Poor Mrs Melley is in hospital.'

Yaya used to say that you knew when an English person was posh because they made their words last for a very long time.

Lucinda, who lives next door to Mrs M, says she can't really ('rarely') help me at all. She doesn't know very much about Mrs Malley, since Norman and she have only had the house a couple of years and only ever come at weekends. She's aware that Mr Malley ('Mr Melley') passed on not so very long ago, but as for any other close family, she's afraid she simply doesn't know. Fiona and Stuart on the other side might have some idea, but to be honest, they're second-homers too, and she suspects they're not terribly close to Mrs M either.

'Surely she must have a mobile telephone with her important numbers in it?' Lucinda says as I thank them and leave.

You'd think so, wouldn't you. But there isn't one on the hall table – or in any of its drawers. Still, it seems a good idea to check again, as Wordsworth and I come back into the cottage, and he toddles over to stare sadly at his bowl, as if he can't believe it's empty again. There certainly isn't a mobile phone here. Only a vase of flowers and the old-fashioned type of phone with a long, curly lead to the wall.

It's not even a push-button one, it has a dial, one of the ones that you have to stick your fingers into to turn. There's no sign of a computer, either – and I'm checking all the rooms now: living room, kitchen, dining room, a bathroom and the toilet which is in a different room, the little bedroom I slept in and the one which must be Mrs M's with two single beds. There's a hairbrush and a box of tissues and some creams on a dressing table. I felt bad looking in Mrs M's bedside table drawers, but it's for her own good. Anyway, there was nothing helpful. Just a box of some pills called Pepto-Bismol and a book of crosswords. There's also her handbag at the end of one of the beds. It's a shiny blue one with a big gold buckle, and inside is a little black leather book, with gold on the side of the pages and gold letters spelling 'Addresses'. It has pages from A to Z with handwriting in it, except not so much Anne to, I don't know, Zoe, but more like Alderton, Penelope to Walton, Helen. And there's nothing that says daughter or son or niece or cousin or next of kin or whatever, but maybe you never write that. Yaya was always just *Yaya* on my phone. Not that she ever answered it. Yaya didn't like mobile phones. They were spying on us. Or giving us brain tumours. I forget which.

When I went to Auckland the first time, I told Yaya she needed one so we could speak to each other. She said she was being two times punished – by me going away, and by me making her have this terrible thing. She never picked up when I called her. I don't know if she was making me suffer, or just couldn't work out what to do with it. She never rang me either. But at least I was the only number in her contacts when the hospital had to track me down. Finding Yaya's next of kin was not a problem.

'Right, Wordsworth, let's start at the beginning,' I say, like he really understands what I'm doing. And to be fair, the look he's giving me now, it's like he really does.

Mrs Malley's address book has heaps of names, but some have a line through them, and the letter *d* with a date. In fact, Mrs M needs to do a bit more crossing out, I reckon, because the first two numbers I call (it feels nice, turning the dial on the old phone, and it makes a funny whoosh sounds as it moves back into place, like I'm in an old black and white movie or something) – Alderton, Penelope and Atkins, Jean are answered by people who tell me they're new owners. Alderton, Penelope has emigrated to be with her daughter in Canada and Atkins, Jean, died three years ago. Adams, Susan answers though and I explain about the stroke and about how I'm trying to track down family or close friends.

'So sorry but I don't believe I know her.'

I tell her Mrs Malley's first name is Mary. From Little Piddleton. And that she lives in a pretty cottage with white flowers in the front, near to the wood.

'No. Sorry. I don't know a Mary Malley, although I do know Little Piddleton.'

I tell Adams, Susan about Mrs M having a basset hound called Wordsworth.

'Wordsworth. But he's – oh, you must mean Harry's friend? Yes, I heard she took the dog. And she was a Mary. I hardly know her though. Harry – Harriet – brought her along to help out at a jumble sale I organised a few years ago. Yes, Mary Malley. I asked if she'd mind running the toy stall and she said she'd rather do the tombola. She told me I'd done it all wrong and that she'd have only allowed tickets with a zero at the end to win, rather do than any five as well. Also she thought we should have left the raffle draw until later in the day. Mary Malley. Of course. She said we must swap numbers so I could call her if I was ever organising a fundraising event again.'

'And you never did?'

'Call her? No.'

Adams, Susan is almost certain that Mrs M had no children. She's sure Harriet said as much. But she wouldn't know about any other family or friends, she's afraid.

'I only met her the once. Good luck though. You're a friend of hers, did you say?'

I'm about to say yes, but Wordsworth is watching me and my cheeks feel warm and itchy.

'More her house sitter. I'm looking after the dog.'

NED

L AST SUMMER, I DID the London to Brighton cycle with Bella and Toby. Hilary too. Toby's parents must have been looking after Henry because we made quite a night of it, with a hotel on the front and fish and chips on the pier and pints in – goodness – a fair number of pubs. Between us we raised more than a thousand pounds. Toby with that stupid joke. 'Good thing we're staying at The Grand tonight, guys, because we've only gone and raised a bloody grand. Geddit?' It wasn't strictly hilarious, even the first time. Toby never could take his ale.

Macmillan. That's what we were all donating to. Me because of Dad, Bella in memory of her great-uncle. And Hilary's father was having treatment for prostate cancer at the time.

It was the first time for the others but my third. I'd done London to Paris in 2014 too.

I cannot see my legs turning because my head is facing the ceiling. But I can hear the soft purr of the machine and I can feel the motion. Left knee up, right foot down, right knee up, left foot down. Round and round. I tell my eyes to close. I would so like to be able to close off the view of strip lights and curtain rail. I'd like to picture fields and lanes and a stream of other bikes moving ahead of me, with Bella directly in front, pedalling hard in black Lycra. I'd like to will away the sanitised hospital smell and block out the words of Becky, the physiotherapist, and breathe in cowslip and sunshine and exhilaration.

Come on eyes, close. Allow me this one little fantasy.

'That's brilliant, Norton. You're doing really well.'

Of course I'm doing well. The machine you've placed on the bed and strapped my feet into is turning automatically. It is plugged into the electric socket at the wall. None of the effort is mine.

'There's a lot of research about the benefits of the cycling motion for patients of . . .'

Please. I don't want to know this now. I want to feel. Close. Eyes close.

Above me, the line of electric light is harsh and white.

'. . . and in fact, in the last hospital where I worked, they found . . .'

Come on, eyes. Please.

They close. My eyes. They actually do it. I told them to close and they closed. I closed my eyes. And the brightness of the ceiling light turns into the dancing red-black of the inside of my eyelids. My legs are still cycling and I let my brain play its film. Left knee up. Right foot down. Right knee up. Left foot down. Round and round.

London to Brighton. Or London to Paris. French villagers came out to clap and call encouragement. 'Allez,' they shouted. Round and round went my legs.

'Good stuff, Norton. We'll keep this going for a few more minutes. And over time you can build up the time to keep those muscles active.'

Spin classes in the gym. More Bella's thing than mine, but good now and then, for working up a sweat. I'd ache after, too, though not as much as after the bike ride.

Left knee up. Right foot down. Left foot down. Right knee up. Round and round. When I was still me, I didn't know how much I loved what my body could do. I just did it. Round and round. Pedal, pedal, pedal.

How old was I when I learned to ride? Four or five, I suppose, with Dad holding onto the back of my bike – I can picture it now, shiny red and so grown up – and then not holding it, but running along beside me. Our street was wide and straight, with palm trees on either side. If he and Mum had stayed together, I'd have grown up American, I suppose. 'I'm doing it, Dad. Watch me! I'm doing it.'

Dad in cut-offs and a white T-shirt. 'Awesome stuff, little man. Keep going.'

'Perfect, Norton. And we'll keep going just a little longer.'

I never wanted to stop. Even though it made me very tired. I wanted to keep on pedalling and pedalling and pedalling. 'One more minute,' I'd beg, when Dad said it was time to stop. I remember once, keeping going until I could pedal no more. The feel of my father's shoulder beneath my cheek, as he carried me back home with my bike beneath his other arm. And that night, in bed, I could still feel my legs moving.

Left knee up. Right foot down. Left foot down. Right knee up. Round and round.

A knocking. I think about opening my eyes. They do not open.

'Excuse me. Is this Norton Edbury's room, please? The charge nurse said to come, but I don't want to interrupt.'

Softly spoken.

The thoughts in my head shift like a projection caught in the light. From the tanned blond of my father to the closely cropped grey of Maxwell.

Becky tells him it's fine, please come in, because this is the last thirty seconds, and Maxwell says what an interesting machine and that he's read about the therapeutic benefits but never actually seen one, and Becky agrees and says how nice to meet him and says goodbye to me.

Open, I tell my eyes. And they do, but only the tiniest bit, and then they close again, so I don't catch a view of him. Just the briefest impression of a shape above me. I can fill it in though. Kind eyes. A face that wrinkles in all the places where my mother's does not. An expression that will be concerned, but calm.

'Oh Ned,' Maxwell says. 'Just look at you.'

MRS M

I CANNOT BELIEVE WHAT I am hearing myself say to the consultant. The shame. A word I have never once, in all my life, uttered before this moment. A wicked word. And to a doctor. What must he think of me?

What is worse is that I do not even know I'm going to say it until I hear it coming out of my mouth. That's the most awful thing about it. I'm listening to what he's saying and I'm thinking that he reminds me rather of Dr Bryans. Old Dr Bryans, of course, not young Dr Bryans. Thick hair and understated spectacles, and a very fetching handkerchief in his pocket. So few men wear them these days. Red with white spots, and silk rather than a cheaper alternative. One can always tell. Roger preferred a cotton handkerchief. Unfussy, he said. He thought silk was for, well, those types who preferred handbags to briefcases, he said. I told him that he needn't be so vulgar and that silk was perfectly masculine. He always preferred a simple square fold, which is what this doctor is wearing. Personally, I've always rather liked a two point but Roger was so terribly set in his ways.

This doctor's name is Mr Douglas. He has a Scottish accent but he seems capable. He doesn't use too much medical jargon as so many doctors seem to.

'Normal to be extremely tired and not to feel like yourself after something like this. The scan shows that the stroke has caused damage to three small areas of the left frontal lobe. Our team will help you to work out how you've been affected and what strategies and therapies we can best bring in to help you adapt. Brains are remarkable things, remember, and good recoveries are possible at any age, though it's important to be patient and to realise that . . .'

Very like old Dr Bryans, except without those eyebrows. Harriet always said how terribly sweet he was, it being her first job, and he never scolded her when she brought in the wrong notes or double-booked his patients.

'. . . very likely that some activities such as moving and speaking might feel a bit different. I hope you understand?'

Yes, I do understand. Everything is going to feel a bit different. It does feel different. And he is quite right. I have been very tired and there are a lot of things in my – you know – that I can't – not really. And I'm still not completely sure that – well, anything. And I know I'm going to say a thing. And what it's going to be – I think – before I say it – is, 'Thank you,' or 'Yes, I see, doctor,' or 'Much obliged, Dr Douglas.'

But that is not what I say. I smile. I think I do. My face still feels so odd. But I believe I smile. And I open my mouth to say something. The right thing. The thing that a lady such as myself knows to say. And what comes out is the other word. The awful word. The nasty, shameful word.

I smile at the consultant – or such is my intention. And I say very clearly, 'Wanker.'

KIKI

'WORDSWORTH SAYS HELLO. WELL, you know, he doesn't say it – imagine that – but he, you know, is sending you the look he does with his eyes. You know, this one.' I'm doing a really good impression but she doesn't smile. She just stares, kind of at me, but kind of through me.

'And he says you don't need to worry about him, because I'm taking care of him. Which is what I wanted to talk to you about. Unless there's anybody else that you think should be doing it? I've been walking him too. So unless you – you know – don't want me to, he's fine.'

She doesn't reply, just stares, so I carry on.

'Like I say, if there's no one else that you need me to call then I'm happy to keep the house safe. I mean just say otherwise. But I thought it would put your mind at rest to know someone's keeping an eye. You don't have to, like, pay me or anything. It's quite nice anyway, you know, nicer than the pub.'

Yaya always told me I talked too much. 'Chatter, chatter, chatter, little Kiriaki.' Sue says it too. Well, what she says is it's OK to allow the odd silence in a conversation. But Mrs Malley still isn't saying anything. Her hand is over the sheet on her chest, with a cannula in it. She's looking at me though, like there's something she wants to say. It's like she's trying to move her lips. I wait. But she's still not speaking so it's me who talks again.

'Was there something you wanted to – sorry, I – I mean, don't feel you have to, honestly. It's nice, your cottage. Lovely. But the hospital have been asking about any family or friends you want us to get in touch with. What's that?

'"House"? Was that it? Don't worry. I know it's hard to talk. Your brain has had a really big shock. You just need to concentrate on getting yourself better. That's what I'm telling you, that I'll keep the house safe. I've been keeping the door locked, too. I know you had it open, but I don't think that's the best idea. I mean, I'm not saying—

'Here. Let me sort out your pillow a bit. That's better. And, look, I brought in a nightie. I hope you don't mind that I went into your drawers to get it. I just thought it would be nicer. And some slippers too. I don't expect you'll need those for a while yet, but I'll give them to the nurses.'

She doesn't nod or smile or say thank you or anything. So I tell her about the flowers.

'I brought some flowers, too. From that wooden wheelbarrow in your garden. Except the hospital don't allow them so I had to give them to a woman who was coming out of the exit. She said they'd look pretty in her kitchen. It was a shame though. I should have realised, maybe. It was the same when I went to see Yaya – my grandmother. Except her flowers were just from the bus stop.

'That's why I know how difficult it is for you. Because Yaya had a stroke too. Not the same, of course, they're all different. But it took her a long time to recover. Or not recover because she never really did, but it was ages before she was able to leave the hospital. That's what I'm telling you, even if you're here for months, you don't have to worry about the cottage. Or about Wordsworth.'

Her lips are really moving now, but I can't work out the sounds she's making.

'Sorry, Mrs Malley? No, don't get upset, it's bound to be a bit hard to get the words out. You know, just while your brain recovers. Is that "cat"? I don't know anything about a— Or cap?

'Cap? You mean – silly me, I forgot. I was just trying it on. I didn't want to . . . I hope you don't mind. It was just that the box was there in your spare room. *"Harriet's stuff"*. I thought there might be something to tell me who I could contact for you. Because of Harriet being your best friend. But it was all scarves and things. And this. Such a lovely colour. I'll put it back. I was just, you know, trying it on.

'But listen to me, rabbiting on about berets when there's something much more important to tell you. I've read the poem. The bucket list. And I'd be proud to help you do all those things. Because you still can. You can have those chips in a fancy restaurant and sunbathe in the nude, like it says. And the hippy festival. That's kind of what I'm here for too. Glastonbury. I've always wanted to go. Sue said I'm a bit obsessed. I'd say we'd go together, except it's impossible to get a ticket. Honestly, impossible. We could go to another festival maybe.'

I can't tell what the look she's giving me is, so I keep on talking.

'And once you're feeling a bit better, I'll take you on that shopping trip, too, like in the poem? And go for a drive in a fast car. And maybe dye your hair. What colour did it say? Pink?

'No, don't try to talk any more – the nurse said you mustn't get excited and I told Vicar I'd go and find him. I'll let you get some more sleep now. But, like I say, don't worry about your house or about Wordsworth. They're both safe.

'Here, let me give you a kiss. What's that? I'm sorry, that sounded like—

'Well, that was very clear. And I know exactly what you want to tell me. Fuck as in "Fuck It". "The Old Ladies' Fuck It List". Don't you worry. I'm going to help you tick off every single thing on it. You can count on me.'

NED

THE AIR ON MY skin is a breath of joy. This is what the world feels like. It has still been here, all the time, waiting outside of the hospital walls. It smells green. It smells like being alive. It's not raining now but I can almost taste the rain that I heard during the night. This is the world, and I am in it.

In my mind I am throwing open my arms towards the sky. The body won't do that, of course. It's propped in this wheelchair, head lolling against a headrest, staring up at grey sky and red bricks and a sign that says The Sunshine Unit for Neurological and Stroke Rehabilitation, *Garden of Hope.*

Turnalope Place.

'Nice to be outside, I would guess?' Tammy is my favourite of the nurses here. She has a smile that never looks forced and her tone is never too bright. If she's knackered, she tells me. If she's pissed off with one of the other inmates, she grumbles.

'Your stepfather will be back shortly. He suggested coming out here. He thought some fresh air would be good for you and we're all loving the new garden. It's nice for us as well as the patients.'

I don't remember Maxwell leaving. I must have fallen asleep. Not that he'd have seen the difference, I suppose. My eyes are open now, and as Tammy wheels me in a half circle, I can see a bench beside a raised wooden planter. It is filled with bare earth and there are rows of flowers in Styrofoam, waiting beside it. An old man in cotton pyjamas is digging clumsily with a trowel in one hand, while the other arm hangs. Next to him, a younger man in blue scrubs is offering him a pink plant. A sweet pea, I think. Or a snapdragon? Maxwell will know. He loves gardening.

'He seems nice, your stepfather. He wanted to know everything about your treatment. It's good to have someone knowledgeable around. You're lucky.'

Lucky? It's a funny way to look at it.

Maxwell certainly is knowledgeable, though. He's helped me understand what has happened to me better than anybody else. He described it all slowly. The bleed was in the lowest area where the brain meets the spinal cord, and if I think of it as the part of the brain which controls messages to everywhere else, it no longer works. With no messages telling it to move, the body does not move. Sometimes, a haemorrhage in this area leads to the entire body being paralysed, while the mind continues to function normally. This is called locked-in syndrome because, essentially, those who have it are locked inside their own bodies. In these cases, though, patients will generally be able to blink and to move their eyes up and down. It is the one function that will be spared.

What makes everything more complicated in my case is these other areas of damage in my brain, which the doctors assume is due to the football injury. They think these may have contributed to a greater lack of awareness. So although I'm no longer in a coma, they believe I could still be in a vegetative state, not really aware of anything around me, or a minimally conscious one, where I have limited awareness of the world, but my capacity for thinking in the way in which I used to think has gone.

It is not always easy to diagnose which of these states a patient is in. From scans and other tests, the neurologists don't think it's altogether impossible that I am in a locked-in state, except that the lack of clear response by blinking or eye movement leads them to feel that a vegetative or minimally conscious state is more likely. Assessment is ongoing.

'The most important thing,' Maxwell told me, 'is that there are documented improvements from all of these conditions. People have come out of vegetative and minimally conscious states. Coming out of a locked-in syndrome is rare, but recoveries happen. Brains are amazing things. They find new pathways, new ways of working. I'm not saying you'll be able to step back into your old life, but there's so much that is worth working for.'

Maxwell started telling me about another young man who'd been in a coma after a rugby match. I don't remember the end of the story. I must have drifted away before he finished.

Tammy's stopped talking. There are noises of cars nearby, and the encouraging comments of the young man to the older one, 'That's very good, Mr Donaldson. So if you can dig just a tiny bit deeper and let me give you this to plant in. What's that – call you Irvin, you say. That's my uncle's name. You don't hear it very often, do you.'

There is a sudden sourness in my throat. It is the taste of self-pity.

How can it be asking for too much to blink? Just to blink.

To show the world I still exist. Or not quite me, perhaps, but what is left of me. I'm not asking to run or to ski or to swim. To blink. To have somebody ask me, 'So is your family from Scotland? Blink if so,' and to be able to tell them, 'Yes, they are.' Or actually, not – I have an English mother and my father was American, but there are Scottish roots a few generations back. Is that asking too much? For somebody to acknowledge that some tiny bit of me is in here still.

My name is Ned. I am still here.

I blink.

I do it. I fucking blink.

Tammy must have seen.

But Tammy is not looking. She is turning her back at this precise moment and saying to somebody who is blocked from my view, 'Hello. Can I help you?'

For fuck's sake, look at me. I am blinking. My name is Ned. I am right here. Look at me.

Tammy is turned away, listening to this stranger say, 'Thank you. I think I'm a little bit lost. I'm meant to meet somebody at the hospital chapel but I reckon I've come the wrong way.'

That accent could be Australian but I think it's New Zealand. '*Mint* to meet someone.' My mother had a boyfriend from New Zealand after she and Maxwell split up. Steve? Or Dave maybe. But for heaven's sake, Tammy, forget the lost stranger for a moment. Look at me. I'm blinking. I'm fucking blinking.

'The chapel's round the other side of the unit, actually. If you go back out of the garden . . .'

Stop it, Tammy. Look at me. Look at me. Now. My name is Ned. I need you to look. Look at me. Look. Now. I am here. Look.

'If you follow signs to Cardiology, then . . .'

'I think your patient needs you.'

'I'm sorry, I—'

'Your patient. All that blinking means he needs something, don't you reckon?'

'Sorry. You mean Norton?'

As Tammy turns back towards me, I have a view of the stranger just beyond her. A red beret with two brunette plaits. Round glasses.

'Norton? Hang on, Norton from the paper?'

I blink. Again. Just like that. I blink.

'Pilates Ned? Ned 30? That's what his friends call him – Ned.'

I blink.

There's a squeal, and a shriek of, 'You're blinking!' from Tammy.

And I blink and I blink and I blink and I blink.

MRS M

I DO NOT KNOW WHAT has come over me. I have never been one for histrionics, as anybody who knows me would attest. Yet the more I attempt to pull myself together, the harder I seem to cry. I feel so undignified, not least, I'm afraid to say, because this is not a few ladylike tears. My nose is running. I can taste it.

'One does not say snotty, if you please, Roger,' I always tell him. 'One must say "congested".' But just look at me. I'm dribbling, too. I can feel it on my chin. My arm, for some reason, does not have the strength to wipe it away. Mary Malley, you pathetic old woman. Whatever would Roger say?

'Nurse, bring me a tissue,' I call. Except those are not the words that come out. I'm not sure what those words are. They do not sound like me. They do not sound much like words. Why can I not do this one simple thing? I can't even—

There are thoughts in my head. And yet, when I try to grasp them, to pin down what it is I'm thinking, they – go. I cannot find those – things. The things I want to – to – thing.

I want to tell myself to pull myself together. Only, as the nice doctor said, it's normal not to be myself right now. Only to be expected. 'Mary, you've had a little stroke,' I remind myself. But thank goodness Vicar and Harriet weren't here when I began this childish crying. I should have died of shame if they'd seen me this way.

Where did she go? Harriet? She was here a moment ago, talking about her dog. That silly creature she insists on making such a fuss of. I wanted to tell her that she didn't need to stay in my house, since she has a perfectly nice home of her own. Except it wasn't there. The thing. I couldn't. House. It wasn't there. She was wearing that hat. I remember asking her when she bought it. 'Whatever next? A string of onions?' But she insisted it was snazzy.

Come to think of it, she was not herself either. Harriet. The glasses. New, I suppose. But there was also – the things. The voice. The way she— and I don't suppose Harriet would have come, because—

Because—

Oh, bother these stupid tears, and this congested nose. I really could do with a handkerchief. I rather think I have to ask the nurse for a bedpan, too. So undignified, but I really think I must. I must call. I must find the – thing – in my – the thing.

But it won't come. The thing in my – the thing – to say. Just a noise. And there is no nurse. And I need to.

Harriet is dead. It can't have been Harriet, now can it. And I am a disgusting old lady, drooling. Control yourself, Mary Malley, for heaven's sake.

But I need the nurse. I *need* the nurse. With the bedpan. Right now. And I'm trying to call, but what comes out of my mouth is obscenity and tears, and then laughter.

I am laughing like a madwoman. Like a lunatic. Like some common fishwife. And, finally, the nurse is coming. But it is too late and there is a smell. Revolting. Shameful. I am so sorry. So awfully sorry. Yet, I do not seem able to stop laughing.

KIKI

'**Y**EAH, NAH. THAT'S UNKIND. She's not so bad when you know her.' This is what I'm saying as I'm pulling the pint, because I can't let him say such things.

His cheeks are pinker than when I served him his last one, which was number three. Robert is a builder who has a pest control business as a sideline. Sturgiss Pest Patrol. His wife cleans the pub on Monday and Thursday mornings, but she never comes in outside of work. She's at home now with their three small children and his mother, most likely. Sarah is his wife's name. Sarah and Rob Sturgiss. Turgid Sturgiss, Meredith calls him. Turgid Breast Patrol. I think she was at school with him.

'But I do know her. I've known Malicious Malley a lot longer than you have.' He's leaning across the bar and the fruity smell of beer and something that's maybe cabbage hits my nose. 'And she's a bossy old bitch.'

I shrug and start polishing glasses that don't need polishing. It gives me the chance to step out of his breath and to move my chest out of his sight. Even with my back turned, he starts a story about being eight years old, and Mrs M reprimanding him for his ungainly manner. Those are the precise words. 'Robert Sturgiss, why must you insist on carrying yourself in such an ungainly manner?' I have to pretend that I have a cough at this point, because the impression is really very good, but also because Mrs M was quite right. He's six foot something now, with a belly but skinny legs and feet that stick out almost sideways in worker boots, and arms that hang by his sides so that he kind of waddles when he walks, like a kind of spoonbill, maybe, or some long-legged duck.

I'm not really listening though, because in my head I'm still replaying what happened earlier. You know when something happens and you just can't stop thinking about it. Norton Edbury from the newspaper being there in the garden. Pilates Ned. I couldn't really see him at first because the nurse was in the way. I was just asking her where to go, and she was starting to answer and she must have moved or something, because that's when I saw him blinking away, and so I knew he must want something.

I didn't recognise him until Tammy squealed his name and, 'You're blinking!' She kept asking him all those questions, like blink if he could understand her, blink if he knew where he was, blink if his name was Norton, blink if he'd rather be called Ned. Even the old man planting the flower couldn't stop watching. And then Norton's stepfather arrived and he kept thanking me, like I was the one who'd made it happen.

'How did you know he likes to be called Ned?' That's what he wanted to know. I told him about the photo in the paper with the *Ned 30* birthday top. I think he was pretty impressed I'd remembered it. To be fair, I was pretty impressed myself.

Maxwell's the stepdad's name. I hope I didn't offend him by asking if he was Norton's grandfather. It was sweet of him to buy me a coffee and say he'd be happy to give me a lift into the hospital whenever he was going in. He comes through Little Piddleton anyway, he said. He gave me his number.

They were going to talk to the doctors again, and Maxwell said that now they'd have to agree that Norton, Ned, is fully aware of what's going on around him. They'll document it all and get a proper diagnosis.

I'll call Maxwell tomorrow. Perhaps he could take me in to visit Mrs M again. I could pop in to say hello to Norton-Ned, too.

'Do you know what else your wonderful Mary Malley did, Kiki?'

Rob Sturgiss is leaning so far over the bar that his head is practically touching the beer tap. He tells a story about confiscated footballs and then starts on another one about him being in trouble with the old vicar because of changing a few words of the Lord's Prayer. 'Our Father who fart in Heaven.' Bob Sturgiss shakes his head. Just a little joke. No reason for Mrs Malley to create such a fuss. He was suspended from cub scouts and his mother was mortified.

Rob Sturgiss orders another pint. His eyes watch my chest as I pour it.

He's been in every night this week. I'm guessing we're almost at the point when he starts asking what brought a nice girl like me over from Australia, then maybe another pint off whether or not I have a boyfriend. There's nobody else in tonight, or else I could go and collect empties. But there's not much to do except listen.

I wasn't meant to be working, only Meredith was invited to a party last minute so Mervyn said I had to. He couldn't, he said, as he always plays bridge on Mondays. I don't think Wordsworth was happy I was going out. Maybe that's why he dug that big hole in the lawn.

'So, Kiki, what's a smart young Kiwi doing working in a village pub over here?'

Right country at least.

'I was born in England. Not too far from here. Technically, I'm a Brit.'

"Nd so what brings you back?' Just a tiny slur on the 's' of 'so'.

I wonder what he'd say if I said, 'Well, Robert, since you ask, I've come to track down a man called Stan Douglas so I can ask him why he poisoned my mother.'

But I don't say that. Instead I roll out the normal stuff about broadening my horizons. 'Also there are some festivals I need to go to. Glastonbury, if you know anyone who's selling a ticket. My family worked the festivals when they were young. I haven't had the chance to go to many. I want to, you know, find my roots.'

'You'll end up staying here. You'll never go back now.'

It's not clear from the gaze whether he means me as a whole person, or whether this comment is for my breasts alone.

Rob orders another beer.

'There must be a boyfriend, Kiki? Some lucky man?'

No, Rob. Neither they nor I have one currently. Same answer as when you asked three nights ago. We've never even had a long-term relationship, in case you'd care to ask that again too. Just the normal embarrassing one-night stands with blokes as drunk as you, and mostly as boring.

'But surely you should be somewhere more exciting than house-sitting for that old cow? You're not a bad-looking girl, Kiki. You know, if I wasn't married . . .'

Oh, please.

We've worn out the 'I'm not planning to settle down for a few years yet' conversation over the last week or so. So instead, I lead us back to, 'She's not so bad when you get to know her.' And Turgid Sturgiss tells my chest a few more stories about Mrs M ruining his childhood.

TWO WEEKS LATER
NED

'AND BABY, YOU PROMISE me you're doing OK? Really?'

I blink.

'That's so great to hear. And your therapists? They're working you hard?'

Blink.

'And you really don't need me back there again just yet?'

I blink and blink again.

'Next month, though, honey, I promise, because I so want to see you again. I'd give anything to be there with you right now. But Sadie says this lunch with the Korean director could be really positive. Because Korean cinema is having such a moment, which means this project could be actually very important. You get that, don't you, Norton? Not just artistically important, but culturally important too.'

Silence.

'You get that, hon? Tell me you do.'

I hadn't realised she was waiting for an answer. I blink.

There is a moment more silence.

'And they're looking after you? The nurses. They're being kind to you?'

I have the impression that my mother finds these Skype calls harder now she knows that I understand every word. She has to create openings. It takes effort.

Meanwhile, on the chair between the stand with my various drips and the monitors which trace whatever of my bodily functions they trace, sits an obscenely large pink teddy bear with a T-shirt that says *Congratulations*. Toby brought it in. I presume it was a joke.

'Sorry about the T-shirt,' he said, as the bear preceded him in through the door. 'It was either that or *I Love You*. And well, I like you, Ned mate. But wouldn't want you getting the wrong impression.' Honking laughter.

He's been all right, actually, Toby. His visits are different to Bella's when there's lots of arm clutching and insistence that I'll walk out of the hospital on my own two feet. They were here at the same time the other day. Toby set us a quiz. Yes/no questions or multiple choice – one blink for a, two blinks for b, three blinks for c. Mostly football and rugby and music questions, so I beat Bella twenty-three to nine. The sad truth is that it was as near to fun as I've come since going in for that header and then waking up to find that I was wired up in intensive care.

'Maxwell's been there a lot, I imagine?' My mother cannot keep the resentment out of her voice when she says his name. Does she expect a blink in response, I wonder?

Yes, Mother, Maxwell has been in every day. He's pored over my notes with each doctor on the team. He's discussed plans and strategies with the physios, speech therapists and occupational therapists. He has started researching new technologies, living and mobility aids and communication methods. He explains everything to me slowly and patiently and without sugar-coating and makes certain that I have all the information I need. He told me that the diagnosis of locked-in syndrome is an encouraging one in that it tells everybody that my brain is still functioning intellectually, but it is not such good news in that the incidences of recovery are few and far between. He has brought me examples of those who have also been struck down like this and who have learned to move a finger, or regained some mobility in their heads, or their legs, or who have found their voice, or some semblance of their voice, again; those even who have walked and run and gone back to living their lives. But he has – kindly, gently – made sure I am aware that for all of these exceptions, there are many more who have remained paralysed in all of their body, except those muscles that allow blinking and the upward and downward motion of the eye itself.

For now, he says, we must be grateful that this ability has been returned. It is a small thing that will make a big difference.

The neurologists can still not say definitively why I was unable to do it at first. Bruising to my brain from the goalpost perhaps. I still can't believe that was not a winner. I swear my head was on the ball. Sam took the perfect corner. A brilliant cross. All I had to do was tap it in. The perfect set-up for the perfect header and it would have put us ahead. In my mind, I was already celebrating the goal.

I can feel it still. Not the impact, though that too because it really hurt. But that sensation of jumping. Of throwing myself through the air. Leaping in the sheer determination of scoring the goal. The yells of the others, cheering already. The bending and stretching of muscles. The exhilaration of a working body.

Despair lurks, like a thug, in the corners of my brain. It is an effort to keep out of its way. I am sticking to the lighted paths of my brain, clinging to the joy and triumph of my blinking. This small thing that will make a big difference. I must avoid the shadows, from which hiss the frustrations. Jumping. Running. Playing. Thrusting my body into the air for a head to hit a ball.

I can blink. This is big. I can blink.

'Norton, hon, you OK? What's with all the blinking? That's not yes or no? Is that good, honey? What are you telling me? You're OK, baby?'

Blink.

There's a knock at the door. I cannot turn my head. I cannot call, 'Come in,' but the door opens anyway. 'Hi there. I – oh you're busy, sorry. I was visiting Mrs M and thought I'd say a quick hello. I'll come back another time, eh.'

With my head positioned straight ahead towards the laptop screen, I cannot see the person talking. But the computer must pick it up too, as my mother seems to hear the voice.

'What's that, Norton – there's someone with you? Listen, baby, I need to be going anyway. We'll Skype again tomorrow or the next day though, yes?'

Blink.

'I love you, Nortie. Do you love me too?'

Blink. As if I could respond in any other way.

'Bye then, my darling.' There is a flurry of kisses blown into the camera as my mother's mouth fills the screen before it goes blank.

'I didn't mean to interrupt your call. Shall I leave?'

Blink. Blink.

'Two blinks. That's "no", yes? Ha. Thank you.' She sits at the end of the bed. In her defence, there is a large pink bear in the only available chair. She leans forward, bringing her face right into my line of sight, and she smiles. 'But, you know, I didn't want to intrude. It must be nice for you to talk to your mother. Or, well, you know . . .' She's smacking her hand against her forehead and her cheeks have become pinker.

Kiki Moon seems to have marched herself into my life.

My existence was surreal enough already. I have to keep presenting myself with objective evidence that it is actually real; this is objectively a hospital, and here are my mother and Toby and Bella acting as I would expect them to act, and here are the medical team, hired and trained by the NHS to deal with such a complicated neurological case as I have now become. Here is the catheter and the nappy and the blood pressure monitor and the feeding tube. Here is the MRI and the CT scan and the electrodes stuck to my scalp to measure brain activity. It is a cliché to say that my life right now feels like a dream, and yet it is hard to accept that anything else is a better alternative.

But here, also, is this Call-me-Kiki with her 'don't mean to intrude' as she plonks herself down on my bed, with her glances, as if she's expecting to be told to leave at any moment. The first few times, she came with Maxwell, and mostly just sat quietly or answered when he brought her into the conversation. But this is the third time she's come in on her own, saying she was in the hospital anyway, visiting her elderly friend. I'm not sure I've ever met anybody who talks quite so much. Almost every word she says she blushes, but then she keeps on going.

She's been watching my YouTube channel, she says. She loves my songs.

'I'm going to try some of your Pilates stuff too. But I'll need a mat. I couldn't do it on the bed in the pub. It's way too saggy and the springs spike you, but there's not enough room on the floor. Maybe in Mrs M's living room. There's enough space there, I reckon. Sue used to do it in our living room. Sue was always talking about how fantastic Pilates was for keeping her core muscles tight. I reckon she has the tightest core muscles in the North Island.'

Sue? Sorry, but Sue who?

Kiki's only trying to make conversation, I suppose. And only one of us can do that.

'You don't know who Sue is though. Sue was my landlady in New Zealand. Or, you know, my friend.' When she says 'friend' her eyes dart to the side, as if she's worried I might ask her to prove it. 'She'd love your stuff on the internet. When she replies to my emails, I'll tell her all about your *Pilates, passion and practice*.'

Norton Edbury's three Ps. Kiki's staring at me like she's waiting for some sort of acknowledgement. I blink.

'Sue'll love it. And I reckon it's really great now for you. Bet it helps?'

Hmm. Not sure the Pilates part is quite so helpful now that every single muscle in my body, other than a couple in my eyes, is paralysed, quite possibly permanently.

'Muscle memory and the right mindset, that's what I mean. Positive thinking. Sue always said positive thinking was important.'

I blink because, well, I might as well. Kiki grins.

How was it her who spotted my eye movements in the garden that day when none of the people who should have seen them had seen them? Let alone coming right out like that and calling me Ned, as if we were old friends. 'Ned Pilates,' she called me.

'I've been talking to Mrs M – you know, my old woman – about your videos too. She's still not talking that well right now though, so I don't know what she thinks. I've been telling her heaps about them. You know what it's like when you're the one doing all the talking, eh?'

No pause. I don't think she realises the irony.

'I've told her how beautiful your songs are. I don't know what she usually listens to, but I said I'll play some to her next time I visit because she'll really like it. I told her it's the sort of music

anybody would love to have somebody write for them. Not –
I mean – that anybody would write any sort of music for me.'

Her eyes turn from me towards the teddy bear. It looks like
she might be blushing again.

MRS M

WHEN I WAS AT school, we had a physical education teacher who was called Mrs Thrower. All us girls thought it was a funny name when her job was to teach us rounders and netball and javelin. She had a whistle which she'd blow if we weren't working hard enough. I remember our gym classes, Harriet and me doing our squats or star jumps or skipping and Mrs Thrower blowing that whistle and yelling, 'Another minute, girls. And put a bit more effort into it or you'll all do it again. Mary Penhaligon and Harriet Wright, I'm looking at you.'

*

'That's very good, Mrs Malley. Let's try a few more steps.'

This is the same hospital where Roger was brought after his fall. And it's here where Harriet came in for that scan because of her stomach aches. She never went home again.

'Can you lift that foot up any more than that?'

Does the stupid woman not think that's what I'm trying to do? 'Lift that foot up' – it is simple enough for her to say. Look at her. She probably runs marathons at weekends. In any case she looks far too young to be a – whatever these people are. There seem to be so many of them. Physiotherapists. Occupational therapists. Speech therapists. Neuro-physiotherapists. Psychologists. Or is that another therapist? A psychotherapist? Stroke nurses. Rehabilitation nurses. Social workers – social worker, I ask you. Do I look like somebody in need of a social worker? Do I resemble an abandoned baby or a battered wife? I shall tell them, 'I have never taken a hand-out in my life, so I do not see why I should suddenly be in need of a social worker now.'

And all of this blasted fuss over my next of kin. I suppose that must be because they're expecting me to die. Well, I do not intend to oblige them on that account. And this obsessing over whether or not the Kiki girl will be living with me when they let me return home. Silly child. She does babble so – Pilates and passion and this young man she can't seem to stop talking about. Daft if you ask me, since, from her description, he's little more than a vegetable.

In any case, I most certainly did not invite her to make herself at home in my house. Granted, it is advantageous for her to be looking after the dog and I should hate him to be taken into kennels, but she did not ask for my permission to stay. And, technically, that makes it squatting, does it not? Trespassing at the very least. As soon as I have all of my word-things back, my word-things, I shall tell her I have no need of her.

KIKI

THE BACK TYRE HAS a puncture. Even after all that pumping up earlier, look how flat it is. My poor legs. It was at the back of the shed, behind the lawn-mower. Such a pretty bike though. I felt like I should have been wearing a lacy dress instead of these cut-off jeans and high tops.

That noise from inside is Wordsworth. He must have heard me. He's taken half the paint off the door already with his scratching. When Mrs M sees it, it'll be off to the re-homing centre for both of us, I reckon.

Right, key in, and cue tail. You'd think I'd been gone for weeks the way he's jumping up even though I'm telling him, 'Down,' in my sternest voice.

This dog needs to go to training classes – look at how he's sticking his nose in my bag, and ignoring me when I say, 'Leave it, Wordsworth.'

He's right though. There is dog food in there. That and some pittas and pasta and tomatoes and garlic, lemon and olives. And chocolate biscuits, lemonade and crisps. And a drinking glass, to replace that one I cracked the other night. Well, actually, I had to buy two because they only sell them that way. They're not quite the same, but a glass is a glass, right?

And the good news? Here, let's get this stuff into the kitchen and put some more water in Wordsworth's bowl.

Wow, thirsty dog. 'The good news,' I tell him, 'is I'm all yours tonight, Wordsworth. No boring pub. We'll do a lovely walk, once my legs recover.'

Meredith's working – and I won't be on the phone half the night again because I've gone through all the numbers in Mrs M's address book now. Or the only ones left are ones like *Williamson, Tony (plumber)*, and I don't think he'd know much about her family. Same with *Renton, Simon (electrician)*. Maybe I should tell Mrs M about the call to *Thorne, Marion*. She was so rude. When I told her about poor Mrs M's stroke and said I was trying to locate family, she said, 'I'm her second cousin. Is she dead?' She sounded disappointed when I said not. I asked her whether she might want to visit the hospital to spend some time with Mrs M, and she said, 'So you're not a lawyer then? She's not dead?'

When I asked if she knew of any other family, she just said none that she knew of and hung up.

But I reckon maybe she is Mrs M's next of kin. I checked through the desk in the living room, and there was an envelope that says *Last Will & Testament*. I've never seen a real one before. Yaya didn't leave one at all. Not that she had anything to leave really, and anyway there was only me. My mum left a will. Yaya said it was because of her having started that law course. She didn't have any money to leave, but she had something more precious and that was me. Yaya said how clever my mum was, because the will said she and Gramps would look after me if anything happened to her.

Mrs M's will doesn't say anything about anyone looking after her children. But if she had any they'd be sixty-something now anyway, I reckon. Her will doesn't say anything about any other family at all, just everything to Roger Malley. She can't have changed it when he died.

Vicar doesn't think there were any children or grandchildren. So maybe one day this lovely cottage will go to that Marion Thorne. Maybe even Wordsworth will go to that woman who can't be bothered to ask which hospital Mrs M's in.

It's a beneficiary. That's the word, isn't it? Wordsworth could be Mrs M's beneficiary. You hear about that, don't you, old women who leave everything to their dogs. But maybe I can't talk because here I am talking to him out loud, like he understands what I'm saying. I'm telling him, 'You'd be a very rich little dog, wouldn't you. What would you spend all that money on? Sausages?'

I've been thinking about that cash. Six thousand pounds – it's enough to go to every festival in Europe. Or to buy a diamond dog collar and a lifetime supply of steak. What would Yaya have said if she'd seen all that money sitting there under the sink?

Anyway, I wasn't going through Mrs M's private stuff in the desk. Or only trying to help. There were some photo albums too. I think Wordsworth wants to see them, because he's following me back into the living room and hopping onto the sofa when I pick them up. Old photos are for looking at, aren't they, because why would you keep them otherwise? I used to tell Yaya I wished we had more photos. I would have loved to have had more of my mother. Especially her.

Some of ours were in frames. That one of Yaya with Gramps, him with long hair and a moustache – with that huge motorbike, an actual Harley, and the sea behind them, in their flares and vest tops. Yaya's thin, and her hair is black and loose. She's beautiful. Their wedding picture too, in another frame, next to the lamp on her bedside table – Gramps with a bootlace tie and Yaya in a green velvet dress over a stomach that's as round as a ball. She kept a box full of pictures under her bed. Lots of them showed a baby or a little girl with curly black hair. I'd always have to check the backs to see if it said Ioanna or Kiriaki.

There were lots of photos of festivals. Some were black and white and some were colour but they were all pretty grainy. There were lots of stages, with crowds around them, and bands – except they were just tiny people. I'd look at them for hours. I'd ask Yaya, who's this? What year is it? Which festival? But mostly she wouldn't remember.

There was only one photograph of my mother with me: actually there are hardly any of her after about sixteen, which is when she went off to be a new age crusty. I used to say, 'Was she like me, Yaya?' And Yaya would say, 'Yes. Always talking, always wanting the things I said she couldn't have.'

Most of my photos are in a box that Sue's keeping for me, back in Auckland. But that one of me with my mother is in my bag at the pub. Her hair is bleached, but I reckon she did it herself and it's pulled up in a plait so you can see the dark roots. She has me in her arms, holding me so I'm sort of sitting on her hip, and we're both looking towards the camera. Behind us, there's a hut – or you can only see half of it and of a big sign over its door, that says '& Sun-Catchers' in Gothic letters.

That photo's pretty old, but not as old as Mrs M's here. Wordsworth really does want to see the album, I reckon, because when I pick it up from the table he leans right against me and puts his head on my lap.

'Look how neatly she's stuck them in,' I show him, and she really has, with these little paper corners, and these beautifully written captions: *Mother and Father wedding, 1934. Mother and me, Minehead, 1942. H and me, Pewsey, 1946; Picnic with H, 1949.* I think Harriet's H. Because see the nose – same woman as *Harriet and Eric wedding, 1953.*

Mrs M looks so smart in this one: *1955, Touch Typing Contest, Cheltenham*. Those little gloves. And look, this is Mrs M's wedding. 1955 too. She doesn't look very happy, does she? And look here's—

Wordsworth looks like he's studying the picture. But then there's a noise, like a ringing melody, and I'm asking him, 'What's that noise?' Which shows how often anyone calls my phone. Because what else would it have been?

'Merv, no doubt,' I'm telling Wordsworth. 'Let's guess. Meredith's got another party so he's asking me to work. Now, where did I put my bag. Here – oh it's . . .'

The caller ID doesn't say *Mervyn*. It says *Maxwell*.

My voice sounds too bright, you know how you can be when you answer the phone. 'Hello, Maxwell. Is everything all right?'

He tells me, 'Don't worry, Kiki. Nothing's wrong. I was just wondering if you fancied a spot of dinner at mine. I'd appreciate hearing your thoughts about a few things. I'd be happy to pick you up and drop you home afterwards.'

Two basset eyes are saying don't go out. They're saying isn't it walkies time? They're saying I promised.

NED

HILARIOUS. ABSOLUTELY HILARIOUS.

Ha. Ha. Fucking ha.

Girlfriend in a Coma stops on a twang of Morrissey. Toby is already chuckling to himself. 'Just wait for the next one, Ned, mate. This one's even better.'

The sound of synthesised chords starts up a rhythmic four-four beat. I know it, though I can't put my finger on it yet. Toby's grinning.

What is this song? I know I know it. I'm sure I'll kick myself. Figuratively speaking, of course. Here we go. I *do* know this intro. And, '*Words don't come easy* . . .' Of course.

Toby honks.

'Get it, mate? *Words* don't come easy.'

I blink. Toby laughs more and says, 'Exactly!' And then he pauses. 'It's only a bit of fun, you know that. It's only because I know what a sense of humour you have. You do know that, don't you, Ned? You do think this is funny?'

And if I blink twice now? What then, Toby, if I communicate that actually, no, I don't find it particularly amusing? What if I were to blink twice and watch the look on your face as it computes that it might not technically be your place to decide what is and what isn't humorous about the situation in which I find myself and that maybe you can't impose jollity on somebody whose future has been squashed.

It's tempting. Two blinks and I could watch the change in him, from a bouncy puppy to a kicked one.

But there could be no rowing back. I could not sit here doing my victim face, and then dig him in the ribs and say, 'Got you.'

Like everything else, jokes have become something that my role is to accept passively.

There will be letters, though. Soon. There will be a board, with the alphabet, and I will select the letters with my gaze – letter by letter by letter – to make the words, and to put together the words, word by word, to make the sentences. I. W-i-l-l. B-e. A-b-l-e. T-o. T-e-l-l. J-o-k-e-s. Again. S-l-o-w-l-y, though. And not quite yet. Just soon. I am in the hands of experts. The speech therapist and the neuro-ophthalmologist – now why, I wonder, did that job never make it into the Happy Families cards? Mr Bun the Baker, and Mr Brain-Eye the Neuro-Ophthalmologist. For now though, my eyes ache and throb after a day of blink-once and blink-twice. 'Yes' and 'no' wear me out. I am tired.

'You do know it's all a bit of fun?' A note of anxiety in Toby's voice? I wait a few more moments before granting him the blink. Perhaps I'm not incapable of winding him up after all.

How would I be if the positions were reversed? If Toby were the one, propped up in a hospital bed, motionless and expressionless? Would I make jokes and playlists? Would I sit with him, just the two of us, or with Bella, or Hilary maybe, week after week, trying to lift his spirits? I like to think I'd bring my guitar and sing to him. It would probably drive him round the bend.

It wouldn't be revenge, because we would never have done it this way round. There would have been no insensitive playlists for me to gain payback for, no *Schitt's Creek*, no oversized teddies. No gratitude for all these daft gestures either.

Bella visited earlier. And Maxwell. He left first. He suggested they might both like to eat with him tonight but Toby said he had Hilary to get back to and at the exact same time, Bella said she was sorry but she couldn't tonight. I have a feeling Maxwell might have given them some sort of sign to suggest that they should not stay too long. I do sense them assessing me constantly for fatigue, or pain, or depression.

No Kiki today. Not that there was any reason to expect her, except that she so often does pop up – apologetic about intruding while marching straight in with all those stories about Yaya and Sue and this Stan Douglas who she believes killed her mother. How can she not even know how her mother died? There I was thinking my family was a messed up one.

It doesn't sound like she has the first clue where to start looking. But there's a lot Kiki doesn't seem to have a clue about – not that it stops her talking about it. All these stories about Mrs M and Wordsworth and cracked glasses and holes in the garden. She hardly draws breath.

She even questioned Tammy about Mr Douglas the consultant after Tammy mentioned something he'd said. What was Mr Douglas's first name, Kiki wanted to know. And when Tammy said it was Hamish, Kiki demanded whether she might know if he had any brothers. As if Tammy'd know.

Maybe Maxwell was right. I think I am tired. Toby and his so-very-funny playlist are exhausting enough. Perhaps I didn't need a load more stories about Yaya's prophecies of happiness in England or about the oddballs at the pub. Although Kiki drops in these properly wild nuggets. Yaya being in labour while Bowie was playing his dawn set at Glastonbury – do I believe that? It's quite the story.

'I'll leave you to it then, mate.' Toby gives my shoulder a rub. 'See you in a few days.'

I blink. As he disappears from my line of sight, 'Words Don't Come Easy' fades out and there's a moment's silence before the strumming of an opening riff: E minor 7, E minor 7, A minor. I know this one. In my mind, my fingers stretch across the strings. You bugger, Toby. I can't see him now – my view is of medical monitors and ceiling – but I can feel him watching me as the singer's falsetto comes in to let me know that I can tell by the way he uses his walk, he's a woman's man, no time to talk, and Toby sings along tunelessly to the 'ah, ah, ah, ah' of 'Stayin' Alive'.

MRS M

S OME OF IT IS genetic. One is either born with good genes or one is not; I count myself lucky, and of course I do have Mother to thank on that account. Mowing her own lawn and weeding the churchyard into her nineties. And now here am I and they all say that I am recovering remarkably well for somebody of my age. Mr Douglas says he is most impressed by how fast I appear to be improving.

But it isn't only genes, surely. There is that element of personal responsibility. Take that Olivia in the corner bed. She doesn't appear to do anything but complain. Today was the second day that she's refused to even attempt to use the walker. Surely she could have tried just a few steps, if only out of respect for the poor physiotherapist. One or two steps, surely. If I can do it then she can at least have a go. She's only seventy-five, and it's not as if she's the only person to whom this has happened. And then there's that awful daughter who, so far as I can see, comes at visiting time and does nothing but drink Coca-Cola and grumble about the buses and the weather and the government and her feet.

I have half a mind to tell this Olivia that she must start putting a bit of effort into her recuperation, otherwise there is no point in her carrying on. Listen to that whimpering. That's hardly going to help. Earlier I overheard the daughter talking to that psychologist woman about antidepressant tablets, saying her mother's having a difficult time coping. Does she not think it's hard for all of us? Does she think I find it easy to discover myself in this situation? Does she suppose that Mrs Bamford in the end bed is here because she has chosen to be? Poor Mrs Bamford. I don't believe she even grasps what has happened to her, the way she keeps calling out for Nanny.

I should very much like to give that daughter a piece of my mind. But that is the problem with so many of them, they seem to think there is a pill for everything nowadays. I am quite certain my mother didn't run to the doctor for a prescription when Father was killed in Normandy. And what about Harriet, when Eric ran off with that awful Ruth Skinner from the Upper Piddleton choir alto section? Although now I think about it, she may have had a little something, but what she did not do was take to her bed and refuse to try.

I myself have been through times that have tried my faith. Those years where every week seemed to bring another invitation to a christening, and the receptions afterwards where you could hardly move for prams and pushchairs. The glances and the comments about whether Roger and I might be next. I shall never forget the time when his senior partner's awful wife said how surprising that we hadn't yet welcomed our own little patter of feet and Roger came out and said, 'Unfortunately Mary seems to be barren.'

I cannot say how close I came to walking right out at that moment. But I stayed. Because life gives us these tribulations.

Prayer and perseverance, that's what Mother always said, will always pull one through.

'A difficult time coping.' And therefore, what? Look, here she starts again, Olivia. What is it now, I wonder. Water, bedpan, painkiller, light on, bedjacket off? How can it be that she is unable to so much as move her hand when the occupational

therapist asks her to hold a ball during her session with him –
Amir, pleasant young man – yet she blatantly has no trouble
ringing the alarm bell for the nurse all night long. Either she is
incapable of using those fingers or she is not.

Harriet always said that there were two types of people in
the world, those for whom the glass was half empty and those
for whom it was half full. 'Harriet,' I used to say. 'It is not a
matter of the glass being half empty. It is about realising that
one cannot simply assume that there will always be somebody
to fill it back up for you again.' Perhaps, I suggested to Harriet,
the division is in actual fact between those who drain their
glasses, with no thought for what might happen when they are
thirsty later on, and those who appreciate the value of having
a drink at all and choose not to squander it willy-nilly. Harriet
told me that it was only a silly metaphor. 'Lighten up,' I seem
to remember her saying. As if she were quoting from a self-
help book, or were an American.

'Lighten up?' No, Harriet. Sometimes one simply has to
accept that life is not all full glasses and guaranteed happiness.
Look at me. I lost my husband and my best friend in the space
of two months. Does nobody imagine there were not days
when it would have been easier for me to remain beneath my
quilt sobbing than to pull myself together and open up the
church library for the community? Just because one does not
go around talking to every Tom, Dick and Harry about one's
feelings does not mean one is unaffected.

I sometimes feel that I may be the only person left who
does not feel the need to tell the entire world about my
'demons' and my 'mental health'. But despair is not the
prerogative of the internet generation. We have all had our
share of pain, only some of us are a little better at keeping
a dignified silence.

Listen to me. Because I too should like a fresh glass of water, in fact, so I too shall ask Nurse – since you have already summoned her, Olivia – for attention. But listen to this, since you seem to think you are the only person having a difficult time. I know she is a nurse. I call to the nurse. And the word that comes out is, 'Cook.'

So I try it again. 'Cook.'

She crosses the room from Olivia's bed, and she does not correct me even though we both know that I have said the wrong thing. She asks, 'What can I do for you, Mrs Malley?'

Listen to me, Olivia, forcing myself to do this, instead of whimpering about how cruel life is, listen to me asking for a glass of water. Except not 'glass'. That does not wish to come. That one. It is there. I do know it. But I cannot say it. But 'water'. Tonight I can say that.

This is not easy. It is not dignified. It is not fair.

And yet I have said 'water'.

And earlier tonight, at a quarter to seven, I took the walker from beside my bed and I walked to the lavatory. One hundred and three steps there. One hundred and seven back. Twenty-eight minutes it took. Yes, I was pathetic and mortified at having to make such spectacle of myself. It hurt my knees and my feet and my hands and my wrists and it made me feel quite humiliated. But that is what I did.

None of this is easy. But when last week, or whenever it was, the Welsh doctor showed me those pictures of a round smiley face at the top of the page beside an empty white circle, and at the bottom a sad face next to a grey circle, and between the two, equally sized white circles going down the page with increasingly large grey circles inside them, and when she explained that the grey in the circles represented how depressed my mood was and where would I place myself, well, I did not point to the empty white circle with the smiling face, because that would have been ridiculous, but nor did I point to the fully grey one, because no doubt then they would have insisted that I too take pills. No. I pointed to the circle in the middle – the one which was half filled with grey. Or half empty, I suppose. Because, Olivia, if one allows oneself to believe that the entire circle is grey, well, then I am quite certain that grey it shall be.

Prayer and perseverance. One must accept that element of responsibility, or else give up.

Tomorrow, when that little language therapist with the lisp – really you might have thought she should have been able to cure herself of it – comes back and shows me that picture of the dog, I shall not only write the word *d-o-g* – with handwriting that looks as if it might be a two-year-old holding a crayon, but I shall say it. I shall imagine the word, as I see it, and I shall say it out loud. This time, I shall not say 'cat'.

They are coming back. Slowly. Those things. My words. And the next time that Kiki makes a visit, I shall tell her, 'I am sure you mean well, Kiki Moon. But my house is my house and my dog is my dog and my life is my life. I do not need you.'

KIKI

JUST LOOK AT ALL of this – the meadow stretching downhill to the stream and the bright wildflowers growing through the long grass, with my frog gumboots swishing through it. And there's the white tip of Wordsworth's tail as he chases his new friend Hector, who's spotted a rabbit. Wordsworth is slower, barking at him to wait.

'Wordsworth! Come back!' I'm calling, because how would I ever explain to Mrs Malley if I lost her dog? 'Wordsworth!'

It's lovely here. Open wild space that smells a bit like back home on a warm evening by the lake. Yaya always told me how beautiful it was over here, and this field, with the old stone farmhouse up at the top there, is pretty much her dream. I can picture Norton – Ned – out here, with his guitar, writing his songs because I think I've seen him exactly here, in this field, in one of his videos. He's walking and talking, and then sitting on a rug spread out on the grass, him with Annabella next to him. She's lying down with her shiny hair and her skin with no freckles, and picking daisies while he's playing one of his lovely songs. She was at the hospital this afternoon, Maxwell said. She's there a lot but I've never met her. She and Ned must really love each other though, mustn't they? Those songs he writes, they've got to be for someone special. Can you imagine? To have somebody love you like that, and be able to put it into music too.

'Wordsworth, Hector, come!'

Look – here's one good dog, racing right back at the sound of his name, like something in a dog food advert, and then here's Wordsworth behind him with his ears flapping. What a surprise for him when Maxwell pulled up in that lovely old car with the roof down and Wordsworth gave me those sad eyes, like, 'You're leaving me again', and Maxwell told him, 'Up, boy.' He got to sit on his own blanket in the back, like he was some English lord, with his ears blowing around.

It wasn't the car Maxwell normally drives to the hospital. This one's like something from a classic movie. I wish Yaya could have seen. It made me think about that poem Harriet wrote for Mrs Malley, the bit about a car with a Jaguar on its bonnet – though a red car, not black like Maxwell's. I'll check it when I get back. I told Maxwell all about it. I didn't mention that the poem called it a fuck it list though. I said its title was 'Old Ladies' Bucket List'.

There's Maxwell now, see, waving from the building on the other side of the field. The annexe he calls it, where Ned lives. I recognise the yellow stone wall from the YouTube videos. Maxwell loves Ned being here, he says, whenever he comes back from his other home which is in France, by the Spanish border. He spends most of his time there now, at his hideaway up in the mountains. Or he did.

He speaks both languages fluently too, Maxwell does. French and Spanish. That's three languages with English. And also a bit of German, though he's rusty. Four languages. He wasn't boasting, even. It was me who asked. I can't even speak Greek, except for a bit of swearing and a few phrases like 'you wicked, naughty girl' and 'you precious, beautiful child'. I told Maxwell I was rubbish at languages. We didn't learn one at school, only a bit of te reo Māori and some phrases in Chinese and some sentences in French. But I was always the one who pronounced everything wrong. Maxwell asked about whether I'd been to university so I told him about that nursing course in Auckland, and having to give it up almost straight away, when Yaya had her first stroke, so that I could go back and look after her.

'Maybe that's why you're so intuitive with Ned,' was what Maxwell said.

Hector's seen him now, and he's racing so fast, I can't keep up. It's funny to see Wordsworth joining and wagging his tail and jumping up like he's known Maxwell all his life too. The annexe used to be Maxwell's surgery before he retired.

'Please do come in. I'd appreciate your thoughts.' The door's open, because he's been collecting up a few bits for Ned while I was walking the dogs around the grounds. Normally I'd feel awkward about going inside like this. It's Ned's home so I don't really like the idea of being there without him knowing, especially when it's already a bit awkward, me staying at Mrs M's, and especially when his guitar is in one corner of the living room and his yoga mat too, rolled up and leaning against the bookcase. But Maxwell wants my opinion. He's thinking about what modifications he might make so that Ned could come home from hospital eventually, not that anybody has any idea yet when that can be. Maxwell wants to know what I think.

'My main worry is the stairs,' he says. 'Even if Ned does regain an element of mobility, the chance of it being enough to use the stairs is slim. In all likelihood there will need to be provision for full-time care too.'

I know my reply doesn't really mean anything. It's just like, 'mmh'. But it would be rude to say nothing and I don't know what else to say. I'm trying not to stare at the photo frames above the fireplace. There's one of Ned with Maxwell. Maxwell's hair is thicker, and grey more than white. Ned's is shorter, spiky rather than shaggy. They're in ski clothes and sunglasses, sitting at a bar on a snowy terrace in front of a blue sky. There's another one of Ned standing on a bridge, high up above a valley, with a harness around his waist. There's also one of a man who looks just like Ned, except older, in his forties maybe. Has to be Ned's dad, unless he has a much older brother. You'd think he'd have a photo of Annabella too. Maybe there's one by his bed.

'It will be easier to discuss this with Ned when the speech and language therapists have established more sophisticated communication methods. But I want to think ahead. I can't work out whether it will be reassuring to come back to his own home, or whether it might be more upsetting than looking for a different solution. What do you think, Kiki? Would you want to come back to the home you'd lived in before? Or would that be too painful, do you think?'

He's looking at me like I'm the sort of person who knows about these kinds of things, not just some barmaid in frog wellies. And I don't know what to say, but I really don't want to say, 'I don't know,' because of the way he's looking at me, like he needs me to say something.

'I don't know.' I want to look away but that would be rude. 'A bit of both maybe. I mean, it will be painful, I reckon. But you can't change what's happened to him and this place is lovely. He's lucky to have it. And lucky to have you looking out for him too. He'll know that.'

This is maybe the most rubbish answer anyone's ever given to any question ever, but Maxwell nods, and says, 'Thank you, Kiki.'

NED

KIKI THIS, KIKI THAT. Kiki, 'something so endearing about her, don't you think, Ned? And a surprising appetite. She'd never had hotpot before.'

Thank you for this, Maxwell. It sounds a very cosy dinner. Perhaps you should adopt her. In case you're interested, my menu option was a bag of goo pumped through a tube in my nose.

'She was so excited by the Jag. I'd suggested she bring her wellingtons in case of rain, and she appeared in this pair with frog faces on the toes. To my mind they were the sort of thing a five-year-old might wear. Perhaps they're fashionable though. Did I already mention that she only agreed to come when I said that her basset hound must come too?'

And this makes her the perfect house guest? Wears bonkers boots and brings her dog to dinner. So charming.

'When I suggested she might like to stay over in the barn as it was rather late with all our talking, I thought I must have offended her. She stared at me for such a long time and I assumed that I'd made an awful faux pas because even at my age, I suppose one could give a young lady the wrong impression.

'It was nothing like that though, thank goodness. She said, "Let me get this right. There's this house, there's Ned's annexe and there's a barn too?"'

Maxwell, don't tell me that's meant to be a New Zealand accent?

'Apparently her grandparents had an old barn somewhere in the Mendips. Before they emigrated. Her grandfather reno-vated it. Did you know that for most of her childhood she lived in an old school bus he'd converted too? I suppose she's already told you that. Parked up on blocks between a forest and a lake, in one of those static home sites, like a holiday park. Bohemian types, I imagine. They made their living picking fruit and then working at festivals. Kiki's mum was born at one, she says. And died at one too, according to Kiki, although – well, she's told you about this Stan Douglas. That's why she's so desperate to find a Glastonbury ticket. I think she feels it might connect her to her past. I do wish I could help her.'

Neither of us says anything for a moment or two. That is to say, Maxwell is quiet. And I'm trying to decide whether this is pointed. He might know I had a ticket to Glastonbury. A ticket I will not be able to use. Is that what all of this is about?

If I was still me, I should already be excited about an upcoming long weekend of music and freedom and of stepping outside of all rigidity and rules. The chance to lose myself in an expanse of happy people and to throw structure to the wind. I love Glastonbury. Maxwell knows this. Is this the question that is hanging like unpicked fruit between the two of us?

Sorry if so, Maxwell. If you came out and asked it, I'd have to tell you that Bella's already spoken to organisers about whether there's any chance of changing the name, given the circumstances.

'Anyway, Ned, has the speech and language therapist been round yet?'

Blink. Blink.

I have had physiotherapy this morning. Half an hour of the bed bike for arms and legs. And I believe I'm due an MRI at some point, though I'm not sure if that is today. Speech is later this afternoon.

'Have they told you what time to expect her?'

Blink. Blink. Blink. Blink.

Four o'clock, Pom's bringing an alphabet board to start practising with. But then again, she was due at ten yesterday and actually came at two. I think time might be different in hospitals, or this one at least. I've never lived in any others.

'Well, perhaps I could go and ask Ros whether there's any reason we shouldn't go out into the garden for a bit. It's a nice day out there.'

Ros is the charge nurse.

And I don't mean 'live', for heaven's sake. You don't live in a hospital – you just stay in it.

MRS M

SLOWLY THEY ARE COMING back. The word things. The words. Not always in the right place. But slowly, there are more of them when I need them.

'So, two bedrooms. And are both of the bedrooms upstairs?'

The picture which she is holding up to me is of a house. It does not look like my house but I do not suppose that is important. All three of these people are watching me, waiting for my answer. Two of them are wearing the uniforms of medical staff. The third is in trousers and a blouse. She is the one talking now. She is sitting in the chair beside my bed and making notes on a clipboard.

'Yes,' I tell them. 'Both bedrooms are upstairs.' Except these word things do not wish to come out. They are near. But for now, it is better to point to the picture, to the upstairs floor. I do it with the other hand. Not the one I want to use. Not my best hand. I could do it with that one, but not just yet. It feels too heavy.

'I see. So there are two upstairs bedrooms in your house. And what about bathrooms. How many bathrooms do you have?'

I have one bathroom with a separate lavatory. There is also a lavatory downstairs. 'Please refrain from calling it a toilet,' I always had to tell Roger.

Harriet called it the loo. Or occasionally, the bog, when she wanted to tease me because she knew how I hated it. Though sometimes she'd put on an American accent and call it the restroom. 'Do excuse me, Mary, I have to use the restroom.'

I manage 'one'. I say the word and I hold up a finger. One finger. It is not the best finger, because of that one being too heavy to lift easily for some reason. However, this feels to be an acceptable compromise. The staff understand me, as was the intention.

'One bathroom. Perfect. An upstairs bathroom is that, Mary?'

I nod my head. I put my finger on the picture. I forgive the overfamiliarity of the use of my Christian name.

'I see. And is the toilet in the bathroom?'

No, the lavatory is separate.

But for some reason the word I hear myself saying is, 'Yes.' And so I have to shake my head with some decisiveness to show them.

I try again. 'Yes,' is the word that I say once more, though it is not the word I wish for. So I shake my head again.

'So they are separate? Is that right? The toilet and the bath in two different rooms.'

I nod my head and I do a thing which I despise, which is to hold up my thumb. I'm looking at my hand doing it. Poor old hand with its veins and paper skin.

'And are they upstairs or is one of them downstairs?'

They are both. The bathroom is upstairs. There is one lavatory next to it and there is also one next to the kitchen, beneath the stairs. I know that I can tell them this, but the words do not want to say themselves. I use my finger – the wrong finger – to point first to the upstairs and then the downstairs of the house in the picture.

'One up and one down? Oh, that's very good. We will do some stair exercises and work on making you stronger, but for a while at least, after you go home, you may well find it easier to stay downstairs if it's an option. Some people choose to make up a bed in their lounge.'

Roger always said 'lounge'. 'Roger,' I used to tell him, 'a lounge is to be found in an airport or a public house. I think you will find that what you are referring to is a sitting room.'

'What about your cooker, Mary. Do you have an electric cooker or a gas cooker?'

She is lifting the picture of the house and showing me a different page where there are different types of cookers and boilers and baths and showers and taps.

I have an Aga but that does not appear to be an option here. The word is there in my brain but it is not proceeding to my mouth. 'Come along, Mary,' I tell myself. But it does not want to come along. That is why I am now pointing at her pen and taking it, but with the hand that has never done my writing, so the letters look the wrong shape.

'Age?' the one in the trousers asks.

I shake my head.

'Aga.' It is me. It is my mouth. The word is there.

'I see, Mary. Well done. So you have an Aga. I'll have to add a picture for that, won't I.' All three of them are grinning at me. I'm glad that the word came, but I think I might be ready to stop this now. It is actually rather an effort.

I point to a bath with a shower above, and to a carpet for the sitting room and to a wooden floor for the kitchen. And, yes, I tell them with the finger that I have a garden.

'Any pets?' The pictures are of a cat and a dog and a rabbit and a mouse-like creature which I imagine is a hamster. The dog does not look like Wordsworth. Its ears are too short and its legs are too long. I should imagine it is a spaniel of some sort. But it will have to do. I nod. I point. I hope that Wordsworth is all right. He must be wondering where I am.

'A dog. Ah. I love dogs too. Just the one?' I nod. My head feels heavy. I would very much like to sleep now. I hold up one finger.

'That's perfect, Mary. And you say you live alone? So there won't be anybody there to help you when you go back home? You will be in the house all on your own. Is that right?'

I would like to close my eyes. My head is full of stairs and baths and dogs and a voice with an accent telling me that it's 'happy to help', and that it can 'stay for as long as you need me'. And I would like to clear all of these thoughts out of my head. I should like to tell these three hospital staff that really there is no need for such a silly old fuss. I should like to stand up and pop on a skirt or some slacks and a nice blouse. I should like to say thank you for all the concern, but I had better be going. It is a Tuesday which means the church library will be opening soon.

'Mary. Will there be anybody else in the house to give you a hand when you leave hospital?'

I shake my head, and I tell them, 'Yes.'

KIKI

'WHAT, YOU? YOU HAVE a ticket?'

The way Meredith's looking at me you'd think I'd just announced that Prince William is planning on leaving his wife so that he can marry me instead.

'Not an actual ticket,' I tell her. 'But somebody's trying to sort it out for me. They're hopeful. Fingers crossed.' I'm holding up my crossed fingers.

Rob Sturgiss is waiting for his pint and Meredith has her hand on the beer tap but she hasn't pulled it yet. She's too busy giving me that look.

'People pay thousands for tickets. They're gold dust. I've been trying to find one for months. You don't just pick one up at the last minute. Not unless you're a millionaire or a pop star. You said you were broke.'

That face. She's shaking her head like there's something wrong with the world. She seems to have forgotten Turgid's pint. He's shaking his head too, on the other side of the bar, but I don't think it's for the same reason, because he's saying, 'You wouldn't catch me dead at one of those things.'

She's finally remembered his drink but she's still looking sideways at me, saying something about not thinking it would be my thing anyway and that I've never mentioned it before. And that's just wrong, because I talk about it a lot. Like heaps. Maybe she hasn't been listening.

'Actually, my mum was born at Glastonbury. I reckon it must be in my blood.'

'Your mother was born at Glastonbury? The actual festival?'

Is it awful that I'm enjoying this a little bit?

It's just that usually Meredith looks so bored by everything and now she's saying this to me and at almost the same time, saying, 'Oh shit,' because the beer is running over the top of the pint glass so that she has to give it a wipe with a towel before passing it to Rob. But even while she's giving him his drink, she's still looking at me. Nobody ever looks at me like that.

'In 1971. In a camper van. My grandparents loved the festivals, you know, like the Isle of Wight. They worked at lots of them, setting them up and running food stalls and picking up rubbish. You know how they talk about the festival families? And it was the year when Glastonbury was a free festival. David Bowie played. He was meant to be on in the evening but there was a bit of a mess-up and he ended up playing at about six in the morning, as the sun was coming up. And Yaya – my grandmother – was actually going into labour right then. So there she was, having contractions and listening to him singing. So, yeah, my mum was born at Glastonbury.'

Actually, it's a bit of a fib because she was born in the camper van a few miles outside of the festival. Gramps thought they should get to a hospital even though Yaya had a sudden demand that he drive to Glastonbury Tor, which is a hill that's meant to be very spiritual. Except my mum arrived too quickly to do either. She was born with the camper parked up on the side of the road.

I don't bother saying that part. But I think I'm blushing. I'm not used to people looking at me. Maybe it's lucky that Vicar comes in, shaking his umbrella, and another customer – I don't think I know his name but I remember he likes dry cider and pork scratchings – comes back to the bar at the same time, so Meredith and I are both busy for a bit.

Vicar wants a shepherd's pie and half a bitter and also to know, please, how Mrs Malley's doing today. He heard from his friend Antony – the chaplain – that we'd talked. Vicar has been meaning to visit again, he says, but he's been so terribly busy.

'You know how it is,' he says, and I tell him I do, which is true, because it's been a busy day for me as well. Maxwell dropped Wordsworth back at the cottage, not in the lovely old Jaguar, but a Volkswagen. Still, it was nice of him. And so kind to let me stay in the barn. Barn, though? More like a penthouse with a coffee machine and power shower. Really sweet. Then he drove me to the hospital but it wasn't visiting time yet. It's all right for him with Ned, because he's family. But I had a few things to do anyway, like the bank and the charity shops, picking up a few bits. When I went back at 2 p.m., which was visiting time, Mrs M was fast asleep. But I had a long chat with Chaplain. Maxwell had told him I was around, he said.

After that I thought I'd pop in and see Ned and Maxwell. But I was turning onto the corridor and I almost bumped into the fiancée. It was definitely her with that lovely hair. She was heading towards Ned's room. I decided he didn't need me there too.

Anyway, Wordsworth needed his walk and I had loads of chores, like checking my emails, in case Sue'd come back to me, and checking out the festival stuff. Because I'm not lying to Meredith.

I watched some of Ned's videos again too, because now I've seen where they're filmed it was interesting to look at them again. I had to come to the pub for the Wi-Fi, because Mrs M doesn't have it and my phone plan's so rubbish. Even a tiny bit of data costs heaps. My phone's really bad too. Like,

Maxwell was asking me last night if I'd read his texts about when he's going into hospital next week. I hadn't seen any of them. If I had any money I'd buy a new phone. But at least my laptop works fine and there's Wi-Fi at the pub. So it's not just the vicar who's been busy.

Vicar says he's going to sit down and asks if I could bring over his shepherd's pie when it's ready. I say of course and I nip into the kitchen quickly to take it out of its packet and pop it in the microwave. I'm not really paying any attention when Meredith says, 'Is she in England then?' I can't think what she's talking about.

'Your mum? Is she in England too? Or still in New Zealand? Does she get free tickets to Glastonbury because of being born there? Is that your secret?'

When people ask me questions about my mum I never quite know what to do with my face.

'She's dead,' I say.

Meredith starts giving the bar a wipe. Rob Sturgiss looks into his pint.

That ping is the microwave telling me Vicar's dinner is ready. And while I'm taking his shepherd's pie to him, a group come in. Not locals, I don't think. They're arguing loudly about Brexit and Theresa May and they all want different drinks, so it's one white wine, one pale ale, one gin and slimline tonic and one grapefruit juice. And then the cider man comes back for another cider and a bag of pork scratchings – his second – and Rob Sturgiss asks for another pint and Vicar orders another half. It's busy for a Tuesday. Meredith doesn't say anything else until Rob goes off to the loo and then she says, 'Was her name something festival-related?' And I don't know what she means because I'm thinking about gin and half pints.

'Your mum. Like Emily or Eavis or – I don't know – Pyramid? If my baby was born there, I'd call her . . .' You can see she's thinking. 'Shangri-La.'

I tell Meredith my mother was called Ioanna. 'Like Joanna but spelt with an I,' I say. 'It's Greek.'

She looks a bit disappointed, but Rob Sturgiss is back and wanting pint number four and Meredith says she'll collect up the empties, so he's only left with my chest to talk to.

At the end of the night, when we're cashing up and everyone else has gone, she says to me, 'My mum's dead too. She died last year. Her name was Sue.'

NED

PILATES, PASSION AND PRACTICE. My three Ps. When I was still me, I believed that these three things would carry me through my life and keep me fit and focused and happy. I believed in them enough to spout on about them on social media and in the pub.

I did know deep down, even then, that these things were really no more than emotional wallpaper. Because, when you break it down, when you strip everything else away, our mind is nothing but an empty room. It is how we are born, each of us, every single one, with our own empty room to fill. We can plaster and paint it or wallpaper it, in whatever way we choose: magnolia gloss or bare bricks spray-painted with graffiti. Still the same room. We can fill it with sofas and scatter cushions, or antique furniture too expensive to actually use. We can give our room a functional makeover – turn it into an indoor gym, say, or a DIY studio or a study or a snug. We might redecorate over and over, or we might stick with our familiar old surroundings, but we will be left, essentially, with the same room. We only get that one room.

'First row? Second row? Third row?'

Blink.

'OK. So the first letter is in the third row. Now let's go through the letters. Stop me when we reach the right one. I? J? K? L? M? N?'

Blink.

'Excellent. So that is "N". Now the next letter. I'm going to go just a little faster. First row? Second row?'

Blink.

'Perfect. Second row. Here goes, E?'

Blink.

'Fantastic. So we have N-E, so now, third letter . . .'

Pom is one of the speech and communications team and if I could still laugh, she would make me do so, often and out loud, with her constant enthusiasm and her oversized smile. I wonder if her choice of career has anything to do with her own quite noticeable lisp. It's the sort of thing that children are always bullied for, like Sean Stevens in my high school. Poor Sean. All that mimicking when the register was called. I hope Pom never had that.

Pilates, passion and practice. My mantra. My very own way of filling that empty room. The Pilates thing came from my mother, which was strange given that I've rejected every other fad she ever pushed upon me. She'd discovered it through a dance friend in Beverly Hills in the eighties and I have vivid memories that include mats and stretches which she'd hold like a frozen ballerina.

Pilates. You could say it's been the one love she's remained faithful to. When she was doing her exercises, I could run my remote control car in circles around her while pleading for park trips or snacks or bedtime stories, and there would be no sign that she'd even heard me. Later, when Dad was dying, it made me angry to watch her. 'That's not exercise,' I'd tell her, with the disdain of a fifteen-year-old who knew everything about the world. Anybody could lie on their back and raise their legs. Like everything in her life, she was just going through the motions. Faking it.

And so she took me – sneering in my hoodie – to a studio called The Pilates Palace, where a trainer named Rhett showed me that there was more to the discipline than lifting your legs a few times.

For me it consists of connecting with the core of myself, of working from the inside out; it's about finding my inner self, which feels fairly ironic now. Now I can't even feel those core muscles, let alone push them to their limits. But there you go. For me Pilates was about being in control. For my mother, I think it was the attempt to hold onto a body that wanted to race away from her.

The three Ps? Prozac and pink gin appeared to be her other two. At that time, anyway. But for me, Pilates, passion and practice. It's therapy talk, of course, but who says motivational jargon does not motivate?

Passion, for me, means music and poetry, it means philosophy and friendship and love, and all the things that turn an existence into a life. Practice is knowing that nothing comes without work. That effort is what matters. That dedication brings meaning. *Passion and practice.* This is what fills my empty room.

'First row?'

Blink.

'OK, so along the first row. A? B? C? D?'

Blink.

'Right. That's D. So we have N-E-D. Next letter? First row?'

Blink.

'OK. A? B? C? D? End of word?'

Blink.

'Good stuff. So that's N-E-D-end of word. Ned. See how quickly you've picked that up. And as you can see, each of the rows is a different colour. See that. So this first row is red.

And on the red row, we have A, B, C, D, end word. Got that? Then the second row is yellow. And the yellow row has E, F, G, H, end sentence. Easy? yes. And you see too that each row starts with a vowel. So red row, it's A. Yellow row, it's E. Now blue row starts with I. Then J, K, L, M, N. Then the green row starts with the vowel O, then P, Q, R, S, T. Then the last row here, that's white and we have U, V, W, X, Y, Z.

'It may feel like a lot now, but with practice, you'll hardly have to think about it. Blue six, yellow one, Red four. N-E-D, Ned.

'I hear you play the guitar, yes? This is *much* easier than that. A bit of practice. Easy-peasy. OK, Ned's friend, you want to try now?'

I can sense Bella flinching as she tells Pom, 'Fiancée,' before she moves into my line of vision and takes the grid which Pom is holding out towards her.

'I see. Congratulations,' says Pom.

Bella's eyes narrow a little at Pom's mispronounced 's' sounds, but she asks if Pom would mind videoing this moment and thanks her as she passes her her phone.

'This is such a breakthrough, Norton. Now you can say all those things that you've been waiting to say. These letters give you a voice again. How incredible is that?'

I don't respond. I could perhaps spell out V-E-R-Y-end word. It wouldn't take too long, I suppose. Or I could respond with I-N-C-R-E-D-I-B-L-E-end word, which feels quite an under-taking. But I think the question was a rhetorical one anyway. Except that Bella then laughs and says, 'So, Ned, here we go.' And sits up straighter. And she's looking at the alphabet grid as if she's waiting for a reply. She says, 'I'm feeling a bit emotional right now,' and puts her hand on mine – I can feel the gold band of her ring on my skin. She watches, with expectant eyes.

Pom has stepped to the side, so I can see neither her nor the iPhone that is capturing this – but in my mind I'm imagining the whirr of an old-fashioned movie camera and a film director in 1920s garb lifting a loudspeaker, ready to call for 'action'. Nobody says anything. I'm waiting for the question, only there doesn't seem to be a question.

'So – remember – we need to ask first row, second row, third row . . . ?'

There's that slight tensing around Bella's eyes, although she's still smiling.

'Oh yes. Silly me. So Norton, is the first letter from the first row or the second row or the third row or the fourth row or the, er, fifth row?' She has the board turned to check it, which means I can't see the letters, though it's not rocket science – apart from remembering the first two rows only have four letters each, with 'end word' coming at the end of the first and 'end sentence' at the end of the second, and of course I do know that each row begins with a vowel so it's not hard to picture which letters are where. That's not the problem.

What does she want me to say? What do I want to say?

'Never at a loss for words,' is what Maxwell used to say about me, often shaking his head.

I don't remember any situation, ever, where I was unsure about the thing to say. Sad, angry, guilty yes, but never unsure. And here I am, when it actually matters. I am being thrown this flimsy lifeline back to a tiny part of me. And I do not know what to say.

In my life – my old life, my real life – my words were not planned because they didn't need to be. They were like movement, unforced.

Bella moves the board so that I can see it better. It is clever. User-friendly. I can see that. But imperfect. There is no question mark – no indicator of when I am not stating but asking. Or exclamation mark so that I can – well – exclaim. And no apostrophe. Going forward, all of this is going to grate. Maybe we should discuss this straight away. It would make sense.

But Bella is capturing this for posterity. Do I really want my first utterance to be recorded as '*punctuation*'? I could spell it out now, although she does not seem to grasp that she should take me through the rows again, and slower to give me time to blink. Fourth row, second letter – P, fifth row, first letter – U, third row, sixth letter – N, and so on. There is a part of me – the part that loved watching old *Monty Python's Flying Circus* with Maxwell, and read his *Hitchhiker's Guide to the Galaxy* – that is tempted by the surreal unexpectedness of the answer. Poor Bella, waiting for a proclamation – something about love or gratitude or the power of strength and endurance – how cruel would it be instead to produce a word about the grammatical insufficiencies of this communications tool?

Bella is waiting.

I blink twice.

'Two blinks is no, Norton. What do you mean, "no"?'

Second row, Bella, come on. Either you have to walk me through it or I need to find a way to tell you.

'I wonder if that's two blinks for second row? The yellow one.' See, Pom gets it.

Bella's smile falters just a tiny bit before she nods and pushes back some hair which has come out from behind her ear. 'Of course. Silly me. So, Norton, second row?'

I blink.

'First letter? Second letter? Third Letter? Fourth letter?'
Blink.

'Fifth – oh, no, was that fourth letter. *Fourth*. Second row, wasn't it? So that's E-F-G-H, that's H? Right?'

Blink.

'Wait. One blink. Is that first row? Or is that one blink for yes?'

I'm not sure I can help with that one. Pom suggests offering up the row options again to clarify. And keeping it slow. And that maybe it might be easier to say each letter in the row out loud.

'Oh yes. Right. So first row? Second row?'

Blink.

'OK. So E?'

Blink.

'Is that E, the letter, or were you just saying yes to second row?'

I don't blink, so as to avoid confusion. But Bella gives me a look. 'Is it E, Norton?'

I blink.

'OK. And so that's – wait, what was the first letter?' There is a furrow of concentration in between her eyebrows. 'H, wasn't it? So H-E. 'He'. Who is 'he'? Which 'he' are you talking about?' She turns away from me, towards Pom, I presume. 'Who does he mean by "he"?'

'Maybe ask for the next letter. This is why there is the box to indicate the end of the word. To establish if the word is finished.'

Bella nods. But her expression is not so dissimilar to when I tried to explain exponential growth.

'I didn't realise this would be so difficult. So this one will be another letter or maybe the end of the word. You understand that, Norton? Don't worry, darling. We will get there. So is it in the first row? No? Are you sure?'

I do nothing.

'Then there must be another letter. I see. Second row? Third row?'

Blink.

'So it is in the third row. Is it J? K? L?'

Blink.

'Right. So L. H-E-L.' She glances to the side, and her smile makes a reappearance.

'And – here we go again – first row? Second row? Third row?'

Blink.

'Third row. I? J? K? L?'

Blink.

'L? That's L. That's two Ls. So it spells H-E-L-L. "*Hell*". My poor Norton. I know that's just how it must feel. But together we'll get through this. You'll see. I've found so many cases of people who've recovered. Who can talk again, or even walk. Darling, this is just the beginning.'

'Maybe best to check the word is finished. Just to be sure.'

'Sorry?' I wonder if Pom notices the frown. 'You think – well, OK, let me ask Norton – Norton, is that what you're telling me that you feel? Hell? Do you mean "hell"?'

Perhaps it would be easier just to say yes.

Blink. Blink.

'No. There are more letters?'

It might have been better to have kept my eyes shut.

Blink.

The muscles in her cheek twitch and she looks away. She's blinking now too. Her face did the same thing when I told her I wasn't sure that I wanted to marry her anymore. Just before the tears came. She insisted that she knew I loved her and that she'd had moments of doubt too. She said she refused to let it end like this, when she knew it wasn't what I wanted. She said give it a month. We'd talk after that, and if I still felt the same, then so be it. But she knew we'd come away stronger because of it. I owed her – I owed us – that month.

Two weeks after that, I went to head a ball and headed a goalpost instead.

'OK. So first row? Second row? Third row? Fourth . . . ?'

Blink.

'Fourth row. Fine. O . . .'

Blink. I do it quickly.

'O is the letter. Hell-O. Hello.' She is silent for a moment. And then the light comes back into her eyes and she smiles. 'Norton, that is so you. Only you could find just one silly word – "Hello" – that means everything. "Hello", because you don't want to make a fuss or a song and dance. "Hello", because of course it's the first thing you'd say. "Hello", because you're back. Norton Edbury is back.'

She puts a hand on my cheek as she kisses me. I feel her lips and the brush of her breath and I smell Chance by Chanel as she whispers, 'I love you, Norton, darling, you know that, don't you?'

MRS M

ONE CAN ONLY SUPPOSE that the primary motivation in planning this garden was a therapeutic rather than a horticultural one. There are a number of such elementary mistakes. Take those hydrangeas. Anybody with a modicum of gardening experience could tell you that they need larger containers. Their roots will become crowded in no time. As for those geraniums, they will not receive anything like enough sunlight in that corner. Still, the lavender is rather magnificent.

It is a jolly enough little space and it is a nice change to have some fresh air, even if this silly wheelchair does make one feel rather a cripple. Still, I must not complain. Chaplain was sweet to bring me out here. A nice surprise, although he's insistent that it was all that Kiki girl's idea. She's been telling him all about my green fingers and my beautiful garden, so Chaplain says. I trust she has been watering it since she appears to have taken up residence. It's too much to expect that she's done any pruning I imagine, but in any case, I shall be home soon. In a week or so, I understand, which is something Chaplain is keen to discuss.

Such an earnest little face. Roger always thought there was something weak about a man with curly hair, which was unfair. It's not as if they choose it.

Chaplain seems convinced that I must be terribly anxious, which is sweet of him because of course I shall be absolutely fine. I suppose some tasks may be a little harder, unlocking doors, opening cupboards and unscrewing jars. Possibly cooking and cleaning and washing and carrying. And the stairs may be a little tricky for a while. And it's true that I do become terribly tired at the moment. One adapts, though.

'Ron told me that you were widowed last year? I imagine that must have been challenging to adjust to?'

Ron is Vicar, the Reverend Ronald Wilkes. It seems this chaplain has spoken to just about everybody about my well-being. He looks very young for the job. But then again everybody does these days. Harriet used to laugh about it. I visited her when she was in this hospital and she said to me, 'Do you know, Mary, I'd swear the oncologist is not old enough to be out of Boy Scouts. Every time he comes on his rounds, I want to laugh because I picture him in short trousers with his little toggle on his scarf.'

I had to tell her that what she meant was a woggle, but she wouldn't have it. She'd put her hands over her mouth and shake her head and say, 'Stop, Mary. We can't say such things.'

And now it would seem it is not just the doctors who are becoming younger, but the clergy as well.

He has positioned us so that I am protected from the sun, but this means that he is sitting on a bench with it shining into his face. His hand is over his eyes.

Was it challenging to adjust to losing Roger? It's strange but I don't recall it terribly well. I suppose it must have been, but Harriet became ill so soon after, and then Wordsworth needed to be looked after. I suppose the only polite answer is that, yes, it was challenging. Because anything else seems disrespectful to Roger and not awfully Christian.

I tell myself that I can say it. I picture the word – that Chinese girl, the speech therapy one, with the lisp, says it helps to do this, and so I visualise the letters, Y-E-S, and I do not hurry it.

'Yes.' I'm nodding too. And it's only one word, but it is the right word, and that is pleasing. Prayer and perseverance, as Mother always said.

I want to say also that Roger and I were married sixty-three years. That unlike today's couples we understood that marriage was a contract and not a game which one stops playing. I'd like to tell Chaplain that after he died I did not know how one went about paying the gas bill or how to use the remote control for the television set or the timer on the boiler, but that also one of the first things I did was to drive into Trowbridge and buy five pairs of slacks. Roger never liked trousers. He said he preferred a lady to dress like a lady. I must, however, accept that I am currently harbouring certain restrictions.

'But . . .' That word came with no trouble. I try to say 'that' and 'is'. I am calm. Slow. I picture. But they do not come. However the word 'life' is clear. 'But . . . life.' It will have to suffice.

Chaplain is nodding. 'How very true. And Ron tells me that you are active in the church. Perhaps that is of some comfort?'

It seems a good time to repeat Mother's mantra, except only the 'prayer' part comes out and for some reason I cannot quite say the word 'perseverance'. But, given the present company, the response seems to work.

'I so agree, Mrs Malley, prayer can bring such comfort. Perhaps you would like to pray with me now?'

He goes down on his knees, here, on the paved ground of The Sunshine Unit for Neurological and Stroke Rehabilitation's garden, but not before telling me to, please, stay where I am. I do however close my eyes, bow my head and put my hands together.

'Our Father who art in Heaven,' he begins.

I join in. 'Hallowed be thy name.' And I recite every word. It comes slowly but with hardly any stumbling and as I reach 'Amen' I open my eyes, and the sun is shining, bathing this man of the cloth in brightness, and he is smiling at me. I do not want to think the word, because it is so overused and one finds it almost blasphemous how quick people are to claim everything is a miracle – the birth of a baby or the recovery of an uncle from a bout of pneumonia – and yet this does feel rather remarkable.

And then something else happens. My hands are still folded in my lap. And I feel something on my fingers. It is wet. It is cold. And I glance down and it is a nose. Two dark eyes are looking up at me from under droopy eyelids. And I can hear the swish from a wagging tail.

I'm not altogether certain if I do manage to say it out loud because it is such a surprise and one doesn't always know, in the heat of the moment, but in my head if nowhere else I'm shouting, 'Wordsworth!'

KIKI

WORDSWORTH'S EAR KEEPS FLAPPING and slapping against my arms. He seems happy though, and with his mouth open like that he looks like he's smiling. Mrs M is smiling too. I think it's the first time I've ever seen her do that. I mean, not that she scowls, it's just that her face doesn't normally look as if it has anything much to smile about. Normally she looks like she's tasting something sour.

But not now. Her hair is blowing a bit, being in the front of the car. We're not going that fast, but it's a sunny day, and the road is quiet, with fields on both sides. And the best thing is that this was my idea. Not the Lord's Prayer thing, of course, though that's incredible. Maxwell reckons that happens more than you'd think. He says it's all about the way the brain works and Antony – should I call him that? Or Father Antony, maybe? Or Your-something? Not Your Majesty, of course, but maybe Your Grace – says he's known other stroke survivors who were finding speech difficult but could still sing songs. This is the first time he's come across it with a prayer though.

They're going to talk to the speech and language therapist about how it might help. Antony's heard about a music therapy session that's being trialled at the hospital. It's not just for stroke patients. But maybe it could be good. And Maxwell says maybe there's a local choir or music group for people with her language problem, after she leaves. Aphasia, it's called. But isn't that crazy? That you can't say 'dog' but you can say a whole prayer. Maxwell says it's because there's one bit of your brain whose job is to find the right words and carry them to your mouth so you can say them. And there's a different bit of your brain whose job is remembering music and poems and hymns and those things that you learn by heart. And one bit is on the left and the other is on the right. And because it's a different bit of brain, one bit can keep working when the other is damaged. You can still find the words for a song because they don't count as words, they count as a tune that you already know. So it's the music area of your brain that looks after them, and not the words area.

But the rest of this was my idea. Bringing Wordsworth in to see Mrs M and her coming out for this ride in the lovely car. Silver Jaguar on its bonnet, just like in the fuck it bucket poem. I mean, it was Father Antony who spoke to all the doctors and it's Maxwell who's driving, but it's still my plan.

When the dog rushed up and licked her, it was perfect. You could see she didn't have any idea until she looked down, and then it was like – boom. I'd be feeling so proud now, except there's this bit in my tummy that feels sick. You know, when you have a knot. And you tell yourself not to worry about it, and just to not think about it, but it's like your body keeps reminding you. Because Antony and Maxwell keep saying these nice things, like how kind I am, and how thoughtful. And I'm feeling really good, except then I keep thinking, 'But am I?'

I reckon what I am is confused. Because am I kind? Really? Am I even a good person? Maybe I'm not. I took something – removed something from Mrs M's things. And I shouldn't have just taken it. I should have talked about it to her first. But I didn't do that. I just took it. And I'm too ashamed to say anything to her.

And now it looks like I'm really going to Glastonbury. Antony says his father knows someone, and it really, honestly looks like I might be able to go. And that's brilliant. Except now there's this knot in me.

And, no, I don't really want to say what it is because I don't feel like talking about it. But I can't just tell myself to forget it and relax. So even though I'm smiling and chatting, it doesn't feel as perfect as it should. Although it's still great that Mrs M is enjoying herself. That's still good.

From my seat, I can see her really well, because her face is turned to look at Maxwell. And that's the side of her that doesn't smile so well right now, but even from this sideways view, you can kind of see she's – and I want to say it, because really, well, look at her – happy. I can't see Maxwell's face from here. I can only see the back of his head, where his skin is pink underneath the white hairs. But if I lean forward, I can hear what he's saying, under the sound of the car and the wind. It's blowing my hair about too. I feel like Wordsworth with his ears.

'. . . my family home. My father was a GP too, and I took over from him, though I lived in Herefordshire with my first wife. Other than that, my surgery was there, at the end of the garden, right up until I retired on my seventieth birthday, nearly ten years ago now. These days, I spend most of my time in France. Ned's looked after the place for the last few years, which works for both of us.

'And you, Mary? Have you always lived round here?'

Maybe it takes a few moments before Mrs M gets out her 'yes' but that's pretty good because a couple of weeks ago she was having a problem saying anything. You can tell she wants to say something else, because she's moving her lips and Maxwell is waiting. And it's only two or three seconds and Mrs M says 'life'.

'All your life?' I can see a bit of Maxwell's face now, because of him turning towards her as he asks. And while I'm looking at him, I'm thinking about how old he is, because if he was seventy when he retired and that was nearly ten years ago, he must be almost eighty. And he was telling me about skiing near his place in France last year. Yaya was seventy-six when she died. Or seventy-seven maybe. She never really liked to say. She always said numbers didn't matter, only people. But I can't imagine her skiing or even walking her dog around the woods like Mrs M does. She could talk clearer than Mrs M can now, except Mrs M seems to be getting better and Yaya got, well, worse. She stopped making sense.

'Antony, are you from these parts too?' Maxwell only turns his head for a moment, because he's driving. And I'm not sure if Antony – Chaplain – has heard him. Because it's quite difficult to hear, with the car's roof down. And maybe you don't need to say Father Antony, or any of those Your Grace things. But I don't want to get it wrong, so it's easier just to repeat the question, without using his name at all.

'Maxwell asked if you were from these parts too.'

'Goodness, no. Originally from Hackney, in east London.'

Hackney is where Stratford is. And I'm too busy telling him about the mistake, me thinking it was the other Stratford, and being shocked that it wasn't all little cottages and pretty theatres, and had nothing to do with Shakespeare and he's laughing – actually they're all laughing, even Mrs M. And we're driving along in this fantastic old car. It's like something that

James Bond would drive. It's sunny and Wordsworth's ears are slapping against my arm and for a moment I can't remember when I ever felt this happy. And then I think about the thing I've done, and the sick feeling is back.

NED

'THEREOF ONE MUST BE *silent.'* If we agree with Wittgenstein's Tractatus *that reality exists only outside of language, then we must also agree that truth exists only outside of thought. Discuss.*

'The real statement is *not* cogito, ergo sum, *I think therefore I am, but* cogito, ergo sum invalidus, *I think therefore I am powerless.' Discuss.*

Once upon a time, I stayed up late into the night writing essays about philosophers and philosophy, about meaning and truth and the value of humanity. I read Russell and Locke. I believed, for some reason, that what Norton Edbury, at that point aged twenty-two, one individual out of the seven and a half billion human creatures on our planet, had to say about Wittgenstein's opinions on language and power had some intrinsic, if small, value.

In the corner of my eye, a white line on a green screen tracks the invisible fluctuations of my body; it peaks up in a mountain top then falls to a flat line, then up it goes again.

If I was back in the time before now, I would take all those essays about relativism and absolutism and utilitarianism and structuralism and existentialism and postmodernism and positivism and I would rip through them. I would keep on tearing and shredding until the pieces were confetti.

I would take the laptop upon which I had typed them and throw it against the nearest wall. Who gives a fuck what Wittgenstein says? Screw Nietzsche. Screw Sartre and Heidegger, Camus and Derrida. There is *no* point.

True power? It's screaming until your lungs hurt. It's hurling that computer as hard as you can and hearing the smash. It's staring at yourself in a mirror before hitting your head against the glass, again and again, until it breaks and cuts and your flesh is bleeding. It's throwing yourself from a tall building or under a lorry or into the sea. Power is a rope from the light fitting, it is the hose from the exhaust pipe, it is guns or pills or razor blades. Power is not philosophy. It is death.

The line on the screen rises and falls and waits a while and rises and falls again.

Young, stupid student, with your Kenco coffee and your Ziggy Stardust poster. One day you will discover that the most fundamental foundation of life was, in fact, only that, the capacity for death. That was your most basic human right.

But by then it will be gone. Powerlessness is a life which you have no capacity to end. Murderers in prison retain the option of a hunger strike. But even that is denied to me. Could I stop breathing? Could I do that now?

I tell myself, 'Do not breathe.'

I concentrate on what it takes, clamping shut my lips, putting a dam in place in my nostrils so that they refuse any air coming in. I think about halting those traitor lungs. I will them to be still. *Do this one thing for me, body.* Nothing happens.

Just the noise of outside, cars some way away, voices in the corridor that are not distinct enough to understand. An afternoon that feels more summer than spring, through an open window, making my skin prickle. No breeze. I should like to sit up straighter, rearrange my sheet. I'd love to stretch.

It's one of those sorts of afternoons that, in my other life, made you want to grab some cold beers and a picnic rug and maybe a frisbee or a football.

Those lines on the green square of the monitor rise and fall. Below it, greetings cards are lined up in rows on the table beside my bed. *Thinking of You. Get Well Soon. In Our Thoughts.* If I could, I would sweep my arm through them. Pictures which depict sunrises and beaches and trees and flowers. Inside are messages telling me how strong I am, or how somebody's father or wife or aunt or brother has been through something like this and triumphed. One card encourages me to find a place for God in my soul. Five of them arrived this morning, four from total strangers and one from a girl I dated for about three minutes in university. Tammy opened them for me, holding each one up for me to see. 'Somebody's Mr Popular,' she said.

It is because of Bella's video. *Norton Edbury, Return of a Hero.* She posted it on my YouTube channel yesterday. Or the day before, perhaps. I haven't seen her since, though I have watched it. Maxwell played it for me earlier, Bella holding up the alphabet grid while reading out the letter 'o' and saying, 'Hell-O. Hello. Norton, that is so you. Only you could find just one silly word – "Hello" – that means everything.' And then the music comes in – bloody Adele – and with it, old footage of me riding and running and talking and doing Pilates and playing the guitar, and lying on the grass and laughing, interspersed with scenes showing tubes in my mouth and medical monitors and my mother sobbing. Cutting between the two depictions of me, with dates and information popping up on the screen.

'*Norton Edbury was a son, friend, fiancé, musician, poet, teacher, athlete and social media star in the making. He had his whole life ahead of him. Doctors warned he was unlikely to ever recover consciousness. He was believed to be in a vegetative state, incapable of recognising the world or people around him. But Norton understood EVERYTHING. Locked-in syndrome robs you of your ability to move or speak but leaves your intelligence and understanding intact. Norton Edbury is a prisoner in his own body. But there is something he has to say . . .'*

My face. But thinner. A mouth that is open in what could be a grimace or a smile, but lacks the animation of either. No movement of muscles. No response beyond the upward roll of my eyes. The me I saw on the screen was an inanimate reflection. A death mask of the face that's watched me from the mirror all my life.

And Bella smiling again – holding the alphabet board towards the camera, kissing me. *'"Hello", because you're back. Norton Edbury is back.'*

But Adele? Bella? When you made me all those playlists in our first months together, did you not think there was a reason that I skipped through Adele every time? Remember? Coldplay and Katy Perry, too.

Lionel Richie would have set the sentimental landscape, surely? Or The Beatles? 'Hello, Goodbye'? If you had asked my opinion, I'd have suggested 'Comfortably Numb' by Pink Floyd – the live recording of Bowie duetting on it with David Gilmour. The Royal Albert Hall, 2006, his last UK performance. That would have been really good actually. Although *The Wall* was never Bella's cup of tea. She said it was too ugly and that it needed to decide if it was a cartoon or not. Toby hated it too. Why couldn't I watch normal films like *The Bourne Identity* or *The Hangover*, he'd say.

Bella won't make it in today. Busy with meetings. She rang Maxwell this morning, and asked him to tell me she was sorry, and told him about uploading her video to YouTube.

'So much energy, that girl,' Maxwell said when he relayed the message.

Maxwell is not here right now either. Something about playing chauffeur for Kiki's Mrs Malley. He was laughing when he said he hoped I didn't mind and that he wouldn't be gone very long.

Why would I mind? I'm terribly busy today, actually. I'd have found it hard to find a moment for you, what with all this breathing. No, off you go. Have fun with Kiki.

Tammy has been in a couple of times. Goo tube-feed. Blood pressure. Nappy change. The usual. She asked how I was feeling. I told her F-I-N-E-end word. She wondered if I fancied some television perhaps, but I declined. No thank you, Tammy. I may be suicidal but I'm not desperate enough for *Loose Women* yet.

'All right then. I'll look in again in a bit.'

The clicking of a closing door.

Get Well Soon! says one of the cards, in orange capitals. The picture shows a family of rabbits waving at one little rabbit who is sitting up in bed. Presumably not with locked-in syndrome. That's probably a little niche for the greetings card industry. Myxomatosis, perhaps.

Get Well Soon. It seems unlikely. Still, it's probably not easy to find a card that says *Get Some Basic Motor Functions Back Soon* or *Get Acquainted With Your Communication Systems Soon* or *Get Used to Your New Physical Limitations Soon*.

Toby brought me one that said *Get Well Soon You Old Git*. It made a change from rainbows.

When the door opens again, I assume it's Tammy, coming back to take a temperature or perhaps to share a bit of gossip about one of the other nurses. But then I hear, 'Hey Nid,' and after a few seconds, Kiki's face comes into view. 'Hope you don't mind me barging in?'

She's already sitting herself down on the side of my bed. I can see her reaching out to the side, and then her hand comes back into my eyeline, holding up the alphabet grid.

'So this is the talking board.' It sounds like she's saying it as much to herself as to me. 'Sweet.' But then she is looking at me, right at me. Brown eyes through round glasses.

'Maxwell's just gone with Mrs M and the chaplain to speak to someone about music therapy. He won't be long.'

She closes her eyes for a moment.

'Ned – you don't mind me calling you Ned? – listen, you're really smart. And I hope you don't mind me coming in here, you know, like this. Just say if you do. Because I like coming, but only if you want me here. The thing is, Ned, I went to your home. I mean, I didn't just go there. Maxwell invited me. But, still, I hope that's OK with you?

'That's how I know how smart you are, see – not that I wouldn't think it anyway, but I saw your bookcase, with all your books about logic and philosophy and ethics and stuff. So I'm thinking you'll understand, and I don't know who else I can talk to. Because I've taken something. Or not taken it so much as – I don't know – re-homed it. Retrieved it. It was in the wrong place anyway, that's the thing. But now I'm worried it was wrong of me to not say anything.

'Except now these good things have happened. Mrs M said a whole prayer. And Antony reckons he can get me a Glastonbury ticket. How lucky is that? Lucky, lucky, lucky. But . . .

'Ned, if I tell you do you promise not to tell anyone else?'

She's leaning in towards me and for a bizarre moment I think she's going to kiss me. Then I realise she's about to whisper something in my ear. Her cheeks are blushing.

'Ned,' she whispers. 'I was looking through Mrs M's cupboards and I discovered. . .' She pauses. 'I discovered. . .' She sighs, 'I discovered. . .'

Even if my power to talk had somehow suddenly returned to me, I think I'd still be speechless at what she says next.

MRS M

THERE IS A TUNE in my head. Now what on earth is it? Buoyant, happy singing about dancing and hearts flying and, although I am here in my hospital bed, this joyous melody keeps playing in my mind. And I can't quite think what it is. Not a very *me* song, I shouldn't have thought. Smiling, swirling, happy exhaustion, a young woman falling back onto a bed with an irrepressible smile. Oh yes. I know. 'I Could Have Danced All Night'. By Lerner and Loewe, if memory serves me well.

Now, why is this song stuck in my brain? Harriet did so love that film. Everything Audrey Hepburn did, in fact, but especially *My Fair Lady*. When she called around for tea she'd often inform me that she had washed her hands and her face. 'Before you "came", not "come"', I would correct her and she would insist that, no, the unforgivable grammar was because she was quoting Audrey Hepburn as Eliza Doolittle. Not that she sounded anything like a poor cockney flower girl. I had to tell her that *My Fair Lady* was an unnecessarily sentimental retelling of George Bernard Shaw's *Pygmalion*, and as for that film about breakfast at Tiffany's, well, it was a load of beatnik nonsense. But now – despite that Olivia whining on to her daughter in the opposite bed about how unfair life is, and the daughter moaning back about feet and buses, and Mrs Bamford's snoring from the end of the room and some ghastly comedy blaring out from the television of the new lady opposite – I find that song playing itself to me in my head.

Perhaps it's these new pills the doctor has prescribed for me. I have a feeling that I am actually smiling to myself. Goodness, whatever would Roger have had to say? He never was the greatest fan of the movies. He preferred historical documentaries. Well, sorry, Roger, but you are not here now to shake your head in baffled disapproval. And smile I shall.

Of course there is a logical explanation. Mr Douglas explained it after I kept embarrassing myself with those bouts of laughter and crying. Shamefully inappropriate but, he said, a recognised effect of the stroke. Medical. Not liability, but lability. Emotional lability. That may be what I am suffering from again now since I can think of no other reason that I should find myself singing musical numbers in my head, even if my eyes are rather difficult to keep open. Or perhaps that's it. A dream creeping up on me. It has been a rather long day.

This is how I felt after that shorthand typing contest in Cheltenham. January 1955. I'd been put forward by Mrs Ryle, who ran the typing pool where I worked. I was second runner-up in the contest – to this day I do not comprehend how I misspelled 'contingency' – and afterwards we were taken to a tea dance and treated to champagne. I was nineteen years old and ever so elated.

I do wish Harriet might have met Maxwell. How she would have loved his car. They are terribly impractical though, convertibles. Roger always said that their mechanics were prone to failure. And the insurance is so much higher. Still, it was rather delightful to feel the breeze on my face.

Oh dear. There go my eyes again.

How terribly pleased Wordsworth was to see me. Such wagging. And that was another sweet thought too, the wool she brought. Kiki. With the cardboard rings that she had cut herself. Sweet of her. She'd talked with the occupational therapist and then bought the wool and the card and cut out the shapes.

'This way you can make a pom-pom or two, for Wordsworth's jumper. Like in the poem. About your friend having a basset hound and you having one too, and knitting them jumpers because of being mad old ladies. Not that I'm saying . . .'

She does always look so on edge. But that was terribly generous of Harriet. Kiki. Goodness, one does feel tired when one is in hospital. And what a long day it has been.

But this suggestion about my hair is going too far. Over my dead body, I told her. Even if it does wash out. Even if it's not permanent dye. Just a pink spray. Even if Harriet says . . . Kiki . . . even if—

A car journey is one thing, pink hair is – I shall put my foot down.

I shall just have to tell Harriet that – Kiki that.

I think I shall keep my eyes closed now. But she must understand that I am not about to become a punk rocker at eighty-four.

She actually didn't sing any of the songs herself, of course. Audrey Hepburn. Harriet would never have it though. She said you could hear that it was her voice. But she didn't sing them. Not a single one.

KIKI

'MAYBE YOU SHOULD GO out the front if you're going to smoke.'

I'm not sure why she's looking at me like that. It's not an unreasonable thing to ask. I'm only the house sitter, and I don't think Wordsworth likes the smell either because he jumped off the armchair and left the room as soon as she lit it.

'But it's raining. And it's not like Mrs Malley is even here, is it?'

'No, but it's just . . .'

Meredith is looking at me like I'm the one being unfair. I should say too bad, she has to go outside or else not smoke, but I don't suppose it's going to do any harm.

She smiles and blows out smoke. 'Ashtray?'

When she said about a drink after work, I thought she meant a quick one at the pub. I didn't realise that she meant here. Really, I was planning to hurry up to my laptop, because I finally found a clue. It was Maxwell's idea. He told me about the Companies House website, and how it had a record for everybody who has a stake in a listed company. I told him I didn't think that my mum would have one. I didn't reckon a crusty eco-warrior student would list a company. I was blown away when her name came up. It was a company called Sammy's Glass Art.

So really, that's what I should be doing. Finding out more about Sammy's Glass Art. But then Meredith asked if I fancied a drink. And she's normally so busy with her essays and her uni friends so it wouldn't have been very fair to say no, just because I don't officially live here and The Fox and Hounds is the last place she wants to hang out after work.

I don't reckon Mrs M will mind that I've borrowed a bottle of wine. I'll buy one back at the supermarket tomorrow. I thought I'd get one for Maxwell too, to say thank you for everything. Mrs M can't have been that bothered about this bottle, because it's pretty dusty and it was just stuck in the back of the dresser, like it had been there for heaps of years. Domaine Margaux it's called. Maybe they'll have it in Tesco.

I'm not normally the biggest fan of red wine, but this one isn't so bad when you mix it with lemonade. Meredith gave me a bit of a funny look when I did that and said no thank you so maybe it's only Yaya who drank it like that. I'll have my next glass straight.

There don't seem to be any ashtrays in the kitchen, but there are saucers which have the same flowery pattern as the teacups. Wordsworth is waiting by the back door, watching me look through the shelves.

'You want to go into the garden?'

He looks at me.

Any question you ask him, he gives you that look and you find yourself imagining what his reply is. *Yes, Kiki, I'd very much like to go into the garden. Thank you for asking.*

'No more digging though, you little mole. What's Mrs M going to say when she sees the mess you've made?'

I reckon that look is a promise. He wouldn't dream of digging any more holes. If he somehow dug any at all, it must have been an accident. I open the door for him, just as Meredith is yelling to ask if I've got that ashtray and if I'm talking to somebody out here.

'Nobody,' I call back. 'Just letting the dog out.'

It is pretty wet out, to be fair; no wonder Meredith didn't want to smoke outside – and Wordsworth stands there for a bit when I open the door, like maybe he doesn't need to go out after all. But then he waddles into the garden with his tail sticking up.

'Ta.' Meredith takes the flowery saucer. She has the old cookery book on her lap, the one Mrs Malley dropped when she collapsed. *Mrs Beeton's Household Management*. It was on the coffee table. Now it has a line of ash on its cover which Meredith brushes into the ash-saucer. Her nails are painted blue and she has silver rings on her fingers and thumb. She's looking at her glass. 'Fill-up would be nice.'

When I was young, I used to play 'friends' – quietly in my room, so that Yaya didn't hear me. I didn't have enough chairs, so most of it was imaginary. I had a doll, like a Barbie but not an actual one. She might have been called a Nicki, or maybe a Vicki, and my Cuddles Bear, and they played the part of the friends. I can't remember what names I gave them but we had great conversations. I did the most talking – although really it was in my head – and they did more laughing and agreeing. But I knew to listen and laugh and agree too. And if there was ever a pause in the chat, I'd pick up the bowl of crisps – well, really it was my pencil pot – and say 'Cheesy Twist, anyone?'

There aren't any crisps here. I did have some Monster Munch but I already ate them all. I wasn't expecting Meredith to come.

She carries on smoking while I pour her wine.

'I like your nails,' I say. Sue always said that talking to people was easy. You just show an interest.

Meredith doesn't say anything back to me, she just takes a puff on her cigarette. But she kind of nods too, so I ask her, 'Did you paint them?'

'Yup.'

I haven't quite finished my wine and lemonade, so I drink that and pour myself another glass, just wine this time, and I'm not quite sure why I'm doing this, but I'm holding it up and giving it a big old sniff. I saw Maxwell doing it when I had that meal with him.

I don't think Meredith is going to say anything more about painting her nails so I tell her, 'I painted mine green. For that festival before I got here – I think I told you about it. It was in Glastonbury, or very near, but it wasn't anything like the real Glastonbury. I painted my nails green for that. I sprayed my hair green and put green make-up on my face, but then I got dumped in a service station and walked miles in the rain. That's how I ended up here and got my job in The Fox, so I'm not complaining. But the festival was nothing like I thought it would be, and the guys who sold me the ticket disappeared as soon as we arrived, and then, you know, like I say, the woman dumped me at the service station. Anyway that's why my nails were green. I wanted, like, a theme.'

The wine's not so horrible. I'm wondering if Meredith is going to say something now, but she doesn't seem to have anything to say. So it's me talking again.

'There's still a little bit of green on them even now – look, there's a little fleck on my thumb. I scratched it off, but not all of it came off.'

I can't work out what Meredith's look means. Like, is she even thinking about nail colours, or wondering why she's wasting her time here with me? Or is she thinking the wine's really good? When I go to the supermarket tomorrow, I'll buy some crisps as well as the wine for Maxwell and for Mrs M. Or some pistachios, with shells. I could put them in bowls. Although Mrs M will be home quite soon. They might be too fiddly for her.

'I should have bought some of that stuff from the chemist, for taking off nail colour, you know, like the stuff you buy that – you know, that what's-it-called?'

'Nail polish remover.' She's lifting her eyebrows.

I always know when I'm blushing because it makes my cheeks itch. Yaya said she knew if I was scared or angry or shy. Just by looking at me, she said.

I smell my wine again and give it a spin round the inside of the glass, like Maxwell did. Maybe I should say something like people do when they talk about it being a cheeky wine. But I did that once, when Sue had some friends over for a meal, I can't remember what I said exactly, something about it being a cheeky wine or about cherries or liquorice maybe. Sue said afterwards maybe leave that for people who knew what they were talking about. So now I just have a glug and neither of us says anything for a little bit.

I'm wondering about what else I can say about Meredith's nails, but she says, 'Did you get that Glastonbury ticket yet?'

I haven't got the actual ticket, but I have been promised it, like definitely – and so then she's shaking her head and saying she can't believe it and about them being gold dust and if there's any way I can find another ticket . . .

She stubs out her cigarette in the flowery saucer, and takes another one out of the box and also a packet of Rizla papers and a clear plastic bag. She licks three of the papers together and puts them flat on the Mrs Beeton. I'm trying not to stare, but she's torn open the cigarette and she's shaking tobacco onto the papers and I know what that is. I should tell her not to. It's Mrs Malley's house. But I'm still working out the right thing to say, and my glass is empty again. I fill it back up, and hers too, and I take a quick drink before saying, 'There's a festival the weekend after that might be fun too. I mean it's small, but it's only half an hour away on a bike?'

It's a funny look she's giving me, while she's holding her lighter under a little cube of black. Yaya used to bring in flowers from the woods and put them in a vase, but she always forgot to take them out, and they'd start wilting. That's what this smells like.

It smells like Sue's flat in Auckland too. Whenever Sue rolled up a joint, it made me think of dying flowers.

'What festival?' Meredith is licking the cigarette paper, and I should really tell her not to smoke that in here. But I'm wondering how to say it without being rude. And you can hear the rain outside now against the windows.

'It's just called, like, the name of the town I think. But there's music. Some students of Ned's are playing. I told you about Ned. I thought it might be . . .'

She's ripping a corner off the Rizla packet and rolling it between her fingers.

'Dad'll say you have to work.' There's a clicking noise of her lighter and it's too late to say not to smoke it, because she's taking a draw on it, and with her other hand she's holding out her empty glass for more wine. 'Anyway I'll be out with friends. If it was Glastonbury, I could work something out. But this sounds lame. I'm bound to have other things on.'

She's talking with her mouth hardly open, and then she blows out a mouthful of dying-flower smoke. I don't know what I'm going to do if she offers it to me. I should say no. I'm Mrs Malley's house sitter. And I don't like it much anyway. I smoked a little bit, in Auckland with Sue, but I ended up talking too much.

I'm not sure if Meredith is going to offer me some or not. Maybe that was only Sue being generous. I'm trying not to look too hard, so she doesn't think I'm staring, but when I do, she has the joint in front of her and she's gazing at it, like she's studying it. And she's closed her lips like she's trying not to tell a secret.

These glasses can't be as big as they look, because mine seems to be empty again so I pour us both more wine and when she passes me the joint, I forget about saying 'no' and just say 'ta'.

Having smoked a bit with Sue means that at least I look like I know what I'm doing. I don't splutter or anything. And then she says, 'So there's no way you might be able to get any other tickets? You don't think maybe your contact . . .'

I'm still trying to keep my lips together with the smoke still in and I say to her that, really, I think there's only one ticket. But she can't really hear me because I'm trying so hard to not open my mouth, so she says, 'What?' And I say it again but now it's like suddenly my chest needs to get the smoke out and I've started saying 'just one ticket' but now I really need to cough it out, and I have to thump myself on the chest. Meredith starts laughing. I do too, even though it's not really funny. I don't want to look like I can't take a joke.

I say, 'Only one ticket,' again and I take another puff, but not such a deep one. Meredith starts giggling again when I pass it back to her so I ask her what's funny and she says she's wondering what Mrs Malley would say if she saw us here in her lounge. I need to breathe out quickly. Because I shouldn't be smoking this stuff in Mrs M's living room with Meredith Paterson. But then I remember her smiling in Maxwell's car, with the roof down. She said thank you afterwards. 'Thank you, Kiki.' She said another word too. I think she wanted to say a whole sentence, but she definitely said that word, because I repeated it and she did a thumbs up. The word was 'fun'.

And so now I'm thinking about her bucket list poem – 'all the fun we've had' – and that maybe she'd think this was something else for the bucket, fuck it, list.

Meredith is holding out the joint to me again, so I take it. 'She's not as bad as you think. I was wondering about taking her to a festival too. That little one I was talking about.' I'll be all right taking a bigger drag. I'm not going to choke again. But then Meredith does this funny face.

'You're taking Mrs Malley to a festival?' I think it's the first time Meredith has ever actually looked at me so hard, like directly at me. She's looking right into my eyes, with this look on her face. The look is so funny. And I can't help it – I'm breathing out all the smoke through my nose because suddenly I need to laugh. Because I can see why she'd find it so surprising.

And I'm already laughing when Meredith says, 'It's Glastonbury really, isn't it? Mary Malley's going to Glastonbury with you. With her handbag and her umbrella. You're going to see The Killers and Janet Jackson and Billie Eilish and Miley Cyrus and . . .' She's trying to say another name but she can't because it's like every time she tries to say it, it makes her laugh. 'And – and – and—'

She's making me laugh more too. Because she just keeps saying, 'And – and – and.' And she's crying, because of laughing so hard. There are actual tears on her face. I'm having to wipe tears out of my eyes too. I don't even know who The Killers and Billie Eilish and Miley Cyrus are – Janet Jackson I know, of course – but I'm thinking about Mrs M at Glastonbury with her handbag and her umbrella, like Meredith says. Mrs M standing there, the way she does, with the crowd dancing around her. And Meredith is still trying to say this other name, but she just can't get it out, just, 'And K-K-K, and K—' and I'm laughing so hard I can hardly even say, 'Who?'

She's pressing her lips together, like she's trying to calm herself down enough to say it right this time.

'And—' I can see her lips, like they're twitching to try and keep her calm. 'And—' She lifts her hand up in front of her like she's patting the air. '*Kylie Minogue!*'

We look at each other for a moment not speaking, and then she snorts out of her nose and her mouth at the same time. And I don't know whether it's this which is funniest, or the thought of Mrs M watching Kylie Minogue – because yes, I do know who she is. And I'm seeing Mrs M dancing along with Kylie wearing that long white dress with the hood. I splash wine from my glass onto the sofa because I'm shaking so much, so then I drink the rest of it quickly and Meredith holds her glass out towards me but when I try to pour, the bottle is empty. I'm holding an empty bottle over her empty glass and it sets us off even more.

She says something else, but I don't understand. It's like 'My culkee one ooka.'

So I say, 'Your culkee what?'

And she shakes her head and says, 'Mi-chael Ki-wan-uka. He's playing the Park Stage. He's the best. You must know him, the theme tune from *Big Little Lies*? He's epic.'

I always hated it at school when someone asked me if I knew somebody or something and I didn't have a clue what they were even talking about. Do you say it or not say it? And I'm trying to make up my mind – she's waiting. Or maybe she's not, because then she says, 'How come you can afford a ticket suddenly anyway? I thought you were broke?'

She asks it so suddenly that I don't know if I should be relieved not to have to answer about Michael Kiwa-whatsit.

She's not laughing anymore, just looking at me. And I'm still holding the empty bottle. I put it down and it's really quiet. There's just the noise of the rain outside.

'Just lucky. It will probably rain all the time anyway.' I'm looking at the bottle. 'I mean, doesn't it always rain at Glastonbury? Mrs M will need that umbrella. She'll—'

The rain outside.

Oh bugger.

'Wait, Meredith. I've left the dog in the garden.'

This sets Meredith off giggling again, but I'm already through the living room door. Poor Wordsworth. He'll give me a bad look. I'll have to get a towel from the bathroom.

The kitchen door needs a bit of a shove so I come bursting out into the garden. It can be stiff when it's very wet. I often leave it open during the day, when it's sunny. But it's dark now, and bashing down with rain.

No sign of him. I shout, 'Wordsworth.'

No movement.

'Wordsworth. Sorry, boy. Come.'

Nothing.

There's only the moonlight and some street light from the lane outside, so it's really hard to see anything. The shadow in the corner by the cherry tree could be him. It looks a bit dog-shaped, so I'm walking towards it, calling his name. And then my foot catches and I nearly fall. One of the holes he's been digging. A new one. The shape isn't him anyway. It's two plant pots with some flowers.

'Wordsworth.'

He's not under the hedge. That's where I'd have hidden if I was a dog. He's going to be so cold. Maybe he'll need a bath. Do you do that to dogs? Baths?

'Wordsworth!'

It's not that big a garden. I can't think where else he'd be hiding. Down the side alley, maybe? 'Wordsworth!' Maybe he's gone down here – and—

And the gate is swinging open. It's tapping against the frame and then swinging back open. Bugger.

The gate Mrs M always complained about, every time I brought him back. What was it she called him? Whodunnit, the master of escape. The gate is open and Wordsworth isn't here.

'Wordsworth!' How can my T-shirt be soaked already? And my hair. And my glasses. I'm looking through blurry splats, running now. The front garden is lighter, because of the lamp-post on the corner. But he's not here. And I'm yelling as loud as I can, 'Wordsworth!'

None of the other cottages have any lights on. Everyone's asleep, I reckon.

He's not in the lane.

'Wordsworth!'

The woods and fields are to the left, but it's pitch black that way. He won't have gone there, surely. He'll have gone towards the pub. Turned right, towards the pub. He won't have gone to the woods and out of the village. Not in this rain. He'll have gone the way he always has before.

'Wordsworth!'

Except, of course, that first day. When I first arrived. I was walking from the other way. From the left, from the fields. He was coming that way then.

'Wordsworth!'

What if I can't find him? What if he's gone? 'Sorry, Mrs M, I was getting stoned in your living room and I left your dog in the garden in the pouring rain, and he ran away.'

Please have gone right. Wordsworth. Please come back.

My glasses are so splashed that the light from the street lamps is making patterns on them. I'm running through splats of light. Rubbing my glasses on my T-shirt doesn't help. There are smeary shapes around the shapes of houses and trees and the high street into the village centre, and I can just make out the green and the pub. It's on the corner with the main road on the other side from me. I can't quite see around the corner yet but I'm nearly there.

'Wordsworth.'

I can hear something from round the corner. Like clanking and jangling from just beyond the pub. Maybe it's the pub sign, being blown in the wind. But I don't think so. It's another familiar sound. The noise of the heavy machinery and the construction trucks that come past.

I'm running as fast as I can and I'm nearly at the corner now by the pub. I can see the road on the other side, through my smeary glasses. I can make out a truck – one of those massive dumper trucks – coming along the road. It's yellow and it's going faster than you'd think one that size should go. I'm nearer to the pub now, not quite there, but nearer, and I can see round the corner.

There's another shape in the road too. I can't see it clearly because of my glasses. But it's a dog shape. But that can't be Wordsworth. He'd move. He wouldn't just sit there in the middle of the road. He's not that stupid.

The dumper truck is clanking on and it's nearly at the pub. And the dog-shaped shape isn't moving. And I yell, 'Wordsworth!'

There's a noise, a howl. And I scream again.

But the basset shape is right there in the middle of the road. And the digger is really near now. It's huge. With its huge wheels and its enormous spade thing in the air. The howl is louder. But then I can't hear it because there's the screeching noise. It's the brakes. Splashing on my face. It's so loud. I can't hear my own yell. I'm shouting so hard my chest hurts. I'm screaming, 'Stop!'

But the truck's going too fast, and the road is too wet. Even though the brakes are screeching the truck's still moving. I have to put my hands over my ears.

It's slowing down. But it's still moving.

'Stop,' I scream again. But there isn't time.

I can't watch this.

It's too late.

I can't stay and watch.

All I can hear is screaming brakes as I turn and run.

NED

I T IS NOT MAXWELL knocking on the door. If it were
him it would be *tap-tap-tap*, three firm raps in quick succes-
sion, equally weighted and then a count of three before
opening the door. And this doesn't sound like any of the nurses
either. They all have a polite but hurried tapping – although
Tammy sometimes does give the door quite a bash if it's the
end of a particularly long shift. Toby never knocks. He swings
open the door, with a 'Don't get up', or a 'Not still lying there
are you, Ned, mate? Anyone would have thought you've nothing
better to do.'

Kiki, then? She said she'd be in this morning, before going
along to a musical therapy session with the old woman. This
tap tap-tap tap is probably her. She and Maxwell have been
discussing whether I could do some sort of therapeutic music
too. He seemed enthused by articles he'd read online. The
effects can be 'remarkable' from what he says.

The door is opening too slowly for it to be Tammy and it's
not Rachel, either. Rachel does it swiftly, very business-like,
and somehow manages a particularly loud squeak. I wonder
if the hospital design in the squeak especially for those, like
me, with our reduced states of responsiveness. Maybe the
squeaking door is the medical equivalent of polite throat-
clearing. Not that there's much I could be interrupted doing
these days.

My bet is on Kiki.

I wait for the 'Hey, Nid', and those eyes which will peer everywhere but right at me, as she sits herself down on the side of my bed and reaches for the alphabet board.

I picture her peering around the door, hesitantly. I'm already anticipating her, 'Hope you don't mind me barging in?'

Actually, there are a couple of things I want to say to Kiki. Because we had quite the chat yesterday, after her confession session. It was exhausting, actually, what with all that spelling. I haven't had a conversation like that since I've been in here. My eyelids still ache. I've been thinking about it though, and I want to tell her that—

'Norton, darling. I'm sorry I didn't come yesterday, my love, but I was so busy.'

Not the padding of trainers across the polished floor, but clicking heels. How did I not recognise Bella's knock?

'And I have meetings all morning today again. That's why I'm so early. I'm just nipping in. I've missed you.'

Bella kisses the side of my mouth that is facing upwards. It's what my head does now. Lolls to one side or the other. Her hair brushes across my face and the silver bean on the chain around her neck taps my chin. I find myself imagining how it would feel to kiss her back.

'I have good news, Nort. You remember Francis Rafferty? Raffer Productions. I worked on that commercial with them, you remember?'

I wish I could laugh and clasp my chest and say, 'Not the Raffer Productions ad?' because only Bella could have been so proud of being an unpaid runner on a dog food commercial. You'd have thought it was *The Lord of the Rings* she was working on. If it could, my mouth would be stretching itself into a smile now. Annabella Hopkins has never been one to give up on a dream. She added TV production skills to her CV although no more TV projects have come along.

'I had lunch with Francis yesterday. He's so on board. He's really excited about this project. He thinks it's a shoo-in for a commission.'

This project being me? Francis Rafferty is the brother of Cressida, who was Bella's closest school friend and is now a receptionist in her father's chambers.

'He has this contact at Channel 5 and he's going to set up a meeting. He's really confident, Norton. How exciting is that?'

Let's just say I can hardly find the words. But Bella's eyes are so bright, I can't help but feel a pang of gratitude.

'It would be a first step to getting your story out there. Darling, it will put you on the road back to real life.'

The alphabet board is right there, on the table – the one on wheels so it can be pulled over to me easily, the one a few inches from her hand. If she lifts it up, I can ask her how. How is the telling of my 'story' going to take me anywhere close to the life I once had?

'So much comes down to attitude. You taught me that. And it's what I said to Francis. All this is just going to make you – us – stronger still.'

She has a lovely voice, Bella. Captivating. If you were to choose an instrument to convey it, it would be the oboe. Breathy, seductive. Vibrato espressivo.

'Do you ever think sometimes things happen for a reason?'

Bel, that's hardly one of those blink once for yes, twice for no questions.

Bella is looking up towards the ceiling so that I can no longer see her face. My field of vision stretches from the collar of her blouse, with the top button undone, to the nook in her neck, where her necklace hangs. Smooth skin. I breathe in her perfume.

Silence.

She reaches out and wraps her fingers around my hand.

'It's the only way that any of this makes any sense. Good things can still come. We just have to make them happen.'

Her face lowers again so that she is looking right at me.

'What you've been through is unbearable. But don't you see how it has made us understand things that maybe we were both too stupid to see?'

I can feel her eyes on me. I cannot look away.

'Norton, when you said all of that stuff about calling off the engagement, I was hurt. I didn't understand why you were saying it. I think I do now.'

She wraps her other hand around mine too, so that both of her hands are clasping me. Her elbow leans on the roll-out table and she's bending closer over me. Her silver bean pendant is in front of my eyes and I don't seem to be able to make them not focus on it, even though it is too close to do so comfortably.

There was a thing that Maxwell showed me once – if you put your index fingers so that they're touching on the tip of your nose and look at them, then your eyes just see one index-finger sausage floating. The silver bean is like that. I'd like to bat it away. It's a silver sausage floating while Bella's words play in my ears.

'The other day, Toby was telling me about becoming a father, about how he felt before Phoebe was born – about feeling so trapped that it was as if he was a prisoner waiting for execution. But then when it actually happened, he said it made him see that nothing else in life would ever matter so much. He realised that that was why he had been so scared in the first place. Because of how much he had wanted it all along, too much to admit it to himself. Because it mattered too much.

'I think that's how you felt too. About marriage. The thing is, I was scared too. And now I'm not. Things are clearer now. There are two things I want, to make television that matters, and to be with you. That's what I mean about this happening for a reason. Don't you see?'

She cradles my head, with her cheek against my forehead. Her skin is warm and I feel like a baby being rocked.

I only realise she's crying when she brings her head back down to where I can see it and crouches beside my chair so that she's on the same level as me. She makes a little sound that could be laughter as easily as it could be a sob, and says, 'Sorry. What am I like?'

She wipes her eyes. 'I've looked on the internet. And I've been there when Maxwell was talking to the doctor. There's no reason we can't. We can still . . .'

When Bella is not here, I can tell myself there is something unexceptional about her beauty. It lacks anything exotic. There are no characterful flaws. But the truth is she is simply beautiful. When I was still me, I would sometimes do a double-take at the reflection of the two of us in a shop window or bar mirror. Now, her eyelashes are shining with tears.

'There's no reason why we can't have a family, my love.'

Those eyelashes blink, slowly, as if she's readying herself for something.

'Of course, I'll have to go on top. Though I'm sure you won't see that as a problem.'

I beg your pardon.

I'm sorry?

Is that a joke?

Bella made a joke. Bella?

There is a noise. It is coming from me. From my silent body, my powerless mouth, there is a noise. It is the first noise that has come from me since I woke into this distorted life. It is like a snort or maybe a hiccup. It is neither, but it is still something.

A joke. Bella?

Has she ever told me one before?

Funny stories, yes – or stories with a humorous edge. But a joke? She has made me make this noise. An elephant sound. Or more seal, perhaps? Walrus? I'm doing it again.

She doesn't mention the noise. She's giggling though so she must hear it. Bella made a joke.

'That's what Toby said. He said, "Of course you will have to go on top, but I'm sure old Ned won't mind that."'

Toby's joke. I see.

Still. Bella told it. She made me laugh.

My noises have stopped. I'm looking at her – well, straight ahead towards where she is – and she's looking at me. I don't know what I want to say, really, but I wish she'd offer my alphabet grid. I blink a few times in the hope she'll realise. But instead she leans in to me and says, 'I know.' She kisses me, her lips soft against mine. And she tells me, 'You see, Norton, good things do come from bad things. You and me, the future. It's all ours.'

She kisses me again and I close my eyes. There is a prickling under my eyelids and I feel a tear escaping.

'You're crying. My darling, you're—'

Tap, tap, tap, tap. Four polite knocks. Tammy's knock. I hear the squeak of a door opening and Bella jumps back up quickly as my nurse comes in to check on me.

MRS M

'**N**ICE TO SEE SOMEBODY smiling round here. One aspirin, one clopidogrel for you, Mary my dear. Something good happen today to make you so happy?'

It is a terribly jolly accent that Sunny has, 'some-ting good'. I wonder where she comes from. I suppose one should say, what her ethnicity is, these days. Or should that be 'heritage'? They change the rules so often, I don't know how one is meant to keep up. It so often feels safer not to try. It will be one of those African countries, I imagine, one of the former colonies, or perhaps somewhere in the West Indies. Somewhere hot, in any case.

It does so happen that I am feeling rather chipper today. I had a dream about Harriet. She was driving us in a car, although then it seemed to be a boat. One of those terribly fast ones. And we both had on long silk scarves which were blowing in the wind. Of course in actual life, I should never wear a loose garment around my neck whilst being driven on either water or road. I don't for the life of me remember where we were, just that it was very enjoyable and that I felt – well, I suppose the word is happy.

And this morning, my occupational therapy session was most pleasing. I could squeeze the foam balls tighter than the last time, and I could lift my arm above my head. I managed to hold a cup of tea with very little spillage and to sign my name on a piece of paper with a ballpoint pen. It was not the tidiest signature, but still, progress. I rather think I shall be allowed home soon. Mr Douglas says I am nearly ready. I walked to the lavatory with the walker in a mere eighty-seven steps, earlier. I did need a little nap afterwards, but it is less arduous than it was.

'Your pills are in here, Mary. And let me give you some fresh water.' She has the jugs and the medication on her trolley. The pills come in those tiny white cardboard cups. Rather like oversized thimbles.

I start to reply. I know precisely what I wish to say, however the word is unwilling. I can feel it there in my brain but when I open my mouth, it refuses to make the journey. But I should say the word. Manners cost nothing, Mother always said. Only the word will not be caught. And so I try a different method.

I hesitate to call it a song since it is from a televised commercial. Ditty would be more accurate. Or should that be jingle? I believe it was for a brand of chocolates. Harriet used to sing it at me sometimes, when a simple thank you would have sufficed.

'Thank you,' I sing now – imperfectly, perhaps, but I manage it. I thank Sunny, 'very much'. In fact there are three 'very's. It may not be tuneful, but the message is successfully conveyed.

Sunny is laughing now and not merely the forced friendliness of the ward nurse. One can generally tell. She is shaking her head and saying something about my being priceless. Goodness me, but Roger would be horrified to see me singing television commercials to an overseas heritage nurse person. He would have said that I was making quite the spectacle of myself.

Yet there is something so rewarding about her laughter that I find that I too am laughing. Somehow one can't help but see the funny side. Harriet would most certainly have done so.

'One has to laugh,' she liked to say. Even after all that surgery. Even when the doctors kept delivering more bad news. 'You have to laugh, Mary. There's no point crying.'

Sunny moves on towards the next bed with a wink, and a, 'no, thank *you*, very much Mary'. In actual fact, I should rather like her to stay for a little longer. She might be interested in knowing about the music therapy class which I shall be attending shortly. A stroke of great fortune, since this is a new initiative for the hospital. Something of an exciting pilot, I understand. I'm rather surprised that Kiki has not yet arrived, in fact. I expected her earlier today.

Perhaps Sunny would also be interested to hear about my peculiar decision. I suspect she would find it quite a shock. I have decided that I shall agree to having my hair coloured pink.

Oh, I know, Roger will be turning in his grave.

'Mary,' he would say. 'You appear to have lost your mind.' I can picture the expression – like the time I served up Harriet's vegetarian couscous recipe on a Saturday night. Well, perhaps I have lost my mind. But, Roger, it is only hair. You may not realise that for the last forty-odd years of our marriage, I had it coloured at the salon every two months, with an additional rinse every fortnight.

I haven't bothered since you've been gone, actually. You might say that I have let myself go rather to seed. But, Roger, I am eighty-four years old. I shall not be around to make a spectacle of myself for many years more, so if I have a desire to make an old fool of myself, I shall jolly well do so. And I could tell you another thing, it was really rather delicious, that couscous. Not that you had the manners to even taste it.

I wonder where she has got to, young Kiki. Taken Wordsworth for a long walk before coming in, no doubt. He is rather prone to dawdling. She will be here any minute. My session is in half an hour and she did say she would be here.

She will be terribly excited about my hair. I'm looking forward to seeing her face when I tell her.

KIKI

U P. UP. UP. THE chain is cold in my fingers. Legs out, stretching back, so that I'm almost lying flat. And then I swing back my legs under me, and lean forward in the seat. Down. Down. Down. And again.

'*How long will you stay on this swing? You know it doesn't solve a thing?*'

Go away, Mother. You're not even real.

The rain is heavy. My clothes are stuck to me. My face is so wet I'm not even sure if I'm crying anymore.

'*Go and dry yourself inside. You know that only cowards hide?*'

I. Am. Not. Talking. To. You.

When I was little, Yaya always knew where to find me after an argument. The playground was by the lake, next to a picnic area. There were the baby swings with bars to stop small children falling out. But the swings I liked best were the tyres on ropes. I would get one swinging as high as it would go, until it was swinging up and back to almost horizontal, and then curl myself up inside it.

Yaya never came straight away. I think she knew I needed to do a lot of swinging before I was ready to talk to her again.

This swing is just a normal wooden one. Just a seat. Not a tyre.

Underneath me is a puddle. When I started on the swing, it was just a patch of wet, but now it is all over the ground underneath me. When I finally get off this thing I'm going to have soaking feet. I should have worn my gumboots. Then I could have jumped right into the puddle like a toddler, splashing everywhere.

Up. Up. Up. Down. Down. Down. Legs out straight, legs back, body up, body flat.

Yaya never tried to force me to come down. She'd just wait, with her arms crossed.

The thing was, when I started swinging on my tyre, I was always so angry. Everything was Yaya's fault. It was her fault that my classmates never asked me to play with them or go to their houses. The only parties I ever went to were when the entire class were invited. And why did Yaya not take me to libraries or cricket clubs, or buy a television or a computer or let me be a Brownie or have my hair cut by a real hairdresser? Why were my clothes and my shoes always different to everyone else's? I never knew the TV shows or the bands they talked about. I didn't understand their jokes.

Yaya gave me the wrong food too. However much I begged for Babybel cheeses, she gave me pulses and rice wrapped in vine leaves. I never knew the games they played. It was all her fault. And nobody understood what she said, not even me half the time. All those years she'd lived in England and New Zealand – how could she not even get the language right?

But when I finally stopped and got out of my tyre and back onto my feet again, the hate was always gone.

Up. Up. Up. Down. Down. Down.

The rain makes everything smell fresh and green. It smells like home.

The chain has a squeak. It sounds like the brakes on the dumper truck, not so loud but the same sort of sound. What do you call it? What does Ned say, in his videos, when he's sitting there in his cut-off jeans, with his legs tanned and his guitar resting on them? Pitch? The pitch of a braking truck driving towards a scared little dog.

Up. Up. Up. Squeak. Down. Down. Down.

Why am I even here? What did I honestly think was here in England? A brand new life? Instant happiness? Kiki Moon, you didn't even know that there were two Stratfords. And you promised Mrs M you'd look after her house and her dog.

Poor Wordsworth.

Up. Up. Up. Squeak. Down. Down. Down.

And even then you couldn't do the right thing. What happened to the 'I would have been a nurse if my grandmother hadn't got ill'?

Wordsworth, I'm so sorry.

They say after you die, you can still hear what's happening around you because your hearing's the last of your senses to stop working. Sue told me that. I could have talked to Wordsworth about – I don't know – rabbits in the woods and food in his bowl and digging holes in the garden. I could have told him stories about stealing biscuits and dragging cushions off the sofa or my socks out of my bag and hiding them behind the greenhouse. Maybe I could have sung him a song about going for long walks, instead of running back to the cottage and screaming at Meredith to get out, and then phoning Maxwell and waking him up sobbing down the phone.

Then curling up on the bed in my wet clothes, with my hands over my head. Somebody was downstairs knocking on the door. Maxwell, I reckon, trying to find out what was wrong. Or the police? Is it a crime, to let your dog escape and then gap it when the poor animal gets run over?

Can you go to prison?

I stayed in my bed, with my hands over my head. And that's when she started up, with her stupid rhymes, like *if you don't go and answer the door, how can you know what they're knocking for?*

Up. Up. Up. Squeak. Down. Down. Down.

Eventually the knocking stopped. But I couldn't bear it anymore, with my clothes cold and wet, and my phone buzzing and her going on about *is this not a little extreme? Sometimes things aren't as bad as they seem.*

I'm so sorry, Wordsworth. I'm so sorry, Mrs M.

Up. Up. Up. Squeak. Down. Down. Down.

Time to leave, leave Little Piddleton. Leave England.

Jump off, into that big puddle. Back to Mrs M's cottage. I haven't got much to pack but I should do some tidying. That wine I spilt on the sofa and the ashtray, and there's a lot of dog hair everywhere and heaps of washing-up. And there are the holes in the garden and the grass needs cutting again. I'll have to go to the pub too, to pick up my other stuff.

Hopefully Merv won't be up yet. Or Meredith. I'll leave a note.

And I'll send a message to Ned. Not that he'll care. He won't even notice I've gone. But I want to tell him thanks for listening yesterday.

I'll go back to New Zealand. I won't stop in Auckland though. Sue hasn't replied to a single one of my texts, or emails. She won't care.

Home, then. No Glastonbury. Meredith won't believe I'm sacrificing my ticket.

I don't suppose I'll ever know who Stan Douglas was or what really happened to my mum. Ironic – just when I thought I was on to something. My mother was a director of Sammy's

Glass Art & Sun-Catchers. What difference does that really make? Really? Even if, by some miracle, the company's still there and someone still remembers her. Even if they can tell me why my mother was poisoned. She doesn't magically come back.

And Glastonbury? It meant a lot to my family? But they're not here. There's only me.

Maybe I could get that job back in the Lake bar. Now that I know how to pull a good pint. Maybe I could rent a unit in the park, and—

So much easier to run away. Braver to find the strength to stay?

Mother. I am not listening. You're nothing more than a shimmer of light in the rain.

Then, Kiki Moon, it is your own self you must listen to. You know deep down what you should do.

I can't stay. If you'd seen that truck and heard Wordsworth howling, you'd know that.

The swing is slowing down. I've stopped moving my legs. I'm just sitting, letting it lull itself to a stop.

There are people you have made promises to, don't they deserve more that this from you?

Mother. Do you never let up?

But, what – I just disappear? All those promises, and I just go? I told Mrs M I'd take her shopping when she's strong enough. And that we'd to a festival together. And on holiday. She said she didn't want go to – but I said I reckoned she'd change her mind. I promised we'd tick off everything on the fuck it bucket list. I've even bought the hairspray.

And suddenly, what, I'm not here and Wordsworth is gone?

I'd want to know what happened.

I mean, I'd hate me. But I'd want to know.

OK.

So.

Water splashes as I step off the swing.

NED

THE BURN OF MUSCLES being pushed beyond their limits. The pelting rhythm in your chest as your lungs and heart strain to propel you further and faster. The banging of blood in your ears and breath in your throat. The salty taste in your mouth. The slapping of feet on the ground and the splash of mud against skin.

It's still not enough. You force yourself to give more.

Running. Not jogging. No nice gentle run, this is full-out flogging my body to push through the pain, driving myself to be as fast as I can be. Down the hill from Maxwell's front door to the stream, slipping in mud and finding my balance again in time to hurdle over the water. Landing in long grass and starting up the steep hill on the other side. No time to breathe in those smells of cows and chimney smoke and hedgerow flowers, forcing myself forward. Faster. Stretch further, Ned. Push harder. Arms working in time – just pausing quickly to wipe sweat from my brow, without breaking my stride. Once I reach the top of the hill, I will race to—

'Very good. Can you feel how we're working to stimulate those muscles, and to rebuild them gradually? Feel it, yes. Let's keep this going for another fifteen minutes? How is that for you? Feels OK?'

I want to stay here in these fields, with my legs thumping the ground, carrying me to the crest of the hill. But the fields have gone. I open my eyes. I blink once for 'Yes'. Head held in place by cushioning, I see legs moving in this wheelchair, feet strapped in to the motorised pedalling machine positioned in front of it, turning without my input. Kneeling by those feet, I see Pom, smiling encouragement. That wasn't her talking just now, though. That was this new physio, Mikey. He's standing behind her, watching both of us, muscular arms crossed. Easy smile, broad shoulders, Northern Irish accent. Together he and Pom present the multidisciplinary team. Physical exercise together with communication practice. She has the alphabet board held up ready, inquisitive look on her face. *Do I want to say something?*

Blink.

'OK. First row? Second row?'

Blink.

'E-F-G-'

Blink.

'G. First row? Second row? Third row? Fourth?'

Blink.

'O-'

Blink.

'G. O. Right. First? Second? Third? Four—?'

Blink.

'Fourth row. O?'

Blink.

'Wow. You really have the hang of this now, Ned. G-O-O. Is the word Good?'

Blink.

'Right. First word "Good".'

Blink.

'Perfect. Next word. First row. Second row. Third row. Fourth row?'

Blink.

I spell out T-O end word, M-O-V-E without misunderstanding. Pom grins.

'Good to move? I bet.' That's Pom talking, but Mikey starts speaking at the same time, 'Don't you worry, champ, this is just the beginning.'

And then they look at each other and laugh. And for a second, I feel like I'm laughing with them too. Pom looks back towards me. She smiles.

'I'm planning to work you far harder than this though,' Mikey says.

Pom holds up the grid, offering it to me. G I tell them. O. O. D. End word.

The big Irishman takes a step closer to me and puts his hand on my shoulder. 'So, champ, you know what we need to do now?'

They're both looking at me. I blink twice.

'I think we need some goals. Know what I mean?'

Goals? The New York Marathon, perhaps? Kilimanjaro? An appearance on the next *Dancing on Ice*?

'We both know you didn't ask for this. But the way I see it, if you don't get determined now and set yourself some pretty impossible goals, you're not going to be pushing yourself as hard as you need to be. See what I'm saying?'

There's a glance at him from Pom – a slight tensing in her eyes – that makes me think this is not a pep talk NHS physios are trained to be delivering. But he's gazing at me intently. Blue eyes. Early twenties. Similar age to Pom. He's a handsome boy. 'Time to get determined, champ. See?'

He reminds me of someone. *Pilates. Passion. Practice.* Yes, Mikey, I believe I see.

'So, what are we saying then? What's the goal?' He looks from me down to Pom. She's waiting too.

R I spell. *U. N.*

'Run? That's the spirit. So, we have a goal now. It is not going to be easy – but by fuck, Norton Edbury, we are not going to give up until we *run.*'

I blink and blink and Pom gives me her questioning look, grid aloft.

Fifth row. Third letter. W. Second row. First. E. First row. Fifth. End word.

'We.'

There really needs to be a question mark on this board. And an exclamation mark. And a smiley emoji would be good too.

'First word "we". Next word, Ned?'

Blink. Blink.

'We.' They glance at each other.

'Just "we"?' Pom says. 'We?'

And then Mikey snorts. 'Quite right, champ. It's not "we", it's you. I'll just stand right here and tell you what to do. The hard work's yours. But I'll make you a deal. You accomplish that goal and *we*'ll go on that run together. You and me. I'm not giving you any head starts, mind.'

I'm not sure why he's laughing now, but I like that he is. Pom too. And then there's another noise in my ears, like a confused seal. I suppose that must be me.

*

Pom pushes me out into the garden, reeling off one happy adjective after another, 'encouraging', 'great', 'fundamental', 'important'. She's so excited about my laugh. Not that it was a laugh. But my something. I saw it in her face – and the way she and Mikey were beaming at each other, like the proud parents of a baby who had just said its first word.

'. . . exploration of vocal avenues, along with all the ocular-based augmentative and alternative communication techniques we've been working with and are looking into. It expands the potential for expression and . . .'

It's a sunny, still day. The sky is unbroken blue after the night of non-stop rain. Pom has to steer me around a puddly patch on the concrete path.

'. . . and given how quickly you've picked up the basics of the alphabet grid, we can start looking at some more sophisticated strategies of . . .'

It's nice to be with somebody who cares about their job. I remember that sense of buoyancy when one of my music students at the school really got what I was trying to communicate. A cliché perhaps, but it was satisfying all the same. They sent me such lovely cards and letters. *We miss you, Mr Edbury.* I wonder who they have covering for me. Although covering is probably not the right word. I don't suppose I'll be back soon.

Best not to cling to false hopes.

And yet – feel that sunshine, listen to Pom's bright chatter. And there's Maxwell, on the bench there. He hasn't noticed me yet as he's looking the other way. He's talking to an old lady who is a yard or so further on, in my line of sight, holding a rake and pressing some pink flowers – begonias perhaps – into the earth of a tall planter. The occupational therapist with her is called Amir, apparently. I think I recognise him, though I didn't know his name, but now Pom is calling out, 'Hey, Amir. Hello, Mrs Malley. How was music therapy?'

I see. This is the famous Mrs Malley. She looks like she should be in a vintage copy of the *Beano*, brandishing an umbrella at the children who've been pinching her apples. Except that she's wearing carpet slippers and a lilac dressing gown.

And except that it rather looks like she's smiling at Pom. It's a frozen-on-one-side smile, but who am I to talk?

Mrs Malley continues to grin like this, and for a moment, I'm thinking maybe she didn't hear the question, but then she says, 'Good.' The word sounds laboured, but she smiles wider and opens her mouth again.

'Thank you very,' there is a slight movement of her lips as though she might be counting or singing silently to herself, and at the same time, she waves the garden trowel in the air, 'much.'

'Excellent,' Pom says – and a jealous little boy inside me takes note. But then she turns to Maxwell and says what a positive hour I have just had in terms of both the physiotherapy – she's sure the new physio, Mikey, will have plenty to report on that – and the communication.

'Mikey,' Maxwell says, shaking his head. 'I don't believe I've met him.'

'Oh, he's very good,' Pom comes in, almost before he has finished his sentence. She giggles. 'I hope Ned thinks so too.'

I blink. Once. *Yes.*

'This amazing thing happened. Ned, shall I get out the grid? It's your news.'

Blink. Blink.

'No? But you're happy for me to tell your father?'

Maxwell glances towards me and I see the hint of a smile. *Blink.*

'So, Mikey and I were laughing about something silly and out of the blue Ned surprised us both by joining in.' She nods at me. 'He laughed too. Which is so positive because that possibility of sound production is—'

'Good news indeed.' Maxwell jumps in. 'How incredible a human brain is when it tries to repair itself. Baby steps, my boy. Baby steps.'

I'm trying to make a sound right now to show him how right he is. But the sound does not choose to come.

The old woman is waving her trowel in the air and she says, 'Per-sis-tence.' She pauses between syllables and it looks like she's trying to say something else – her face wrinkles in concentration – but there are no more words. She rocks her head back and forward a little and closes her eyes and she says 'prayer'. It sounds almost as though she is singing it.

Persistence and prayer. Goals and baby steps. Pilates, passion and practice. What a motivational lot we all are. The sun is bright. I'm breathing in the smells of freshly dug-in flowers.

Maxwell says, 'Well done, Mary.' She opens her eyes to look at him and then down at the soil which she's been patting with her other hand.

Mary? One drive in his car as a favour to Kiki, and now it's 'Well done, Mary'?

'Thank you very ... much,' she says, looking down at the planter.

*

You wouldn't know from looking at him that Maxwell hardly slept last night – at least that's what he told me as he rushed into my room earlier, full of apologies for having to leave just as soon, but he was accompanying Mrs Malley to a music therapy session because Kiki had disappeared and he didn't want the old woman to worry.

'Long story,' he said. Something about being woken up by a hysterical phone call and a midnight drive to her village but there being no sign of Kiki. Something else about a lorry and a dog and the pub. I couldn't quite keep up.

'Where has she got to?' he kept saying. And, 'I hope she hasn't done anything foolish.' He'd hoped that he might have found Kiki here at the hospital, but she was nowhere to be seen.

'Saint Maxwell,' my mother used to yell when they fought. 'You think everyone wants to be fixed by you.'

Mary Malley's head is up again. She's staring at me this time. Gawping, you might say.

Mary Malley whose bucket list Kiki rabbits on about. Ride in a sports car: tick. Maxwell fixed that for her. And now here he is, rushing off in the middle of the night to try and fix some digger-driving-over-dog drama and searching for Kiki all night, yet still turning up to take this elderly woman to music therapy sessions.

I'm thinking how much I'd like to go for a drive in Maxwell's open-top Jag right now, how much I'd love to be tucked up in the grounds of his lovely farmhouse, in my own little house, in my own bed.

Think positive, Ned. I can breathe. I can blink. I have twice made a noise that sounds nothing like laughter if we're honest, but is at least not silence. The sky is blue. The air is soft. And if you don't get determined, champ, then how will you ever get anywhere?

I blink and I blink and I blink again.

I want to go home.

MRS M

H E'S NOT AS HANDSOME as in the YouTube video that Kiki showed me on her computer. But he wouldn't be, I suppose, now that he's so dreadfully handicapped, if that is something one is still permitted to say nowadays. Probably not. Naturally, I am far too polite to stare, as some might be tempted to do, but it is rather sad to see nonetheless, with his arms and legs tucked in and strapped up, and the padded support keeping his head upright, and that facial expression of – well – there is little of an expressive nature, if one is quite honest, certainly nothing in common with the video of that young gentleman playing his guitar in those dreadful denim shorts which I am quite certain were not hemmed.

His eyes are the only thing that he can move, so I understand.

Harriet and I went to the zoo once when we were – let me think – fourteen or fifteen – and I remember a gorilla looking out at me, with his hands gripping the bars, and being struck by pity for the creature because it looked so human. One couldn't help but believe that there was an intelligent being imprisoned in the body of that beast. There's something of that about this young man, too. One has to wonder if perhaps it might have been easier for him to have not come round at all.

This chap retains all his wits, so young Kiki insists. But one must ask oneself if that is not more of a curse than a blessing.

And I understand better than most. Just look how long it has taken me to plant out one single bedding plant. An entire garden at this time of year is going to demand a Herculean effort. I fear that Kiki Moon will have let it all go to rack and ruin.

Such an inconvenient time for this to happen. November would have been preferable. But there are others worse off. I must remember that.

Another begonia. Yes, Amir, I am aware of what I need to do with my trowel. I have been planting begonias longer than you have been alive and if you watch, my hand is doing it correctly. It just takes a little time and I am somewhat distracted by this conversation.

What a shame Kiki had that migraine but what a kind gentleman Maxwell is to accompany me to music therapy in her place. Perhaps he would like to come for tea when I am back at home. I wonder if perhaps he might appreciate a drop of Roger's Scotch. Lucky, now that I come to think of it, that I did not waste it on marmalade.

Would it be appropriate to ask Maxwell to stay for supper? It would have to be a simple affair since I fear chopping anything too finely might be a stretch. Perhaps a poached chicken breast with beans from the garden.

Before she leaves, Pom-Pom turns Norton Edbury's wheelchair out of the sun, so that he is facing Maxwell and so that I can only see the side of his face. In any case, I have more begonias to plant out into this earth.

'Just two more,' says Amir, though it is rather difficult to concentrate on the conversation, if one might call it that, which Maxwell is having with Norton, whilst planting at the same time.

It appears that each word must be spelt out letter by letter. It cannot be a very efficient system because each one of those letters appears to be on a different line and it takes an age.

One would think there would be an easier way. And really, Maxwell might speak up a little because it is something of a strain to make out everything that he is saying. I have excellent hearing for my age, as I used to remind Roger, when he had the cricket on at full volume. Yet even I have to listen hard to make the letters out. G-O-end word. H-O-M-E-end word.

'Go home.'

Amir is asking if perhaps I should like to go back inside, just as Maxwell is telling this poor young man how he would love nothing better than to take him home, and that he is researching everything that can be done to make it happen, but that he has to understand that he has rather complex needs and that his welfare must be the priority.

And here I am, with the trowel feeling very heavy all of a sudden, and thinking also how very much I should like to be in my own garden. Mr Douglas says soon. A social worker is going to do a visit to assess, he said. Social worker – I ask you. Yet here I am – and the hospital garden looks rather pretty today. I am still alive and there are five newly planted begonias in this box.

Maxwell is talking to this young man about 'patience' and 'improvements' and 'adaptations'. And then a strange thing happens. I hear my name being called – or rather the abbreviation that Kiki will insist upon using. I really should tell her to stop.

'Mrs M.' I hear her before I see her. She's coming from the side where the ward is, and at some speed. It is something of a surprise, since Maxwell told me she was not feeling well and would not be visiting this morning. In truth, she should probably have stayed in bed since she looks dreadful. Her face is flushed and her hair is a terrible mess. It looks like she slept with her plaits still in. She is wearing a strange combination of a shapeless orange T-shirt and pink stripy shorts of the kind one wears to ride a bicycle. She is panting as if she has run all the way here. I do wish she would not yell 'Mrs M' like that. I suspect half the hospital can hear her.

'The nurses said you were here,' she says, and then she stops and stands, saying nothing for a moment. And then she bursts into tears.

'I'm so sorry,' she says. 'Sorry, sorry, so, so sorry.' I can only assume that this strange behaviour is due to whatever illness she has come down with because although, admittedly, I was a little disappointed not to see her earlier, it was only a session of music therapy.

I should tell her to pull herself together, except that the words do not feel like being said. She continues to sob, sorry this, sorry that. She is rambling so much it is quite incoherent. Perhaps she is delirious. She is ranting rather about wanting to do everything right and about my cupboard and my next of kin and never having had any luck and how she needed it – whatever *it* is – more than I needed it. And about a punishment for her taking something without asking, and about the awful thing and being so sorry – so, so sorry, and it being all her fault and how she'll never forgive herself because now Wordsworth is—

Maxwell has taken a step towards her and is putting a hand on her shoulder. Really it is rude for her not to have acknowledged him or Norton. He says, 'Stop. Everything is all right,' and then he says a most curious thing. He says, 'Wordsworth is at mine with Hector. He's safe and well.'

Wordsworth?

I fail to see why the whereabouts of my hound should be worth mentioning, or why Wordsworth should be anywhere but home in the first place. Perhaps Kiki had to work last night, but a dog can be left for an evening without worry. She may be taking her duties rather too seriously. She is staring at Maxwell with the strangest of expressions.

'He can't be.' She is shaking her head and her look is quite manic. 'The digger . . .'

If by 'digger' she means Wordsworth it is a very apt nickname, since he does have that terrible habit. Is this why he has been taken to Maxwell's home? Has he made such a mess of my lawn that he has been sent away in disgrace? I suppose I shall have to put down grass seed when I return, but removing the dog does feel somewhat like shutting the stable door after the horse has bolted.

'An extraordinary escape, according to the pub landlord. The wheels were so high they passed right over him. The driver was very shaken.'

Now I really am confused. What driver? Is this pub landlord that he is referring to Mervyn Paterson? Has he been involved in a road traffic accident? Is that what has upset Kiki? If so, what has that to do with Wordsworth?

How vexing not to be able to make my questions into words. Here I am, with my mouth open, yet unable to speak, a pathetic old woman in my slippers and dressing gown. All I can do is wave this trowel and stare from Kiki to Maxwell and back again.

'*Tell me what is going on*,' I am demanding, except that these thoughts remain inside my head.

I find myself thinking again about the message that Norton Edbury was spelling out to Maxwell on that alphabet board of his just before Kiki burst into the garden. *Go home*, that was it. Letter by painful letter. My goodness, but I too should like to go home.

For all her strange expressions and her ridiculous clothes, this Kiki must care about my home an awful lot if she is so upset by a little digging in the garden. Look at her with her hair such a mess and her cheeks so red. Such an emotional young woman. Like Harriet used to be.

There is a song in my head which I remember Harriet singing one day when she was about to leave – Harriet making one of those Harriet jokes – and her insisting that it was by Dvořák and I had to tell her that of course the tune was Dvořák, but that in actual fact the words were written by an American pupil of his. And then Roger came out – which was rare as he tended to keep himself out of the way when Harriet was around – and asked why she was singing the Hovis bread advert, so I had to correct him as well. 'Roger,' I said, 'even you must know that this is a melody from the New World Symphony.'

This is what I am recollecting. And this must be why I find myself, without strictly planning to do so, singing aloud, '*Going home, going home, I am going home.*'

I am waving the trowel in time, rather like a baton. Kiki is watching me. I'm looking at Maxwell. Maxwell is glancing at Norton, although I can only see the young man's profile, what Mother used to call a proud nose. But as I sing, he turns his head ever so slightly, presumably to watch me.

'Ned!' Maxwell jumps to his feet at this. 'You moved. You moved your head. Did you feel it? Did you mean to do it?'

Actually, it was a *tiny* motion, hardly anything. The most minuscule of movements. But Maxwell is clapping as if it is the last night of the proms. He is repeating, 'Ned, Ned, Ned.' And Kiki is all smiles again suddenly.

Nobody has so much as mentioned my song. Luckily, I am not the sort to take offence.

ONE WEEK LATER
KIKI

WORDSWORTH HEARS THE TAXI before I do. Sometimes he acts like he can't hear at all – like when I'm calling him from the bottom of the field or shouting at him to 'drop' when he's run off with one of Mrs M's cushions, but for other things – like me opening a packet of biscuits – he has the best hearing in the world. He's Super Hearing Dog. All he needs is the little cape.

Now, he's lying in the sun, with those little legs stretched out behind him. And Hector is next to him. Their backs are touching. Wordsworth loves it here. He loves it so much he doesn't even do any naughty digging, maybe because it's so much bigger – more a field than a garden, and no fences. He just races around with his friend until he's too exhausted to race any more. That's him snoring now. I think he'd move in here quite happily, not that we've been asked, but I've got my job at The Fox and Hounds and I still need to look after Mrs M's place, otherwise what sort of a house sitter would I be? Anyway that's his home.

But he's looking pretty comfortable, and I'm on a wooden sun chair, leaning back with my laptop resting on my knees – or, you know, more on my lap. That's why it's called a laptop, I reckon. The sun's out, and when I look up, there's the big field in front of me and the lovely old farmhouse behind me. And it smells like a summer's day should smell.

What would Yaya say now?

She'd be so stoked to see her little Kiriaki, sitting in this English country farm-garden-field. And guess what, Yaya – I really, truly, honestly am going to go to Glastonbury. It's properly definite now. So see, all those things you talked about, I'm really doing them.

And even though it's out in the countryside, the Wi-Fi is good here and I've got Ned's face on the screen in front of me. It's not one of his old videos though, it's the one Annabella did – with this woman singing 'Hello' in the background, and Ned spelling the word 'hello' out with his eyes choosing the letters, and telling her that he loves her. I've heard the song before. And there are all these clips of him doing other things, like running, and playing the guitar, and lying in the grass – just down on the field, where I can look right now. I'm thinking about them, him and her, being right here, on a big white rug, with her hair resting on his legs, and him singing her one of his songs, and it makes me ache inside a little bit.

It wasn't like I was even looking for this video. I was just checking my emails to see if Sue had maybe sent one yet or if there are any messages about Glastonbury. Because I really am going. Definitely, really, actually going. Except I don't want to jinx it by looking too much. And I also went back onto the Sammy's Glass Art & Sun-Catchers website but it's the same message saying the workshop will be closed up for the summer and a list of the festivals they'll be at during that time. And I did heaps of googling, too – but there are just people saying what lovely glass things they've bought. Nothing comes up about my mum or Stanley Douglas. Just the reviews and the festivals. Glastonbury's the closest and the biggest. Maybe I'll try and find Sammy's Glass Art & Sun-Catchers. I probably should.

And then I just put Ned's name into a search, just to – I guess I don't really know why – just to see. So that's why I've got this up now.

And that's when Wordsworth hears the taxi – or not taxi, it's more an ambulance. But a private one, maybe. Maxwell's been on the phone heaps this week, organising it, and making sure everything would be suitable. So I guess that's what Wordsworth hears now. It's so quiet here, you always know when any car is coming up the drive – and he goes running and woofing round to the front, with Hector jumping up and following him.

I have this odd feeling, like I shouldn't be here, like I should climb up a tree or hide or something. Because shouldn't it be just Maxwell and Ned? Maxwell said he wanted me here, but he's not even invited Annabella, and she's Ned's fiancée.

Sue always said there were a few things I needed to remember: like it's OK to pause when you're talking and not fill in every single little silence, but also that you shouldn't always assume people mean what they say. Maybe this is one of those times. I mean, how do you tell?

Annabella doesn't even know about Ned coming here. Maxwell said he wanted to keep it all simple. He had to jump through a lot of hoops – that's the way he said it – to persuade the hospital to let Ned come out at all, even though it's just for an hour. They thought it was too soon, he said, and it's only because he's a doctor himself that he got them to say yes in the end. But he said it was fine for me to be here. I'm never any fuss, he said – he'd like me here. It sounded like he meant it. I'm not going to actually run and climb a tree.

Anyway the motor has stopped. They're getting out, I reckon.

I should have put on some different clothes. I mean, these dungaree shorts are so comfortable, but Meredith says no self-respecting adult would even think about wearing them. I should have put on something a bit smarter. Too late now, but I'm shutting my computer at least, because it would look pretty sad to be watching videos of Ned when Ned arrives.

My face is hot and itchy. That's the sun.

Let's put this laptop under my seat and sit up straight and – here they come – smile like I've just noticed them. And – yes, Wordsworth, you know I'm here, you were with me one minute ago. I don't need licking like you've been away for weeks. Maybe I should stand up. Or will that look daft? It's Ned, not the Queen. But is it rude to just stay sitting? Like I've made myself a bit too at home. I can hardly shake his hand and I don't think I should give him a kiss.

What is it with my cheeks? Maybe they're sunburnt.

'Hello, Kiki. Look who's home for an hour or two.' Maxwell's smiling.

I still haven't decided about standing up even though now I'm starting to do it, but then I'm also kind of changing my mind and starting to sit again. But now I think that will look even odder and so I'm standing again. And then I realise it must look like I'm doing some strange dance. Or a curtsy. And I still haven't even said hello, so I do it now, 'Hello Maxwell. Hey Ned.'

Maxwell smiles, with a nod. Ned doesn't. But he does make a sound, from the back of his throat. Like, maybe, he's saying hello too, or else, maybe laughing at me for trying to curtsy.

I must have looked pretty stupid.

'I wasn't trying to curtsy. I just couldn't decide if I was standing up or not.' The words are out just as I'm thinking I really shouldn't say it out loud.

My cheeks are so hot. I think this is probably one of those times when Sue says it's best not to talk, except Ned can't say anything at all, so sometimes you find yourself doing it a bit more when you're with him.

'Sit down, Kiki' – Maxwell's laughing. 'Why don't I make us a nice cup of tea.'

I tell him that I'll do that – but he shakes his head and says us young people should relax in the sunshine and he'll pop the kettle on.

Maybe I should point out to him that Ned can't drink anything, so it will only be Maxwell and me drinking the tea, and I'm not that bothered anyway but he's already gone inside. There's a big jasmine bush by the back door. There's one at Mrs M's too. Yaya used to collect up jasmine flowers to make tea. I made a cup for Maxwell last week but he said he might stick to English Breakfast if I didn't mind. I'm starting to tell Ned about this, but I don't finish the story, because, well, he has more interesting things to talk about than tea. He's travelled all over the world and been paralysed in a coma. Nothing exciting has ever happened to me, unless you count Yaya dying and me coming to England. Who cares about stupid tea anyway?

So that's why I stop in the middle of my sentence. I'm saying 'jasmine', and then I just say, 'doesn't matter'.

The alphabet grid is on the low table between Ned's wheel-chair and my lounger. I pick it up and hold it up for him. Wordsworth puts his head on Ned's knee, like he wants to know what he has to say too.

Ned doesn't do anything. No blinking, no noises, nothing. Maybe he's waiting for me to ask a question, but I don't really know what to ask. So instead I just say, 'Anything you'd like to say, Ned?'

NED

‘ANYTHING YOU'D LIKE TO say, Ned?’

This is not what I was expecting. 'Bet it's great to be here, Ned?' maybe. Or 'good to be out of hospital for a bit, eh?' Or the trusty old 'nice day, isn't it?' Something that could be answered with three- or four-letter words – G-O-O-D, maybe, or Y-E-S. Or G-R-E-A-T if I wanted to push the boat out. Because it does feel g-r-e-a-t to be out of the hospital, away from The Sunshine Unit for Neurological and Stroke Rehabilitation. But 'anything you'd like to say?' stretches, open as the field around me.

The dog's head is on my knee, staring up from under basset folds of forehead. Kiki is watching me too. Their eyes are the same dark brown.

Anything I'd like to say?

Can I even remember what it was like to talk without having to think about what I was going to say next? To open my mouth and just do it. The gift of the gab was what Toby always said I had.

Anything I'd like to say?

People always commented on my accent. I used to like it, if I'm honest. An interesting accent was the pay-off for a childhood of upheaval, from Los Angeles to the Cotswolds along with stints at a home counties boarding school and university in Scotland. I sounded very English, friends told me, but with hints of the transatlantic.

249

Anything I'd like to say? Kiki Moon, you cannot imagine.

Behind her, the grass stretches down to the stream and the old willow tree. Hector is playing in the long grass. Hector who I have known since he was a puppy, who I taught to sit and to lie down and roll over on command, who would keep pace with me if I went running or cycling in the local lanes. Closing my eyes for a moment, I feel myself pulling myself upright and giving my feet a bit of a tap on the ground to shake out the aches and the stiffness before racing down to join him. *Arriba, arriba!*

I studied Spanish and French in school. I was pretty good at both. Giving my Spanish a run-out was one of the things I loved most about backpacking in South America. '*Hablas muy bien,*' I was told by waiters and waitresses. 'You speak well.'

I open my eyes again. Wordsworth is ambling down the hill. Kiki is still watching me from the sunlounger. 'Daft question, eh? Sorry.'

Blink twice for no. Not at all daft. Just big. Bigger than I am used to.

I used to pour my feelings into music. Leaning back against the trunk of that weeping willow down there, or right here in the wooden lounger where Kiki is sitting, hugging her knees, or across the field, on a rug in front of the annexe – my home. I used to sit for hours with my guitar, working out the melody of my thoughts.

'It's good to see you here. I mean, having seen it in your videos. Because they're sweet, especially the songs you write.' She's blushing, not just her cheeks but her throat all the way down to those ludicrous dungarees. 'It must be amazing to make up something so perfect.' I'm not sure why she's screwing up her face like that.

'I'm jealous because I don't have any talents. I can't sing or, you know, paint or write poems. I'm terrible at sports. Merv says I even pour a rubbish pint. That's what I mean. You can do all of it and not everybody's that lucky.'

Lucky?

She's turned away to gaze down towards the dogs by the stream. 'Sorry. I talk too much. You should tell me to shut up.'

I think perhaps I'd like to laugh. And actually, there is something I want to say. I blink a few times, but she's not looking. I've not quite mastered the noises yet. They seem to come when they want to. But I tell myself I am going to make a sound. I dig into my throat. I summon it.

No noise comes, but she turns towards me all the same. 'Sorry, Ned. Did you want to say something?'

She holds up the alphabet grid. 'I'll try not to be too useless with the letters,' she says. And she isn't.

I tell her row two, third letter – G. Fifth row, first letter – U. Third row, first letter – I. Fourth row, sixth letter – T. First row, first letter – A.

'Guitar?' She grins at me and I blink once for yes, just as there is the clink of china knocking together and the clearing of a throat behind me and then Maxwell steps into view, carrying a teapot and cups on a tray. Biscuits too. A shortbread selection. God, I miss biscuits.

'What's that you two are talking about?' he asks.

Kiki looks into my face. 'I think Ned would like us to fetch a guitar,' she says. And I blink once for yes, because that is exactly what I want.

*

'Comfortable with your bed like that?'

Blink.

'Light off now?'

Blink.

'Music too?'

Blink. Blink.

'Righty-ho. So keep the nice music on and just the light off?'

Blink.

'Night then, Ned.'

Night, Tammy.

The nice music is playing on a repeat loop from the iPad on the table. Maxwell recorded it on his lovely old Gibson. It is perhaps not the most sophisticated tune ever written, but all things considered, I am pleased. Exhausted, too. My eyes ache. There was a time when Maxwell first taught me to play and he would spend hour upon patient hour helping me to perfect my fingering. This felt like going back to those long nights, except harder, with me having to blink for every chord root and key, before even bringing in the rhythms and the configurations. And there was Kiki, shaking her head, smiling, and saying it sounded like we were speaking another language.

'Like this?' Maxwell would ask. And I'd blink my answer. *No, try A. Yes, nice. Separate out the notes.*

All of that effort for – what? – these few bars. Sixty seconds, maybe, of music, waiting for lyrics and a melody. But still – this is something I have done. That chord change for example – that's choice, as Kiki would say. Maxwell is a lovely player – it's nice. It reaches the end and starts again. We need to change the dominant seventh in the third bar, I think. But still.

My eyes are sore and heavy. I can feel the breaths from my nostrils tickling my lips and I am dribbling. The music is beginning to feel like part of me and I'm picturing the field again, with the stream at the bottom and Kiki Moon shaking her head and saying how incredible to make music from nothing. And she's running down to play with Hector and

Wordsworth. I am following her, running after her with the long grass around my feet. And I can hear the music and I can smell the meadow. And I shout to Kiki that I've thought of something, that there's something I need to say . . .

*

My eyes open again to darkness. There are some words whispering to me in my head, too. *I lost my voice but found a tune.* I should write it down. I'll forget otherwise. I should turn on the light and grab a pen while it's fresh in my mind. But I'm so tired. Maybe I'll just close my eyes for a moment more.

MRS M

OGER'S WHISKY SEEMS TO have vanished. In the cabinet where there used to be his twenty-one-year-old rare island malt, is something which calls itself Highland Fling Blended and appears to be from Tesco. There are forks in the knife drawer and vice versa. My curtains are hanging loose, as if I was in possession of no tiebacks. There are dog hairs on the sitting room sofas, along with dark stains that one can only guess might be some sort of spillage.

I distinctly doubt that there has been any dusting done in my absence.

However, the bouquet of carnations in the vase on the kitchen worktop is a thoughtful touch. And the baking smell that greeted me is explained by the cake beside it – an attempt at a Victoria sponge, rather messily iced, with the words 'Welcome Home'.

'How very sweet,' says Amir, the occupational therapist. 'Look what your carer's made for you.'

I concentrate on my reply and manage to say, 'Not carer', and 'sloppy'. Because, technically, Kiki Moon is merely to be a temporary helper and dog walker. If she were a real carer she would not be leaving me this Sunday when she goes to the Glastonbury Pop Festival, now would she? An informal helper is what she is.

Also one can see that she has not allowed the icing to cool sufficiently before piping on the lettering. This is why the colours have bled so.

Still, it seems to have met approval with Wordsworth's sense of smell, since here he is, all of a sudden, tail wagging away. He seems altogether more interested in the cake than he does in my return.

And really, it is me doing Kiki the favour, since no young lady in her right mind would voluntarily lodge at The Fox and Hounds if there was a comfortable alternative. I believe that she is there working at this very moment, so I shall wait for her arrival rather than offer Amir a piece of cake right now. In any case the arrangement is only for a few weeks, before she embarks on her European travel, by which time I shall be recuperated enough to live on my own.

'You should come with me,' she said the other day, quite out of the blue. 'What do you reckon, Mrs M? We could go travelling together.' Or rather what she said was, 'We could go, like, travelling together, eh?' I have been meaning to speak to her about her English usage. It really could do with improvement.

She made reference to Harriet's silly poem again – this time the part about new countries and new food and that nonsense about sunbathing in the nude. I had to explain that it was Harriet's fruity sense of humour, not something she was seriously advocating – because, my goodness, what would Roger have said about that? – and that anyway I was not about to take up backpacking at my age.

I doubt whether I should be eligible for insurance in any case.

'So, Mrs Malley, you have the grab frame in the downstairs toilet and you're quite sure that you will manage without a rail by the front door?' Amir is being terribly thorough in his home assessment. 'Shall we have a look at the garden together now?'

The bolts and handle on the kitchen door are rather harder to open than they used to be, however I achieve the objective eventually. Wordsworth runs straight out. He doesn't seem to have much concern that I am obliged to go slowly with this dratted walking stick.

The jasmine around the windows has grown and, my goodness, the clematis will need some cutting back. It is also abundantly clear that a naughty hound has been intent on digging up the lawn while I have been away – all those bare patches where the earth has been scooped back into holes. Still, I suppose one should be grateful that the grass, what remains of it, appears to have been satisfactorily mown.

KIKI

GLASTONBURY FESTIVAL.
The actual Glastonbury.
Just look at it.

It's incredible.

And I'm really here.

Ned – I hope you can see this – oh, no, wait, that's wrong, there's nothing flashing on this phone of yours. Let me see. That's the camera. That's right. So – let's see. Video. Is that it? Numbers moving. That's it then? Yes, I've got it now.

Glastonbury.

Just look.

Here, let me turn your phone in a circle like this – see that? It is bigger and louder and more colourful than anything I ever imagined. It's just so huge. I mean, Yaya said it was huge. But it's huger. It smells of doughnuts and spices, and sewage and farm and smoke and candy floss, and it is so hot. And everywhere you go and everywhere you look, there are people dancing and laughing and singing and walking and sitting and talking and – and music and noise and so many people – and look at this, Ned. Can you see this? Can you see?

I've been here an hour and I am still just walking around, with no plan, because I don't know where to go or what to do. There was an old film that I watched with Sue, back in Auckland. It was about this boy who had no hands but only scissors and he learns to use them like fingers, I can't remember why, but there's this young woman and she loves him. And there's this bit where she's standing with her arms out wide and she's looking up at the sky and she's spinning around. And there's snow falling on her, but really, it's ice from a snow statue that the boy is making with his knife-scissor-fingers. And she's just spinning and spinning with all this white ice snow falling. That's how I feel now. Not the snow, because it's so, so hot – but like I'm spinning. All around me are jugglers and rainbow colours and fishnet tights and sequins and glitter and smiling and people holding hands and gumboots and dusty feet in sandals. And I need to think about where I'm going and what I want to do, but I can't. I can't think about anything. I'm just watching, not even knowing where to look, because it is just so big.

How did Yaya never tell me it was like this? She said it was big. She said it was huge. Enormous, she said. So maybe OK, she did try to say it. But this is like a whole country. It's a different world.

Maybe it's just as well that Chaplain, Antony I mean, could only get me this ticket for Sunday. I don't really mean only – it was him who said only. His father knew one of the artists who was playing today and I had to arrive at the same time as the crew. Antony said he was sorry it wasn't for the whole festival. What a thing to say, because it's the sweetest thing anyone has ever done. Meredith would have killed me for this ticket, even if she tried to tell me that it's not such a big deal because it's only for the one day. Then she asked who the band were, and when I told her she said, 'Never. They're legend.'

Anyway, if I had four days of this, I might have exploded. Just look at it. Look at me.

If Yaya could see me, she'd cry.

She always talked about this. Our family story. You see that little girl wearing the Spiderman suit, the one sitting on the shoulders of the man in the tutu and the Viking helmet – that's about how old I was when I was last here with Yaya and Grandad and my mum. Yaya always promised we'd come back.

Well, Yaya, I'm here.

*

So this is going to be the end of the recording because the battery is flashing, and I reckon it means all the power is gone. But, Ned, you've seen most of everything, I think. All those massive fields with all those stages and people dancing and all that music. And the theatre and circus bit, I mean, that was epic. So hot though. It gets hot back home but you don't have all these people around with no shade. It's lucky Mrs M gave me this hat otherwise I'd have poached. I've been to the Green Fields and the Healing Field and the Greencrafts Village and that place with the naked people hitting each other with branches and the tent with the opera singer and the Beatles. Not the real Beatles, of course. But they were really good.

And now I've climbed up to the top of the hill, here, by the Glastonbury sign, to show you this view. I mean, just look, this view. I hope I've filmed it OK. I think I had my finger in the way a bit but then I worked it out.

Your phone is so clever. I have to buy one like this. It even shows me how far I've walked – this heart button here, well, you know of course – and, look at that, 13.2 miles. Thirteen miles. Lucky I didn't wear my gumboots or I wouldn't be able to walk at all now. My feet ache enough in these sandals. But – wait, wait, wait – Ned, you told me to show you what I wore and I completely forgot. Hang on. So. Let me see if I turn the phone round like this then you can see – Mrs M helped me choose. She pretended she wasn't interested but then she gave me this hat of Harriet's. And this scarf too. It's—

Oh.

The phone's dead.

Bye then, Ned.

That's probably better though. Because it's time to stop wandering around, doing this – whatever you call it – blog chat FaceTime thing. Because I do have something important to do here. If I'm really going to do it.

Which I am. Of course.

I've walked past four times already.

So.

Maybe now is the time.

Definitely. Now.

If I'm ever going to.

It's quite a long way back though.

If I go.

It's all the way back down the hill. Through the Sacred Space and the Green Fields into the craft village. Between the wood-whittling workshop and the friendship bangle tent. It's not easy to spot if you're not looking out for it. It's smaller than both of those pitches, and it doesn't have so many stands out the front, so you don't really notice it.

If I hadn't looked at the website and known that it would be here, I would never have come across it. Not by chance. I might have walked past it, and looked at the pieces of coloured glass hanging on the front of the tent. Even then, I'd never have noticed the sign. It's written in old-fashioned church writing. Sammy's Glass Art & Sun-Catchers. If I hadn't been looking out for it, I'd have walked on past without seeing that.

Not that I have looked at it yet, really. Just to see if it was there. So that I knew where to find it. But I was going past anyway. I was too busy to really have a proper look. And I couldn't stop straight away. I didn't have time to go in, or talk to anyone. Because of Ned needing me to do the videoing. I'd promised I would. So, really, I just had a glance. Or four glances. Because I went past four times.

Sammy's Glass Art & Sun-Catchers.

The writing – & Sun-Catchers – is the same as the sign behind my mum in the photo when she's holding me. I didn't realise that the first time. But it definitely is. I thought it when I went past the second time. And the third, I was even more sure. And on the fourth, I was certain. No question. It's the same.

Was this where Stan Douglas worked? Did my mum work with him there? Is that where they met? Before he poisoned her?

But look at me here, standing still, with the festival drifting past me, and me doing nothing, except getting out my water bottle because, you know, it is so hot. And the exit is just a little bit further up the hill. And I'm really tired. Knackered. But, do you know what I'm thinking about, just suddenly? I'm thinking about Wordsworth. I'm thinking about a scared little dog with a truck coming down the road at him. I'm thinking about the brakes making that horrible noise.

And now I'm picturing Mrs M, lying on the floor of her lounge with the fuck it bucket list poem and Mrs Beeswax's Housework Tips beside her. That might have been it. No more Mrs Malley. I'm thinking about Ned too, and how he was playing football one day, and then couldn't even move or speak the next. Just like that.

I have a glug of water.

There's a bashing of drums and a cheer so loud it feels like it's inside my ears. It must be a band that people like a lot, because everybody starts hurrying towards the stage, which is down the hill and to the left. I'm being jostled and pushed as the crowd decides it wants to go that way.

The Green Fields are the other way – they're down the hill too but to the right – and that's where Sammy's Glass Art & Sun-Catchers is. And I don't know who Sammy is, or why my mum was once listed as part of his company. Probably they won't even remember her. It's a really long time ago. I guess I'll never know if I don't ask though. I have to squeeze myself into spaces between people and shout, 'Excuse me,' over the music, every two or three seconds as I start heading that way down the hill.

NED

THE TOP OF THE Park Stage Viewing Tower is cut off by a pink finger-shaped blur, magnified to fill practically the whole of my iPad screen, which leaves just a glimpse of the twenty-metre-long rainbow ribbons.

'So, Ned, here you can see – oh, bugger, my silly thumb again, eh.' The picture rotates and lurches like it is on a rollercoaster. There is a flash of big round glasses, a straw hat and then the Glastonbury sign and a group of men wearing swimming trunks and flippers, with masks and snorkels.

Please, Kiki, stop for a moment. If I'm not mistaken that's Damon Albarn singing behind you and – wait, that's only the legendary Paul Simonon on bass. Paul Simonon, Kiki – of The Clash. *The Clash*. He's an actual living legend.

Kiki, turn around please. For once in your life show me the stage. Let me hear the band.

'And if we walk up the hill, look at these people over here, they look pretty happy, eh?'

For pity's sake. Simon Tong on guitar. Turn the camera round now. Please. At least let me see.

'But back this way, you'll love this even more. I need to show you the teepee village, Ned. It's epic. There's, like, this amazing feather art. And there's this old man who plays drums on tortoise shells. Back in five.'

And off moves the camera, with unknown faces and unexpected outfits trooping into shot. And then all I can see is a rhythmic bounce over earth and feet. I suppose she's forgotten that she's still filming because I have a minute or so of pink jelly sandals and dirty toes with green nail polish and then another 'Bugger', and the screen of my iPad goes blank. Still, well done Kiki, for working out how to send it to me.

'Perhaps not a great threat to Spielberg. But it looks like she's having quite a . . .' Maxwell begins.

There's a ping. He peers and turns the tablet back for me to see.

'An Instagram post from Annabella. Or am I meant to say that she's posted another one to her story? Would you like me to open it?'

I blink.

Maxwell presses on the screen while also averting his eyes. Her outfit is a gold bikini top with a denim mini skirt and cowboy boots. Hair in plaits. Glitter on her cheekbones. Toby has a tie-dye bucket hat and tank top. Toby mate, good to see you're making the most of my ticket. I trust Hilary doesn't mind being left with the children all weekend.

That's Bella's friend Cressida, pairing the Hunters with the sequinned dress. And the man with the beard, bare chest and T-shirt slung over his shoulder? Her brother, Francis Rafferty. Leaning into the group selfie.

#Glasto2019 #BillieEilish #PyramidStage #RaffaProductions #MissYouNorton #WishYouWereHere

A line of heart emojis and smiley faces.

Blink. Blink. Blink. Blink. Alphabet grid, please, Maxwell.

But Maxwell is still looking away. Ever tactful. Although perhaps it's more than that. He's doing that thing, where he pinches his chin between his thumb and his forefinger.

He's been floating out thoughts for my approval all afternoon. *Do you think she's found the place yet? She will go, don't you think, Ned? Do you think she'll wait until the end of the day or go first thing? Do you think she's maybe already gone? Do you think she'll be terribly disappointed if they can't tell her anything?* Pinches chin. *It is the right thing for her to do, don't you think?*

Let's hope so, Maxwell, given it was your idea to check out the Companies House website, otherwise she wouldn't have known that this sun-catcher shop even existed. And it was you, Maxwell, who talked to Antony in the first place about how going to Glastonbury was so important to Kiki. But given she's talked about it since the first day we met her, I can't see that it's a bad thing.

He's doing it again, the chin-pinching. And he looks at me. 'But do you think she'll learn anything?'

MRS M

WASHES OUT WITH JUST one shampoo though, so only Kiki and Wordsworth even saw it. However, she is going to buy some more permanent dye next week. Can you think what Roger would have said? No doubt he would have blamed you, Harriet. He did always think that you were rather a bad influence.

I should have told him, 'Why yes, Roger, Harriet is an extraordinarily bad influence. That is why she is my friend.' I do wonder why I never said that.

Here. I brought some branches of jasmine. I wish you could smell them. Did you know that one can make tea by infusing the flowers? I've grown rather partial to it, although it's hardly Earl Grey. Bear with me – this poor old hand struggles rather now. Not the most elegant flower arranging, but it shall have to do.

Now where was I? Oh, yes. The hat. Your hat. A wide-brimmed boater with a lemon-yellow band – do you remember the one? Very fetching it looked. And I gave her that old Jaeger scarf of mine, the one that I discovered in the strawberry patch after wicked Wordsworth buried it. Well, I was never going to wear it again, but it still has those wonderful colours. She used it as a belt, which was rather ingenious I thought, around a pinafore dress which she had bought in a charity shop. It's surprising, actually, what interesting finds she comes back with from those places. The shoes I was not so certain about. They resembled something a toddler might splash around in, but I suppose the intended look was fun as opposed to elegant. I do wish you could have seen her, Harriet.

She was so excited when Maxwell arrived today to give her a lift. And nervous, I think. She has this notion that one of the stall holders knows something about how her mother died. I think that's why she was fussing so much about me.

She kept asking if I was quite certain that I would be all right without her. I had to tell her not to be so ridiculous and that I would be perfectly fine. I told her to go and enjoy herself. No doubt there will be stories for days to come.

And next weekend she is most insistent that I shall accompany her to a local festival. She says she will make garlands for us, which, Harriet, is altogether your fault. That silly old poem. Kiki seems to have acquired this notion that I wish to wear flowers in my hair.

KIKI

SAMMY'S GLASS ART & Sun-Catchers.

There is a chair outside the hut, a wooden deckchair with a stripy seat. It's empty, though, so maybe they've finished for the day. I'm probably too late. There are some metal frames, hanging from chains on a board, with patterns of coloured glass inside, triangles and circles and waves and squares. But there's nobody there, unless maybe they're inside. There's a curtain that's pulled shut. I'll be able to see better when I get a bit closer. Not that there's any rush. I'll do it in a minute.

I'm watching from this stall opposite which sells wind chimes made out of strips of drinks cans bent into spirals. I think the owner must be the man smoking his roll-up and humming to himself. He doesn't look like he cares whether I want to buy one of his wind chimes or not, even though I've been here for a really long time, tapping them to hear their clinking because there's no wind. It's still so hot – I keep having to take my hat off to use as a fan – and that makes the wind chimes clink too, but otherwise they're silent unless I'm tapping them, but mostly I'm just looking around at the people going past.

Sammy's Glass Art & Sun-Catchers.

The chair is still empty. Maybe they've gone to watch a band or buy some food. It must be dinner time. I'm pretty hungry after all this walking. The heat makes you tired and hungry too. So I guess I've missed my chance for Sammy's Glass Art & Sun-Catchers. Otherwise, there'd be someone there, you'd think. I'll go over and check in a moment. But after I've finished looking at these wind chimes. No big rush.

The next stall along is a potter's wheel. A woman with dreadlocks has a lump of clay between her hands. The sign says 'Fire-powered wheel' and I can smell the smoke from the logs that are burning beneath the wheel. It's clever how it makes it turn. And the lump of clay is rising up into a tunnel. I'm watching it grow taller between her hands, and she pulls it wider and it wobbles and warps. But then the sound of tambourines and flutes makes me look up and in the corner of a field, there is a man and a woman. She's wearing a wedding dress and he's in a suit jacket, but with football shorts instead of trousers, and they are walking towards me, with their arms out straight in front of them, holding hands, and their hands are wrapped together with ribbons. There is a group of people around them – five or six of them have tambourines and another has a flute. Two others are holding branches over their heads as they walk. And when they are right in front of me, they stop, and they kiss. Their friends cheer.

The potter looks up from her wheel and calls out, 'Happy handfasting.' The couple smile at her and then they carry on through the field, with their friends dancing along behind them. I'm watching them go and then I turn my head back, still thinking about the word 'handfasting' and also about how hot she must have been in that dress. One of the ribbons from around their hands, a green one, has fallen onto the dusty ground. And I'm just thinking how it looks like the shape of an S, when I realise there is someone sitting in the chair in front of Sammy's Glass Art & Sun-Catchers. A moment ago,

I was thinking how hungry I was. Now, it's like my stomach is suddenly full.

It's not Stan Douglas though. Because it's a woman.

Not that it would have been him. He's probably in prison still. He'd have been jailed for life, wouldn't he. For poisoning my mother.

I've always imagined he'd be very tall with dark hair and a handsome but angry face, thick eyebrows and maybe an earring. No reason except I have a feeling that's what he looks like.

This woman has brown hair that's rolled up and clipped on top of her head, except for some bits that have escaped out of the sides. Those bits are more grey than brown. She's wearing a black sun top and a long skirt and she's holding a mug in both her hands. She looks, well, normal. I really don't think she can have anything to do with my mum being poisoned. And it was twenty-two years ago. So what am I meant to say? What am I even going to—

Kiki, what is all this worrying about? There's only one way for you to find out.

I can't feel her. No star dust. No glimmering. Just the voice. It's like it's only me thinking it – like it's just in my own head.

But she's right.

There is only one way to find out.

I'm going to go over. Right now. But I'm so thirsty. And there's only the tiniest bit of water left in my bottle. So I gulp it down. I'd like to go and fill up my bottle. But not yet. Because I'm going to do it. I mean, I am doing it. See, I'm walking over. My mouth feels dry and my stomach feels sore.

She's looking down at her cup, but maybe she hears me, because she turns her head. I should have decided what I was going to say though, because I think she's about to ask if she can help me and I find myself saying the first words that come into my mouth, 'I wonder if you knew my mum? I think she used to be part of this company. Ages ago. She died. My name's Kiki Moon. My mum was called Ioanna. Like Joanna but spelt with an I. I think my—'

'Kiki Moon?'

Her chair is quite low so I'm staring down at her. It's like her whole face is staring back at me. 'You're Kiki Moon?'

I'm hot, and so thirsty. I want to take my hat off to fan myself, but I have my hands in front of me and I'm squeezing my thumbs tight, like I'm waiting for something to happen.

'Kiki. Wow. Yes. I can see it in your face.' She takes a sip from her cup, with both her hands around it. 'I didn't know you were even in England. I didn't—' She pauses before she speaks again.

'I'm Sammy. I'm so sorry. You must hate me.'

Then she starts crying.

*

Yaya blamed Sammy. After my mother died, Sammy kept trying to phone Yaya to talk. Yaya refused to speak to her. Sammy wrote letters trying to explain. I think somewhere in my brain, right at the very back of my memories, I can see Yaya ripping a sheet of paper into pieces and saying angry things in Greek.

I wish Yaya was here now – in this wooden hut, at this camping table, drinking a bottle of beer too and listening to what Sammy has to say. Maybe even Yaya might have listened. Because every time I think Sammy's stopped crying, she starts again.

'Jo wanted to show me it could be done. We'd started making these sun-catchers, you know, little glass pictures of the sun

or the moon or flowers or animals, like those ones up there,'
She points to the wall behind. There are little round glass
pictures of flowers and butterflies and rainbows. I know what
a sun-catcher is. I had one in my window when I was little. It
had two stars and a moon.

'They were for hanging where the sun would come through
and catch the colours. Jo's idea. They were for children, and
Jo was the one who sold them. She was brilliant with children.'

'Did you call her Jo?' Yaya always used my mum's full name,
although mostly she said 'your mother'. *Do not give me that
look, Kiriaki. You have the same naughty eyes as your mother.*

Sammy smiles, although she's still crying. 'Jojo mostly. That's
what she would sing to you, *'Jojo loves her Baby Moon.'*

She's quiet for a moment. There's an electric fan on the
table, it whirrs and creaks as it turns towards me. I feel the
air on my face. Then it moves back the other way. Sammy
starts talking again. 'I'd make them – the sun-catchers – in my
studio and we'd sell them alongside my bigger pieces of glass
art. But Jo had this idea of turning it into more of a craft
activity – letting children choose their own glass beads to go
into frames, so that we could fire them for them to buy and
take home. I had to keep telling her that it was more complicated than she thought. We'd need to transport a glass kiln to
all these different festival sites and find power sources and
shelter. I'd suggested during the winter we could buy a port-
able kiln and work on the idea. We were too busy all summer
for something new.'

She breathes in slowly and out again.

'She was always so headstrong though. Jo never liked to let
an idea go. And she'd seen somebody using a fire pit to fire
pottery at one of the shows we'd done. I'd explained to her
that pottery and glass were very different and what worked

for one wouldn't work for the other. But she seemed to think that I was just being precious. She laughed about me not liking change and said she'd had to push me to sell the sun-catchers in the first place, which was true. I'd made the first one for you, you see, and Jo had insisted other children would love them too. She said I was too much of a head-in-the-clouds artist and I needed her to spot opportunities.'

Sammy's standing up, but it's only to go to the little fridge and take out two more beers – she passes one to me. 'I was at this arts festival up in Cumbria and Jo wasn't due to be there. But she wanted to surprise me. She left you with your grandparents to drive up and join me. Except by the time she arrived I'd already shut up shop and gone for some food with friends. If she'd just come to join us, she'd have been fine. But she had this stupid idea in her head. She'd brought an old barbecue with her, and she fired it up and she put these glass beads inside some of our sun-catcher frames and lay them on fireproof sheets and then had them sitting directly on the coals. I think she pictured me coming back and finding that she'd managed to do this thing she'd been talking about. Maybe everything would still have been OK, but it started raining so she wheeled the barbecue over to my camper van.

'The flames were already out, but you know how the coals stay white-hot and smoky. So she put it under the van's awning, out of the rain. She must have thought it was all right there, because she had the door shut. But the camper's window was open. And it was a windy evening. And—' She's looking up at me. 'You know what carbon monoxide is?'

I nod. I don't know much but I've heard stories.

'Carbon monoxide is a poisonous gas. You don't see it or smell it but that barbecue was churning it out and the wind was blowing it through the window. And Jo was – Jo was sitting in there – doing these sketches of designs, because she was so certain that her idea would work and that she'd have this lovely surprise that would prove how silly I'd been to doubt her. And all the time, she was breathing in these fumes.

'By the time I came back, she was unconscious. She died in hospital the next day. And you know what the stupidest thing is?'

There was a cat in the upstairs flat in Auckland and it used to watch me coming up the stairs. Sammy's eyes are like that. I shake my head.

'The glass in those sun-catchers cracked. Exactly as I'd always told her it would, because of course the heat doesn't— Sorry, Kiki. Doesn't matter. But your grandmother blamed me. She didn't really understand about the carbon monoxide, she only seemed to take in that it was smoke from my coloured glass that had blown in and killed Jo.'

It's awkward to have her giving me that look again. Because it's like she's trying to ask something with her eyes and I don't know what. I'm thinking maybe this is one of those times when Sue would say I shouldn't talk for the sake of saying something. So I don't. I just listen.

'And then there had to be an inquest, up in Cumbria where she died. The verdict was death by misadventure. But until then your grandmother had assumed that Jo and I were just workmates who shared a flat. Just friends. The inquest meant, of course, I had to answer all these questions about us. And I think that was the final straw. I don't think it was a moral thing. But I think she felt I'd – I don't know – taken her daughter away from her, because of there being this thing she hadn't known about her. Something Jo had chosen not to tell her. She hated me after that.'

Hold on. What was it Yaya hadn't known?

I hope I'm not staring, I don't want to be rude – and maybe I should say something. Because this feels like – I don't know – a moment. But – wait – did you think I knew this, Sammy? Because I didn't know. I don't think so. I didn't even know you existed before today. I should say something? I probably, definitely should. But, give me a moment. Because I'm not, you know, shocked. I'm just a little bit . . .

You spend your life thinking one thing. Or not even thinking it. Just assuming. And I just need a moment.

Sammy's stopped talking. I reckon she can see I'm trying to put all my questions in my head into order. Because this is fine. It's different. But it's fine. But what about Yaya? What about my book of secrets? Where even is Cumbria? I didn't know very much about how my mum died, but I did know where it happened. That one thing. I even wrote it down. *Glasonby*. Six-year-old spelling, but I was only little.

The sun-catchers on the wall are hanging from nails by ribbons. The bigger frames are more – what do you call it? – abstract, just shapes and colours and lines. You think you can see a picture of something in there, you just can't quite see what it is.

'My mum died in Glastonbury. Yaya and Gramps both said that.'

Sammy's shaking her head but with smiling eyes. 'No, not Glastonbury. I think maybe you heard it wrong. The arts fair was in a little village called Glassonby. Jo and I made jokes about how similar it sounded. It's near Penrith. It's very beautiful. There are stone circles there.'

I'm looking at the neck of my beer bottle. Not drinking.

'Is that why I couldn't order the death certificate?' I say, half to myself. 'Wrong place. Pam said I needed to do a wider search. Except the website didn't have it either. You'd have thought it would have shown.'

Sammy's reaching out and touching my arm. 'Which name did you use? Moon? You know about the deed poll, right? You know Jo'd changed her name?'

Too much. Sorry what, Sammy?

I'm on a merry-go-round and it's heaps too fast. I can't even focus on what I'm seeing. I can't even say, no, I don't know anything. All I can do is just stare and watch everything I thought I knew blur as it spins. No I didn't know about a deed poll. Nobody ever told me. Except, as I'm spinning, I'm hearing echoes of Yaya's voice. 'Deep hole.' 'Why did my Ioanna have to change?' Maybe they did tell me. Or maybe I listened, when they didn't know I was listening. I just didn't understand.

Glassonby. Deep Hole. It's like that moment in the cartoons when the character's running, and they've gone right off the end of the cliff and they keep going. Run, run, run. But then they look down. And they see there's nothing there.

All those lies Yaya said about my mum – killed by a fire, a camper van accident, leaking gas – perhaps they were all true. She just didn't realise I didn't understand. She thought I knew.

'What did she change her name to?'

Some people have ways of looking at you and it makes you feel calmer. Sammy's like that. She has a very calming face.

'Did you ever hear about the Newbury bypass? Or the protesters who chained themselves to trees to try to stop them being cut down?' And then she smiles. 'Of course you didn't. You were only a baby.'

'Crusties, you mean?' I say. And Sammy smiles.

'If you like. Though we saw ourselves more as protesters. Because it mattered. These trees being replaced by roads, it mattered then because if we could have . . . Anyway. We'd both been moved on a few times and some of our friends had even been jailed. I suppose you know your mother wanted to be a lawyer. She'd have been a really good one too. Well, it was her idea – the deed poll. She came up with it. A whole group of us did it. We all changed our names to Free. Your mum said it was only a gesture but it was like a fist in the air. If any of us were arrested again, and they asked for our name, we'd say our name was Free, and it would be true. And if they arrested a whole lot of us, they'd ask us each, and we'd all give them the same answer, 'We are free'. We'd chant that at them sometimes when they were trying to bring us down from the trees.'

Sammy pauses.

'But your mum never did anything they could lock her up for. She would never have let anyone take her away from you.'

There is concern in her face. Maybe I'm looking a bit lost even though this feels like a good thing to know.

'Ioanna Free.' I'm saying the name out loud, and feeling a bit less giddy. I swallow some of my beer. I'm spinning less.

My mother died in an accident after she breathed in carbon monoxide. And she'd changed her name, which I reckon was the glitch in finding her birth certificate. Not just me being a total dodo. She changed her name because she was clever, and good. My mum loved trees. And she loved me. She wanted to wave her fist, but I was her Baby Moon.

I hold the bottle of beer against my forehead.

But what about Stan Douglas? What about him? He can't have poisoned my mum if this is how she died. So where does he fit in?

The fan turns towards me and puffs out air. And I take a gulp of my beer.

And I realise something.

I realise I've always thought Stan Douglas was my father. Not consciously. Not once have I thought it through to myself like this before, never, 'Stan Douglas must have been my father'. Never consciously. But deep down, it's what I've thought. That there was this man who poisoned my mother because – I don't know – she didn't love him enough, or she loved him too much. Some dramatic story. Tragic. Romantic.

And I'm starting to ask Sammy, 'Who was Stan Douglas?' And Sammy's looking at me like she's never even heard the name.

It's a knot in my head. A tangle.

Except even as I'm repeating the name and hearing myself saying it out loud, I can hear Yaya in my head, whispering it to Gramps that night. 'How can I move on when our Ioanna was poisoned by Stan Douglas?'

And I know. Even as I'm saying it again.

Because I stop halfway through: 'Stan D-uh-glass'.

I say it again to myself, 'Stan d-oh-glass'. And of course. Of course.

Yaya, whisper-sobbing in Yaya-ish to Gramps. And me, a sleepy six-year-old, listening to her, and then writing down what I heard. Or thought I heard. My secrets.

Stan Douglas never was Stan Douglas.

Stan'd (little sob) uh-Glass. Not Stan Douglas. Stained glass. Stained glass poisoned my mother. No wonder Yaya told me I was making it all up.

'Another beer?'

I nod. As Sammy's kneeling down to reach into the mini fridge, I see something. There's a tattoo on Sammy's shoulder. Two stars and a moon. When I was little, the sun-catcher in my window had this same picture. You know how sometimes you talk before even knowing you're about to speak. That's me now, 'Look at your tattoo'.

Sammy passes me the beer and, for a moment, her hand is on it and mine is too. She nods and turns around again to show me the tattoo better. 'Second star to the right. This was the design of that first sun-catcher, the one I made for you. Jo had the same tattoo. She had this thing about Peter Pan. But you must know that? She used to – here – wait, let me show you.'

There is a bag hanging from a hook on the wall, next to all the glass pictures. The bag is woven from string and beads and Sammy pulls out a leather purse. She opens the purse and she takes out a photograph. My mother is wearing a short green dress with a skirt that has lots of pieces of material that are shaped like leaves. On her head, she has those things – boppers, maybe? – like two bouncy stems sticking up from a band, with gold stars on the end. And on her shoulders are big gold wings. She's holding a little girl – me. They both look really happy. We look happy.

Sammy is saying I can keep the photograph. She says she has the negative and when I ask what a negative is, she laughs and says, God, that makes her feel old. She says, wait, she must give me her card, too, then I'll have her number – and I let her take my number too, so she can call me. And why don't I come to the studio once her crazy summer's over.

I'm still studying my mother and me. Because this was really her. All this time.

'Did she speak in poems?' I ask.

'Poems? She wasn't as eccentric as the outfit suggests. It was just a thing she did for the kids because they thought it was – wait, you mean, like *"our sun-catchers will catch the light – and find the second star to the right"*. Yes, yes, yes. You're absolutely right. For the children who came to the stall. The kids loved it. My God, Kiki, I haven't thought about that in years. She'd do it on the protests too. Her and Ziggy seeing who could come up with the best rhymes. Like *"We are right. We are free. You'll have to pull us from this tree".*

She's smiling and shaking her head and saying how funny to remember that. And when I ask her who Ziggy is, she says, 'Ziggy's your father.'

And if there was a merry-go-round in my head before, I'm suddenly in one of those fairground rides that sends you flying up into the air and round and over and under until you don't have the first clue what's happening.

*

It's funny how time moves. It doesn't feel like I've been talking very long, but it's dark outside when I hug Sammy and leave the hut. I have the photo and Sammy's card in my bag, and my head is so full of all of this new knowledge. So many things to think about, but I can't even think where I should be going now.

All around me there are people and colours and sounds and smells.

Maxwell said he'd be happy to come and pick me up. But I don't think that's fair on him. And I don't know if I'm ready to leave.

There is one thing that I do know for certain. I need a wee. All that water and beer. But look at that queue, the doors ahead swinging open and then the next person going in and us all shuffling up one, trying not to breathe in too deeply – and you see the feet as they sit down or stand up and I'm all but hopping. So all I'm thinking about is getting to the front and it being my turn and – my God – what a relief when I do and it is. When I come out again, I'm still not really thinking straight, just letting everything bounce around my head. Because there's so much bouncing around in there.

Ziggy wasn't my father's real name. It was Mark something, Sammy thought. Dixon or Nixon – Sammy couldn't remember because everybody only ever called him Ziggy. She said she'd ask around. Someone might know.

Everyone liked Ziggy. He and my mum were great friends and she'd always said to Sammy that ending up in bed with him was one of the drunkest, stupidest things she'd ever done.

'She was glad though because it meant she ended up with you,' Sammy told me. 'But she was in London when she found out she was pregnant. You know that's where she moved for her studies? She tried to get in touch with Ziggy but he was never easy to find at the best of times. It turned out he'd gone off to Canada – I think, or Japan maybe – to protest against the clubbing of seal cubs. It's horrific what – anyway, nobody saw him for years. He didn't know about you. I don't think he knew about what happened to Jo until years later.'

I'm coming out of the festival dunny and the sink is like one long farm trough. And as I'm washing my hands, I'm still thinking about all of this. I had a dad. His name was Ziggy. When I told Sammy how Yaya said she couldn't tell me anything about my father except that he was one of the crusties, she laughed and said, well, fair enough. I asked what he looked like and she said average white boy with dreadlocks and a holey jumper, although somebody she knew said they'd run into him at a festival about ten years ago, and the hair was cropped short and receding. She didn't have a clue where he was now though. 'Ziggy wasn't the Facebook type,' was what Sammy said. Maybe somebody would know something but best not to hold my breath.

I'm not holding my breath, but I'm kind of lost in my thoughts, trying to picture what he might look like, and I realise I'm still standing here with the water running over my hands. And there's someone next to me. She's tall and blonde and she has her hair in plaits and a straw hat on, a bit like mine, except probably heaps newer. And maybe I would normally be too shy to say anything, but it's been quite a day, and when I realise who it is, her name pops out of my mouth, 'Annabella.'

She gives me this does-she-know-me look. Because of course she doesn't.

'Sorry. You don't know me. I'm just Kiki,' I say. 'Ned's friend. Norton's. Or not friend, but I've met him heaps of times at the hospital.'

I wonder if Sue would say this is one of those times when I shouldn't be talking so much, but it's fine because this Annabella is smiling and giving me a hug and saying, of course, she's heard all about me, and asking if I'd like to come and have a drink with her friends.

ONE WEEK LATER
NED

L IFE, WHAT HAVE YOU done to me?

For the last week, all I have heard about has been Glastonbury, Glastonbury, Glastonbury. I have listened to the stories, and watched the video clips, and looked at the photographs. I have yearned and envied and resented.

And here I am, being wheeled from the mobility taxi to the village green which, along with two nearby fields, comprises the summer festival of Paddocks Knowle. Or rather Fête-stival, as the welcoming banner proclaims. No doubt some committee member is particularly proud of that brainwave.

But even this feels too loud. Too open. Too busy.

It feels too much.

It is drizzling, in that non-committal English way. The air smells of hay and petrol lawnmowers. 'All You Need is Love' is being massacred by a brass band somewhere on the other side of the green, and is competing with fairground-type organ music and children's laughter, which I'm guessing is coming from the bouncy castle. The organ music sounds like an old-fashioned merry-go-round, but it's probably just a recording. If I could turn my head, I would look to see where it was coming from.

I am here because my music students from St Gilda's School are giving a performance at 3.35 p.m. and have invited me to watch. Maxwell knows the head teacher, Mrs McCready.

He had everything to do with organising this excursion. Kiki had already roped him into bringing her with Mrs Malley – hence why I am being chaperoned by Antony and Mikey. It is generous of them as they are both doing this in their spare time. Once again, I am aware my complex needs have meant a lot of planning. The consultant wasn't keen. I should be grateful. No, no, I *am* grateful.

'My pleasure, champ, it'll be fun,' Mikey told me in the taxi. 'Pom might swing past to say hello too.' In my old life, I think I would have had a lot of time for Mikey. It is him who is pushing me now, holding a golf umbrella above me. A pair of young women do double-takes as we pass. Their gazes bounce off me and fix on him and there is a twisting feeling inside my chest.

Antony is at my side, and between them, he and Mikey are giving the running commentary, 'Look, a raffle. Perhaps we should buy a ticket. It's for the village youth group.' That's Antony.

'A bottle tombola. Never again. I won a bottle of crème de menthe on one of those, once, and downed it all. I vomited mint-coloured puke.' That's Mikey.

As if my big day out was not exciting enough, Bella floated that she might be bringing Francis Rafferty along with a cameraman. 'Isn't that amazing?' she has asked me more than once in the past few days, offering me the chance to share my 'journey', in the same way that a cat might proudly bring you a dead mouse. *Norton's return to village life*. There is no sign of them yet, though. Perhaps an emergency dog food commercial came up.

The wheels of my chair bump and bounce on the earth. I bump and bounce too, and bodies pass me on the left and right or step out of my way, while faces make that concerted effort to neither stare nor be caught looking away. It's what I used to do not so long ago and it occurs to me that perhaps I am living through some sort of retribution. Perhaps I did die after all and this is now Hell presenting itself as a village fête.

'Look who it is.' Antony's range is from sympathetic listener to eager enthusiast, which is where we are now. 'It' is Maxwell, in linen trousers and a short-sleeved shirt which I have never seen before. It has a green leaf print that may not be quite Hawaiian, but nor is it his regulation white or grey. He is arm in arm with an elderly lady whose white hair has streaks of vivid pink. There is a daisy chain circling her head. The last time I saw her she was in a dressing gown and pointing a trowel at me. Now she has one of those hospital-issue walking sticks with the three little feet in the other hand, and is wearing a Barbour jacket over ivory trousers, and a pair of very strange wellington boots. They have frog faces on the toes.

Kiki's boots are black and about as conservative as any item of clothing I have ever seen her wear. I can only assume a welly swap has taken place. But she too has new pink streaks in her hair, along with a daisy chain of her own on her head. She is wearing a green plastic poncho.

'Ned, you're here.' Look at her, bounding like she is skipping over a rope. I can't imagine Kiki Moon was ever on the school athletics team. 'Hi Antony. Hi—?'

Mikey and Kiki introduce themselves to each other and Kiki pulls the alphabet grid from the back of my seat without checking whether I have anything to say right now. This one's a slightly different model that Pom thought would be good for me. The letters are arranged the same but they're in clear plastic, so it's like Kiki and I are looking at each other through a window, just with the letters stuck on it. Pom has added in a question mark and a smiley face, which is to say I'm joking. Kiki holds it up. 'What's up with you then, Ned?'

It's like having a puppy. You don't have the heart to say no and watch the ears go down. She's waiting. Just beyond her, a mother and a young child have stopped. They are licking ice creams and staring at us.

Sod it. Here we go.

Third row, fourth letter – L, third row, first letter – I, third row, third letter – K, second row, first letter – E, end word. L-I-K-E. Fourth row, sixth letter – T, second row, fourth letter – H, second row, first letter – E, end word. Second row, fourth letter – H, first row, first letter – A, third row, first letter – I. Fourth row . . .

'Hair? So is that "Like the hair"?'

Blink.

I glance up towards the smiley face.

'You mean, like, you like the hair? Our hair? My hair and Mrs M's?'

Blink.

Big grin. That imaginary puppy's tail would be wagging now. 'I'll do yours too, eh, Ned. I was trying to convince Maxwell he'd look good but for some reason he seems to think it wouldn't match his, like, style. I'll bring some dye in this week, eh. Maybe not pink, but, like, red or orange. What colour do you fancy?'

Third row, sixth letter – N. Fourth row, first letter – O. First row, fifth along, end word. Fifth row, third along – W. First row, first letter – A. Fifth row, fifth along – Y.

'No way?'

Blink.

'But you'd look great,' Kiki says at the same time that Mikey's saying he'll do it if I do, and how about blue, and Antony is saying, not him, though he's sure it would be most fetching on the rest of us. Maxwell is saying nothing, but he's smiling. They're all smiling.

Maybe I'm smiling too. Just not with my face.

'We made you a daisy chain. And one for Antony. Sorry, Mikey, I didn't know you'd be here. I can go and pick some more daisies and make you one quickly now if you like.'

Antony insists on donating his daisy chain to Mikey, so there is a lot of laughter as Mikey skips all the way around the chair, in his gym top and daisy crown, for me to see. The child with the ice cream is so fascinated that he has stopped licking it and is standing completely still, watching us, while melted Mr Whippy drips onto his fingers.

'And here's yours,' Kiki leans in towards me with it held in her two hands. I feel it being placed gently on my head. 'There. How perfect are you now, eh?'

With her hands still either side of my head, she kisses my cheek. I'm not expecting it, which must be why I feel a sudden little jolt of surprise in my tummy, like a camera lens clicking.

'Oh no.' She's laughing. 'Silly me. Our daisy chains are stuck together. Stay still a moment.' Her breath tickles against my ear.

I breathe in shampoo and soap smells, and something that I think is patchouli, and I feel her fingers in my hair, untangling us. 'Nearly there. Wait. Wait. OK. You're free.'

When she stands up, her cheeks are pink. For a moment, none of us says anything, and I'm not quite sure what that look that Kiki's giving me is, but then an announcement comes over the tannoy system thanking the Paddocks Knowle brass band for their Beatles medley and informing us that St Gilda's School will be starting their performance in five minutes.

*

Lucy Harrison is over-pressing her guitar strings more than ever and Tilly Carter-Smith's wrist is too slack on her violin. The ensemble is all strings apart from Elisa Hurst on the trombone. Elisa's performance might best be described as enthusiastic. Overall, the squeaks and the false starts make me think that perhaps Beethoven's 'Ode to Joy' is not thrilled at being chosen for the Class 9A band. The timing is not entirely right either, but then I suspect Mrs McCready has never conducted a band before. She was a chemistry teacher before becoming head. Still, the girls look as though they are enjoying themselves and hopefully it's too loud up there for them to hear how many of their audience are talking amongst themselves.

It is gallant of Mikey and Antony and Maxwell and Kiki to applaud as loudly as they do when the passage comes to an end. Even Mrs Malley is tapping her stick with her hand. The girls all look a little confused by the experience. Such conflicting expressions when I was wheeled up to the front of the field, from Tilly's look of shock to Katherine Nontwich's overexcited waving. It was the first time any of them have seen me since I was assessing their scales and arpeggios.

Now Suki Nathan – one of my guitar students – is coming to the microphone at the front of the stage and Mrs McCready is stepping out of her way to let her speak.

The world goes dark, apart from thin streaks of light, as I feel my face being covered, and the sound and touch of a kiss on my head.

'Hello, darling. Nice daisy chain. Sorry we're so late.' As Bella takes her hands from my eyes, she comes in front of me and gives me another kiss, this time on my lips.

At the same time, Suki, is saying, 'The 9A string band have one more song to play and we'd like to dedicate this one to Mr Edbury. Oh, gosh, sorry sir! I didn't mean to – sorry.'

Bella steps away from me, to laughter from all around us, and a few cheers. And this is when I realise that there is a cameraman behind her who is filming me, before panning round to Suki on the stage. Poor Suki looks as though she's forgotten what she meant to say next. She's looking down towards us, not speaking, but then she looks around to her classmates and back to the front, to me.

'We have one more song to play. Sir, you always said that the music all of us liked was rubbish and that one Bowie was worth ten Biebers. So, sir, we'd like to play this for you now. Because – well, sir, you'll always be a hero to us.'

I'm not sure even the great man himself would recognise his epic hit, played by three violins, two guitars, a viola, a cello and a trombone, as an instrumental, except for the chorus, which they sing with gusto having reworded it to, 'Sir you're a hero, just for 9A.' And yet, the stupid thing is that I'm having to tell myself that I must not cry. The bloody camera keeps moving between the performance and Bella's face and mine.

There's a hissing behind me – 'Don't forget disclaimers for the kids.' I'd like to tell Francis Rafferty to shut up.

The audience are giving this song more attention and there is applause at the end. Mrs McCready turns to the microphone and begins to say thank you to the girls of 9A, who planned this all by themselves. This is when Bella begins waving her arm and walking towards the stage, shouting, 'One minute. Please.' The camera is following her, climbing the steps in her tight jeans. 'If I might,' she says to Mrs McCready, who looks a bit baffled but lets Bella step into her place.

Bella blinks and smooths her hair. She bends closer to the microphone. 'I want to say Norton Edbury is my hero, too.' There are cheers and whistles.

'My name is Annabella Hopkins. On my twenty-eighth birthday last year, Norton asked me to marry him and I said yes.' More clapping. 'Since then so much has happened. Many of you might have heard about Norton's accident. Doctors don't know if he will ever walk or talk again, but to me, he is the same Norton I fell in love with.' More cheers.

'Norton, I've come up here to tell you that I've promised that we will share your story, and we will. And earlier today, I went to St Mary's Church in Paddocks Langley and talked to Father Sullivan there.'

She pauses. I have a dawning realisation of where this might be heading.

'On the twentieth of March next year I will turn thirty. I already know what birthday present I would like. The church is reserved for 4 p.m., at which time I am hoping to become Mrs Annabella Edbury. That is, Norton, if you will have me?'

People look from her to me. And when there is no reaction from me, they look back to her.

'One of you down there, grab his alphabet thing. Kiki – could you do that, please. Norton, darling, on my birthday next year, will you marry me?'

I cannot turn my head to look at the field of strangers around me, but I can sense every eye watching. There is a firm pat on my shoulder. I think it is Mikey.

Kiki steps into my line of sight and reaches for the communication grid from the back of my seat. She lifts it so that it's in front of me, but steps sideways so she's not obstructing my view. I can see the stage through the clear plastic but I can still see the letters. And to the side of my field of vision, I can see Kiki.

She has a strange look on her face. Bemused perhaps. Because does Bella not realise that 'yes' or 'no' are answers I can actually give without needing to count through the alphabet? What's wrong with one blink for 'yes', two for 'no'. Maybe this is what Kiki is thinking. Why would I need to spell out my answer, letter by letter?

But maybe Bella thinks it will give the moment more weight. Maybe it will encapsulate our journey better.

Kiki waits. She is looking down at the grid, not directly at me.

Bella waits.

I am lucky. Honestly, blessed. Bella is a good person. She's decent. She's beautiful, and she's ambitious and she loves me. She must do if she still wants me, even like this. That is not something I could have hoped for.

And – OK – I had my doubts. Yes, I tried to call things off. But Bella is right. Just cold feet. I would have changed my mind. And if not – well, I would have regretted it afterwards. And, after what has happened, most women would have been grateful to have been given a way out. Bella has been there every step.

I am lucky.

But as I begin to spell out my answer – fifth row, fifth along – Y – Kiki's eyes lift towards me. And there is a feeling in my stomach that is a little like falling.

MRS M

HARRIET USED TO ACCUSE me of being insensitive, which was unfair. All her rabbiting on about intuition and emotional intelligence. I believe she read articles about it in *Woman & Home* magazine. She used to say to me, 'Mary, you've always been far cleverer than I, yet you rarely pause to consider other people's feelings.' I had to tell her that the correct form is 'cleverer than me' and that, actually, it is kinder in the long run to say what people need to hear, rather than what they want to hear.

Take Harriet herself. After Eric left her for that dreadful woman, I had sympathy, of course. But eventually I had to say, 'Harriet, the moment has come to stop eating Walnut Whips and guzzling Scotch. You must move on.' There comes a point at which the measure of friendship is pointing out failings. 'Wallowing,' I told her, 'is not productive.'

Harriet said that perhaps polishing Roger's golf clubs was not productive either and that I should think about moving on myself. Of course that was merely Harriet being touchy. Roger had not left me for a member of the choir, after all. Anyway, he never liked me to touch his clubs.

In any case, Harriet was wrong. Look at me here, in Maxwell's Jaguar – with the roof up, because of the rain, but the windows open and the wind blowing in my hair – him driving and Kiki in the back seat. Do you not think, Harriet, that a person lacking in emotional intelligence would be unaware of how quiet that young lady is now? Maxwell has been the only one talking since we left the fête. Actually, it is rather fascinating to hear about the Basque network of resistance fighters who helped wounded allied pilots across the mountains to San Sebastian at the end of the war. And it is enlightening to learn a little about his research in artificial communications. He and little Pom have been looking into various technologies which might enable Norton to express himself through a smart tablet. They sound most ingenious. Maxwell also says he's going to teach me how to use E'mails, because goodness knows it took him long enough. So it's a most conducive conversation, albeit with him doing most of the talking. But in the normal way of things, all that one would be hearing would be that garbled flow of hers, 'Like, raffle and, you know, eh, morris dancers.'

Instead, she is gazing out of the window at the countryside. I do see this.

Harriet, do you think an insensitive person would have noticed her expression when Norton's fiancée came down from the stage and kissed him?

Nearly home. The turning takes us back towards Upper Piddleton, then it's left at the crossroads once we have come through the woods. What a clever back route Maxwell has taken. Perhaps Kiki will give Wordsworth a little trot while I offer him a cup of tea and a biscuit. I rather think that before she leaves for work, however, I shall have to sit her down for a chat. It is rather difficult – this dratted stroke and the words that will still not come – but she needs to hear it, and if not from me then from whom?

'Kiki,' I shall say, 'there will be other men and they will be far more suitable. You have spent half your life being a carer already.'

'Kiki,' I shall say, 'this is for the best, you shall see. You came to Europe to have an adventure so jolly well have an adventure, young lady.'

'Kiki,' I shall tell her – and to be honest I am rather looking forward to seeing her face when I do this – 'you suggested we might go on holiday to Greece together and I said it was a foolish idea. I said I was too old for such things. Well, I have a little surprise for you. I think perhaps I should like to do it after all.'

If that does not put the smile back on Kiki Moon's face, I do not know what will.

KIKI

MEREDITH DOESN'T LOOK TOO happy. Giving me these filthy looks, and every time I ask her something, she just snaps, like now, when I ask her if the pint glasses have gone on to wash and she just says, 'Nope,' and turns away.

What is up with everyone? Did I miss the message that today was act crazy day?

First there was Annabella doing her marriage proposal up on the stage – which was great – lovely – but still, pretty odd. Not that it wasn't all very – well, I'm thrilled for them, of course. Delighted. But they were engaged already, so was it really worth such a fuss? And it was meant to be the schoolgirls doing their thing for Ned up there, really. Their moment.

Then there was Mrs M, and I don't know what was going on with her either, because most of the time it's an effort to get her to say anything but today she was all, *sit down, and let's talk.* I had to say I was sorry but I didn't have the time. I think I'm a bit too tired, maybe, because it takes quite a lot of concentration to listen to what she's trying to say, and anyway I'd told Merv that I'd be at work early this evening.

But now there's Meredith, slamming bottles into the fridge and saying, 'So you didn't feel like meeting up?' And I don't know what she's talking about, so I say that but she gives me this look like everything bad that has ever happened in the world is all my fault.

'I cycled all the way to your crappy fête and you didn't reply to my text.'

I don't even know what she's talking about. She didn't send me a buggering text. So, like I say, it really must be every-body's-gone-mad day. But when I tell her I didn't get any message from her, she says, 'Yeah, right, sure,' and stomps off to clear tables.

And that's why I hand her my phone when she comes back. She's the one who's got this wrong, not me. 'Look for your-self,' I tell her. And I'm not trying to be – what's the thing everyone says? – passive-aggressive or any other type of aggressive. I'm just not in a very good mood. And I didn't get a text. I really didn't, so it's her who's made the mistake and not me. She must have sent it to someone else. But she just gets on with wiping down the bar. Meredith never wipes down the bar.

And when Turgid comes up to order a pint – his number two – she's still wiping so I serve him. And I reckon he can tell that something's up because he hardly says anything. He just says 'ta' and takes himself off to a corner without even sneaking a gawp at my chest, or hardly at all. Meredith mutters, 'Pervert,' and then she says, 'What piece of crap phone is this anyway? It's prehistoric.'

I can't remember what type of phone it is. There is a name written on it but I'm not sure what it is without looking. 'A BooWoo maybe? A HooWoo?'

Meredith snorts. But she's the one who's holding it so how would I know? Do I look like a mobile phone expert?

'You don't even have a password?' She says it like I've come into the pub without my clothes on. I shrug and say nothing.

'Anyway, it doesn't prove anything. You don't have any messages. I mean not a single one. You obviously just deleted it.'

I hope the look I'm giving her is as superior as the one she's giving me. It's not as if it's my fault there aren't any messages. The stupid phone deleted all the old ones, the ones from Sue back in Auckland and from her when I first arrived here, asking how I was. And the ones from Siobhan, the ratbag landlady in Stratford, about her room. All of the texts just disappeared. They must get rubbed off after a while. And I haven't had any messages to keep, not for weeks. Maxwell and Merv always phone. And Sammy. She phoned me last week. She didn't text. Nobody texts me.

'But – hang on – what settings have you even got this on? You've – hang on, your message preferences here – you've, why would you even do this? You've disabled your incoming messages. Was there a reason? Because why would you otherwise? It would be daft. Did you honestly mean to disable your texts?'

How do I answer that? I didn't even know that you could disable your texts. I wouldn't have had the first clue how to do that. I don't want to lie but I don't want to look stupid. So I don't answer, I'm just doing this thing, like shrugging. Like, I don't even know what I've done.

'You did, didn't you?' She's giving me this funny, hard stare. 'You've blocked all your messages. What was that about? Angry ex? Or that Stan you were always talking about? The one who killed your mum? Or a stalker? You're a dark little horse, Kiki Moon. Is that why you came to Little Piddleton? You know you can block just one number? You don't have to block them all.'

I'm a dark little horse? I'm trying to empty the dishwasher with a mysterious air. But at the same time I'm remembering something that I'm definitely not going to mention right now.

When I got to the festival – the horrible one – the guys who had sold me the ticket wanted to pitch their tent but I was dying for the loo – so they promised they'd text me where they were. So I could find them again. They never did.

But, now that I think back, I dropped my phone. It was in my pocket and it fell out when I was in the stinky dunny and trying to perch and to hold my shorts away from all the surfaces so they didn't touch anything. My phone landed on the ground and came apart. And when I tried to put it back together it was all: *set-up incomplete* and all sorts of boxes with on and off. But I was hurrying to see what the festival was like – this was before I knew it was just loud and rubbish – and there were hundreds of people waiting for the nasty loo, and I put my phone in my bra to stop it falling out again. And when I got out of the way and checked if there was a message to say where Peter and Paul were, there was no text – no texts at all, even the old ones that had been there – but lots of the set-up options had ticked themselves in my bra. I just pressed *finish set-up* and sent them a message to ask where they were. I went to look for them. And they weren't anywhere. They never messaged me back saying where to meet. But if Meredith's right and I'd put some kind of block on my phone, maybe they'd tried to text. Maybe they thought it was me who was ignoring them.

If that's right, I could have met up with them after all, and had somebody to spend the weekend with, and then gone back to London with them, and not hitched a lift and been dumped at the service station and walked for miles in my frog gumboots. I wouldn't be here in Little Piddleton, with Meredith giving me this strange look and Rob Sturgiss on his way back for pint number three.

Now I think about it, when Sammy called me after Glastonbury, she did say something about a message and had

I not seen it, but she also said her phone could be glitchy, and not to worry because we were talking now. I reckon it wasn't her phone that was glitchy.

When Meredith asks if I want her to turn my messaging inbox back on, I try to make my face look like it knows something, like I'm – that word they say about the Mona Lisa? I tell her, 'Yes, please. I think it'll be fine,' and I say, 'now.'

Enigmatic. That's the word.

NED

'RIGHT. SO THIS ONE?' Toby is in full swing now. We have had Marlon Brando as the Godfather as well as a questionable Boris Johnson. Bella has provided Britney Spears – though, strictly speaking, singing her best-known song makes it more difficult *not* to guess. Now Toby is running his hand through his hair, sticking his chin up, pouting and affecting a phoney transatlantic twang. 'Be more me. That's the way to live. Be inspiring. Be perfect. Be like me. Live your life through the Ps – Pilates, passion and practice. Oh, and partying. And pizza. And pretty women. And penetrative—'

'Toby!' Bella cuts him off.

That accent was nothing like me, anyway, Toby, you utter bastard. Though Bella seems to think it's funny.

I blink five times for fuck off.

'See how fast you can get this one, mate.' Already grinning to himself in anticipation, he sticks his chest out and bats his eyes rapidly at me. 'Nid! Nid! Look at me, Nid. I've got, like, kooky hair and stupid shoes and I, like, tell my life story, like, to everybody I, like, meet, eh. Nid, I love you. Don't marry her, Nid, have me.'

Come on, Toby. That's a bit low.

'Not funny!' But Bella's squealing makes it sound like she thinks differently. 'Leave Kiki alone. She's sweet. In her own way.'

'She's a headcase, Bel, and you know it. Rambling on about living in a bus with her Greek gypsy granny, not knowing her mother was a lesbian who dressed up as Tinkerbell and killed herself by barbecuing glass. What was all of that about? She must have been on drugs. And those clothes. Like she was dressed by her granny on acid. Where did you pick her up anyway, Ned? Hospital's psychiatric unit?'

'Toby, don't!' Bella's laughing. 'Norton didn't pick her up anywhere. She just sort of latched on, didn't she, Nort? But she's always around so there must be something you like about her?'

This sounds like one of those does-my-bum-look-big-in-this type of questions, superficially neutral but in actual fact a field of hidden mines. One wrong step and . . . boom.

I'm not going to play this game. Sorry, Bella, but no. Granted, Kiki is a little, well, left-field and, also true, she did somewhat attach herself to me at the beginning. But she's not a bad person. If you'd seen how upset she was when she thought the dog had been run over. And did you have a good look at the old lady the other day, with those silly wellies and the daisy chain on her head? Did you notice how much she was smiling?

The alphabet board is being held in front of my face. Thanks Toby. I hadn't realised it was that sort of question. But Bella is watching with an expectant look. What were you asking again? About Kiki latching on – about why I might like her being around. Come on, you two. You don't even know Kiki. It's not fair.

Not fair.

Third row, sixth along – N.

Not fair because Kiki is the one person I've ever met who isn't expecting you to be something or do something or say something, but just wants to know about you and how you're feeling and who you really are.

Fourth row, first – O.

Not fair, because Kiki Moon listens when nobody else does – when everybody else just wants to be told that you're OK, or you're surviving, or you love them or you don't blame them for carrying on with their life. And, do you know what, that is what I am going to say. Sorry if this is a 'yes your bum looks big' but N-O-body else listens like her. Nobody else.

Change of tack, and be ready for the spelling, because it's true. Nobody else does listen.

Except.

'N-O. No? Mate, that's brutal.'

'No?! Norton that's awful. Poor Kiki.'

Blink. Blink. Blink. Blink. I haven't finished. I didn't say end word. For heaven's sake, you two. There's a 'b' and an 'o' and a 'd' and a 'y' and four more words.

But they're laughing too much to notice, and then Toby is doing more of his horrible impression. 'Nid, Nid, I dream about you when I'm picking flowers with my imaginary fairy godmother. I want to marry you and we'll have lots of little fairy frog babies.'

They don't react to my blinking – both enjoying the joke too much – and I concentrate and I strain and there is a noise. I make a noise. And Toby says, 'Now even you're laughing, Ned. Hear that, Bel?'

And then Maxwell comes in and asks what's so funny and why Kiki isn't with us. He says he left her in the corridor because he had to take a phone call from an Augmentative and Alternative Communication charity. She said she'd pop on ahead and he'd catch up with her here.

MRS M

I SHAN'T BE HERE LONG, Roger, I came by with some peonies for you and some for Harriet. White ones. So many people favour the pink but these are particularly beautiful. They seem to have flourished, despite my having been in hospital. And that smell. I think I prefer a peony to a rose. Not that you'd have known the difference.

As you see, I am recovering. Slowly and imperfectly. This stick is a dratted nuisance, and this leg does drag so. As for my speech, well, I know you would have said that it made a change for anybody else to have a word in edgeways but if you must know it is the most bothersome thing about all of this. Vicar was here just now and I attempted a discussion about when might be a good time to return to my church library duties. I could tell he did not understand the half of what I was asking. He just kept saying, 'Marvellous. Marvellous.'

Still, one must not complain. I was in the hospital for music and speech therapy last week, and Pom let slip that Olivia is back in the acute unit. Another stroke, so I believe. So one must count one's blessings. Which, Roger, is why I am going to go to Greece. Yes, I know. What was the comment you made when I mentioned how I might like to take a cruise one day? Something about *Shirley Valentine*. Oh, and, 'daft old bat'. Still, I should prefer to be a daft old bat who has seen the sun set over the Aegean Sea and eaten octopus cooked on charcoal flames. I know, Roger, that you will tell me that I will not like octopus, but I rather think that I shall. Maxwell says that it is quite delicious, grilled over the fire with a simple squeeze of lemon and some freshly ground pepper. And if it makes me sick, well – so what – at least I shall have tasted it.

You see, my mind is made up. More than made up, Roger. I have a plan and you will not like it. Harriet left me some money. Or 'gave' would be more accurate. Six thousand pounds. In cash. I rather think that it was money which Eric had put in their safe and which Harriet chose to remove before he had the opportunity to reclaim it. This was before your fall and before her illness. Our 'adventure fund' she called it. She had no wish to put it into her bank account since she did not trust herself not to spend it. She said please might I look after it instead, so that when the time came, it would pay for some old lady misbehaviour. The things dear Harriet said. You remember that poem – or rather, you won't, of course, because I never showed it to you.

Anyway, I could hardly have told you. You would have objected on the grounds of some tax implication or other. You might even have insisted that the money be returned to Eric, and that would not have done at all. So I popped it under the sink, amongst the cleaning products, in an old tin of stem ginger shortbread. It was *most* unlikely that you would notice it there. I did try to return it to Penny, of course, after Harriet died, but she would not hear of it. So there is six thousand pounds just sitting there still.

Can you imagine Kiki's face when I tell her. She hurried off to the pub yesterday evening before I had the chance. And this morning she was out early with Maxwell to visit Norton.

But, actually, that is all for the good. Because now, I am able to go home and take out the money, so that I can be waiting to surprise her with it. Perhaps I shall pick out the atlas from the bookcase and open it to the appropriate page. 'Kiki,' I shall say. 'I wish to speak to you.' I shall not let on straight away what it is about.

I shall say, 'What is that you see here on the table?' She will be confused, no doubt. She will think that I am scolding her for something or other. And then I shall say – and I shall keep it slow, I shall picture the words before I say them – 'Greece is beautiful, I hear.' And I shall say, 'Where should we stay?' I shall show her the money. And I shall say, 'My treat.'

I should have asked Maxwell to pick up a brochure from a travel agent. What fun that would have been. But I do not wish to impose too much. He is already contacting British Telecom on my behalf to install that wireless Wi-Fi. When that is operational, I shall be able to consult a computer from the sitting room. Maxwell is going to help me learn how to do so. Kiki and I shall make plans before we go. We shall do it online.

That, Roger, is known as surfing.

I shall need some new clothes. Perhaps even some swimwear. And I thought a kaftan. Harriet always insisted they were the easiest garments to wear. Very forgiving. I believe there is one in that box of her things. A purple one. If I thought I might manage the stairs, I could be wearing that when Kiki arrives back. Can you imagine the look on her face. Or would that be going a little too far?

You once said that you would divorce me if I ever wore a kaftan. After we had accidentally watched that silly programme about what to wear or not to wear. You know the one, with those two obnoxious women. 'Mary,' you said, 'if you were ever to wear one of those, I should divorce you.'

I suppose that is no longer a worry with which I need concern myself.

KIKI

ISN'T IT FUNNY HOW you can wake up one morning and feel like everything is going to be good because there's a text on your phone from Sue in Auckland, that she sent at 3 a.m. – except it was normal time in New Zealand – saying, *Only you could block all your texts Kiki Moon you daft dodo. Buy a new phone FFS. Thought you'd fallen into a black hole. I sent a billion texts and didn't hear back. And no I didn't get your email. Guessing you had my email address wrong too (underscore not dash?!) Big news. I'm getting married next year. You're invited of course. Come back soon and help me plan? You can have your old room if you want – wedding's costing a fortune so I could do with the dosh. Hope England's good? Not too much rain? ;o) xxx*

And then when you come out of the shower there's another one from Meredith saying, *Testing Testing. Haha. See you at work later. Mx.*

Then, just now, in Maxwell's lovely car, when he was pulling into the hospital, my phone made a ping sound, and there was another one: *Hi Kiki. I'm away in Europe for a few weeks but see you when I'm back in August if you're still in UK? Sammy x*

Three texts. And 'x'. That's a kiss. Maxwell's giving me a glance from the wheel and asking, 'Good news?' But it's not really news – well, the Sue getting married is, but not the Sammy text. But, yes, it's good.

Maxwell's in a pretty good mood himself. He and Pom have been talking to a charity who know about these laser systems which track tiny eye movements and turn them into letters and words on a computer, like Ned's alphabet grid but electronic. So Ned could do it himself – or just him with the computer. He'd be able to write emails and even texts, without other people having to do it for him. The phone he lent me when I went to Glastonbury wasn't even his newest one and that was pretty amazing. So I guess maybe he could send texts with this eye thing. So long as it wasn't to someone who'd blocked them without realising – ha ha.

Anyway, that's who's calling Maxwell, just as we're going into the unit – this eye-talking technology expert person – so of course he needs to take it. Maxwell says he'll catch me up in Ned's room. And the nurses on reception – Rachel and Tammy – recognise me, and say hello, and why don't I go on in. And I'm coming up to Ned's door and I pause, just for a moment, thinking about Annabella and her big proposal yesterday. I was in a funny mood then, I don't know why. But today I'm going to tell him properly, congratulations. I'll tell him about Sue, too, about being invited to her wedding, and what a coincidence. Not that I'm expecting to be invited to his. Probably it will only be close friends and family. Still, it's funny to hear about two weddings in twenty-four hours.

I'm at his door and I can hear some laughing. It sounds like Annabella, so now I can say congratulations to both of them. The happy couple. Unless, maybe I'll go back and see if Maxwell's finished on his call yet, because maybe I should wait if she's there. Maybe I'll just pop to the loo. I don't need the loo, but just for a minute until Maxwell's finished on the phone.

So I'm walking past Ned's door quietly – the loo's at the other end of the corridor – but I hear another voice from inside. They're really not very good at keeping the noise in, these doors. You'd think they'd be better. It's Annabella's friend, the one who was at Glastonbury with her. The tall one who sounds like a goose when he laughs. That's what I recognise first. The honking. And the voice too. He has quite a distinctive voice. Except he's talking in this really odd way. He's doing this stupid accent with a whiny voice.

He's saying, 'Nid. Nid. Look at me.'

It's funny the way you realise something. It's a bit like when you throw a ball up in the air, and it's going up and up. And then there's this moment – and it's not quite going up anymore but it hasn't started going back down either.

He is saying, 'I've got kooky hair and stupid shoes' – and it's like this is that moment. The ball is about to start falling but it's not done it yet. He's saying, 'Nid, I love you.' And he's laughing. And even before Annabella says my name, I'm realising what he's doing.

He's pretending to be me.

He says I'm a headcase and that I ramble on about living in a bus with my Greek gypsy granny and about me not knowing my mother used to dress up as Tinkerbell and killed herself by barbecuing glass. He says I must have been on drugs when they saw me.

'Where did you pick her up anyway, Ned? Hospital psychiatric unit?' That's what he says.

I should go. Quickly. Maxwell will be here any second, or one of the nurses will. I can't just stand out here. So why can't I make my feet move?

Annabella is laughing even louder, and saying about me latching onto Ned but she's saying there must be something he likes about me otherwise I wouldn't be around so much.

I need to go. Before Maxwell arrives. Now. Right now. Maybe I'll come back in a little bit, and try to act normal, like I haven't heard anything. Like I haven't heard them ask Ned if there's anything he likes about me. Because Maxwell will wonder where I've gone. Maybe I'll go and splash some cold water on my face. But I must go. I must stop listening.

Except I can hear Toby saying, 'First row, second row third row – first letter . . .' – so that must be Ned's grid – and it's an N, and then it's an O. And they're laughing even more.

They're laughing because Ned has spelt out N-O. No, there's nothing he likes about having me around.

He's even spelt it out. If they'd just asked, 'Is there anything you like about having Kiki around?' he could have just blinked twice for no – for nothing at all, he liked about it. But that's not how they asked it. 'There must be something . . . ?' Toby asked. So Ned's had to spell it out. N-O.

He hasn't done 'end word', but there's this big pause so probably he did it with his eyes. Probably they're pointing to 'end word' and he's blinking. You don't need to actually say it. That's what he'll have done.

And that other noise is Ned. He's laughing too.

There's nothing he likes about me being around. N-O. Nothing. And they're all laughing about it.

Maxwell will be here, any moment. I can't be here, listening.

The loo is at the end of the corridor but the door out to the garden is before it. And there's another way out of the hospital from there.

NED

'WHERE'S KIKI?'

Bella and Toby are looking at each other like children who have been caught out by a teacher and who are now putting on their most angelic faces, while trying not to snigger. Maxwell is clearly confused, I can hear it in his voice. 'She was coming right here. I suppose she must have nipped to the loo. Or maybe she bumped into one of Mary's therapists. That's possible I suppose, but . . . oh, one moment. My phone is buzzing.'

I love Maxwell. He is calm and organised and I tend to forget he is eighty years old. But he does that thing that old people do where a call or a message is an event. He's doing it now, stopping everything to read it.

'She's texted. How peculiar. I hope she's all right. She's had to hurry away. Something she'd forgotten to do.' He pinches his chin. 'She had a text from her mother's friend while we were driving here. I wonder if it was something to do with that. Anyway. Kiki says sorry.'

'What a pity,' says Toby, and I could thump him.

There is a taste in my mouth that feels like shame.

In any case, Kiki will be back soon enough, no doubt. This afternoon maybe. I've thought of some words for that tune of ours. They're not perfect yet, but maybe if she writes them down, we'll be able to knock them into shape.

MRS M

THAT BLONDE PHYSIOTHERAPIST, REBECCA, I believe was the name, would insist upon referring to the issues that I am having with my hand as spasticity and I have to say that I did not like that term one bit. *Spasticity*. Why can one not stick to the word *contraction*? That, after all, is what my hand is doing. Contracting.

It is not that I do not appreciate their time or understand that their exercises are beneficial. But one seems to spend one's every waking hour doing nothing but opening and closing and pressing and stretching. And still this hand chooses to remain contracted when I actually need it.

Do you know, Wordsworth, that it took me more hours to make that pom-pom on your collar than it used to take me to knit an entire cardigan? Dratted hand. And will you look at this vase of flowers on the table with all the foliage on the inside with the blooms facing out and all the wrong lengths. Kiki tries, but it is frustrating not to be able to do these things oneself.

Now, let us give this lid one more go. I know I can do it. If I bring it here to the edge of the table and wedge it with this bothersome hand against my body, then with this left hand, I must surely be able to—

Why are you looking at me in that way, Wordsworth? There is no food in here, I am afraid. As you shall see if I can just – bother, bother, bother. I shall be exhausted from struggling with this rotten thing. Oh, but it is vexing to be so useless. I shall – oh, here we go. Wordsworth, I believe it is coming. Finally.

Funny little dog, you shall see what we have in here.

Can you imagine what Kiki will think? What fun, when she arrives back and finds ... ?

Yes. Here we are. It's coming. It's coming. 'I have had an idea,' I shall tell her. 'I think you will like it.' And – aha. Open sesame!

Now, Wordsworth, you will not believe your eyes but in this biscuit tin we have a whole lot of—

Of—

We have—

But—

*

I am not waiting for Kiki. Quite the opposite, since I am not expecting her back for some hours yet. I only happen to be in the front garden when the taxi cab draws up, because I am in need of fresh air.

There was – and of this there is no question – six thousand pounds in the shortbread tin beneath my sink. It was there when I was rushed into hospital one month ago. And now that tin is empty.

One should not jump to conclusions. Yet I did not have the stomach to remain in the dining room, with the dratted thing right there on the table. Empty. Quite empty. Besides, the wisteria is in need of attention, although I have foolishly forgotten to bring out my secateurs. So here I am on the step, leaning on my stick and watching a plump old bumble bee buzzing around the flowers without a care in the world.

There must be an innocent explanation, yet there is a tightness inside me – that same tightness that I used to feel when I had spent the day braising steak or marinating lamb for Roger and his golfing partners, and then he would telephone to say that they were going to eat at the club instead.

'What is wrong with you?' he would say when he arrived back.

'Nothing,' I would tell him, though I trust my voice conveyed that it was not what I meant at all.

Harriet always said that I should just tell him. But, lest we forget, mine was not the marriage which ended in divorce.

Mr Bumble Bee is not flying solo in his nectar-gathering activities. There are one, two, three, four, five of them. What is the collective noun for a bee? I do know this. A swarm of wasps. A colony of bees, I believe. Yes, that is it.

This is what I am doing on my doorstep, watching this colony of bees making merry with the wisteria, and I have such a tightness in my stomach. There is an empty Fortnum & Mason biscuit tin on my dining table. There was six thousand pounds in that tin when I was taken away in an ambulance. Six thousand pounds which had been left in my safekeeping by my dearest friend. It was our 'adventure fund'. In fact, no. That is not what Harriet said. It was our fuck it fund. And now it has disappeared.

I am not expecting Kiki back here so soon – she cannot have been gone more than an hour – so when the taxi cab pulls up, I am somewhat taken by surprise. And yet, as she steps out, and as she dips into a pocket of her shorts and pulls out a banknote – I cannot see from here of what precise worth – and receives the change, I am reminding myself about not jumping to conclusions. All the while, that knot in my stomach is twisting tighter. And Kiki looks shocked to see me.

I may be old but I know a forced smile when I see one. And when she says, so very sweetly, 'Mrs M, what are you doing out here, eh?' and says it without meeting my eye, the feeling in my stomach becomes uncontainable.

That was my money. From my friend.

Kiki – tell me that, how can this be?

Because money does not disappear into thin air. It does not evaporate from inside closed tins.

The word is out before I can stop it, 'You . . .' It is clear and clean and angry. But the next word does not follow it.

Stay calm – you must not try to hurry, Pom says.

'You . . .'

You took something from me. I would be shouting this if my body allowed. *I let you into my home and you took my money.* I should like to scream it at the top of my voice. So what if the neighbours hear?

Instead we both wait – while my brain fishes for the word to fling. My stomach is tight and my shoulders are tense and I *want to shout.* But I must wait for the word to come. I must not hurry it. From the blank look on her face one would think that butter would not melt.

'Took . . .'

Something from me. Something from me. Something from me. It was Harriet's and she wanted to share it with me. And then I was going to share it – Harriet's fuck it fund – with you, but you took it *from me.*

Something from me. Calm. Think it, picture it, calm, calm Mary, say it.

'Something . . .'

Her face looks shocked. 'I took something? Like, what, Mrs Malley? What did I take?' Her eyes are wide behind those spectacles, as if she does not have the slightest idea to what I might be referring.

I search for the word and the one that comes is 'cupboard'. It will do. I am almost shouting it, despite telling myself to be calm.

'I took something from the cupboard? Is that what you're saying?' Does she think I will be fooled by the vacant expression? But then her mouth drops open and she puts her hand across her mouth. 'Oh. God. Of course. I should have told you, Mrs M. I was going to, really I was, but it was, like, you know, awkward.'

Awkward? *Like, I know, awkward?* Can the damn girl *never* speak properly?

'I was, you know, waiting for the right time. Because I knew you wouldn't mind. I mean, I didn't think you were going to do anything with it.'

Kiki is blushing. Laughing, too. Not even denying that she took it – *laughing.*

'I'm glad you know now. I was just, you know, ashamed. But it was just to bring me luck on my travels. A bit of a giggle. Sue in Auckland says it's lucky to take something that someone else has given you.'

Given? A bit of a giggle? My money. Here I am, banging the ground with my stick in the frustration of not being able to say what I need to say. Kiki is looking at me while I thump the doorstep with its three stupid legs, and the only dratted word that I can pull out is, 'Money.'

She gives me the big wide-eyed stare again. 'Money? No, I'm talking about my . . .' She's blushing. It is so curious, is it not, how some people seem so prone to it. I, personally, have never had an issue with it but Harriet used to do it when she was upset. Kiki's cheeks are a ridiculous pink. 'My . . .' Her face is scrunched up, like she's eating something sour. 'You know . . . like, knicker . . . thong . . . G-string. The red one. I mean, I wasn't going through your cupboards. Not snooping. I, just needed to see if I could find anything about your – you know – next of kin. For the hospital. You were unconscious and they didn't know who to contact. And I don't know how I even left it here. I mean, it must have fallen out of my pocket, that first day. When Wordsworth found me in the rain. And it wasn't, you know, for wearing. It was only something that Sue gave me. It was like a joke maybe, but, like, a lucky one too. Or maybe it was meant to be a St Christopher but she gave me the thong instead. But still, a talisman. I didn't think you'd, you know, mind if I – oh. No. Money, you said?'

Now I am bewildered. I'd quite forgotten about that hideous item of – I hesitate to call it clothing. And, as I am trying to work out what on earth this has to do with the removal of Harriet's fuck it fund, the expression on Kiki's face changes to one which is as much alarm as epiphany.

'The money under the sink? But I explained . . . I told . . . No, but maybe . . . I am so sorry. Oh, Mrs M. I should have spoken to you again then. Because I did tell you, right after I did it, but maybe you weren't taking much in then. You were still in hospital and I reckon you were still quite confused. I didn't take your money. I just moved it. Because Yaya always said never underestimate a thief. Yaya said they always look in old tins and shoeboxes. She said they always look above the washing machine and in the cleaning stuff, underwear drawers too, and they're checking for something that doesn't fit. And under the sink. She actually said that.

People assume they won't look there, so that's where they go first.

'Yaya sewed her money and her jewellery inside cushions. That's the best thing because nobody ever looks there. But I didn't want to pull your cushions apart. Then I had this idea. Maybe you remember that frog bag – the one I had when I first arrived here. You remember, like a big tennis ball with eyes and you said it looked like a dog toy. I thought that was somewhere a thief would never look. Never in a million years. So I hid your money in there, and I left it with Wordsworth's other toys. I did tell you and I thought you'd understood. I thought I saw you nodding. Because genius, eh? No burglar would ever check in there. That's where it is. I'll show you.'

It is not often that I am lost for words – but if I have understood correctly, Kiki Moon has taken it upon herself to hide my money amongst Wordsworth's chew toys. What can one say to that?

I need a few moments to take on board that she is waiting for us to go inside. The door is unlocked and Wordsworth rushes up, wagging as if we have been away for days.

'Let me show you,' Kiki tells me.

The dog's possessions are kept in a straw basket, between the hall table and the stairs. Kiki kneels beside it and lifts out a stuffed duck, which she puts on the table, followed by an orange rope, a beanbag and a squeaky mouse. She lifts out a soft yellow ball, a pink blanket and a small sheepskin cushion, and then holds up Wordsworth's spare leather collar. The basket is empty. No frog bag. No money.

'I don't—' She's shaking her head. 'It was here.' I have never seen eyes so innocent as Kiki Moon's as she tells me, 'I promise it was.'

I have a sudden impulse to kick her. It is so powerful that it is all I can do to refrain. I press on the handle of my stick. I hold my breath and clench my teeth. I can feel the acceleration of my heart as she looks up.

It is not even the lying – though that is maddening enough. What a fool I have been. What a fool she has made of me. Daisies and hair dye and those ridiculous wellington boots. How everybody must have laughed at me. Let alone a holiday in Greece! What was I thinking? As if a young woman in her twenties would choose to travel with an old woman like me.

This is what they say about people of my age, is it not, that we are vulnerable, easy to trick. We are easy targets.

'Mrs M, you have to believe me. I would never—'

An image flashes into my head – my stick sweeping down onto her head. I urge back the rage which is building inside.

She would never what?

Kiki, what happened to my crystal tumblers? Or to Roger's whisky? And what about our 1987 grand cru? I lean all my weight onto the dratted, stupid stick. Kiki, what happened to my money?

'You must know you can trust me, Mrs—'

'Go!' The word explodes from me. No need to visualise and prepare. I raise my left hand, as if I am about to slap the air. My fingers are shaking. 'Go!'

'I . . .' She bursts into tears, shaking her head.

There is no pity in me for Kiki.

'Go,' I tell her again. I keep my eyes on Wordsworth. I will not look at her, as she walks to the front door. He follows her, but turns back towards me with a puzzled look and his tail down.

The door bangs shut.

Wordsworth will not miss you I want to shout after her, *and neither will I.*

I go to the dining room. The ginger shortbread tin is still there, on the table, still every bit as empty. I sit down and I do a thing which I have not done since my wedding day.

I sob.

KIKI

THE BED CREAKS AS I shift my weight. I lift my laptop and move my legs and then rest it on them again.

There is a flight this afternoon from Bristol to Crete for twenty pounds. Or nineteen pounds ninety-nine, because it's always something ninety-nine, isn't it. Like that's the law. Or there is a flight to Auckland that takes forty-eight hours and twelve minutes, with a transfer in Amsterdam and one in Singapore. It costs one thousand seven hundred and twenty-three pounds. In economy.

I always told Yaya I'd go to Greece one day, to see where she was born. It would be an adventure. That's what I should do. I'm here in Europe, after all.

But what's the point? What am I going to do? Meet friends, find happiness? Really?

Bristol to Auckland. I press book ticket. It asks for my details. The money has only been in my bank account a week.

Twenty-one years Sammy looked after that money in case I came back. My mum's savings, it was nine hundred pounds, all in an envelope sewn into a cushion. Sammy put it into a high-interest account when Mum died. It must have been really high, because that's a lot of interest. Three thousand pounds, Sammy put into my bank. That's why she phoned me after Glastonbury – when her text didn't come through – to check the right details for the transfer. That's the thing, Mrs M. I didn't need your money. Well, maybe when I first found it I did. Because then, if I'd found a Glastonbury ticket, I wouldn't have been able to afford it. So, yes, when I found it I might have needed it. But I didn't take it even then.

The booking page asks for my passport details. It's in my bag beside me. I have to hold it close to my face to read the numbers.

And why would I have hung around to look after your dog? If I'd taken your money would I really have come to visit you in hospital whenever I was free? Shopped for hairspray and brought you wool for pom-poms? Brought Wordsworth into the hospital garden and taken you out in Maxwell's car? Spent all that time practising peeling potatoes with you and doing your talking exercises and brushing your hair? Do you not think that – perhaps – I'd have gapped it right away and got as far away as I could?

Confirm payment the box on the screen says. I breathe out so loudly I can hear it.

Did it not occur to you, Mrs Malley, that if I was the thief you think I am, I'd have been pretty stupid to have stuck around with a mean old woman who never ever says thank you?

Confirm payment.

I press *YES*.

The springs creak as I stand up.

Goodbye spiky, saggy bed. Goodbye little room. Goodbye window nook.

I'm half expecting my mum to pop up now, with some rubbish about being a coward to run away and having to stay and face the day. But nothing. Just rain on the window.

Through it, I can see the road where the truck went over Wordsworth. There's a big puddle there now. I could walk to the main road and wait for a bus, but it only comes every other hour and I've probably missed it. Anyway I left my gumboots at Mrs M's.

The cab driver from the hospital gave me his card earlier. Maybe he doesn't pick up heaps of Kiwis because he recognises the accent straight away and says he's not far and he can be with me in five minutes.

Time to go.

*

I managed to come in earlier without being spotted, but – wouldn't you know it – Merv and Meredith are both behind the bar now. He's saying, 'Where are you off to with that backpack?' and she's saying, 'What's up? Kiki, you've been crying.'

Turgid Sturgiss is here too, watching from a bar stool. From the red face I'm guessing pint number three. An early start. A couple of other tables have drinkers at them. I don't know any of them, but they are staring too, maybe just because everyone else is. Or maybe it's Stare at Kiki Day.

It feels a bit like being an actor. Like being on the stage with everyone waiting to see what I'm going to say. I have that feeling, like when you're about to be sick.

'I'm leaving,' I say. 'I'm going home. To New Zealand.'

'But Keeks. You can't do that.' Meredith says 'Keeks' – nobody's ever done that with my name before. I reckon yesterday I'd have loved it, but now all I can think about is that she was at Mrs M's house that night while I was out looking for Wordsworth. She was there. And now the money is gone.

Maybe I said something without meaning to, about where I'd hidden it – you know, let it slip – or maybe that's why she came round in the first place. Or maybe she just found it by chance, thinking she could be helpful by bringing one of Wordsworth's toys to help get him back. Maybe she found it then and it was too much temptation.

Nobody else has been alone in the house. The gardener came that once. And Maxwell for a cup of tea the other day. But Mrs M was with him. Only Meredith has been there on her own. Meredith and me.

So if it wasn't me who stole the money, you don't need to be a genius to work it out.

Merv is telling me I won't be paid if I leave without giving my notice, and Meredith's giving me this stare like she doesn't have a clue what's going on.

And looking at them, all cross and staring, with the fox pictures on the wall and the fireplace and the wood tables and wobbly chairs, I feel like I suddenly can't breathe.

What was I even doing here all this time? Mrs M thinks I'm a thief. Ned doesn't like anything about me, N-O, no. And Meredith – all that stuff with the texts and the 'x' and the 'how about a little drink?' I was stupid enough to think maybe – just maybe – she wanted to be my friend.

All she wanted was the money.

I should confront her. I should tell her what I think of her. Call the police even.

But what's the point?

That beeping outside will be my cab.

'You're not seriously leaving?' Turgid asks the question to my chest. 'You know you'll miss us if you do.'

'I doubt that very much,' I say, and I walk out into the rain.

SEPTEMBER
NED

Mr and Mrs Arthur Hopkins request the pleasure of your company at the marriage of their daughter, Annabella, to Mr Norton Sebastian Edbury at St Mary's Church, Paddocks Langley, on Friday 20th March 2020, at 4 p.m., followed by dinner and dancing at Ragbury Hall. Carriages at midnight.

Dear Kiki – Ned asked me to add a note to say how much he'd love you to come. Such a shame you had to hurry back to New Zealand. It would be great if you could make it over. PS: Ned also insisting I remind you dress code is smart and strictly non-frog. He says you'll understand.

Annabella

MRS M

Mary Malley [mmalley1935@gmail.com]
To: Kiki Moon
Subject: To Miss K Moon

Wisteria Cottage,
Thursday 19th September, 2019

Dear Kiki,

I hope that this E'Mail will reach you safely, since I am very much a novice still in this department. I have my own Lap Top now, as well as my BT wireless Wi-Fi system. Maxwell has been extremely patient in teaching me the basics. As a young lady I learnt to touch-type at the Pitman School and achieved a respectable speed, so, although my fine motor skills are not what they were, the keyboard is not so alien to me as it might be.

Before proceeding, I must confess that this is difficult for me. We did not part on the best of terms and it transpires that I owe you an apology.

As you will remember, a sum of money had disappeared. I jumped to an assumption which, whilst logical, was unfounded. I accused you of lying about having hidden the missing money amongst Wordsworth's toys. In my defence, it did seem a most unlikely hiding place, particularly for something which was not yours and which you should not strictly speaking have touched. However, I now know that I was wrong to doubt your story.

To my shame, whilst deadheading my dahlias I came across a patch where the earth had been disturbed and where a green strap was poking out. I suppose it must have gone unnoticed while the surrounding flowers were in bloom. In any case, when I fetched my spade, beneath the soil I uncovered that distinctive bag of yours, the one with the frog design. Inside it was the money which I had accused you of taking.

I can only conclude that a certain dog is the culprit. You might remember that he does have a habit of digging. He has buried other possessions of mine in the past. He truly is a wicked animal. However, Wordsworth is not the party who has done the _most_ wrong.

My late husband would have told you that apologies do not come easily to me, yet, on this occasion, I can only offer an unreserved and abject one in the desperate hope that you might find it in yourself to forgive me.

I am so terribly sorry. This money meant a lot to me since it had been given to me by my friend, Harriet, of whom – as I may have mentioned – you do rather remind me.

Kiki, the reason for which I was looking out that money was that I hoped that you might permit me to take you to Europe. I suppose our conversations about that silly old poem had given me a notion that I might not be too old to fulfil a few ridiculous dreams, and I was hoping that you might help me to do so.

In fact – if you can bring yourself to pardon a sad old lady – I have a suggestion.

Please allow me to make amends. I believe that you have received an invitation to Norton Edbury's wedding. I thought *perhaps that if you were coming over to attend, I might offer to pay your passage. I also hoped you might agree to take a trip with me afterwards. I should like to suggest Italy as well as Greece. I should rather like to eat pizza in St Mark's Square and to ride in a gondola. I should be honoured if you would accompany me. Maxwell has said that he would be happy to look after Wordsworth who, by the way, howls every time we go past the pub.*

I believe he misses you.

Once again, Kiki, my sincerest apologies.

Yours,

Mary Malley

KIKI

Kiki Moon [kikikiwimoon@gmail.com]
To: Mary Malley
Subject: To Miss K Moon

Hey Mrs M – good to hear from you.

Ha! Naughty Wordsworth. Should have guessed.

I'm just happy you found the money. And WOW yes I'd love to go Europe with you. What fun we'll have. I can't make it over for Ned's wedding sadly. I've started veterinary nurse training in Auckland and I won't have any vacation then. I'm coming over in June though, working on my mum's friend Sammy's stained-glass stall at Glastonbury. Maybe we could get you a ticket – you'd like the Green Fields.

We could go after that if you're still up for it? We'll eat pizza and ice creams and visit the Pope. And we can ride Vespas and wear sunglasses. Thank you a million again for the invitation. We'll have the best time ever.

Tell Wordsworth I miss him back. Even if he's a very bad dog.

I miss you too. Heaps.

Better leave it there – class to get to. I'll tell you all about it when I have more time.

Can't wait for next summer. It will be sweet.

Kiki x ;o)

24 DECEMBER 2019

NED

Norton Edbury [call-me-ned@gmail.com]
To: Kiki Moon
Subject: Hello Kiki

Hello Kiki Moon,

So, I am writing this with my eyes if you can believe it. Maxwell and Pom sourced a machine for me. Annabella raised thousands of pounds which paid for it. Eye gaze technology, it is called. I have a tablet which tracks my eye movements with a light sensor and translates it to letters on the tablet. It is slow or rather I am. Up to here has taken me three days to write. This is a joke but only just.

Still, it gives me back a bit more of myself.

Bella says you said you will not be at the wedding. Lucky you.

But do come and see me in the summer. Please. Mary Malley has told me about your plans. She was here for dinner yesterday. Her speech is improving and she is walking much better. Her hair is pink again and she was wearing a red beret which I believe I once saw on you? Wordsworth had an orange jumper which she had knitted. With pom-poms. Very stylish. For a dog.

I believe they will join us tomorrow for Christmas lunch. I am here until Boxing Day along with a paid carer called

Terrence and more equipment than you would believe. Still, it is good. With luck I will move out of the hospital in the next few months.

I hope you are happy in New Zealand. I am still unsure why you left so suddenly. Maxwell said about going back to your old room in Auckland, and about your vet nurse course. But I do not understand the hurry, and why did you not say goodbye?

I have been working on more music. I should very much like you to hear it.

Let me know how you are, Kiki Moon.

And Merry Christmas.

Ned

MRS M

I DO WISH THAT VICAR would not do that. I shall have
to have a quiet word, I suppose, since nobody else will.
'A moment's silence while each of us prays to our god,'
he says, with that smug look. But somebody needs to point
out to him that we are in a Christian church. There is no need
to be so inclusive on Christmas morning, of all days. There is
no 'our god'. God is God.

Do excuse me, God, but I do not need to be told to
whom I should pray when I am, let us not forget, in Your
house.

Lord, look after those less fortunate than myself: the poor
and the needy and Norton Edbury. Maxwell insists on making
such a fuss over this new eye-computer laser thing, but it is
hardly the same as being able to walk and talk, now is it? I
did not know what to give him for Christmas. So terribly
difficult because, if one is honest, what can he do? In the end,
I knitted him a bobble hat with the remains of that soft
tangerine yarn from Wordsworth's jumper.

I hope that Maxwell appreciates the driving gloves. I trust
the size eight will fit. Roger wore a seven and a half, and
Maxwell's fingers look longer. Keep him safe, Lord. He has
been so good to me.

I do not suppose that Annabella will care much for the
biscuits, but one must give something. And perhaps I should
not have said that thing yesterday to Maxwell, with Norton in

the room, but it rather slipped out. I was not, of course, implying that she had no character, merely that her presence does not lift one in the same way as other people's.

Lord, keep Kiki Moon safe this Christmas, and would you please make it a happy one for her. I suppose it is summer over there but do look after her. She was such a forgiving soul after naughty Wordsworth upset her so this summer.

I signed her card *from Mary and Wordsworth*. I even added a kiss. And you may tell Roger from me that I may be a batty old lady but I shall sign my Christmas cards as I choose.

I did not, of course, replicate that strange little symbol of hers. A semicolon, a zero and a parenthesis. Maxwell tells me that it is a smiling face doing a wink, but it seems like nonsense to me.

Do tell Harriet I miss her. Every single day. And that I'm doing them – the things she said in her poem. Not all of them, but some. Tell her I wish very much that I had done them with her. Tell her better late than never. I may sunbathe nude yet.

Oh, and dear Lord, I should very much like a ticket for Glastonbury. I saw Antony last week, before my speech therapy class. He may be able to help procure one for me, but he said he cannot promise. Do tell Harriet that if he manages to do so, I shall dance.

Dear God, give me the strength not to tell Robert Sturgiss that his suit is too tight for that stomach and that his hair needs a cut – just look at him over there – or to tell Meredith Paterson that her skirt is wholly inappropriate for church.

And, Father, teach Wordsworth not to howl every time the postman comes to the door. Make him—

Oh. Already? Goodness, but I was miles away. Amen.

We may stand.

Now what is this that Marigold Bennet is massacring on the organ? 'Away in a Manger'? Of all the Christmas carols why must Vicar pick the most childish and saccharine? I shall really have to mention it to him, because if I do not say something, then nobody else will.

1 JANUARY 2020
KIKI

Kiki Moon [kikikiwimoon@gmail.com]
To: Mary Malley
Subject: HAPPY NEW YEAR!!!!!

Hey Mrs M,

Happy happy happy HAPPY new year! Thank you for the Christmas card – where did you find a basset elf? – and for the lovely necklace. And yes absolutely – I'll get a frog tattoo if you get a dog one.

I can't believe 2019 is over already. But I have this strong feeling 2020 is going to be even better. Italy here we come!! If Antony can't sort out a Glastonbury ticket for you, maybe Sammy can get you in as a helper. We could work the stall together maybe? My mum used to dress up as Tinkerbell when she was selling the sun-catchers. We should do that too.

Give Wordsworth a cuddle from me and get ready for the best year ever!!!

K ;0) xxxxxxxx

Kiki Moon [kikikiwimoon@gmail.com]
To: Norton Edbury
Subject: HAPPY NEW YEAR

Dear Ned,
I hope you are well.
I . . .

I don't know what to say.

I'm sitting here, looking at my laptop, and I don't know what else to say.

It's been six months. You've been busy I bet, with this new eye computer thing and your wedding to organise. It was nice of you to email me but I'm not stupid – well, not that stupid. I get it. Mrs M comes round on Christmas Eve so you feel you have to send me a Christmas greeting.

But what am I meant to say? Because I'm not about to, what was it, latch onto you again.

I'll just say Happy New Year to be polite. Because I can't keep not replying to your emails. But I'm tired. Sue's been pouring the fizz like fizz pouring is an Olympic sport, and she's going for the gold. Now she's having a row with Tommo about whose turn it is to choose the next song and their friends Raja and Tix are in this deep conversation about whether truth means the same thing in every language, and Pete and Maia are showing off a trillion photos of their baby and talking about teething and nappies. I said I needed to send some messages before Sue opened the next bottle. I'm already finding it hard to focus enough to keep the letters still on the screen. In fact the whole room is doing a bit of turning. The cards from Mrs M and Maxwell up on the windowsill are not staying quite where they should.

Just *Happy New Year*. And *best wishes*. What else could I say anyway?

Because what difference does it make whether I said goodbye or not? We both know you didn't want me around. And do you not think I'm too busy to worry about it now anyway, with so much going on, and so much to learn, and being back here, with a different life, so why are we even bothering with this? One of my coursemates asked me out on a date, you know? I said no, because he's kind of strange. But I'm just saying. New life. Lots happening.

So *Happy New Year* to be polite. There's nothing else to say. What would I even tell you?

Yes, I've watched a few more of your YouTube videos, but only to check that you're OK. So you don't have to tell me that you can move your eyes a bit more, or your head, just that tiny bit now, just up a bit, and just a bit to the left. I've seen it.

She never says anything about it though. On the videos. About your eyes and your head. Your Annabella, she doesn't say you are making different noises now too, a little bit softer, so that it's more obvious you're trying to say something. She must hear it. But she mostly talks about how you're on your incredible journey and what a hero you are.

And how much she loves you.

It's great of course, I'm happy for you. You know, congratulations. But it makes me feel – I don't know – like there's a big fat lump inside of me. I don't even know what the feeling is. Just sick, sick, sick. And it's not just because of what you said about me – or not said, but you know – about me latching on and being crazy and all of that. It's just maybe because when I look at you, at your eyes, which are just moving that little bit more, and I can see how hard you're concentrating, I'm not sure that she knows what you're thinking. And I think, just maybe, if I was there, then maybe I would.

You know, just maybe. But not from here. I can't tell it from here.

So I think that's what the feeling is. It's just a pity.

I should just say Happy New Year. That's all I need to say – just that and send the email and go to sleep. What I really shouldn't do is let my fingers keep typing, like they're doing some Olympic sport too, like they're winning the gold in tapping out the stupid, drunk thoughts that come along. I'll stop writing all this rubbish because I'm never going to send it. I wouldn't dare. You know it, I know it and my fingers know it. Because, I mean . . .

. . . think it's best if you don't send any more emails and I know you're trying to be kind but it's really better if you don't. You don't have to feel sorry for me because there are some people who have songs written about them and who share people's journeys and there are other people who don't and that's fine because they've always known it anyway and I'm sorry if I bored you and made you awkward, I'm sorry if I latched on. I didn't mean to. But the thing is I don't need the songs and the journey – I just need to not be hurt and I think it's just best and I hope you understand. You don't have to feel bad is what I'm trying to say. I don't need to be your friend. I just need not to be laughed at.

Good luck with the eye stuff. But no more emails please.

Or any more pity.

I love you.

Kiki

Send.

*

The desk is hard as I lower my forehead down onto it. I'm breathing in and out, and my brain feels like it's, what's that word, pulsing. And spinning a bit too. And I've still got that sick feeling inside. Maybe that's why it takes me a while to realise what I've just done.

Because I've just pressed send. *I've pressed SEND.*

Shit. Shit. Shit.

Shit.

What have I done?

Bugger.

New email. Now.

Kiki Moon [kikikiwimoon@gmail.com]
To: Norton Edbury
Subject: Don't read last email. Mistake!

I didn't mean to say I love you. Stupid typing mistake. I was thinking about something completely different. I meant to write Happy New Year and I wasn't thinking. Too much fizz. Ignore that other mail!! Didn't mean to even send. All I meant to say was Happy New Year. None of the other stuff. Just Happy New Year. That's all. K.

20 MARCH 2020
NED

Norton Edbury [call-me-ned@gmail.com]
To: Kiki Moon
Subject: Thank you

Dear Kiki,

Many thanks to Mary Malley and yourself for the tablecloth and napkins. Such a thoughtful gift. No doubt Bella will send a thank you card in good time, but as I could not contain my excitement I am jumping in first.

I am certain that you are opening my emails despite the fact you are not replying to them, so hello Kiki Moon. By the time you read this I will be married. Bella is furious as most guests have pulled out and her director friend is not bringing the TV crew that she was expecting. Bella believes that the world is overreacting and that the best thing we can do is to let as many as possible catch this virus to build up immunity. Maxwell disagrees. He thinks we are about to have the same catastrophe as Italy. I had a slight temperature yesterday and he wanted to cancel the wedding. Or have it in the hospital with nobody else there.

I shall let you imagine Bella's reaction to that.

I wish you could be here but I suppose that would have been difficult now in any case. My mother has not made it over either. I hope that you are staying safe.

Please stop ignoring my emails. I don't know what you think I did but I would very much like us to be friends. I am sending some words I wrote for that tune you helped me to compose. You might remember it. Perhaps you will give them a listen – well, a read at any rate.

Right. Better go. I have somewhere to be.

N

With a glance toward the top of the tablet, the screen offers up the option: *Send this email to KIKI* (kikikiwimoon@gmail.com)? *Confirm?* I blink.

The technology really is quite incredible. There is a noise like a Disney wand being waved as it is despatched.

9.42. This one has only taken fifty-odd minutes to write.

So here I am. If I were able to turn my head to the left I would see a hospital bed in the place where the vintage red Chesterfield used to be, the one on which I proposed to Bella two years ago. If I were to look to the right, the oak table where we were sitting when I told her we should go our separate ways has been replaced by a new metal cabinet, full of various medical delights, along with my motorised pedal machine and a mobile hoist.

Instead, around the edges of the tablet which is positioned a couple of feet in front of my face and attached by a rod to my chair, my view is of the window and the green field beyond.

Am I really going to go through with this?

It was raining earlier but now the sun has come out and a breeze is playing with the willow by the stream. When I was younger, I used to catch frogs in jam jars or buckets.

In sickness and in health? Until death do us part?

I'd let them go afterwards, of course. After I'd watched them breaststroking in confusion from one curved wall to another. I'd pour them back into the water where they'd wriggle out of sight into the weeds. There were newts too. With orange bellies. And dragonflies, who used to attach themselves to each other mid-air.

The thing is that this is as good as it gets for me. It is this or talk to the ceiling for the rest of my days. Besides, Bella loves me. Imagine how devastated she'd be. And humiliated. She wants this. She wants me.

I'm just nervous. It's a big day. Normal, I suppose.

Soon, there will be a new voice function too, for me. Bella was disappointed the new software wasn't ready for today. I can already make speech, though it doesn't quite feel like me yet, and it's slow, of course. Bella kept asking me to try out different options for saying my vows with my synthesised voice. In the end, I told her thank you, but maybe I'd rather just do it the old low-tech alphabet grid way.

She and Maxwell have shared my old videos with a company that says it can clone my voice. They say one day I'll even sing again, though I might have to wait for the technology to catch up a bit. We'll see.

Bella is smart and kind. She loves me and I love her. I do. She's beautiful, too. And she moves so perfectly. She can make even this sad body perk up. No doubt there will be plenty of that in Toby's best man speech. It will be one long running joke about how one part of me is not quite so paralysed as the rest.

Well, so what? I can't run. I can't dance. My food is piped into me still. Mikey swears he'll have me chewing one day but I'm not sure I even want to try again after last time.

And now, the world is going crazy too. It's not just my life that has taken a turn into the Twilight Zone, it's everything. Why shouldn't I gather what rosebuds remain? We'll probably all be dead this time next month.

But it's not what you want.

This voice I hear in my head has an antipodean accent? It is like a wagging finger just out of sight. And I have this sudden image of Kiki Moon, at the end of the field, in her frog wellies and short green dungarees, leaping into the stream and making the water go splash.

'So, mate, ready for this?'

I didn't hear Toby come in. But here he is, crouching in front of me. Staring up. His waistcoat is the same grey as mine, with a white rose in his buttonhole.

What now, Toby? A rendition of 'Get Me to the Church on Time'? Something about the bells tolling?

But no. He's moving the tablet out of the way so we can see each other better.

'You all right, Ned?'

I blink. Yes.

'Good. Good, mate. Listen.' Look at him, running his finger under the neckband of his cravat. 'I want you to know how much I've always admired you.' Glancing away from me, to the corner of the room. 'And how proud I am, you know. Bel's the most amazing woman. Fantastic. Really. Beautiful, clever, lovely, funny – one in a million. You're so lucky. Both of you, I mean it.'

I'm not sure I'd know what to say to this, even if talking was still as easy as talking.

'You do love her, don't you, Ned? I mean, really? She deserves that. You know that?' He's tugging at his collar again.

The eyes come back to mine and there is a look in them that I do not recognise. Hilary and the children have not come today. Paranoid about this coronavirus, Toby said.

I do not blink. Not once. Not twice. We look at each other, until Toby jumps up with a grin and says, 'Right, mate. Enough sentimental nonsense. Let's get this show on the road.'

MRS M

ONE MIGHT HAVE KNOWN that they would choose lilies. Such an obvious flower for weddings and funerals and those ghastly magazine features where celebrities boast about their homes. Though St Mary's does look beautiful, with the sun coming through the stained glass and those vases on either side of the lectern. The organist is so much better than poor Marigold, too. Marigold has destroyed Pachelbel on more occasions than I care to remember.

I think perhaps I shall not tell Kiki quite what a lovely bride Annabella makes. I shall say simply that she looked very nice, without further detail, but, really, that hush of admiration as she walks past. The pairing of silk with the lace is – well – exquisite. One can hardly take one's eyes off her.

Goodness, but how life goes by. Sixty-five years. How can that be? Such a disagreeable heat, and I was so uncomfortable. Terribly unfortunate timing. Harriet used to say that sanitary belts were instruments of torture – terribly crude of her and some things should remain unspoken. She was right, however. One always felt one was being sliced in two by the dratted things. The towels twisted and chafed and never stayed put, and with every step one was damp and worried. Standing in front of all of those guests, in white taffeta. And such an irony, of course. Because stupidly I'd begun to think . . .

Though not the most ironic thing, as it turned out, because of course we couldn't, or I couldn't, or one of us couldn't, or at any rate we didn't.

Roger never did ask why I agreed to marry him so suddenly. He simply assumed that it was because of his letter. What was it that he called me? *Contrary* I seem to recall.

Twice I have asked you in person. Now I am putting pen to paper to humbly request your hand in marriage, one final time. Four years is unnecessarily long for a courtship, and while I have indulged your wish to complete your secretarial training and to put your skills to use in the workplace, I am sure you will be equally happy as a wife and mother. I have admiration for your character, Mary, but the time has come to stop being so contrary and to agree to marry me.

I await your positive reply.

He signed it *Yours Faithfully, Roger* although *Yours Sincerely* would have been the correct form for a letter which started *Dear Mary*.

Had it not been for the touch-typing contest in Cheltenham, I should have replied to Roger that, grateful as I was, I was sorry but I must still decline. But, of course, I did go to the contest and finished as the runner-up – I do kick myself over that misspelling of contingency – and attended a celebratory tea dance where champagne was served.

I suppose I drank too much. I was feeling rather buoyant. I should never have agreed to dancing with a stranger otherwise, far less to a nightcap in the hotel lounge since he happened to be staying in the same one as the other typists and me. One might say that I was terribly naive, which of course I was, but he had such lovely manners. And when I said I was tired and it was time for me to turn in, he asked me if I should permit him to kiss me goodnight.

I should have said no. I was not that sort of girl. My shame was not so much that I did not say no, but that the kiss made me feel things I had never felt previously and have never felt since.

He had told me that his name was Lawrence Hamlin and that he worked for a medical supplier and was passing through Cheltenham visiting clients. After he kissed me, he said that he could imagine himself falling deeply in love with me. He asked me to come back to his bedroom for one more drink. Of course I refused. One did not go back to a gentleman's bedroom. However I did tell him that I would be taking breakfast at eight o'clock should he like to join me. I hardly slept all night.

He did not appear for breakfast, however. At a quarter to nine, I asked at the desk, and was told that no Mr Hamlin was staying at the hotel.

Later that day, I took the train back home, where I wrote to Roger to accept his proposal and to ask that it be as soon as the church might fit us in.

Sixty-five years.

We were married seven weeks later. I did not feel it necessary to tell Roger about Lawrence – if that was his real name. It was one unimportant kiss. Besides, Roger and I had not been engaged and my intention had been to break things off. Nor did I tell Harriet. The only person who knew of my drink in the hotel lounge with a handsome young man was Mrs Ryle, who ran the typing pool and who had been in Cheltenham that day, so it was something of a relief to hand in my notice in advance of the wedding.

Sixty-five years.

When my monthlies did not come that month, I did not worry about an immaculate conception. I knew babies were not delivered by storks – I was not altogether ignorant. And yet, as the days passed, I began to feel somewhat fretful. In those days nobody discussed the actual ins and outs, as it were, of reproduction. Such subjects didn't crop up on *Woman's Hour* as they seem to do nowadays. And I confess I had a passing notion that perhaps there was some aspect of the whole thing that had eluded me, and that the kiss had been somehow more than a kiss.

Very foolish, yet one does allow one's imagination to run away sometimes. But three days before my wedding any such doubts were put to rest. 'On the rag', was how Harriet used to describe those days of the month. Such a detestable expression.

Sixty-five years. How can that be?

Roger, gone, and here we are in a world where young people jump into bed with each other at the drop of a hat, where hygiene products are advertised willy-nilly and one can write E'Mails on one's Lap Top or smart tablet with one's eyes. And yet we find ourselves leaving a space of an arm's length between each other in our pews, and Annabella is gliding past, looking like today is everything she has ever wanted.

Norton Edbury is very smart though, with his buttonhole and his haircut. I suppose he must be happy. At the very least, I do hope that poor Maxwell has stopped fretting. For days it has been whether Norton's temperature has gone up or down, and whether or not the marquee reception might go ahead without the risk of him coming into contact with any surfaces which might be contaminated.

I did say, 'He is hardly going to shake everybody's hand.' But a doctor is bound to take these things seriously. Maxwell fears it may be months before we return to normal. That seems pessimistic but he should know, I suppose.

In any case things must be better by June since I have bought my sarong. Rather a bargain in the sales, and such a jolly blue. And the dates are all agreed for Maxwell having Wordsworth.

Here we go, handkerchiefs out. I presume the lady sobbing is the bride's mother. Same nose. Revolting fascinator.

We are gathered here today. I had forgotten that this vicar has such a strong accent. Newcastle? Somewhere terribly north in any case. And that stoop. Somebody should tell him that it costs nothing to stand up straight. Apart from that, he is rather good. Predictable though. Abiding love, inspirational in the face of such tribulations. To be perfectly honest, it is not as if Norton has had much choice, now is it. Her? Well, yes. She did not have to stand by him. True.

She, Annabella Lucy Hopkins, takes Norton Sebastian Edbury ... How sweet that lovely little Pom is translating for him. She looks quite pretty out of her uniform. Translating? It is his own language, of course. But I suppose it is best like this. It would take forever if we all had to wait for him to spell it out. Maxwell said it was Norton's choice to do it this way.

Who is this horsey type coming up to do the reading – such tiny little print, how is anybody meant to read that? Cressida someone? *Let me not to the marriage of true minds admit impediment.* Harriet could recite all the sonnets by heart. She loved Shakespeare.

Harriet always said how when a ceremony came to the impediment part, she wanted to jump up and shout out a reason. She said it would have been a good thing for most of the weddings she went to. Of course, they never seem to say the traditional words anymore, '*speak now or forever hold your peace*'. These days so much of it is meaningless waffle about going through life hand in hand or what have you. But nobody ever did stand up anyway. Not even Harriet.

Dear me, look at Annabella's mother. One would think, given the current concerns, she would not be waving her handkerchief around so.

Maybe Harriet was right. All these weddings, and generally, one knew that they would never be happy, but one never felt one could say. Everybody smiles and sings and pulls out their handkerchief and then – well – sixty-five years have gone and one's life has disappeared. All those years married and now you're an old widowed lady with your silly hand that will not grip and your foot that will not lift and your mouth that still refuses to always say the right words. And you make the best of it.

Take these two. Maxwell seems unconvinced that this young lady is right for Norton. He has not said as much but one infers. And, poor girl, I am sure she is a terribly nice person, but how is that good for either of them? He will be so dependent on her and there is bound to be resentment.

And there you have funny Kiki. Not a resentful person at all. I don't know what it is about her, but she does make one smile, somehow.

Of course, she is not elegant like Annabella. If that were Kiki, she would be fidgeting and looking around or waving at the guests, perhaps, like the toddlers when Vicar puts on the nativity play.

I shall send her an E'Mail this evening. The wedding was fine, I shall tell her, and the weather kept dry.

Such a strong accent, this vicar. He reminds me of an actor. I forget the name but that one who plays miners and criminals.

Annabella is putting the ring on Norton's finger. And now what happens?

I see. The best man is putting the ring on hers. Maxwell mentioned that she asked him if he might do it and he told her actually he'd rather not.

She's bending down to give him a kiss. So I suppose that is that.

KIKI

I T'S NOT ANYTHING TO do with the wedding that I'm
crying like this. It's just that I'm so exhausted. This essay
is taking forever and there's all this other stuff going on.
Sue says it's nature protecting itself from humans doing any
more harm to the planet.

So it's nothing to do with this video that Annabella has put
up on YouTube. I'm not even really watching it – which is
why I've had to start it again – because I'm mostly worrying
about this essay – with all these books on the desk here that
I should be reading.

Anyway, what can I say? She's the most beautiful bride I've
ever seen. And Ned. He's just—

He's—

I'm so happy for him. For them.

So that's not why I'm crying. Just tired.

And then there's this email from Ned, which he must have
sent before he went to the church, and there's the attachment
which says 'music' and the other one which says 'words'.

I haven't opened either of them yet because I have just been
so busy and I was studying so late and I've just woken up, so
I'm only just getting round to it. But of course there's no reason
not to. It's not like I've been putting it off.

I'll just do it. Now. Just like this. Right now.

So, if I click on the music one – and this play arrow . . .
And . . .

Listen.

That guitar. That tune. I know it. Of course I do. How could I ever forget?

It was Maxwell playing the notes, but Ned telling him what to play. We were sitting in his lovely garden, with the sun shining, and Ned was home just for an hour or two. If I close my eyes now, I can feel the sunshine. There's Wordsworth and Hector on the ground by my feet. And if I look down to the bottom of the field there's that big willow tree and the stream. I can feel the breeze.

Listen to that. So lovely. I curtsied that day. Top marks, Kiki Moon. Your normal coordinated self. Maxwell made tea in a teapot, while Ned and I chatted. He had his alphabet board. It was his first time out of hospital.

There's this other attachment too. *Words*. And it's not that I don't want to open it. I do. But I have all this other work. So really, I should be reading more *Principles of Veterinary Nursing Ethics and Basic Practice*.

I'll look at this words attachment later. Now's probably not the right time. Because my essay is due in in—

Oh, bugger it.

Click.

Dear Kiki,
    You once told me nobody would ever write a song for you.
    So I did.
    I hope you like it.
    N

BABY MOON
By N. Edbury

There are stars outside my window
but for you it's not yet noon,
For you are half a world away,
and I miss you Baby Moon.

I think I hurt you badly
and you left me far too soon
and now I am so sorry,
I miss you Baby Moon.

I cannot sing these words out loud
but you helped me find the tune.
Say that you'll come back to me,
I miss you Baby Moon.

I'm not crying because I'm knackered. I'm not crying because my essay isn't written, or because we're all going to be wiped out by this new virus. Like I said, I'm just tired. But this is the most beautiful thing I've ever read. Or heard. And I'm looking out of my window, and it's such a lovely night, with all those stars and this moon just sitting up there, and Ned is a million miles away and he has this whole new life. And I'm not in it.

NED

M Y WEDDING NIGHT.
Terrence – my now live-in carer – has just left us. I have been fed and cleaned and changed and moved. I am buttoned into brand new cotton pyjamas. Leaning against pillows in pillowcases that may have been a gift. Reclining, you might say.

David Bowie is playing from the speaker. *Diamond Dogs*. 1974.

I have a view of a cloudless night sky. Perfect full moon and stars, above two large vases of lilies on a windowsill. I can smell the flowers from here, sweet and dusty.

My wife is in the armchair just out of sight, though I can hear her chuckling to herself.

'I'll be right there, Norton, darling. I'm just commenting on these pictures of the reception that Toby's posted.'

In the dark sky, the orange light of an aeroplane is flashing out a regular beat as it jets away to somewhere far off.

MRS M

Mary Malley [mmalley1935@gmail.com]
To: Kiki Moon
Subject: To Miss K Moon

Wisteria Cottage,
Thursday 26th March 2020

Dear Kiki,

I hope that you are coping in this strange and distressing time. As you will have heard on the news, we in Britain are now, like yourselves, in what is being termed a 'lockdown'. It sounds rather like a game show. It has been a strange few weeks. Your president lady keeps popping up on the radio and television.

You do not need to worry about Wordsworth and myself. We are very self-sufficient and, although I can no longer help at church or attend my physiotherapy or speech therapy sessions, I do not suppose it will be for too long. They say they will review the situation in three weeks and we can still go for long walks in the woods. I spent the weekend stewing fruit and my freezer is well stocked, although the village store has no flour which is rather vexing. Vicar called past yesterday to ask if I—

We all know who that silly howl belongs to. When Mr Wordsworth wishes to come back in from the garden, it seems the whole village must know.

One minute, dog, while I find my stick. Patience, animal. And it is raining, is it not. Let me pop on these wellingtons. Really I should return them to Kiki. If anyone were ever to call round and find me wearing them in the garden, they would think I had gone quite mad. Yes, yes, dog, but the door handle is so stiff. Here we are.

Wordsworth. Come.

Oh you pesky boy, all that noise and you are not even waiting at the door. Where have you gone now? Off down the side, I suppose, wishing Maxwell had never fixed the latch on the gate so that you could escape off to search for Kiki. Well, too bad for you, you are stuck here with me and – whoops-a-daisy, slippy paving stones down here. I must have those seen to. So wobbly. I nearly tripped. Look, this one too. And this.

Really, one could have a nasty fall. Wordsworth. Do you think this is clever? Making me come out here to—

Ow!

Blast.

Oh, my.

Bother. Oh, drat.

My arm. Ow.

Look, dog, what you have made me do. I shall have such a bruise on my poor bottom. Gosh, but it hurts. That, Wordsworth, is your doing. And this poor arm. And now, if I can just reach my stick . . .

If I can just reach . . .

My poor arm.

My bottom.

If I can . . .

TWO WEEKS LATER
KIKI

THERE ARE NOISES IN my dream but I'm still asleep and it takes me so long to realise there's another noise too. A different one. And I'm not really awake. You know when you're not even quite sure if you are or not. It's not a dream anymore, just sounds and colours or whatever happens in your head when you're sleeping. But my phone is on the floor next to my bed, charging up. And that's what the sound is. My phone ringing. I'm opening my eyes but I haven't got my glasses on, so I'm pressing the screen for ages before I manage to answer it. I'm trying to say 'Hello', but it sounds more like, 'Hmm,' eh. Like more of a yawn.

Maxwell says, 'Hello Kiki. It's Maxwell.' I'm still yawning, until he says he has bad news and then I'm awake. Wide awake.

It's like a jolt.

I can feel it in my throat, like shock. I feel quite sick.

Hello Kiki. It's Maxwell. I'm sorry if I woke you but I have some bad news.

Really sick. Like I can taste it.

Because people don't say bad news unless it's *really* bad news. Not just bad. If it's bad news, but not *that* bad, like, I don't know, there was a big storm and the pub got flooded and now it's going to be closed for a long time, then you don't need to say it like that.

I know it's really bad too because Maxwell doesn't speak again for the longest moment. I'm listening, and I'm feeling sick, and it's just silence. And I *know* – he doesn't want to say it. He doesn't want to give me this news.

He doesn't want to say it and I don't want to hear it.

I want to pull the phone away from my ear and throw it across the room, against the wall above the desk. It would crack and smash and break. I feel so sick – but sick in my chest. Like my heart is ready to just, I don't know, puke.

It's the middle of the night. Maxwell knows what time it is here. He knows he's waking me up. He's calling me with bad news. And it's so bad he doesn't even want to say it out loud.

It must be Ned.

That's what it has to be. The bad news is Ned. Maxwell's been so worried about him – he emailed me last week and said how he was going to be full-time at home in the annexe now with Annabella, but with a carer living in the studio. He wrote to me not to worry about them, that everybody was fine, but I could tell Maxwell was scared because of the words he used, like vulnerable and compromised and shielding.

And now he's calling me in the middle of the night. And he can't bring himself to say it.

It's like when you drop something. That feeling you get. It's like sickness and fear and shock and something more. Like not wanting to believe it. Like you just can't.

When Yaya died I felt sick all the time. And dizzy. The way you feel after flying halfway across the world, jet-lagged. Like nothing was real. Like I couldn't believe it. Like I was floating.

I can't let it be real again. Not Ned.

Because I haven't even emailed him. Since he sent his beautiful song. Not because I didn't want to. Because I couldn't. I just couldn't.

'Kiki,' Maxwell says. 'Are you there?'

He was waiting for me to speak. That was the silence. He was waiting.

I try to say, 'Yes,' but my throat won't say anything. It's too dry. Too scared.

He's still waiting. And if I don't say anything he's going to ask again if I'm here. And then he'll tell me anyway. And I force the words out but they don't sound like me.

I say, 'Is it Ned?'

And I can't bear it. Because that thing I dropped is about to smash – into a million billion pieces, and nothing will ever be right again. It will be broken forever.

I don't want to hear it.

I want to scream as loud as any human being can scream. Or run to the toilet and throw my phone in it. And flush it away. And then stay in bed with my head under my hands and not answer the door or look at my emails. Block it all out.

Ned looked into my eyes. He spelt me his words. He wrote me a song. He married someone else and I'm already a little bit broken. But not like this. I'm not ready.

But I've said the words now. 'Is it Ned?'

And I feel so sick. Because it's coming. Maxwell is going to tell me. He's going to say it now. And then nothing will ever fix it.

Maxwell says no.

'No,' he says. 'No, Kiki, not Ned. It's Mary. I'm so sorry. I'm so, so sorry. Mary's dead.'

*

She did not want me to know.

She thought I'd worry so she told Vicar not to tell me that she was hurt and to tell Maxwell and Ned not to say anything either.

She fell over in the garden in the night and fractured her hip and cracked a bone in her wrist.

She was there until morning, when the vicar called past to ask if she needed any provisions or medicine fetching from the pharmacy. He'd been making calls on his elderly parishioners. There was no answer to the door but he heard Wordsworth barking. That's how he knew.

According to the vicar Mrs M was conscious and, apart from the injuries, she was really all right, if rather cross. He said she was put out at being found wearing my frog gumboots. He called an ambulance. But after putting her wrist in plaster and doing whatever they do with a fractured hip, the hospital sent her to a residential home. For recuperation. They told her she would be at less risk from coronavirus there.

They believe it was in the home that she caught it, because at least eight other residents did too.

'She didn't email me,' I say. I don't understand. Because she'd have done that. 'She didn't call me or email me. I mean, she'd have wanted to do that? Definitely.'

But – Maxwell says – she was on strong painkiller medication. For the wrist and the hip. Morphine probably. She was sleeping all the time, even before she got ill. And then it was just a cough, she said, she didn't think it could be Covid-19, and anyway, she didn't want to worry me. She'd let me know when she was better. Except she deteriorated. Quickly. And what with the morphine, and the weakness and the illness . . .

'Antony called me,' Maxwell says. 'Ron – Vicar – had rung to ask if he had your address. She left you a note apparently.'

I still haven't put my glasses on. The room is a bit fuzzy. I'm staring at the desk and the books in their pile.

'The post is extremely unpredictable at the moment,' Maxwell says. 'I wondered if you might like somebody to scan it and email it over to you before sending?'

*

They must be busy at the care home, because it's not until the next afternoon that the email comes through. At the top is typed, '*FAO Ms Kiki Moon. My deepest sympathies on your loss. This is the letter that Mrs Malley wrote for you before she died.*' It is signed by somebody called Clara.

The writing does not look much like Mrs M's. I know what her writing is like from when I had to search through all her papers. This is more childish. Messier. But she'd fractured her hand, of course. So it would be. Maybe the morphine too.

> *Kiki. Excuse bad handwriting.*
> *Do not be sad. Be happy.*
> *Go to Glastonbury.*
> *Go to Italy.*
> *Do everything and remember the fun we had.*
> *Thank you for being my friend.*
> *Mary ;O) x*

NED

'IT'S NOT AS IF it's a real funeral. It's only Skype. Anyway, I hardly knew her. And I'm sorry she's dead but let's not pretend she wasn't a mad old thing. That hair. And she knitted you an orange bobble hat for Christmas, for Christ's sake.'

I blink twice. I cannot be bothered to get into a conversation about this. Far better for her to go and ride Pampras – since apparently the forty-mile drive to her parents' is within the spirit of lockdown, as is the driving twenty miles further for a long walk with Toby ('he's having all these stupid rows with Hilary and needs some space, and he can't come here, because it's too risky for him to see you'.) They will each take their own hip flasks.

I am not sure Annabella quite understands how contamination works. She likes to remind me that I am extremely vulnerable and must be isolated from everybody else because of my complex needs, but does not seem to understand that those rules might apply to her too.

Terrence has just left – with his hands washed and sanitised and in a gown and mask that Maxwell had stored away from his doctor days. Terrence washes and dries them after every single time he comes in. Such protective clothing is apparently not to be had for love nor money.

Maxwell has only just gone too. He was instructed not to be early. It will only be him, Antony and an old woman from the village. Even for that, Antony had had to persuade the vicar that it was not really breaking any rules, since the ceremony would be by the graveside and not in the church, and since there were no close family or household members to attend.

I am wearing my suit for the second time in a month. Not that anybody will see me. Bella is in jodhpurs and boots. She's shaking her hair, and I have a sudden image of a horse that is raring to be off at a gallop. But she will make sure the livestream is up for me before she goes.

KIKI

THE CAMERA IS AT such a funny angle, looking down at Vicar, at the pink of his head and the bits of hair on the sides which are being blown by the breeze. I can't work out if it's a really tall person recording it on their phone, or if it's attached to a tree or a pole or something. Probably a pole, because otherwise it would be more shaky.

And in the corner of the picture, just beside him, there's the coffin. Except I can't see all of it, just like the bottom end. I think the orange and yellow flowers on it must be the ones I sent, because I said to the woman on email that I wanted something bright. Cheerful. Mrs M would have known exactly what flowers they were, geraniums or roses or whatever. She'd have told me they were wrong, I bet. Inappropriate, she'd have said. She'd have liked the other ones. The white ones. They're from Maxwell I reckon. He told me what they were called. The ones that sound like ponies. He didn't think she'd approve of lilies. I don't know why.

I hate coffins. Your brain can't quite believe that there's someone inside it. I dressed Yaya in her best black dress for hers. I emailed the funeral people about Mrs M, too, but Maxwell said it was probably best not to joke about tuxedos and stockings, given the current concerns and everything. Of course they will have had to wear all the protective stuff, and masks and gloves. It wasn't like normal times. Because I reckon she'd have liked her purple kaftan. She told me she was going to wear it in Italy. Or her new sarong, maybe. But in the end I told them just a skirt. A black skirt and jacket. I told them she'd maybe like the red beret. Harriet's one. She looked good in that.

I don't know if they will even have been able to go and get it though. Things aren't quite normal.

I suppose—

That's Sue knocking. Checking I'm OK, which is nice of her. She's saying she could sit with me or maybe I'd like to go into the living room. But she didn't know Mrs M, so I'm here, on my bed, with my laptop on my knee, and looking down at Vicar's head and half of the coffin. I'm imagining there are loads of people, standing there with black veils over their faces, or black suits. But I don't think it's like that. Maxwell said hardly anyone is allowed to be there at all. Just him and Marigold, even though I can't see them from this angle. Mrs M always said she found Marigold very tiresome. She'd be glad to have Maxwell there though.

There are others watching, like me, on their computers. Meredith sent me an email saying she and Merv were going to join that way. She wanted to check I was all right. She said she missed me and she hoped I was safe.

Ned will be watching too. With Annabella, I suppose. He sent me an email to say how sorry he was. I should have written back.

Vicar's clearing his throat. It's quiet, but if I put my head nearer to the screen, I can hear what he's saying.

'Friends, we are here, though many of us in a virtual manner, to say goodbye to Mary Malley.' I wish he would look up at the camera. Instead, I'm still watching the top of his head.

And it seems a bit rude, but it's all there is apart from the coffin. It's three weeks since she died. Maxwell says it's because there are so many funerals and so many people not working. But it's still hard to think she's really – you know. I can only imagine her being in her cottage or her garden or walking in her gumboots in the woods and shouting at Wordsworth to be quiet.

When someone is a long way away, it's harder to think that anything's changed. You think they're just doing the same things.

'I am not at all convinced that Mary would have approved of this ceremony.' Vicar's pausing, like he hasn't written anything about her and he's just thinking it all up now.

He's still got his head down. 'But then again I am not sure that any ceremony under any circumstances would ever have met with her full approval. Mary was, as you may remember, a woman of opinions, not least when it came to a church service.'

Now he's looking up, at the sky but towards the camera too, because you can see his face and his cheeks are quite red. And it's like he's looking right at me. He's wiping his forehead.

'So I trust that Mary will forgive me today and understand that this current crisis is beyond even my control.' He pauses again and wipes his head, with a smile that's not really a full smile.

'I remember the day I met Mary Malley, eleven years ago, on my first Sunday as parish priest here. At the end of the service, she shook my hand and informed me that my hymn choices were pedestrian and that my homily left a lot to be desired. She said, if I remember right, 'I have always been of the opinion that one should only preach God's word if one's own words are themselves worth listening to.'

The strange thing is how much this actually sounds like her. It's not her voice of course, but it's exactly the way she would have said it. And I'm wondering what Mrs M's going to have to say about all of this. Maybe I should email her to ask straight away before I forget. I hope she's not too cross.

I don't know I'm going to make the noise – half a hiccup and half a sob – until I hear it coming out of my mouth. But when Vicar says, 'Nobody could have accused Mary Malley of suffering fools gladly,' it comes out, even louder. Because I won't be able to ask what she thinks. Not after the vicar's finished. Not later on tonight. Not tomorrow. Not ever.

'But she would pop over with a jar of marmalade and some lemon drizzle cake after she had told you how disappointing your sermon had been. And she was always the first to volunteer when there was a jumble sale to organise, or a church library to be opened. Even if she may not have liked to show it always, there was a kind side to her.'

She was going to take me to Italy. We were going to eat pizza and drink Prosecco. We were going to go to the opera. We were going to ride scooters.

'The sermon is from Revelation 21. It was one of Mary's favourites. "*Then I saw a new heaven and a new earth. The first . . . Jerusa . . . loud voice speaking from the throne, 'Now God's home . . . wipe all their . . . old things have disappeared*".'

Something's gone wrong. I don't know if it's my laptop or if it's their camera or if it's maybe the wind, because there's a loud whooshing noise, and the screen has frozen. I don't think Mrs M would be very pleased.

Maybe she's there in the coffin and she's disappointed.

But she won't be, of course. She won't even know. She'll be able to hear Vicar, even if I can't. She's just thinking what a good prayer. She'll be thinking how terribly *appropriate* it is. And I should have got some tissues. Yaya always said if you wiped your nose with the back of your hand you were a little animal, but if I go to get some now the sound might come back and I might miss an important bit.

So I'm wiping my nose like an animal and leaning closer to my computer screen, but all I can hear is this whooshing, with a few words, like charity and standards and consistent. And then singing, although it's just Vicar you can hear really, and I can't work out what it is, until I hear the word *abide*. She sang it to me once. 'Abide with Me'. She sang it because the words came out easier that way. But her talking was getting better slowly. She said it was much better than when I was there. She told me I'd see when I came back to England. She was even learning some Italian. For our trip.

I'm trying to sing along, but I don't know the words, and I can't really hear it either, so I'm just singing 'abide with me, abide with me', over and over again. But then the sound's a bit better again, suddenly, and the music's stopped and Vicar is saying something about Roger and then about Harriet. He's saying 'abiding friendship' – just like abide with me. Something about loyalty and about a bridge – or maybe he means the card game – and some blackberries but I can't understand it all.

And now Vicar is stepping out of the screen and Maxwell is stepping into it. And I know what he's going to read because it was me who emailed the words to him. He's doing it for me. But it's not working. It's still just '... Mary ... hospital ... car ... friend ...' and I'm tapping the side of my laptop, like that might fix it. I'm leaning right in, and there's a tear dropping onto my keys. I hope it doesn't damage my computer.

Come on.

It's not like I don't know the poem. But I want to hear it too. I'm tapping the side of my machine again but it's still whooshing. And now Maxwell is taking a piece of paper from the pocket inside his jacket and unfolding it. And I'm thinking, *bugger, bugger, bugger*, because I can't do anything. I'm going to have to just watch his mouth moving and maybe be able to hear one or two words.

But now Vicar's leaning in and whispering something to him and they're both looking towards the camera but a bit lower, and Vicar's saying something. Pointing away to the side. Maybe talking to someone. And then there's a voice saying, 'Is that better?' I don't know whose voice, but the sound is clear again. No whooshing.

Maxwell looks up. It's like he's looking right at me.

'As I was saying, I hadn't known Mary for very long but I admired her a lot.' His voice is clear. 'I enjoyed her company and I became very fond of her, as did Kiki who would have read this herself if she could have been here. This is a poem that was written by Mary's dear friend Harriet and I think it shows that there was a side to Mary that not everybody saw. The poem is called – and you will please excuse the language – "The Old Ladies' Fuck It List".'

I'm wiping my nose like an animal, and my eyes too, because otherwise I'm going to cry all over my laptop. That's the thing about crying, you can't help yourself. Your nose is running and you're twisting up your face. But smiling as well. I know every word. I can hear Maxwell perfectly now. I'm saying it along with him, but quietly.

Dear Mary, here's our bucket list
(our 'old ladies who say fuck it' list)

When you and I are past our prime,
That's when we'll claim our rightful time,
We're surely due some misbehaviour
Before we go to meet our saviour,

So here it is – our 'to do' list
(add in anything you feel I've missed).

We'll dye our hair a neon hue,
green for me and pink for you.

A shopping spree, of bling and glam,
We may be mutton but let's dress like lamb!

We'll drive a bright red sports car, silver Jaguar on its bonnet,
We'll fly it past the speed limit and then keep on stepping
on it.

We'll go to trendy nightclubs, named Stringfellows or
Heaven, we
Shall flirt with handsome toy boys (some as young as –
goodness – seventy!).

We'll have nights at the opera and take tea at the Ritz,
We shall dine in three-starred restaurants but demand
they feed us chips.

We'll visit a new country, drink new drinks and eat new food,
We'll stay up until morning and we'll sunbathe in the nude.

I shall buy a basset hound and you shall have one too,
We'll knit them fluffy pullovers, like mad old ladies do.

We'll go to hippy festivals and put flowers in our hair,
We'll dance in fields by moonlight and not have a single care.

And when my life reaches an end,
I'll know we did it well, my friend,
So bury me in something shocking,
– a white tuxedo and some fishnet stockings.

And when I die, I shan't be sad,
Because of all the fun we've had.

He stops. He's looking right up and he smiles, like he's smiling just at me, and he says with a little nod, 'Goodbye Mary. It was an honour to have known you.'

*

It looks like I'm waiting for the email to arrive. Because I'm just here on my bed, with my laptop still open, but with just my picture of Wordsworth – that's my background picture. Sue showed me how to put it on there. But I'm not really looking at Wordsworth, although he's got such a funny expression on, I'm just looking at nothing. Just not wanting to close it, even though it's all over now and Mrs M is buried – not that I could really see that, I just heard Vicar saying that bit about ashes and dust and God. Now I'm looking at nothing. Just looking.

And the email pings.

It's from Ned. I open it straight away. Like I was waiting for it, although I wasn't.

How are you? it says.

And I type, sad.

Send.

Just that. I'm not thinking about how I'm not talking to him. I just send it.

And one comes back – not straight away, he's got to write it with his eyes. But it's only two or three minutes.

I'm so sorry.
I miss you.

There's this pain in my chest. It's right in there, pulling me wide open. And – here we go again – I should get some loo roll. I'm crying onto my laptop again.

I miss you too.

Send.

This time it takes five minutes exactly. I know that because I'm watching the clock in the top corner of my screen. I send mine at 22.26. His arrives at 22.31. That's five minutes.

When this is all better, promise me you'll come back to see me?

I send my reply, before the clock even turns to 22.32.

Yes!

NED

I SHALL HAVE TO WRITE it down in a letter. It would be too agonising to spell it out word by word, with Bella having to piece it together as we go along. This will be kinder. I can craft it very carefully. It won't come out wrong. She won't misunderstand any of it. I shall make sure there is no room for misinterpretation.

Thank goodness for this technology – for which thank you, dear Bella for raising the funds. Never think I do not know what you did.

The funny thing is I think it will be a relief to her. She'll cry of course. But Mary Malley was right. Life is too short to do what you know is wrong.

That's what she said in the note she left with my name on it. I think writing was difficult for her. It is quite a scrawl.

Dear Norton Edbury.
Sorry.
I should have shouted in church.
Life is too short to do it wrong. Better to be happy.
Kiki taught me that.
Kind regards,
Mary.

KIKI

'HEY THAT'S GOOD NEWS at least.' There's a funny sort of echo on my phone, so I can hear myself repeating it in my ear – '*Hey that's good news at least*' – at the same time as hearing Maxwell's reply, 'You wouldn't believe how excited people can be about a trip to the garden centre.'

Mrs M would have been first in the queue, I tell him and I hear him laughing at the same time as my own words say themselves back to me again too ('first in the queue'.) She told me that she'd managed to buy some seeds and bulbs from the supermarket right at the beginning of lockdown. 'Procure them', was how she put it, although the variety had been uninspiring.

I have little faith in these gladioli being glorious, she wrote.

I wonder if she planted them anyway. She probably did. She said she was spending a lot of time in the garden as well as going for lots of walks with Wordsworth. '*Perhaps I should sell him since I understand there is quite a demand,*' she wrote to me. '*Exercising one's dog is one of the activities one can do without sanction, and so dogs are at something of a premium. Even defective ones.*'

I'm looking at my laptop, which is open on the desk with its Wordsworth background looking back at me. I ask Maxwell how the defective dog is doing and he says, 'He has a basket next to Hector's at night, but he also spends a lot of time in the annexe with Ned when Terrence or Annabella are not in there. I think Wordsworth was with him for the streaming of the funeral. He was certainly there when I arrived back.'

Maxwell himself avoids close contact with Ned. He tends to FaceTime him even though their buildings are just across a field from each other. Maxwell feels it's still safest to minimise contact, although an argument could be made that they are one household.

'What about you? Have you been in touch with Ned?' Maxwell asks.

I can hear the pause before my echo tells him, 'You know, just a couple of emails.'

NED

ONCE, I WOULD HAVE stopped her as soon as she came in. 'Sit down,' I'd have told her. 'We should talk.'

But Terrence has fed me and cleaned me and placed me with my body propped and cushioned, and my gaze directed towards the window and a sky that is reddening with the sunset. The door is behind me and I hear it open and feel the breeze of outside. I can't see Bella yet.

'You're not asleep?' The question comes without her crossing to where I can see her. Her voice is light. She can't have seen my email yet. 'Sorry I've been so long, darling. It was just too wonderful to be outside on a day like this. I rode for hours. And then I thought I'd better pop in on Mummy and Daddy – only the doorstep, of course. But then you remember Toby'd left a message asking if I fancied a meet-up on a bench on the side of the A303. I didn't mean to stay so long but he seemed so lonely. He misses you, I think. I was going to let you know I'd be late, but my stupid phone went and died on me and I'd forgotten my charger.'

Oh hell. She hasn't seen my email. *I have something difficult to tell you when you're home. I've written it all on my tablet.*

The tablet is now lying on the table beside the bed. I asked Terrence to leave it there so it would be waiting for her. I wanted it to be there for her, not right in front of me. I thought it would be best if she could read it at her own pace, not have to hear it from my voice function. If I could reach out, I'd pass it to her. If I could talk, I'd say, 'Stop, Bel.'

When I called off our engagement, Bella said the way I sprung it on her was cruel. She said it felt worse because she hadn't seen it coming. I wanted to do better this time. Except she's telling me how happy Pampras was to be given a good run out and how Toby's been struggling with being cooped up at home, and on a different day, I'd be questioning what she and Toby consider essential travel and daily exercise, but instead I'm listening to Bella's voice and footsteps before she appears into a space between the bed and the window. She smiles her beautiful smile and I feel a squeezing inside my gut.

'All OK? You don't need me to fetch Terrence for anything?' I blink twice for no.

Bella bends and kisses my cheek. Her perfume is different. Not the one I bought her. When did she change it?

Bella pats my face. 'Scratchy. You need a shave. A haircut, too, when we're finally allowed one. Or I could try. What do you reckon, Nortie? Would you trust me?' She laughs and brushes a strand of hair from my forehead. 'Short back and sides? Keep some of the length on top?' The pang inside me tightens.

'Or you could grow it. It suits you. Here, let me take a photo to show you.' There is a handbag on a chain across her body, and she unzips it and takes out her phone. She has lifted it almost to camera height before she groans. 'Silly me. It needs charging.'

She disappears again from my eyeline so that I am left with a view of pink clouds and grey sky, framed within the wall and window. I'm guessing there is a phone charger in one of the sockets on the opposite wall and Bella is plugging it in. A little symbol showing a battery will be appearing to show it's working. Will she wait until her message notifications pop up and read them?

'Actually, Norton, there was something I need to say to you.' She reappears in front of me and sits on the bed beside me. I feel her hand wrap itself around mine. 'I wanted to say sorry.' She glances away again. I wait.

It is a moment before she speaks again. 'I've been thinking and I was mean about Mary Malley's funeral. I should have stayed and watched it with you.' Her thumb is stroking a line over the back of my hand. 'I wasn't very kind about her and that wasn't nice.' Her eyes come back to mine again. 'I hope you forgive me?'

I blink. Yes. Of course. There is nothing to forgive.

'And you still love me?'

Bella, please. The tablet is right there. I've strained my soul to write how I feel.

But she's looking at me and her hand is holding mine. Her eyes are asking the question.

I blink.

She lifts her hand and touches my cheek.

'And you know that . . .' she is beginning as I blink again. And again. And again.

'Sorry?' She's smiling still, though her eyebrows have narrowed together. 'What's with the blinking? Is that yes, yes, yes, yes, you love me?' She giggles. 'Or . . . ?'

I blink. And I blink. And I blink again.

'I don't understand what you're saying, Nortie.'

Blink. Blink. Blink.

'Here. Let me get you the tablet. Tell me.'

She's picking it up. 'Right. So. What do you . . .'

My ribcage suddenly feels too tight. I see the hesitation in her face. *Bella, read this.* She glances up at me. Then back to the screen. 'What's this, a surprise? You've written something for me?'

The breaths through my nostrils feel louder as I watch her eyes scanning from left to right and back.

Can I remember what I wrote? Maybe not word for word, but as near as.

There is no easy way to say this but I do not think we can be together anymore. Please understand that I am the stupid fool and that you have done nothing wrong. I am so sorry. You have helped me more than I can say and I will always love you for what you have done. But my love is not what you need it to be.

I can't see her face because she is looking down, saying nothing.

I love you because you are kind and loyal and good but sometimes people need more. I am scared to not stay with you but life is too short to do what is wrong.

Her hand is still around mine, but her thumb has stopped its stroking. I would like to touch her, to say 'I'm sorry'. My breaths sound so loud to me. She says nothing.

I want my facial expressions back. I want to tilt my head to one side and tell her with my eyes, 'This is not your fault.' Except she is looking down.

'We've been married five weeks.' Slowly she lifts her head. I can't read from those blue-grey eyes what question is being asked until she asks it out loud.

'Is this about Kiki?'

I have no means to make an incredulous expression. I am unable to shake my head from side to side.

I close my eyes.

I open them. I close and open them again. Two blinks for no. It is nothing to do with Kiki.

She closes her own eyes. 'I thought you were just sorry for her. I thought—' She presses her hand over her eyes and breathes out hard. 'I should have— That song, for Christ's sake. I thought you were playing around, like she was obviously upset about something and I thought you were just humouring her.' She slides her hand down her face until it is cupped over her mouth and I can hear her blowing air out into it.

She opens her eyes again and stares at me. 'Baby fucking Moon. That was our wedding day.'

It had never occurred to me that Bella read my emails. Did she do it while I was asleep? While I was being washed or fed perhaps? I am blinking now, blink, blink, blink. Bella, let me talk. Offer me my tablet now so I can spell out what I need to say. This is not about Kiki. Let me explain.

'I never once thought – I thought it was you being nice. I mean, Norton, those fucking wellington boots. God, and that email, "*Never contact me again. Happy New Year. Silly me, did I go and say I love you? Must be the wine because I'm such a ditz.*" Don't tell me you actually—? Don't tell me you— I was doing you both a favour deleting that pathetic rubbish. I didn't realise you might actually—'

What email?

Until today Kiki hadn't sent me a single email. What does Bella mean? What rubbish did she delete? What is this '*did I go and say I love you*'?

'I mean, for fuck's sake, Ned,' As Bella lets go of my hand it flops down and slaps my thigh. Her voice is a little higher now. 'Do you not think other people might—?'

She stands up and turns her back, takes three steps towards the window. It is nearly dark outside, except for one long stretch of cloud-pink. 'Do you think marrying you was easy for me? Is that what you think? That I was so desperate that you were my only option?'

She's wrapping her arms around herself, hands cradling her shoulders and rocking slightly. 'I – just – don't – understand. Everything I've done. What the flying fuck can Kiki Moon possibly do for you that I don't?'

Not once since I woke up in this rag doll shell of a body have I felt this powerless. No jumping up to defend myself. No anything. And she has this wrong.

Kiki doesn't give me anything that Bella doesn't. Kiki doesn't tell me how strong I am or insist to me that one day I will be fixed. Kiki doesn't post positive videos to drum up donations and help tell my story. Kiki just listens.

Bella is still staring, like she's waiting for an answer, but without her bringing the tablet back to face me I have no way to tell her this. That this is not about Kiki. I am willing the words to be in my mouth and there is a noise – a muffled sort of moan sound inside my nose. But Bella does not react.

Pilates, Passion and Practice. My old life was better, no doubt. And Bella, more than anyone, believed in it. But even then she – us – was not what I wanted. I tried to tell her that once and I'm sorry that she wouldn't believe it then, but nothing – even this catastrophe that is my existence now – could change it.

I am so sorry, Bella. But the only person this is about is me. And maybe, yes, it's true that although my mouth can no longer smile, Kiki sometimes makes me smile inside. And maybe, although the noises I make now are not really laughter, Kiki sometimes makes me feel like I'm laughing. But that is the point, not her but me – me being a person who has the capacity to laugh and smile again, not just to hope that one day I might be lucky enough to recapture something of what I once was.

'I don't believe this.' There's a wobble in her voice. 'I told Toby you didn't love me. Exactly that. I told him. He said of course you did. He said how could you not. But you didn't. Not ever.'

I blink. Yes! I blink again. I did, Bella, yes. And again, in case she thinks my two blinks mean no. I did love you. I do. I want to so much. This is not what I want either. Give me back my tablet. Let me explain.

She's crying now, breaths catching, and my own eyes are blurring. I can taste the salt of tears on my lips too. I want to take her hands and to say the right words to take back some of the pain.

Though what would I say?

I'm sorry. You did nothing wrong.

Only maybe that was part of it. You never curtsied and blushed or boiled up odd-smelling jasmine tea or talked over Damon Albarn with your thumb covering the phone screen. You never barged in and babbled about borrowing back a lucky lacy thong from an old woman's filing cabinet. You never waggled your hair around to show me a basset hound's ears blowing in the wind. You never hid thousands of pounds in a basket of pet toys because you thought that would keep it safe, or invented stories in your head about an imaginary poisoner and then flew to the other side of the world to track him down, because of something you heard wrong when you were six years old.

Everything you do is right. It's just not right for me.

I'm blinking and blinking. Please Bella, let me have my tablet back to tell you how sorry I am. But Bella is on her feet. She's leaning towards me. She's still crying, but there's anger in her eyes now too. 'I'll tell you something though. Toby doesn't think I'm worth less than some Kiwi lapdog. Toby knows how much I've given up for you. He knows how hard it's been, because do you not think there were times when I could have walked out? Do you think staying was easy for me? I gave up everything to look after you. Everything.'

She's quiet again for a moment.

'Toby knows what I've been through. He says I'm brave to have stayed. He says I'm the bravest person he's ever met, if you must know. Actually, Norton, he says I'm perfect. It's only because we cared about you so much that—

I will myself to make a noise. No noise comes.

You are perfect, Bella. It's me who's not. That's what I'm saying. And who cares what Toby says because he's – wait – what are you saying?

'You know what? Toby makes me feel special. He makes me feel happy. When we went to Glastonbury, it was the happiest I'd been in so long. You weren't there and I was happy. I'd forgotten what that felt like.'

Bella, stop. Explain. I don't understand what you're saying. Toby's my friend. And he only went to Glastonbury because I couldn't. Remember. You took my ticket. All those calls you had to make and the letter from the doctor before they'd change the name. Because tickets are non-transferable.

'And it's not because he can walk and talk. It's because Toby cares about me. And you never did. I deserve better, Norton. I deserve someone who loves me.'

Wait. What are you saying?

'I can't believe this. Kiki bloody Moon. After everything I did for you. She's welcome to you.'

She's turning her back. She's walking out of sight. She can't go. Because I don't understand. And the guilt and the pain and the frustration, and this sudden jabbing of bemused jealousy are like a chemical mixture coming together into an explosion inside me, filling me with a fog of confusion. Wait. Bella. We need to talk about this. Don't go.

I can hear her pause by the wall – unplugging her phone I think – and one, two, three, four footsteps behind me. And then a gust of breeze from outside, and the sound of the door slamming shut.

A YEAR LATER
KIKI

'SO FOLKS, THIS IS Harry, your pilot. We're just waiting here for our slot on the runway before we start this flight to Hong Kong. Shouldn't be very long now, just a couple of planes ahead of us in the queue. And flying conditions today couldn't be better so I'm hoping to make up the time in the air.'

Seatbelt. Mask. Vitamin D tablets. Sue made me promise I'd take one every hour. She's convinced they're going to protect me. Even though I'm vaccinated and I told her how careful I'm going to be. Meredith's picking me up from the airport but then I'm going to stay on my own for ten days. Well, not completely on my own. Maxwell will drop Wordsworth off without coming in himself. Not until all my tests are negative. Too risky for Ned.

I'm worried he won't recognise me. Wordsworth, I mean. Because Ned's seen me on Zoom often enough. Six or seven times a day, sometimes. So he knows what I look like, even with the pink hair cut short. But Wordsworth – he's used to being with Hector now and having that huge field to run around in. He's not been back to the cottage since Mrs M had the fall.

My cottage.

What would Yaya say? Here I am, Kiki Moon, and I've inherited my very own English cottage and my very own basset hound. Maxwell says Wordsworth will be delighted to be back, but, whatever, we can play it by ear.

Play it by ear. Like when you don't really know how to play music from the notes on the page, and you just kind of make it up as you go along. That's what Ned says we'll do too.

Because, well, you don't know, do you? Or sometimes you do know. I know I know. But what if he doesn't? When he actually sees me again. And I haven't said anything. Just that I want to be with him. And he says he wants me to be there too. But we'll have to see what happens.

Funny thing, life. Like Bella and Toby. Ned says he's happy for them, except for Toby's wife and children. Ex-wife, maybe. I still think it's got to be strange for him. But Ned says life's too short to do what you know is wrong.

'Harry here again. So we have our slot and we'll be taking off in just a couple of minutes. So sit back. Seatbelts on and enjoy the flight.'

Right.

Here we go.

We'll just see what happens. That's what we'll do. We'll play it by ear.

NED

'OK, CHAMP, LET'S GIVE the legs another five minutes on the bike and if I put this weight into your right hand here, I want you to tell yourself you're going to squeeze it hard. Ready?'

'Yes,' I tell him, or my tablet does. I'm becoming used to my voice. It has a name. It's called Geoffrey. It sounds a little like Hugh Grant. But it's bizarrely very like my own voice too. It was created for me by a company who used samples from my YouTube videos, mixed with another voice from their database of donated voices. Technology is unbelievable.

The annexe window is open and the sky outside is blue. I tell my hand to squeeze. One day it will, maybe. My head has a tiny amount of movement now. I can't nod it or shake it properly, but what I can do is just slightly more than nothing. Last week one of the fingers on my right hand twitched a few millimetres too. Who knows, maybe in time squeezing will come.

'And let's give the left hand a try, shall we?'

'OK,' I tell him.

Mikey has been in every day this week, bringing stories of new patients – or clients as he calls them, since he set up on his own – who've given themselves injuries trying too hard with lockdown workouts. He brings me updates on Pom too. Her due date is less than a month away now and they're both hoping that restrictions will let him be there, because who knows anymore. But he says he's one of the few people who should be grateful to Covid. He'd still be trying to drum up the courage to ask her out otherwise, and instead he went right ahead and asked her to move in with him.

'Anyway, champ, tell me what's going on with you? Any plans for later?' Mikey's eyes have a glint and I can tell he's smiling behind the mask. 'Seeing anybody nice?'

KIKI

'VICAR SAYS TO TELL you that you won. He says the rules about no planting have been in place since 1923 so you'll be the first in almost a hundred years. The parish council say no trees or big shrubs, just small plants and bulbs. I've taken some cuttings from the lavender bush under the window. I checked with Maxwell that I was doing it right. They're in your greenhouse now doing their sprouting. Propagating, that's the fella. I read about it on this gardening website. Because I thought—'

The sound of the church gate banging is what jolts me quiet. I wait while an old man walks by. He nods at me and I nod back. He has a walking stick and he's quite slow. I'm silent until he's gone past.

'—that some lavender from your garden would make it more like home. Maxwell's going to come and plant it with me when your stone arrives. And Vicar will say some words. You always said lavender smelt lovely so we thought you'd like it.'

I'm still holding a bunch of cut garden flowers. To the old man I must have looked like I was offering them to an invisible person, or to the grass beneath me. The thing is I'd forgotten there'd be nothing to put them in here, like the silver vase that's built into Harriet's stone. You'd have thought I'd have remembered because I talked to the stone people earlier this week.

All I can do is bend down and put the flowers on the ground. They look nice, even though they're just flat on the grass. I tied them with some brown string from the greenhouse. They'll die quicker though, I reckon, without water.

There's lavender from the same bush where I took the cuttings, as well as yellow and white tulips and some pink flowers that I have a funny feeling might be weeds. I made a bunch for Harriet too. I'll take them round in a minute. I didn't bring any for Mr Malley. But he's here next to Mrs M, so he can share hers, I reckon.

I told the stone people she needed her own stone. I didn't want her name being crammed in underneath Mr Malley's on his one, even if that was heaps cheaper. When I called them on Tuesday they apologised about it all taking so long but granite deliveries have been very disrupted. I said not to worry because it had given me more time to get the words right anyway.

'I hope you'll like what I chose,' I say now, and if that old man walks past again he'll think I'm talking to the flowers. 'Maxwell reckoned you'd want something traditional, like from the Bible. Sue thought a line from a song, like maybe 'My Way' or something by Ella Fitzgerald, but I reckoned you'd maybe say that was inappropriate.'

I'm looking at the tulips and lavender and my cheeks are warm. Yaya was easier. She'd always said, 'Just scatter me in the lake and the trees so I can return to nature.' But I'm not sure Mrs M would have wanted that. I think she'd have wanted words on a stone.

'Ned suggested "*small acts of kindness*". That's nice, don't you think? Or maybe not "small" – maybe "little". Yes, "little" I think. And something else too. "Unremembered"? And "nameless". I think that's right. It's from a poem Wordsworth wrote.'

I blink. 'The poet I mean. William Wordsworth. I don't think our Wordsworth writes many poems.'

This is the moment that the old man with the stick decides to shuffle past again. He gives me a funny look, maybe because I'm laughing out loud at my own joke with nobody else there. I watch him carry on past, open the gate and walk slowly down the steps, and while I'm watching there's the sound of a motor and a black Jaguar pulls up.

'Here's Maxwell.'

I'm taking out my mask from my pocket and hooking the elastic around one ear, but not the other yet, because I still need to finish telling Mrs Malley about her headstone. I could just say the words silently, but I want to hear them too.

'In the end, I decided something from Harriet's poem would be nicest though. "*And when my life reaches an end, I'll know we did it well, my friend*". I hope you like it.'

I can hear the sound of a car door closing but I don't turn round yet. I crouch down and lower my voice just a bit.

'And I need to tell you about Harriet's money, because I know she wanted to spend it on the two of you doing all those bucket list things. And then you and I were going to go to Europe. I'm sad we never did that. We'd have had heaps of fun. I think about it all the time, you and me riding on our Vespas.

'Ned and I've been thinking maybe he and I can go one day – you know, when things are more normal. If we can work it out. With Maxwell and a carer and all of Ned's equipment. Then I'll drink a glass of Prosecco in a gondola for you. But I wouldn't use the fuck it fund for that. That's what I need to say now. The way I see it, that was about your memories. It should have been about making memories but now it can't be. So it should be about remembering you instead.'

It's good that I've been doing a bit of Pilates at Mrs M's – I still think of it as Mrs M's – while I was bored during those days self-isolating, because crouching low like this is quite hard work.

'So I hope you won't mind me giving the money away. Because Maxwell and Vicar said such amazing things about the care home where you went, and how lots of the staff had to move in full-time and live there, so they weren't going back to their own families every night.'

I don't mention that Clara who Maxwell spoke to most days when Mrs M was there, and who took the time to scan and email me her message, and one to Ned too, died of Covid three weeks later, or that she had nine-year-old twins. Or that Bisi, the manager of the home who'd become a mother ten months earlier, was in intensive care for almost a month, but is now back at work. It's her I've been talking to.

Instead I tell Mrs M about the memorial garden, and how it was partly my idea. I wanted to do something good with Harriet's money and Bisi agreed it would be lovely to plant a special place for reflection and remembering, there in the care home grounds, with blossom trees and plants that attract butterflies, and benches for sitting and thinking, and a plaque commemorating all the residents, and Clara too.

Harriet's fuck it fund won't be paying for fast cars and foreign holidays, or for nightclubs and marvellous mutton-ladies dressing like lambs. No gigolos. And that's a massive shame. But the whole world is a massive shame right now. And I think this is right.

'They've already started work on it. It's going to be beautiful,' I say. 'I think you'd have liked it.'

'And Sammy – you remember Sammy? – is going to make you a plaque too. A glass one. One for you and one for my mum, and one for Yaya and one for Gramps. I'm going to hang them on a tree by the Glade when I go to the festival. Not this year because they've cancelled it. But let's hope by next year. I know you've never been, but this way you'll sort of be there too. I hope you'd have thought my family—'

'Talking to yourself, Kiki?'

I pull the mask over my other ear as I'm standing up. 'Yeah,' I tell Maxwell. 'Nah. Talking to Mrs M. Don't say she can't hear me.'

He's stopped two metres from me and I wrap my arms around my shoulders to show him I'd like to give him a hug. He holds out an elbow at the same time so I air-tap it with mine instead.

'Of course she can.' It's the first time I've seen Maxwell since he dropped Wordsworth off. He was at the gate by the time I opened the door, with just the dog on the doorstep. Maxwell and I waved at each other and said, 'Hello', but it wasn't like really seeing each other. Now, the creases around his eyes tell me he's smiling and he's quiet for a moment, looking down at the flowers before he asks if I'm ready to go.

'We can pick up Wordsworth on the way? I think Ned's looking forward to seeing you both.'

Maxwell probably can't see how pink my cheeks are because of my mask. I can't see it either, of course, but I can feel it. They're heaps itchy.

'Yes, ready,' I tell him. 'I'll take these other flowers to Harriet quickly first, if that's OK?'

NED

D ID I EVER REALLY listen to the world before all of
this? Or make the effort to smell it? Ha – slow down
and smell the roses, is that what I'm saying? But,
actually, did I ever do that?

I've trekked through South America and backpacked Asia.
I've driven across America. I took hundreds of photos of places
I can still picture, the coves of Nai Harn and the emerald pool
of Krabi, Nepal, Machu Picchu – I see them still, but can I
hear them or smell them?

I saw hummingbirds in rainforests. But did I hear them hum?

I'm outside, in my chair facing down to the stream. I told
my new carer, Jonathan – lovely bloke – I wanted to be on
my own. I can summon him through my tablet if I have to.
It's right here, attached to my chair, in front of my face, and
such an ever-present fixture that I no longer see it unless I
need to. So now, I'm only seeing the familiar slopes and trees.
I'm smelling freshly cut grass and I'm listening to the birds.

Before all this, I would never have known that the bossy
trilling above me was a wren.

Hector's bark – it's muffled because he's inside the main
house – tells me the car's coming before I hear the car. So I'm
listening out for the sound of the motor and I listen to it
becoming louder, nearer, and at the same time I'm hearing
that wren giving out instructions to the sky, and some starlings
singing songs about who-knows-what, and the chirping of

grasshoppers and a fly whining near to my ear. I'm willing it not to land on me.

'Buzz off, fly.' That's a very Toby joke. He emailed me last week. He feels we should talk. I haven't replied. Maybe. One day. But one thing at a time.

The Jaguar's engine has a different pitch to Maxwell's Golf. It's pulling up now. And stopping. Engine off. Hector's barking is agitated and high. And I'd know that howling anywhere. They haven't seen each other for two weeks. Such excitement.

Car doors. One. Two.

Annabella had one of those video doorbells long before anyone else I knew. She used to tease me about how much she loved to watch me when I rang the bell and didn't remember I was on camera. She said she'd see me running my hand through my hair while putting on my most nonchalant expression.

Now I wait. I can't even swallow.

Voices. They're here. I can't make out the words, just the sounds of Maxwell's soft, slow lilt and the twang of Kiwi. She talks faster than him. I feel my breathing quicken a little too. And my heart. A metronome that has been reset to beat allegro.

My lips feel dry.

I can hear two dogs barking out their joy at being reunited, and the wren overhead. The fly has gone. That's good.

I breathe. I wait. And I listen to the voices coming nearer.

KIKI

THE CHAIR IS SET so he's sideways to us, outside the annexe, all the way across the other side of the field. He won't be able to see me but I reckon he might have heard the car. Maxwell and I haven't stopped talking since leaving the church. He's been telling me about how impressive the alternative communication aids Ned's been trialling have been, and how amazing some of the voice generators are, and how human they sound.

'Of course you've heard him on Zoom,' Maxwell says. And of course I have. I agree with Maxwell how incredible it all is, even if Ned says he won't use the voice to laugh. He says there's something too premeditated about telling his tablet to do that.

I've also been telling Maxwell about what I've been up to in my ten days locked away – moving bills from Mrs M's name into mine, and looking to see if any local vets are hiring nurses. I've also been busy on the internet. Because Sammy emailed to say she'd spoken to somebody who knew my father. She didn't have any firm details but this person thought he was going by Mark Dixon these days, and that he was living somewhere in Scotland, maybe on one of the islands. They thought he was farming. It's not a lot to go on, but it's a start.

Now though, we're here. We're just across the field from Ned. Maxwell's pointing out things that we can both see. There's the old willow, remember, and look how happy Hector and Wordsworth are to see each other, and isn't it good that the rain's stayed off.

And I'm agreeing, yes and yes and of course I remember and aren't they funny. And I'm also saying how much I've thought about being back here while I've been away, and how lovely the cherry tree looks, and what the weather app said last week and yesterday morning and yesterday night and this morning.

Sue told me to remember not to talk too much. She also said no curtsying. She made me promise.

'You should think through your entrance in advance,' she told me, before I left for the airport. 'It's a moment you'll tell your grandchildren about one day.'

I told Sue not to be such a daft egg. It's just Ned and me.

But Meredith said the same thing, when she picked me up from the airport and we drove back, with all the windows wide open.

'How've you been, Keeks?' she asked me, even though we've emailed heaps.

I did a sort of shrug, because – you know. But I smiled too, like it sort of escaped. Like an I-can't-help-it smile. Because smiles do keep escaping at the moment. Even while I've been on my own – or not on my own because of self-isolating with Wordsworth too. The smiles. All the time.

'Look at you,' Meredith said. 'Good to have you back.'

Her hair was different. Not black. And she didn't have the same eye make-up. She's nearly not a student anymore. She did her last-but-one exam online a couple of weeks ago.

I felt a bit sad thinking how the last time I'd seen her, I'd thought she must have taken Mrs M's money. She doesn't even know. I need to say I'm sorry. When we can sit down with a drink. They're saying the pubs will be open again soon. Maybe then.

That's when Meredith said about needing a killer line. She did a funny voice and said something about me needing kissing badly. I didn't know what she was talking about, but apparently it was from *Gone with the Wind*. I've never seen it. I said about Ned and me playing it by ear and just being friends anyway. She shook her head and said, 'Killer line, Keeks.'

But it's now already, and Ned's right there. Every step, I'm a bit closer to him. I'm talking to Maxwell and saying how it's looking like this weekend might be a lot wetter. Just normal walking, talking. I haven't even thought about a killer line. Or, OK, I've sort of thought about it, but only in passing and only because Meredith's kept messaging things like *This from Casablanca?* and *Elizabeth in P&P?* and *When Harry Met Sally?* and I've replied that thanks, but like I said I'm just playing it all by ear.

It would have to be really simple, if I was planning one. Which I'm not. But all it would be is just 'hey', or 'hi', or 'hello', or just his name, but with a smile that shows how happy I am to see him, except not too excited, not like it's the only thing I've been thinking about.

He won't be able to see us yet, because we're coming up from the side, with his chair pointing down, towards the stream. But I reckon he can hear us. He can definitely hear Wordsworth and Hector. They're stoked to see each other, because listen to that barking, and they're racing across the field and that's why, maybe, my feet have sped up a bit too. Not that there's any hurry. I'm just talking to Maxwell about the weekend and whether it will rain.

'Actually, I tell you what,' Maxwell says when we're level with the back door of the house, 'I'm ready for a cup of tea. Why don't you go on ahead and say hello to Ned and I'll bring you out a cup too.'

I'm not sure why my cheeks are suddenly so hot but I'm saying a tea would be lovely. And so Maxwell's heading off to do that and I'm walking on to where Ned is. I'm going a little bit faster because, well, I just am.

I won't hug him. Ned. Of course. But I'm nearly there. And I haven't thought about that killer line but I don't need one. I'm just going to say, 'Hey Ned,' or 'Hi Ned,' or 'Hello Ned,' whichever pops out. Nothing from *Casablanca* or *Pride and Prejudice* or *Gone with the Wind*. Just hey or hi or hello.

And here I am.

I'm right beside him.

I could touch him. I could put my hand on his arm or his shoulder. I could stroke his cheek. I could bend down at this very moment and hug him. If we could hug. I could put my arms around him and hold him and rest my head against his.

He won't be able to see me until I step into his line of sight. I take a breath and I take one, two, three steps. And now I'm in front of him. I stop. He's looking at me and I'm looking at him.

He blinks.

Something inside me inflates.

'I . . .' Was that me? I've opened my mouth and all I need to say is hi or hello or hey or Ned or anything. Except what comes out is not a word, unless 'ho' is a word.

Because I'm just about to say my word and he says it first – his tablet does – his Geoffrey voice. 'Hello Kiki.' And he says it just as I'm about to say my line too.

He says, 'Hello Kiki.' And what comes out in return is, 'Ho.' Maybe because I'm still deciding if I'm going to say hi or hey, and hearing him say hello.

'Ho.'

That's what I say.

He's looking at me. And I say, 'I don't mean ho, of course. That's not a word. I mean—' And I pause. My cheeks are hot. 'I mean—' He's still looking at me. And so that's my killer line.

'Ho.'

I'm sort of sighing at myself – because top marks again, Kiki Moon – except the sigh turns into a sort of hiccup, but really it's a laugh. I can't help it. It's the sort of laugh you're trying to hold back except you can't. And I say, 'I'm sorry,' and I say, 'I didn't mean to say "ho", I meant to say—'

Except there's no word. No line. Just an odd laughing sound exploding out of me, and there are tears in my eyes too, and now they're running down my cheeks. But mostly I'm laughing.

I'm smiling and crying and laughing this odd-sounding laugh.

Because I've been waiting for this for so long. And now I'm here.

I'm here. Finally. And the best I've come out with is 'ho'.

And even if I can't hear it, I know Ned's laughing too.

AUTHOR'S NOTE AND THE ACKNOWLEDGEMENTS

'... *that best portion of a good man's life, his little, nameless, unremembered acts of kindness and of love*' William Wordsworth

'*This stroke was a gift, not a curse, you've just got to shut out all of the negativity and see out the heartbreak, then own what happens next*' Howard Wicks, founder of the Locked-In Trust

It's a cliche to talk about a book as its writer's baby but, just like a child, a book has a tendency to take on a life beyond the author's expectations. As a parent, I soon learned that my children were too much their own little people to have any of my parental whims easily imposed. And maybe other authors who meticulously plot every tiny detail have more obedient manuscripts – but my own two book 'babies' have followed their own rebellious path. *Small Acts of Kindness* is quite a different book to the one I planned to write – better for it, I hope.

Back at the end of 2019, if I remember right, I wrote a tentative chapter in which an elderly woman pulls a red thong from her clean laundry pile. I wasn't sure where this would lead but it made me chuckle. I didn't know yet how this item of clothing had made its way into her washing, or to whom it belonged, but I did know that this was going to be a story about unlikely friendships. I also knew that Mrs Malley was going to find her life changed by a stroke and that the re-evaluation which this would bring, though frustrating and painful, would ultimately be rewarding as well.

During my career as a journalist focusing on the human side of health issues, I'd talked with many people who'd experienced unexpected changes to their lives and had needed to find the strength to adapt, including many who'd had strokes at very different ages and in vastly different situations, and who'd been affected in very different ways. I'd also spent time on a stroke unit after my own grandmother's stroke. While, sadly, my lovely Grandma Betty would never recover, my time with her on the ward and in the day room whilst the nurses tended to her, gave me a glimpse into the tenacity of other stroke survivors whose lives had been changed in an instant, and who in many cases now had to relearn skills which they'd taken for granted since early childhood. It takes spirit and guts.

I knew that *Small Acts of Kindness* would be a novel about individuals whose worlds stop for a moment and have to find the way to restart. What I didn't know was that the entire world itself was about to do this same thing. This is a novel which I started writing before Covid – a time which now feels a different age – so if we stick with the 'book-baby' cliche, this is my Covid book baby.

It is no coincidence that Kiki found herself on a pilgrimage to Glastonbury Festival, although I hadn't known this about her when I started writing. I'd been lucky enough to attend the festival in 2016, 2017 and 2019 – and researching this storyline provided an excuse to relive some wonderful moments of 'Glasto' in my head during a scary, restricted time, and to spend hours reading about the early years of Glastonbury and about David Bowie playing there in 1971 to a field of mostly sleeping festival-goers. Writing this book during Covid felt surreal – and losing myself in memories of festival freedom provided a temporary escape from the fear, boredom, claustrophobia and anger.

I want to thank those people who read and fed back their thoughts during my writing of this book, especially Anne and Cath, Emma, Belinda and Tim (I promise Tim, you're not Mrs M, even if I may have borrowed your opinions on a hymn or two) and of course brilliant Ben, who has become quite used to having a computer thrust at him first thing in the morning with the demand: "does this read OK?" And a thank you, just because, to our funny clan of almost-adult Todds, as well as to my parents, Liz and Mike.

A big thank you also to Chris and the group of writers at the All Good Bookshop in Turnpike Lane. I read out early extracts in their interim space before the shop moved to its current spot – and, in between, when Covid pushed us online. Sharing this book as a work in progress and hearing your feedback was much appreciated – thanks guys, and apologies if I'm the one most prone to babbling while drinking all the wine.

I fully intended during the writing of this novel to do what I'd failed to do whilst writing *Hope Nicely's Lessons for Life*, and to record every article, website, blog, organisation, book/ book extract, case study and individual experience that I encountered and learned from. In the end, there were just too many and I am too forgetful. But the personal stories shared, through the Stroke Association and Different Strokes, for example, as well as the shared experiences of those living in a locked-in state, were especially invaluable. People are incredible. People living in locked-in states run companies, have relationships, write books and blogs and give life-affirming presentations which all of us can learn from, whilst living full and important lives. Ned is fictional. But he's also a real star in my eyes.

Thank you to Howard Wicks, founder of the Locked-In Trust for giving his blessing to my using his above quote in my acknowledgments. His words perfectly encapsulate the sense of hope which I wanted this book to convey. Thank you also to the communication disability charity, the Sequal Trust for information on communication aids and to Michael Saguan, staff nurse at the Centre for Neurorehabilitation at Queen Square, for guidance on patient welfare, safety and trips out from hospital.

Thank you to the amazing team at Zaffre for all that you have done to bring this novel into the world – to Emma Rogers for the cover design (I love, love, love, that doggy), to Laura Gerrard for an edit which taught me I was not as knowledge-able as I thought about commas and speech marks, to Salma and Katie and to Melissa, for wisdom and calmness, also to Ruth and to everyone else whose involvement in giving a book the best possible launch is beyond this author's radar. Thank you of course to Sarah Bauer – no longer at Zaffre but to whom this book owes not only its title but so much more. Thank you, Sarah, for all the ideas – you were right in every case. And thank you to my wonderful, brilliant agent, Sarah Lutyens as well as Anna and Tara and the rest of the fantastic team at Lutyens & Rubinstein. I am so proud and so grateful to have you in my corner.

Thank you, lastly, to my two extremely silly doggies, Snoopy and Charlie Brown, for unfailing moral support (I'm not sure all writers choose to work with a dog pal on either side of them, but it's essential practice for me) – especially Snoopy for his inspiration on Basset Hound naughtiness.

**If you enjoyed *Small Acts of Kindness*, you will love
Caroline Day's heartwarming debut novel,
Hope Nicely's Lessons for Life.**

*I don't have any friends, only dog ones, because they don't make you do bad
things. I don't want any human friends, actually. It's for the best . . .*

Hope Nicely hasn't had an easy life.

But she's happy enough living at 23 Station Close with her mum, Jenny Nicely,
and she loves her job, walking other people's dogs. She's a bit different, but as
Jenny always tells her, she's a rainbow person, a special drop of light.

It's just . . . there's something she needs to know. Why did her birth mother
abandon her in a cardboard box on a church step twenty-five years ago?
And did she know that drinking while pregnant could lead to Hope being
born with Foetal Alcohol Spectrum Disorder?

In a bid to find her birth mother and the answers to these questions, Hope
decides to write her autobiography. Despite having been bullied throughout
school, Hope bravely joins an evening class where Hope will not only learn
the lessons of writing, but will also begin to discover more about the world
around her, about herself and even make some (human) friends.

But when Jenny suddenly falls ill, Hope realises there are many more
lessons to come . . .

Hope Nicely's Lessons for Life is a heartwarming, coming-of-age novel about
loneliness, friendship, acceptance and, above all, hope.